The Divining Season

Gwendolyn Paradice

THE DIVINING SEASON

Gwendolyn Paradice

aunt lute books
San Francisco

Aunt Lute Books, P.O. Box 410687, San Francisco, CA 94141
www.auntlute.com

Cover design and illustrator: Shirley Chong
Text design: Sarah Lopez
Senior Editor: Emma Rosenbaum
Managing Editor: Shay Brawn
Production Team: Isis Asare, María Mínguez Arias, Severa Brawn, Georgina Guardado, Allie Rigby, and Golda Sargento

The production of this book was made possible by support from California Arts Council, the Council on Literary Magazines and Publishers, the Poetry Foundation, the San Francisco Arts Commission, Sara and Two C-Dogs Foundation, and the Zellerbach Foundation.

Library of Congress Cataloging-in-Publication Data

Names: Paradice, Gwendolyn author
Title: The divining season / Gwendolyn Paradice.
Description: San Francisco : Aunt Lute Books, [2026]
Identifiers: LCCN 2026000726 (print) | LCCN 2026000727 (ebook) | ISBN 9781951874124 trade paperback | ISBN 9781939904485 epub
Subjects: LCGFT: Fiction | Novels
Classification: LCC PS3616.A696 D58 2026 (print) | LCC PS3616.A696 (ebook)
LC record available at https://lccn.loc.gov/2026000726
LC ebook record available at https://lccn.loc.gov/2026000727

— TABLE OF CONTENTS —

For you, Mom. I wish you could have read this book.

PART I

•

DESCENDING A SPIRALED PORTENT

Girls appear and disappear, but so do women. We know this because blood talks to blood. Since Larissa is welling with new-old blood. Since the scent of blood is past, and present, and future.

We find each other, the women who have been misplaced, separated, given to the bright dawn, to stars, to the falling from night into dawn, to the quiet, to the gone. The opposite of copper-locked is memory.

We are remembering something. We are remembering the sun on our backs, the flies on our arms, the dead toes on our feet.

We are remembering needles made of bone and the voices of women who have disappeared.

We are remembering a girl who once fled from us, who became one of us, who dropped her tongue and stitched another in its place.

Blood is calling to blood.

We find the memory of blood. Along the riverbanks. In the grass-lands. Buried under concrete.

We open our mouths to call to blood and drop dust, and sand, and dirt, while we search for other lost women.

1

We Found You

—Emily—

"I feel terrible for her. It must be awful to be cooped up, confined to the house."

I pause on my way down the stairs, resting my hand on the banister, one foot hovering above the next step. My mother is talking to her aunt, my *great* aunt, though I've never met the woman.

"I don't think it's too bad." My mother's voice carries, low and calm. Her shadow moves along the wall, her body pausing between columns of wallpaper flowers. "Emily is ... unique. She doesn't mind time alone, and she's good at entertaining herself. Keeps to herself mostly as well, but she isn't unhappy. Where is she? Emily?"

I make a noise, humming as I descend, delighting at the buzz in my throat. Stairs creak under me and I try to match the measure of wood to the length of each exhalation.

Mother sits down in one of the oversized chairs that came with Cedar House, framed by its barrel back. She smiles when she sees me, and she tucks a blonde curl behind one ear before reaching for me.

I go to her, but my eyes are on this relative I do not know. Mrs. Habbermire is a mystery yet to unfold, a woman I did not know existed until only a few weeks ago. Mrs. Habbermire, who Mother says prepared this house for us. Mrs. Habbermire, a sister-ghost of Mother's mother. Mrs. Habbermire, the only relative Mother has left, besides me.

"So this, I suppose, is Emily?"

The woman is older than I had thought she would be, white hair thinning and hair sprayed stiff, her pink scalp showing through her bouffant. Even from where I'm standing, I can smell her perfume, something vaguely lilac. She is appraising me, and Mother clears her throat.

Mrs. Habbermire smiles at me then. "Here, girl, look. I've brought you something."

"That's very kind of you, Mrs. Habbermire." My mother pushes me gently towards her. "Emily, say 'thank you.'"

I am about to say just that, but Mrs. Habbermire cuts me off. "Oh, just call me Rebekah. We don't know each other well, but we're family. No sense being formal."

Mrs. Habbermire reaches into her purse and pulls out some items wrapped messily in tissue paper. She proffers them to me, and Mother nods for me to take them.

"Some soap you'll like," she says, handing over two small rectangles.

I take them and put them up to my nose and sniff. I can smell only mothballs.

"And here are some ribbons. For your hair. Such lovely hair ..."

This package is flat and in a shape I have no word for.

"And here, a book. Something to keep you busy, since ..."

I take the book too, but when I do, Mrs. Habbermire won't give it up.

"Thank you," I say, tugging at the volume while trying not to drop what's already in my hands.

She finally lets go. At the corner of her mouth, a small, dark hair is curled, and I sway as I fixate on it, imagining it growing longer, wilder, reaching up to her nostril and attacking her nose.

"Emily?" My mother stands and puts the back of her hand against my forehead. "Are you feeling sick again?"

•

I am aware from the looks on their faces that these women think I am strange.

I'm holding in scarred hands a tray of petit fours, and I am trying to appear delightful. I'm smiling brightly. Making my cheeks into apples. Looking at the women of Mother's new Garden Club through half-moon eyes.

"My daughter, Emily," she announces, sliding her hand behind my head, her fingers lingering on my neck, a pressure that makes my eyes soften and double everything that I see.

I try to fight the dizziness, to stand straight, to look prim and proper, but my bones are drooping and my skin hurts. My brain is too large for my head and I can hear blood like a river rushing inside my ears.

"It's okay, darling," my mother whispers to me, though everyone in the room can hear her. "If you don't feel up to it, you can go back to bed."

I deposit the snacks on the table and retreat to the kitchen, leaning against the wall by the telephone and counting in grey silence the seconds as they pass. Seven. Twelve. Eighteen.

Finally, I hear Mother's voice floating from the parlor, higher in pitch than normal, but these women do not know her well enough to track the difference. "Emily is getting adjusted and has been under the weather. Cedar House," she laughs. "I should have known better."

A voice I cannot yet put to a face says, "Oh, that's a terrible allergy, that cedar. And it's not even cold yet. Poor girl. When winter comes ..."

When winter comes, my mother says there will be ice. It will hang from branches and eaves and we will break off sharp points, melt them on our tongues.

"I know," my mother continues. "If it's not one thing, it's something else." She sighs.

"But of course," Mrs. Habbermire adds, "there used to be more of them, so it could be worse. The cedar trees, I mean. You spring chickens wouldn't remember that, though. Larissa when it was still coming up. Oh, what a sight!"

My eyes swivel and the room goes hazy. I slide to the ground and see small bodies in the warped lead glass of the cabinets. I put my cheek to the tile and feel the grit of dirt and plaster against my skin. I latch on to that voice as it continues talking.

"Well now, let me see ... it was 1910," Mrs. Habbermire continues, "and Mrs. White's father had just cleared a whole new section of land ..."

I stand and edge to the gap in the wall where the doorway has been removed. Peek out to spy the face recalling a time I never knew.

Mrs. Habbermire is sitting with her legs together, stockings slack and gathering around her ankles, the ribs of fabric cradling her swollen joints. She is an old mirror of me, both of us craning our heads to *look*, but I cannot see what she is looking *for*. She is turned towards the empty library. Speaking to no one and everyone.

The other women I only know based on my mother's descriptions. Mrs. Bee likes to talk and interrupt others, which she keeps doing because she wants to talk about the DAR, to which she's just been given membership. Mrs. Tandy has a twitch of the eye. Mrs. Rolf only wears black because, like my mother, she lost a husband in the war; however, unlike my mother, she can't move past it. And then there is Mrs. Daphne, who is a beautiful piece of stone. No wrinkles, not even around her mouth when she smiles, which I find both interesting and disturbing.

I think Mrs. Daphne is searching me out. She says the sun is too bright through the window. She says she needs to change chairs. She keeps moving and attempting to peer into the hallway to the kitchen. She keeps asking about the drop cloths and plaster trowels and the doorways.

"It's an interesting choice," she proclaims hastily when Mrs. Habbermire seems done with her reminiscence. Mrs. Daphne is studying the square boundary between rooms. "I don't think I've ever seen a house without doorways. Just, one room flowing into the next."

I hate doorways. Or rather, they hate me. Mother tells me that in traveling between rooms I've ripped her dresses, shredded door frames, thrown my toys through windows, urinated on hardwood floors. I'd be embarrassed if I remembered anything about this. But I don't. My mother says it's a "positive side" of my condition. She's referred to it this way often—*the gift of forgetting*—but I prefer the term "do not remember" because, after all, they do mean different things.

"Yes, it's quite original," my mother responds. She is holding a cookie but not eating it. "It's quite nice, I think. Such a big house. This way, Emily and I can see each other no matter where we are."

I giggle because this is untrue. It's an obvious lie, since we're only a few rooms away from each other and no one can see me.

I slide my body along the floor, worming my way back to the threshold between me and the women of the Garden Club. I stretch my neck, willing it to be longer than it already is, and steal a glance into the parlor, the women haloed by motes sparkling in the sunlight.

"What have you done with the molding?" Mrs. Bee asks. "It was beautiful, just beautiful. Thomas Gladwell had it brought over from Scotland. Quite a shame to remove it. He put a lot of work into this big old house."

Mrs. Habbermire coughs loudly and reaches for her tea.

Mrs. Tandy's eye twitches. She raises her hand to it.

Oh, Mrs. Bee says, her cheeks flushing red. "I'm sorry. I shouldn't have said anything ..."

The women quiet, something unsaid between them. The lull in the conversation goes on for too long, and since my mother hates pauses, she sews the gap with a new thread. "Larissa seems so different now. Almost like it's an entirely new town." She laughs nervously. "New town. New friends. Emily and I could use some of that good old southern hospitality about now. We had such a trying time up north."

Up north is only one state away, in Oklahoma. According to my mother, I hated it and when I was even younger, I made life there difficult. But like so many things, I don't remember much of it. I don't remember that I would not stop screaming and crying. Mother says that sometimes the tantrums would last all night and all day, weeks even, and that this happened for years.

Then, instead of misbehaving, I began to quiet, and to shrink down in myself. Once, my mother heard my grandmother tell me that I was the ugliest child she'd ever put up with and that she was glad I no longer opened my mouth as much. That woman became wicked about me, and no matter what I did, how silent I was, how separate from her I became, it was never enough. She finally told my mother that the pair of us was too much of a reminder of what she'd lost, and she put a check in my mother's hand and said, *go back to your family*, which she did. And she brought me with her—*the last women of Larissa*, she said, *all together again*—because her family is here, only most of them are under the earth.

•

Because I'm very good at being quiet and keeping people from knowing where I am, I've heard the workers in the house talking about me. I hear and see all sorts of things I'm probably not supposed to. My mother says this is a miracle—my sneak-thiefiness—because she would have never guessed me capable of being so taciturn. Now, in a house where I can move freely, mother and I have made a game of it, seeing who can be the best at sneaking and surprising.

I am winning. Not because I am better at hiding, but because I am better at knowing.

I know how at sunset, the shadows cast themselves among unfamiliar furniture.

I know what stairs squeak, or groan, and I follow the worn parts of the runner in silence.

I know how to bend around walls. How to be laundry. How to become a cabinet. How to fold myself like a turkey onto platters that were left by the people who lived here before, whose belongings would one day be needed by a woman and her daughter who would come with nothing.

I want to surprise the workers right now because they are being quite rude.

Part of the problem with removing doorways, of having one room simply become another, is that doorways and walls are sometimes needed for support, and to decipher how to eliminate them is "nothing like sliding off a greasy log backward," as Earl says.

Earl and John are the men I see most often, brothers who own the company that is fixing Cedar House, but it's Frank and Buster who are chipping away at plaster today, high up on ladders and wearing bandanas over their noses.

"And no one knows," Buster is saying. "I remember Gracie from high school. Good girl. Cheerleader. Homecoming queen for Christ's sake. Never would have thought she'd go and do that."

"I bet George is rolling in his grave."

"Doesn't look a thing like him. Can't be his daughter. Can you imagine what Irene must have thought when she brought that baby home? It's a wonder she didn't throw them out on the street. Son away and dying during the war, serving our country, while her daughter-in-law shacks up with some ..."

"George must be rolling in his grave."

"I mean, I *knew* her. Knew *of* her. Never would have expected Gracie McCallin to do something like that. And then to come back here. Larissa, of all places."

"I bet her parents are rolling in their graves, too."

"Little girl is pretty though. Will grow up real pretty too. But she'll have an albatross around her neck her whole life."

The plaster falls. The room is sandy with it. The men's white arms grow whiter.

I want to jump out and yell *surprise*, but if I do then one might fall and break his neck.

•

Little girls disappear. This is what I learn from the book Mrs. Habbermire brought me.

There is no longer a Mr. Habbermire, and there were no little Habbermires that ever grew into big Habbermires, so the book is now mine.

I've never read a book with so many missing girls: but they're here through all the pages. Little girls losing themselves in the woods. Little girls following strange men to other towns, never to be seen again. Little girls going up with the smoke because of wicked stepmothers who burn them for their beauty. Little girls are locked in dungeons and starving because people forget that they're there. Little girls are eaten by animals. Little girls falling from high windows. Little girls hearing voices singing and leaving their homes during full moons. Little girls traveling long distances and freezing in the snow between towns. Little girls drowning in lakes. Little girls taken by elves, fairies, and brownies, whose mothers are left weeping at empty cradles.

I read these stories while mother is washing dishes. I read these stories while neighbors knock at the door and talk to my mother, handing over casseroles and inspecting how the house has changed, saying things like, "I'm so glad there's life here again" or "Good thing you could see past it" or "I still wonder what happened between the Gladwells."

I read these stories after mother has gone to bed. I read these stories by the light of the lamp in my turret bedroom overlooking the street.

Sometimes the stories creep along my arms and make me feel cold even though I sweat. Sometimes they whisper to me to turn out of my shell, risk the taking of an extra step towards understanding my tendency toward the silence I read them in. Sometimes, I think the stories are trying to tell me something about what people say and don't say, what they're willing to reveal and what they choose to keep hidden, even from themselves.

Each night, I turn off the ceiling fan, and, in the quiet, I hear the drone of cicadas, the crickets chirping. Sometimes I close the book and turn off all the lights and open the window. Sometimes I think I might be a girl who throws off her skin and grows feathers and flies away, never to be seen again.

•

I watch my mother from the kitchen window. The room smells of basil and citrus and it is my job to make sure the sponge doesn't over-bake while my mother attempts to tame the garden. That was her word—*tame*—and I don't think she's succeeding.

My mother's shirt is damp with sweat, a ragged V down her back, spread wide across her shoulders and tapering down her spine. From time to time she stops her work and stands, looking up at what is still left to be torn down or looking down to survey what she's already accomplished.

I get up and dance around the kitchen to songs on the radio. Drink large glasses of water. Slide my hands into padded oven mitts and bathe my face in heat, daring the pan to burn through the layers of cotton protecting me. While the cake cools, I read old newspapers mother has lugged up from the basement, remnants from the Gladwells who lived in Cedar House before us.

What I would *like* to do is go out into the yard. I would like to plunge my hands into dark earth or burrow into it like a beetle. I imagine I could build my own house under this house, one filled with colored pots for snakes. There would be no doorways of course. Only the scent of sweet things in decay.

"Emily?" My mother is in the doorway. The knees of her pedal pushers are brown, and her wide brim hat bobs up and down. Up and down. She has startled me out of my daydreams and is sniffing the air. "Is the cake done?"

I shake my head.

She comes into the house, arms full of vines and small, white flowers, screen door slamming shut behind her. "Do you like them?" She puts the flowers on the table. "How do you feel?" Mother reaches for my cheek and frowns.

"If you like them, I like them," I say, pushing her hand away.

"That's not an answer."

The sound of water rushing. The scrape of metal on porcelain.

I am touching the flowers, the sharp pins of their stalks. My palms are pinpricked, splotches of red blossoming just under the skin. I put the oven mitts on my hands and then spread the clustered flowers around the table. "A bed of roses," I say.

"What was that?"

"Who would want a bed of roses?" I amend. "All those thorns."

"Emily?"

She is giving me that look that says she's concerned. One brow is raised, and her lips are a flat line over which she darts her tongue.

The flowers are deceiving. Looking lush but wanting to bite. I use my mitts as protection and wad them all up, crushing the blooms.

"Emily! I was going to cut those off and put them in water!"

"Yes, but now neither of us can get hurt."

•

I like to vacuum the plaster dust, disappear the refuse into the walls. Take a damp rag and wipe down the arms of chairs and tables. Trace the whorls in wood with my fingertips. Run my hand over rough walls feeling for bumps and divots. Sometimes I pretend I'm Cinderella and talk to mice I cannot see. This only seems to alarm the men doing the renovations. Maybe I scared them away playing make believe, though I think the workers would be silly for fleeing a little girl. In any case, Frank and Buster have not returned since I told my mother what I overheard, her mouth pressing tighter and tighter until in anger she vowed that one day, she'd set the town straight.

•

"Honestly," my mother says, "I think this house might be too big."

"You don't say."

We sit in two wingback chairs facing the street. Outside, two boys ride their bikes. Back and forth. Back and forth. They seem to be interested in Cedar House, and I wonder if they can see us through the window or if the porch's overhang darkens the interior enough to hide us.

"You should get a job," I suggest. "It will give you something to do besides think about how big the house is."

"And leave you here all alone?"

"What's the worst that could happen?" I ask.

"You might get bored," she says, sounding bored herself.

I turn to look at her, but she is looking at her feet, flicking flecks of old paint onto the floor.

"I have things to read," I say.

"Really, you wouldn't mind?"

I shake my head. "Not at all."

"You're too old for that young body of yours," she chuckles.

"And while we're talking about reading," I tell her, "I might mention I haven't seen the paper yet."

"Lord," Mother says, shaking her head. "I swear, you're more interested in that thing than I am".

"It's how I'm getting to know Larissa." I get up and look through the windows to the long side of the porch. The paper is there, a corner of it flapping up in the breeze.

"Like a dog with a bone," she mutters, getting up and opening the front door.

Outside, the boys stop on their bikes. The smaller one says something to the taller one, and he shakes his head in response.

"Here," mother says, handing me the bundle.

I take the paper and unfold it. Read the headline. "Have you seen this?"

She is closing the front door. "Emily, I *just* gave it to you. How could I have time to read it?"

I hold it up and show it to her. It says a girl named Marjorie Kent has gone missing.

•

Within a week, women start appearing in response to Mother's newspaper advertisement for a maid. I like opening the door for them because I can get close, a sickening thrill, knowing I don't *have* to cross through it. It's almost like doors were built to tempt the changes they can bring; the time it takes to open one and step away is the same as a final breath leaving the body.

Mother's asked that I sit in on the interviews. This is a good idea since it's clear by halfway through the conversation with the first applicant that some won't be too keen on spending time in Cedar House.

"You know what happened here," one woman asks, purse held neatly in her lap, cloth gloves scraping over leather.

My mother holds her chin up and says, "That thing? Happened while I wasn't even here. It feels like a brand-new home to me."

The woman looks at her shoes and responds, "Cedar House will always be Cedar House."

My mother elbows me.

The woman across from us frowns, but I'm not sure if she does so because of the house or because of me. I can feel my gums drying. I've held my smile for too long.

•

Mother says Larissa is praying for rain. That east Texas shouldn't be this dry. But while Larissa may be parched, there is a storm inside my body. If only I could splay myself open and water this town.

At night the air feels tinted with static. I toss and turn in my bed, hear thunder low and rumbling. But when I get up and look out the window, there is only darkness. No flashes of bright light cracking the sky.

Sometimes I lie on the floor and take up as much space as I can.

Other times I walk around the house, go into the kitchen and turn the radio on to static, let my ears discern the many voices lost to white noise.

Sometimes I hold water in my mouth, swishing wet sounds, and then spit it onto the floor. Then I clean it up.

Sometimes I open the door to the basement and think about tumbling down the steps into the Gladwells' life, or what's left of it.

Sometimes I stand on the coffee table in the parlor and practice being a cat.

Sometimes I am suddenly in rooms I have not gone to sleep in and then have to rush back to my bed before Mother wakes and finds me.

•

Three days into interviews, my mother's patience has worn thin. I can tell by the way her answers to the women become shorter and shorter. "Where is your husband?" they ask. "Why on earth would you come back to Larissa?" they ask. "And I would also be watching the girl?" they ask.

Through all of it I smile and break open pecans, timing the crack of shell to disturb the silences in which mother takes deep, slow breaths.

I think my mother is about to give up when the right woman presents herself.

I see her walking down the street, cutting through a cloud of yellow cedar pollen. Her swinging arms seem to conjure dust devils that spin themselves into the shapes of women wearing yellow dresses, yellow skirts, yellow matchcoats. They are dancing and dipping and their clothing swishes. They are stomping their feet in time with the woman who is climbing the stairs of our porch. They are bending their hidden knees and coming through the doorway with her. This woman has brought a gift that makes me cough. I can taste pollen on my tongue.

I like Candice right away because she walks into the house without any trepidation, doesn't bat an eye at me, doesn't mention the lack of doorways, and asks nothing about me besides what I like to do since I don't leave the house.

Candice says it took fifteen minutes to walk here from the other side of Grand Avenue and that she likes to cook, even though her husband is better at it because he owns a diner. She has two daughters who have married and moved away.

She smiles a lot and compliments me on how nice I look.

She talks to mother about how Larissa has changed. *Grown like a weed,* she says. They laugh about *small-town Texas* and southern-sounding tongues. Trade stories about *good ol' Roy Baker* who was not a good boy at all, apparently, because according to mother and Candice, he always seemed to be drunk and yelling. *Do you remember*, my mother asks.

Do you remember, Candice asks.

Do you remember? The pollen-wreathed Women who have come into the house with Candice are whispering to me. They are movement in a still image, blurred, their faces like smoke blowing, trying to solidify. They stand around the room and in the foyer, on the stairs. One crouches on a chair, the tips of her toes grabbing at the edges of the seat. Every time I look at one, She shifts. Becomes misty. Shimmers. *Do you remember?* They ask.

"Remember what?" I ask.

Mother and Candice both look at me.

"What was that?" my mother asks.

"Nothing," I say, unwilling to share what I'm seeing, the women stomping their feet, demanding my attention, becoming more real with each passing second. But Mother and Candice do not seem to notice. They talk about remembering when in 1941 the town received its 10,000th resident, a little girl named Abigail, and they stop laughing when they realize neither of them knows where she is now.

•

"I don't think we need to worry," my mother says. "If you never go anywhere, you can't disappear."

I've asked her about Marjorie, and if the girl has been found yet. Mother thinks we shouldn't be concerned because she's sure the girl will be okay. I will be okay, too, she says, because I don't leave the house.

But there are many ways to disappear.

Sometimes I feel like people disappear in the middle of a conversation. One minute you hear them talking and the next thing you know they've gone and come back, or *you've* gone and come back, and something's been missed in the meantime.

Other times someone is in the room with you, and you turn to ask them something, and they're somewhere else in the house.

I think what my mother means is that *we* don't have to worry because if I disappear, she knows she'll find me.

This is not what happened with my father, who went to war in Europe and disappeared. He's the kind of disappeared that doesn't come back.

There are lots of pictures of him around the house, but my mother says he and I never actually knew each other.

There are nights when I think I remember him, but I know these are made up memories because I see them playing like a movie on the backs of my eyelids.

"We'll lock all the doors, though," my mother says. "And close all the windows. And we'll be just fine here."

•

When mother is not here, Candice lets me crack the windows, just a bit, so there's a breeze.

"Just let someone try to get in," she says, brandishing a knife in her hand and shaking it towards an invisible man.

I am sitting at the little table in the kitchen, trying to copy a picture out of the book Mrs. Habbermire brought me. It is of a little girl with a lace apron, holding a candle and looking into a cave. Drawing is difficult because I am not a good artist and because the table is striped with indentations that make the lead of my pencil jump. My sketch is a mess. I crinkle up the paper and start again on a fresh sheet.

"Oh, no, Emily," Candice says. "It looked good!"

She is sweet, trying to make me feel better about my lack of talent. I start to run my pencil over the paper, lightly working my way from the top left corner and angling down across the page, shading the entire sheet and revealing the invisible lines etched into the table's wood.

"I'm glad you're here," I tell her. "It's so nice to have someone ... besides my mother."

Candice sounds like she's choking. "Emily! What a thing to say!" But then, quieter, she adds, "Really though, I'm glad I'm here too."

On the paper in front of me the wood has given up its secrets. The white lines revealed by my pencil shading seem to say HELP ME HELP ME HELP ME, but the words are all jumbled up and overlapping.

"How come you're not afraid of Cedar House?" I ask.

"You know about this house?"

"I know a lot of people don't like it."

"But do you know what happened here?"

"No."

Candice sighs and then is quiet. I think she's trying to decide if she should tell me or not.

"Candice," I say, "I would like to know what happened. I do live here after all."

The Women in yellow are hiding in clocks and in the basement and behind the drapes. One of Them unfolds herself from the bathroom and goes to stand next to Candice.

"A man killed his wife. And then himself."

"Oh. Is that all?"

"Is that all? Emily, murder is a very serious crime."

"Yes, well, it's done and over now, isn't it? A house is just a house."

"Emily?"

Candice has turned her head towards me just enough for me to see her jaw moving. "You won't mention to your mother that I said anything to you about the house?"

"If you'd rather me not, I'm very good at keeping secrets."

"I'd appreciate that."

I fold my HELP ME paper into a square and slide it under my palm.

•

Technically, it's not my mother's turn to host the Garden Club again, but here they are anyway because my mother is desperate for friends.

I help Candice and cut the crusts of small sandwiches, and I do it very slowly because I am trying to concentrate and listen in about Marjorie Kent. Candice is trying to listen to the Garden Club too.

From her station at the counter she is arranging refreshments on a tray, and she says nothing to me.

According to one of the women in the next room, Marjorie's mother is tearing her hair out. Mrs. Bee delivered a pie because Mr. Kent said his wife had taken to her bed, and when Mrs. Bee got there, she found the woman twisted all up in sheets, her pillow scattered with arcs of curls she'd pulled from her head, a nightmarish version of sleeping beauty.

Marjorie's mother has taken to bed and may be tearing her hair out, but she also roams the neighborhood at night. Mrs. Habbermire found the poor woman in her dressing robe—she just happened to be up, checking the doors—and found Mrs. Kent calling for Marjorie, but calling in hoarse whispers into the darkness, and Mrs. Habbermire took the woman into her house and made her drink a glass of whiskey to calm her, put her to bed, and called her husband who came to get her in the morning.

Marjorie's mother has taken to roaming the neighborhood at night, but she's also convinced ghosts took her daughter. Mrs. Daphne heard from the librarian who had an odd phone call with Mrs. Kent that Mrs. Kent wanted to know what books her daughter had recently checked out, what books were still outstanding, presumably still on her person. Mrs. Kent learned that Marjorie was reading about Indians and something called the Killough massacre.

"I know, I know," Mrs. Daphne exclaims shrilly from the other room. "Ghosts. That takes the cake!"

I stand in camaraderie with Candice, helping her rearrange cookies that are already perfectly arranged.

"I'm not saying I believe it. I don't believe in ghosts, of course," Mrs. Daphne goes on. "It's just a poor woman looking for a reason."

•

Tonight, the Texas heat is enough to turn my skin to caramel: tacky and hot. I read a story about a little girl who does not want to grow up. Her friends and family call her Forever Girl because she shirks her impending womanhood, spends her days playing, and refuses to do chores: cooking, cleaning, sewing. Forever Girl fills her days roaming her family's ancestral lands, climbing hillsides and wandering the riverbank and exploring rock caves. This is how she meets the Little People.

The Little People play hide-and-seek with her. They leave her small gifts of bundled twigs, colored leaves arranged into little houses, braids of bird feathers. She leaves them gifts too: sweets from her mother's kitchen, bits of embroidered ribbon, lockets of her hair tied with twine.

All is good and well for the Forever Girl until one day her mother declares that she must go to school. She must grow up, find a husband, get married, have children, and learn to take care of those children, which includes doing all the chores Forever Girl doesn't want to do.

And so the night before the Forever Girl is set to begin her formal education in womanhood, she goes to say goodbye to the Little People. She runs through the hillsides and along the riverbank and to the rock caves and she calls out to the Little People—*Goodbye! Goodbye! I must become a woman now and can no longer come to see you!*

The Little People appear. They hug her shins and weep and cry and tell her she can stay with them. She could be a Forever Girl. And so, she becomes one.

I rest the book on the window ledge, finger tracing the illustration of the Forever Girl surrounded by the Little People. She has an indiscernible object in one hand and is mid-motion, bending at the knees to gather a few of them into a one-armed hug.

No reason is given for her decision to stay, to leave her family behind. This is the kind of story that would bother my mother. One that lacks what she calls *connective tissue*. But I understand that what is private must be held close, lest we give too much of ourselves away to others. There is a risk in opening too deeply, because every opening is also an entrance.

The branches of the cedar tree growing wide against the house rustle, and I look up. I squint at the yard, pull myself away from the window, and put my hands against the glass, ready to slide it down.

Hoo

The packets of green needles part, and from the tangled darkness emerges a small owl, hopping along the arm of the cedar tree, its head low on its shoulders, jutting forward like a stooped old man.

The light from my room reflects in its eyes, and it ruffles its feathers, turning its head.

Hoo Hooooooooo

"Who?" I ask.

You, it says.

And then I can sense Them in the room. The Women in yellow.

The owl stares at me, twisting its head, blinking its eyes.

Remember, the Women whisper.

When I turn to look at Them, my curtain parts. Mother is standing in her dressing gown. "Emily? I thought I heard voices. What are you doing?"

"It's just an owl mother, look."

"Emily, remember? We're supposed to keep the windows closed."

2

Weep Into Your Palms

—Gracie—

Gracie Howard was beginning to feel as if Cedar House was an affected space, and it didn't help that the Gladwells' belongings were everywhere. That was part of the reason Gracie settled on Cedar House and why she told the realtor she'd take it: the house had everything they needed, already in it.

But the wallpapers were gaudy. The dark wooden furniture made every room feel heavy. And the space—the tall ceilings, the staircase, even the transom windows—made her feel small. None of what was in Cedar House was reflective of who Gracie was, and because none of it was hers, everything was a reminder of what had happened there. If Gracie were a different person, she'd be likely to think the house was haunted, what with its constant reminders of its old inhabitants and the way they had died.

The ghost, rather, was Larissa. The town was familiar, but it was also somehow insubstantial, or like it had misplaced itself. It had always been home. Or the idea of home. And now, it wasn't.

Understanding that the Larissa she had returned to was not the Larissa she had left was uncomfortable. Not only had the roads changed—new ones added and old ones repaved, the brick from the streets around the courthouse now hidden by concrete—buildings had been torn down or built up, the air smelled different, and the women she had known had mostly moved away. An entire town had seemingly lost an entire generation of girls.

Now Gracie drove around Larissa. Tried to reacquaint herself with the town that had once been a small stop between Dallas and Shreveport now welling up into something desirous of being a city. She went down the highway and noted the missing cattle, the two new factories where swathes of trees once stood—one with its silo towers and the other with its low, flat roof—and wondered what was attractive enough about Larissa to bring new people here. To bring those who'd left back as well.

She noted the loss of small business. The music store which was now shuttered and unoccupied and the flea market which was now an A&P grocery. The old playhouse, if anyone could call it that, had become a bank. One of the old train stations had been converted into a motel. On a corner where her great aunt had once lived—dead before Gracie was even born—the house had been bulldozed and replaced by a soulless drug store made of sand-colored brick.

It was a stupid idea to come back to Larissa. She could have gone anywhere. Irene would have paid for her and Emily to move to Florida, or Arizona, or Washington. But she had thought Larissa was familiar, and it seemed too hard to start all over again.

Now she knew she had no home, and found it a cosmic joke that the place she had fled at eighteen years old with a ring on her finger was now a place she would never be able to return to, no matter how long she drove the streets, no matter how many lots she parked in remembering her youth, no matter how many times she whispered the word *Larissa*, drawing it out, caressing the roof of her mouth with her tongue.

•

Gracie didn't remember the Kents as being a remarkable couple, but then again, she hardly remembered them at all. In her mind, they were more of an impression than actual people, still young children with blurry faces from her old neighborhood. But as she put up the photos of herself and George, she began to think that the Kents *must* be remarkable people, because they were dealing with the disappearance of their child, albeit Mrs. Kent not so well. And if Gracie knew anything, it was that disappearance was a terrible burden.

Gracie hung photos on the wall along the staircase to the second story. She stood them in silver frames on the bureau and credenza, wondering what photos had been here before hers, feeling a bit like a usurper by displaying her own family on the furniture that came with Cedar House.

She also had photos that she did not, and would not, show anyone. There were three photos of Beatrice. In none of them did she, Gracie's first daughter, look dead. She looked peaceful, sleeping, in the way infants do: all wrinkles and mushed face. These she kept in a small box, with a lock of the child's blonde hair, a perfect replica of her mother's own newborn down, in the chest in her bedroom. The photos were one reason to keep yet another doorway—a barrier between herself and Emily—and Gracie thought about the smart, strange girl that Emily was and how she had asked no questions about why her mother made her own bedroom a place that could not be entered.

Gracie did not believe Emily knew about Beatrice, and if Irene ever said anything in the moments when she was screaming at Gracie's inconsolable child, it was a blessing that Emily could not remember. Beatrice's disappearance was of the worst kind: unexpected and coming on the heels of her birth. Gracie and George knew her, and then she was gone.

She looked down at the photo in her hand, the one taken of her and George the day before he was deployed. There was nothing on her husband's face to suggest he had been thinking about Beatrice, though Gracie could discern her own thoughts written on her body: the way her hand was placed on her slowly deflating stomach, the way her head tipped slightly down towards it.

At times, Gracie wondered what she'd given Emily, if when she held the still unnamed girl against long-emptied breasts the small body took something that was not milk. An erasure. A memory of absence. What did Gracie pass to her if not a desire to forget?

•

She drove by her mother's old house.

She drove by her mother's old house on the way to the market, the library, to the dry cleaners. She drove by it when she dropped Candice at her home one evening, and she drove by it, sometimes, with no errands to do at all, just so she could get out of Cedar House.

A mother cannot tell her daughter she is suffocated by her.

A mother cannot say, *I know girls are going missing, but still, I am compelled to leave you.*

A mother cannot say, *it is my duty to protect you, I know this, but there must be something for me in life besides you.*

And because she could not say these things, Gracie thought it a wonder, a blessing, an intervention, when Emily told her she should get a job.

•

Gracie picked up the telephone and pulled its long cord, opened the door to the basement, and then descended the steps.

Flick. The light shadowed the remnants of the Gladwells' lives.

Mrs. Habbermire picked up on the fifth ring, her voice heavy in the way of someone just waking up, though it was the middle of the day.

Gracie's aunt talked about Marjorie. Little Marjorie who played the angel in the Christmas play last year at the Methodist church. Marjorie who loved the animals at the circus and was enamored with the eyelashes of elephants. Mrs. Habbermire was unloading all her memories of the small girl—everything she knew—when all Gracie wanted to know was if there were any new developments.

"This is just awful," Gracie said, but the words of sentiment sounded flat. "How did this happen," she asked to herself, though Mrs. Habbermire answered her.

Marjorie Kent was last seen by a neighbor—"not a neighbor like me," Mrs. Habbermire clarified, "just someone in the neighborhood"—with her schoolbag that she used in the summers to take books to and from the library. This neighbor saw her at the corner of Myrtle and Connor and Marjorie didn't seem to be in any distress. Then Marjorie didn't come home for dinner. Her father phoned the library just as it was closing—"lucky it wasn't ten minutes later!"—and no one there had seen her for hours. He got in his car and drove the three-quarter mile to the low brick building. In the meantime, Marjorie's mother—"can you believe he didn't tell her right away something was wrong?"—set the table and waited for the rest of her family to return. When Mr. Kent came home, he called the police right away. The police came to the house. They drove all the streets. They knocked on neighbors' doors. Nothing. Not a peep about who might have seen what happened to Marjorie Kent.

"Horrible, horrible, horrible, horrible. There are no right words for something like this," Mrs. Habbermire said.

Above her, Gracie could hear the floorboards creaking. Emily moving from room to room.

"I can't help but think she was taken," Mrs. Habbermire continued.

"Mrs. Habbermire, thank you for sharing this with me, but I really need to go now."

"You lock your house up tight, girl. You are lucky your daughter has that condition."

"Yes, lucky."

A circle of sound from the parlor. The scrape of a chair.

Gracie tiptoed up the stairs and softly replaced the receiver. She could taste bile in her mouth, sour and stinging. She turned on the faucet, tried to vomit as quietly as she could.

•

Gracie knew the house was too much even as she sealed the envelope to mail back the contract. But she told herself she wanted something that offered some form of protection, socially, at least.

Maybe it was wrong to ask what street had no other children. Maybe it was wrong to cloak mother and daughter in the dress of status. But if George's mother taught Gracie anything, it was that money is power, and, even if one had no power, the illusion of power could do wonders.

People still remembered the Howard name in Larissa. They remembered Irene, at least, if not her husband, gone as he was all the time anyway. Gracie and George might have moved away with his mother and father when the oil company relocated, but the town library still had a plaque honoring their donation. The rigs with their black, iron pumps on the outskirts of town were still stamped with rusting H's. And Gracie was receiving cards from people all over town whom she'd never met but who knew the Howards and wanted to invite her for dinner, and coffee, and tea. She'd already received requests from the church and the booster club to support their most recent endeavors.

Irene Howard, if *she* came back, would be as welcome as a skunk at a lawn party. But Gracie didn't think the people in Larissa knew what to do with the dress maker's daughter who went away with the oil heir's family and was now back, daughter in tow, husband dead, and barely any family besides. *Let them wonder if I've become an Irene,* she thought.

Cedar House, she reminded herself, afforded a certain level of protection. From prying eyes, from certain kinds of people looking to thieve, from those who might knock on the door of an average house to sell vacuums or Tupperware. Some might have called the house unlucky because of its murder-suicide, but then again, Gracie thought, if it kept people away, then "unlucky" was a relative term.

•

Emily came into the kitchen with the book Mrs. Habbermire had given her. She looked tired, like she'd barely slept. Her feet shuffled along the tile.

Gracie asked, "Were you up late last night?"

"How late is late?" Emily replied.

"Past bedtime."

"I had trouble sleeping."

Gracie turned and looked at her daughter, drying her hands with a rag. Emily looked paler and was starting to form dark circles under her eyes. "Strangest thing. I thought I heard a slam last night. Woke me right up out of sleep," Gracie said.

"It was probably my window."

"Emily."

Daughter turned to look at mother, her brown eyes framed by furrowed brows. "I'm on the second story. No one's going to bring a ladder to our house in the middle of the night to crawl up on the roof and try to come into the house. Besides, even if someone tried, I'd have plenty of time to see it all happening and call for help."

Gracie knew the girl had too much sense. "I've been thinking," she said, "that I might drive around and take some photos of the town. Have them developed and we can look at them together. I can show you where I grew up and the pecan tree I used to climb and where I went to school. I can take pictures of anything you'd like."

"That sounds fine. I'd like to know more about Larissa." Emily opened the book and was studying a picture. "There are probably lots of interesting things here, aren't there?"

"If you had asked me that when I was your age, I would have said no. But Larissa has grown a lot. Changed a lot. So yes, maybe there are interesting places here now."

"And lots of people too. Probably lots of people here that you still know. If you haven't forgotten them." Emily frowned, but Gracie didn't know if it was because her daughter had picked up on her own nervousness about returning to the town, or if Emily was thinking about all the people she'd forgotten.

•

The drop cloths were gone, and still, there were doors.

Emily didn't need a house with *no* doors, she just needed a house without doorways for where she went. Doorway to her bedroom: gone. Gracie asked Earl and his brother to do that themselves before any of the other workers had even entered Cedar House. Doorway to Emily's bathroom: gone. The brothers put up long, heavy curtains. Gracie thought to let Emily replace them if she wanted, choosing her own from mail order.

Doorway to the parlor: gone. Doorway gone in the kitchen, the dining room, gone.

There were still some doors, like the ones to the guest rooms upstairs, the basement, the downstairs bath. To the library. To Gracie's room.

The real estate agent's eyes widened at the transformation of the house. Gracie wondered if Ronald Toller was thinking it would be impossible for him to re-sell one day.

But even if the door-less house was not to his liking, he was polite, taking off his hat, the hair underneath wet with sweat, which he apologized for.

Gracie introduced him to Candice, and would have introduced him to Emily, too, but Gracie's daughter was in bed again, knocked off her feet with cedar fever, a mystery since it wasn't even the season for it, and her eyes were puffy and her forehead hot. Candice was making Emily chicken and dumplings, bringing her wet rags for her face, and reading the newspaper aloud because Emily kept demanding stories.

When Mr. Toller spied the camera placed on the bench of the hall tree, he said to bring it along. Maybe while they were out and looking at property, Gracie thought, she would be lucky enough to see one of the "wonderful women." Give them something else to talk about. The widow and the man who duped her into buying Cedar House.

Stop it, Gracie told herself, but she couldn't help smiling while getting into Mr. Toller's car.

Before looking at the possible locations for the dress store, they drove around the town. Gracie took pictures of the library and its plaque, the town square, and the courthouse. They stopped every mile or so along her route to the grocery, capturing houses and businesses along the way. She would have taken pictures of George's old home, too, but she didn't want to ask Mr. Toller to drive out into the country.

Instead, she took pictures of her childhood home, a far cry from the house on Woodlee in Oklahoma, Irene's house. Gracie's old house was not quaint by any means, but not obscene either. Yellow brick, two-stories, with a pecan tree and crepe myrtle.

She wanted to knock on the door, to ask if she might take pictures of the rooms, though she was sure they'd be much different now.

"Do you know who bought this house after my mother died?" She asked Mr. Toller, who waited patiently, leaned against the car.

"Let me see …" He counted off the owners on his fingers. "I believe Norman and Bettye Donald live there now."

Gracie was a few steps up the walkway and stopped. "Norman Donald?" she asked. "He bought my old house?"

"He's done quite well for himself. Took over his father's auto business. He and Bettye have two children. I think one older and one younger than Emily."

Gracie stared at the house she once called home. She did not know Bettye. At least she didn't think she did. But she imagined a young blonde woman reclining in the clawfoot tub, her leg propped up on the ledge, smearing herself with bubbles.

What would Bettye say if Gracie told her about the last night *she* ever sat in that tub? The blood turning the water pink? Scrubbing herself raw with a cloth she had to throw away because Gracie had pulled so hard, pressed so hard, the threads came apart?

"What time is it?" Gracie asked, knowing full well what damn time it was.

Mr. Toller checked his watch. "A quarter past two."

"You know, I'm really starting to feel as if I should check in on Emily. Do you think we could reschedule? For the dress shop?"

Mr. Toller tried to not look disappointed, and Gracie found herself suddenly irritable. Hadn't she thrown enough money his way already? She made for the car, reaching through the open window to pull up the lock.

"Of course. Of course. Let me just drive you home then," the agent trailed off.

•

The backyard was overgrown, untamed.

Gracie couldn't stand it. The ruthless abandon.

It must have been well-manicured once, years ago when there was a team of people to subdue it. The Gladwells must have had a gardener. Or two. Or three.

Grass had grown up between the pavers, the paths winding through overgrowth. It was mostly brown now, fragile and thin. Weeds had erupted and dried up everywhere: long lengths of crabgrass, knotweed growing where old leaves had long decayed, large patches of dirt without even the memory of roots.

The only thing thriving were the climbing roses, and they mocked her.

Gracie didn't know what she was thinking. A garden club. Friendship. Working together with matching gloves and straw hats. Radio playing.

She dragged the trash bag along with one hand, crawling on hands and knees and ripping up the ill-kept plant life, ropes of it coming up easy out of dry soil. She could smell herself.

If she had to imagine this yard at its height, it would be a magnificent place. There must have been grand parties here once. Lanterns and melting ice, fruit pies and the clack of shoes on stone.

Gracie thought she should ask Mrs. Habbermire how the Gladwells made their money. She didn't remember the woman saying when she first suggested Gracie buy Cedar House.

"How long has it been sitting there?" Gracie had asked instead, whispering into the phone in the hallway of Irene's house.

"Ah, a few years," Mrs. Habbermire admitted. "Took Mr. Toller some time to track down the relatives. All overseas."

Gracie found it strange that she didn't remember Cedar House from before she'd moved away with George. But then again, back in the day she would have had no business traveling down the street she now lived on. It was out of the way from everywhere she went, and though her mother made dresses for the kinds of women who lived in the neighborhood, it didn't mean she socialized with them.

"Gracie?" Candice was coming outside, shading her eyes from the sun. "Dinner's ready."

"Just leave it on the table," Gracie said, knowing Emily would not be down. The poor girl alternated between lucidity and bouts of fever, maybe something more than an allergy. If it didn't get better, Gracie would have to call a doctor. And Emily hated doctors. "Go on and get home," Gracie said. "I'll clear it all up."

She went back to the grass and began dwelling again on how she hated that dreams died like this—wishes that made sense at the time and only later were remembered with embarrassment.

A garden club. Pshh.

The work of clearing out the garden was tearing her hands, the bending of branches refusing to die, the ripping into green fibers that rejected being twisted apart.

She gave a little yell, stomping her growing pile of refuse foliage.

"You mock me," she said to the undergrowth, to the hedges, to the roses.

When she looked up, she gave another little yell, not believing what she was seeing.

She stepped back. And back again. She put one foot behind the other until she was halfway across the yard, unnerved by the sprawl of the thing she was staring at.

The roses had arranged themselves in such a way as to make a face. Some grimace of a jack-o-lantern: triangle eyes and a wide, stretched mouth, pickle-colored leaves darkening the more she retreated: a maw curving up, smiling its emptiness at her.

•

Gracie went to the library because she wanted Emily to have something to read other than the newspapers and the single, slim collection of stories Mrs. Habbermire had brought her. Emily hadn't said she was bored, but there were so many things Emily didn't say that Gracie felt she often had to take the initiative.

She'd found two books she thought looked interesting and had just checked them out when she noticed the records room. It was vacant, not a soul in it, and Gracie was overcome by a sudden wave of nostalgia for the Larissa she had known, the town that had become distorted in the intervening years.

Gracie went into the space and made her way around, stopping in front of dozens of expandable folders nestled into the shelves. They were labeled "post cards."

The last time Gracie had sent a postcard, or received one, was a few years back when she was still writing with Angela, who was now in Georgia, a nurse, and still unmarried. Gracie selected a random collection and carried them to a sleek, varnished table. The armchair was silent on the carpet. She opened the folder, sliding the contents out in front of her.

Everything in the folder was from 1900-1920: black and white pictures or sepia images tinted with green. The first she chose to examine was of an old cotton compress, bundled pallets of the export stacked in neat rows outside on the dirt. Not a person was in sight. Just acres, Gracie estimated, of product waiting to be shipped. The next was an artist's rendering of Bell Street with its grand, two- and three-story homes, stately columns and sidewalks that dead-ended into still dirt streets. The cedar trees themselves formed neat lines into the horizon, separating the sidewalks from the yards. The next postcard was dull, yellowed with age and no image or picture. It was simply ornamented with red text that spelled out POSTCARD.

Dear Cora. The words had been typed, not written, and the *i*'s were misaligned, a little lower than the rest of the letters. *I'm glad to say all the work is almost done, and soon I'll be able to send for you. There is a beautiful bedroom in the front turret that looks out upon the street. I've saved this for you. I hope all is well and that you are missing me as much as I miss you. We've a new horse too, a roan with a sweet heart and gentle nature. I can see us now, side by side, like in days past. All my Love, Lillian Gladwell.*

She turned the card over again and read the addressee: Cora Bent, Summit Lane, New Orleans, Louisiana. Whatever this message was, Gracie didn't think it had ever been sent.

Cora Bent, from New Orleans. Gracie wondered who the woman was and about her connection to the Gladwells. A cousin, perhaps? Surely someone who knew the Gladwells intimately if they were going to bring her all the way to Larissa at the turn of the century.

She wondered about Cora Bent and where the woman was now, if she had stayed in touch over the years or if this unsent postcard was a precursor to another failed relationship, lost over time and distance. Did Cora Bent know what had happened to Lillian Gladwell? Or, like Lillian, had she passed away?

•

"Where's the rest?" Candice had the newspaper spread out on the table, the pages in disarray. "You know how much Emily likes the newspaper. Says it helps her know Larissa."

"I have those pictures now," Gracie said, trying to distract her maid, but then she decided against asking Candice to show them to Emily. *She* would do that. She had been the one to take them, who knew the stories attached to them. Besides, she had stopped at the library, so she went to her purse and pulled the books from it. "Actually," she said in amendment, "I thought Emily might like something else to read."

Mrs. Candice took the books and eyed the them dubiously. "I think your girl is too mature for this one.'

"What's wrong with *The Secret Garden?*"

"Mrs. Howard, she has me reading the newspaper to her. Doesn't that say something?"

"What about the other one, then?"

Mrs. Candice shook her head, holding up *The Lion, the Witch, and the Wardrobe*.

"She likes fantastical things," Gracie said in her own defense.

"I'll try it," Candice said. "But where's the rest of the paper anyway? She was asking about some article we can't find the beginning of."

Gracie silently cursed herself. "I don't want Emily reading the front page."

"What's there?"

"You haven't heard? They found the Kent girl."

•

Gracie was sitting in bed with *The Secret Garden*. If Emily wasn't going to read it, someone was. Her eyes were drooping and she realized she'd been staring at the same paragraph for minutes now without retaining any of the information. She closed the book, turned off the lamp, and rolled onto her side.

From where she lay, she faced the door, and so when she thought she heard the doorknob turning, her eyes flashed open.

In the darkness she saw a person.

Or a figure.

Or a form.

Her door was still closing, and in the darkness just inside her room was a shape moving towards her.

She screamed, and in the time it took her to blink once, the shape was gone.

Gracie sat up, breathing hard, one hand to her mouth. And then she shot from the bed, rushed down the hall, and threw open the curtains to Emily's room.

Her daughter was asleep. Snoring. Her window open.

Gracie shut it, looking out onto the deserted street. Then she checked the windows in the house—all twenty-three of them—and the two doors. Nothing seemed amiss, but still, she could not believe someone had not just been in their house.

3

It's What She Doesn't Say

—Bet—

"Goodbye Bettye! It was so good seeing you."

Bet wondered if Mrs. Tandy really had been glad to bump into her. It was so hard to assess the women in the Garden Club. Even when she had been a member, before she left and took a job, she felt the women often spoke in codes, never really wanting to say things plainly.

Mrs. Tandy continued along, a bag of groceries hooked in the crook of her arm, a wily squirrel seeming to follow along behind her.

Bet found herself looking left at the intersection and following the tree line all the way down to the library. Odd that she'd never noticed it before, how the trees all lined up. Different sizes, different ages, but still. Like someone had walked the same, straight line down the yards, over time across decades, dropping acorns or seeds until the trees popped up, same distance from the street, in front of each house.

She could almost picture a man behind one of those trees, hiding, listening for the small footsteps of a girl skipping her way home. Maybe singing. Maybe talking to herself.

Bet looked the other way and then stepped into the street.

She passed in front of the historical society where Mrs. Habbermire sat on the other side of the window, fingers punching at her typewriter, swiveling her face to and from whatever document was open on her desk, and Bet tapped on the glass and waved. The older woman waved back.

Then Bet turned right at the square, passing the diner where her boss ate lunch every day, walking by the Richards & Sons law firm, and finally passing the hardware store. Through the window she saw the far wall lined with hooks, draped with rope and supporting gardening tools: hoes and shovels and spades.

She pictured Marjorie Kent's face peering out of a shallow grave, dirt peppering her skin.

"Stop it," she muttered to herself.

"Are you okay?"

Bet turned to see a woman about her age, hair pinned up under a thin scarf and wearing short pants. The woman held a wooden bird-feeder in both hands.

Bet recognized her as Gracie Howard, and reflexively, Bet frowned.

The woman frowned back.

"Are you okay?" Gracie repeated, not a hint of recognition in her voice or face.

To this woman, Bet was a stranger, and she felt oddly grateful for it. "Fine. Fine. I was just distracted."

Gracie smiled then.

The hardware store bell chimed, and a man Bet didn't recognize came out and walked between the two women. He rapped on the hood of his truck before opening the driver's side door.

"Have a good day," Bet said. "I'm going to be late for work."

Gracie nodded, and then she turned away. Bet squinted against the sun and watched her go.

•

At the police station, Bet deposited her purse in her desk drawer, discretely straightened her pantyhose, which were twisting something wicked, and then patted her neck and face with a tissue to soak up the sweat. She opened the window closest to her and then knocked on Marcil's door. He was on the phone but waved Bet in. She sat in the chair across from him and waited with her pen and paper.

"Listen, Dan," Marcil was saying, "I can't just write a check every six months. There's plenty of jobs here. Larissa's exploding with them!"

Dan was the police chief's youngest brother. Bet knew they'd been fighting. But maybe fighting wasn't the right word. More like disagreeing. Dan was in a pickle, had been for quite a while, and Marcil was tired of bailing him out.

"I could put in a good word and ..." Marcil was obviously cut off mid-sentence. He listened. Bet waited in Marcil's silence while he played with the phone cord, wrapping it around a drawer knob on his side of the desk. "Look, Dan. I have work to do. We're going to talk about this, I promise. I'll put a check in the mail today. But it's the last one. Last one, Dan. Then we really have to figure out what to do." He hung up and shook his head. "I'm sorry, Bet. I just don't know what to do with him. He just never listens."

Bet had almost married Dan. Maybe this was why Marcil talked so openly in front of her. She knew something of his younger brother's desperation to be his own man—to revolt against the family legacy of public service and to *make something of himself*—Dan's words. He never did tell Bet what happened with their family and why he was so eager to get away, to not be tied to them or east Texas. Whatever that reason, he was impulsive, had no real plan other than to "not do what the family does." He had a good heart, but he had no vision, which meant he had no security. Bet carried in her body the memory of childhood hunger, and she never wanted to feel that way again, which was part of why she had broken up with him. Bet had wanted a provider and realized too late that a good match was less about money and more about respect and love.

"A risk," Marcil murmured, shuffling the papers on his desk.

Bet discretely tapped her pad with her pen a few times to remind him why she was there.

"I need you to schedule me a meeting with the mayor," Marcil said. "And I need you to find me everything we have on Marjorie Kent. Papers everywhere. Why can't people just keep it all together," he added, clearly frustrated. "Everybody's running around like a bunch of BBs in a boxcar."

Bet thought it an apt description. Ever since Marjorie went missing, the police had seemed even more disorganized than usual. And of course, it was her job to clean up their mess. *Mother at home, mother at work*, she overhead once, as if she wasn't capable of being anything other than a caretaker.

•

Bet had to rifle through five desks, the records closet, and the conference room to find what she needed. The initial report on Marjorie Kent had been taken by Calvin, the follow-up by Dwight, and then various other officers had been dispatched to talk to neighbors and potential witnesses. But it was what she found on Buddy's desk that sent gooseflesh up her arms.

She'd been searching for the statement from the librarian who'd been the last person to see Marjorie, and she did find that, but she found something else, too. In a slim folder were two pieces of paper, both drafted in Buddy's tight handwriting, reports about other girls who'd gone missing.

Bet sat in Buddy's chair and began to read.

A little girl named Georgia Stock had gone missing almost a month ago, on May 28th. Her parents, workers out on Mrs. White's farm, had called to report her disappearance. Buddy even wrote down the time of the discussion, 10:38am. After her, on June 5th, another girl from the farm went missing. Rita Randall. Rita's parents came to the station. They referenced Georgia Stock. At the bottom of the report on Rita, Buddy had written, *maybe girls ran away together*, and Bet knew it was hogwash because a seven-year-old girl and a nine-year-old girl wouldn't have the resources to just take off. Especially not ones from the farm.

Bet felt blood rush to her cheeks and she clenched her jaw. Buddy had barely cared enough to take a full statement, and his theory linking the girls was laughable. This was not the kind of police work Larissa needed or deserved. Bet exhaled slowly, turned sharply on the balls of her feet, and headed to Marcil's office.

"You got it?" He asked. "Give it here."

"So," Bet began, not quite sure how to phrase what she was going to say.

"What? Spit it out. Something's missing? Should have guessed."

"No," Bet replied, holding the messy stack of papers to her chest. "Nothing's missing. It's just ... Marcil. I don't think Marjorie is the first girl to go missing."

"What do you mean?" Marcil put down his pen and rested his elbows on the desk, clasping both hands together.

"I think you should look at this."

•

Bet looked out the window at her boys in the backyard with Norman. They'd all become quite enamored with the Guides program, and her youngest, Alton, wore his badly constructed headdress and sloppily sewn fringed vest with the only patch he'd earned so far. He watched his older brother rub two sticks together in an attempt to start a fire. Bet had made Norman dig the brittle grass out of that spot in the yard and told him to line it with bricks and sand. "You're gonna set the whole place aflame," she warned him.

She was glad for the Guides if only for one reason: it provided her time to be alone.

Many nights, before or after dinner, Norman would sit with Will and Alton, poring over the pages that listed all the badges they could earn, making notes about which would be easiest to obtain (Alton's idea, since he was eager to be satisfied quickly and often), and which were the most interesting (Will's idea, which conflated interesting and complicated).

Her hands pruning in the water—the right glove had ripped and there was no point in only wearing one—Bet listened to Alton's shriek of delight as it pierced through the kitchen. She could not see the fire but had no doubt it was there now, smoldering in the twilight.

She knew it was unfair to have a favorite child, but knowing did not stop her from favoring Will. He'd been a colicky baby but was growing into a good man. Shy and short for his twelve years, he was slow to respond to questions, always thinking through what he wanted to say before answering. He said *please* and *thank you* without having to be reminded, and his grades were good. He especially liked science.

Alton gave her pause because as he aged he was becoming more like his father. He was quick to frustrate, which many seven-year-olds were, but in addition to that he had bouts of intense anger that manifested in screaming and hitting. And that wasn't all that made her worry. Alton didn't seem to know the line between entertainment and cruelty, a lack of distinction she found increasingly unnerving, especially in light of Marjorie Kent's disappearance.

Just a few days ago—the day she'd learned Marjorie was missing—she'd come home to find Will reading in the living room, reclining on the sofa with a book in his hands. Alton was in the back yard with his back to the house, and when she opened the fridge to put the groceries away, a yowl startled her, sending the milk to the floor, the thin, white liquid spreading all over the tiles.

She found Alton outside with a knife in one hand and hunk of skin and fur in the other, his arms scratched and bleeding, his hands coated with sticky blood.

Bet had slapped him. Grabbed the knife. Looked for the cat, who was long gone and would probably not be coming back.

While Alton began to cry, bringing Will outside as well, Bet had simply turned from her youngest and walked calmly back into the house.

Stunned with what she had done—laid hands on her own child—she washed the knife. Then, still dripping with pink water, she'd just thrown it away.

Norman said it was boy's play and that he'd "had a conversation" with Alton, and Will, of course, about the importance of being nice, and kind. But when he said this to Bet, she'd thought *look who's calling the kettle black* and rolled over to face the wall.

There was a tangible distance between her and Alton now. The boy hadn't forgotten what happened, and neither had Bet, which is why she hadn't apologized to him.

She couldn't help but think that event was a milestone of some kind. A marker. An omen. An act that would delineate the threshold between child and man, and that Alton had stepped over, gleefully, into his first act of adulthood with a viciousness that would continue throughout his life.

It wasn't fair to think this, but it didn't stop the thought from occurring. Or building.

In the other room, people on the television prattled. Bet clanked dishes against each other in the sink. The floor at her feet became slippery.

•

"Uh-oh."

Bet had just come into the station and was eyeing the coffee maker when Calvin walked by her.

"Huh?" Bet asked, thrown off by the comment.

"It doesn't look good, that's all I'm saying." Calvin was beating around the bush, plugging his thumbs into his belt loops and looking to either side. He even rocked back on his heels.

"Oh lord, Calvin. Just tell me."

"Over there," he said, nodding discreetly with his head.

Bet looked across the room and saw Buddy in Marcil's office. "What's happened?"

"He's in a world of hurt," Calvin responded. "Really dropped the ball. Marjorie wasn't the first girl to go missing."

"Wasn't she," Bet said flatly, not mentioning that she was the one to point out that fact.

"Well, Buddy never *said* anything, but two girls have gone missing out from Mrs. White's place. And no one's found them yet."

Bet chewed on her lip, wondering if she asked what the progress was, whether or not Calvin would tell her.

"And that ain't the end of it, either. There's another girl too, now. Her parents came up here last night."

"There's what?" Bet asked, her heart beating a bit faster.

"Yup. She went missing before Marjorie, but her family thought she'd run off and gotten hitched. Guess that's not what happened after all."

Bet wanted to go straight to Marcil's office. To find out what the hell was going on in Larissa.

"So he's going," Calvin added, interrupting Bet's train of thought.

"Who? Who's going where?"

"Marcil's letting him go. Firing him. No more Buddy boy. Hey," he said, elbowing Bet gently in her side. "Maybe you could take his place," he joked.

Bet smiled weakly. She'd be better than most of the men working for the police. She had no doubt of that.

•

There was a vigil for Marjorie Kent at the Methodist church to pray for her safe return home.

Summer in Texas meant too many hours of light and at seven p.m., the sky showed no desire to lose its sun, and Alton showed no desire to start following directions. He stood in the backyard, refusing to come in and bathe and instead hitting rocks with a hammer and claiming he was going to find a geode soon. Bet warned her son that if he wouldn't behave, he wouldn't be allowed to go, but the threat had no effect. So she left Alton with Norman and got in the car with Will to make the short drive through the square to the Methodist church just beyond.

Will hadn't said anything either way about a desire to go with his mother. She'd simply asked, and he said he would. He did not say that he *wanted* to.

Her eldest son held a squat bouquet of flowers in his hands. He'd picked them himself, weeds mostly, dandelion blooms, and bush daisies. Bet hadn't had the heart to tell him bringing flowers was akin to proclaiming the possibility of Marjorie's death—flowers were for funerals—but she intended to tell him that it wasn't the best idea. She just had to get to the point where she could say it.

It was Friday night in Larissa, Texas, and Bet knew the town's teenagers would be clustered at the ice cream parlor. Packed in cars at the drive-in theatre. A few wild ones would be taking the long road to the lookout over Milton's pond, which was hardly a pond now—more a broad, mucky indentation in the earth—parked for the coming darkness, waiting to place eager hands over and under clothes.

In a few years Will would be there, at one of those places, laughing under yellow lights, Marjorie Kent not even a memory. That's what happens to tragedy over time, to those people that it only tangentially touches. They forget and move on.

She was not ready for her son to grow up. She was not ready for him to think about women in the ways men do.

"I haven't asked how you feel about all this," she said, both hands on the steering wheel.

Will shrugged and twirled the bouquet slowly. "I hope they find her."

"You know there's a chance that when they do, she won't be alive, right?"

"But maybe she will be."

Yes, maybe she will be, Bet thought.

The lot of the church was full, and Bet had to circle out of it and park down the street in front of the beauty parlor.

Will got out of the car, and after hesitating with the flowers in his hand, decided to leave them on the passenger seat. Bet took his hand.

The lawn of the church was crowded with people, and Bet noticed that there were no other children present. Will must have noticed this too, because he dropped his mother's hand, though he stayed close to her side. Laurel Dawson, impeccable as always, in heels even while she moved over the grass, was passing out small candles anchored in wax paper cups. She had a basket of them.

Bet made polite small talk with the women around her, church ladies she used to call friends. Will said very little, nodding when he needed to, saying, *good to see you again miss so-and-so* and making them smile with his civility.

When the clock tower chimed seven, Marjorie Kent's father climbed to the top of the steps. His wife was nowhere to be seen. Bet suspected it was better that way and wondered how the woman was faring. She'd heard not so well.

Arnold Kent was a big man. His stomach was round under the waist of his pants. His hair was plastered back along his scalp, shining brown, grey at the temples. He thanked the town for coming out, for supporting the Kent family, and pleaded with anyone in the crowd who might know something about Marjorie's whereabouts, who might know something about what happened to her, to call the police.

Marcil Wallace then stepped up beside Mr. Kent and patted the man on the back, saying something too soft to hear, to which Mr. Kent nodded.

"Our officers are working diligently," Marcil began. The chief was in uniform, imposing, sure in his voice—"to find Marjorie Kent.

We've made good headway in the past few days, and now Mr. Kent is generously allowing whoever is involved in this business to identify themselves. Better to speak up now than to have us come knocking at your door."

There was a murmuring in the crowd.

"We'd like to take a moment of quiet," Marcil continued, removing his hat, "to say a prayer for Marjorie's safe homecoming. And for the other girls, too," he added. "If we could all bow our heads."

Bet looked down at her shoes and let the words of supplication creep in one ear and out the other.

No one wanted to be the first to break the silence. The prayer, prayers, silent and spoken to the selves, must have been over. And yet, the quiet.

"Thank you," Marcil finally said, relieving the tension.

As residents of Larissa began turning and talking to each other in somber voices, Will turned to his mother.

"What was he talking about?" Will asked. "Other girls?"

Bet's candle flame was out, the thin black wick curved like a question mark. She didn't want to throw it away. It would look tacky. She carried it with her to the car, thinking she'd rid herself of it at home. "Marjorie was not the first girl to go missing," she finally admitted.

"Then why's the vigil only for her?" Will asked. He kept looking backward, towards the church.

"Well," Bet began, "Marjorie was from Larissa. The other girls ... they aren't really from here."

"Then where are they from?" Will asked, looking over his shoulder.

It was an unspoken rule, or custom, for Larissa to consider Mrs. White's farm as separate from the town. And it was. The farm was county land, but the distance was more than just a boundary on the map. It was part disdain and distrust of Larissa towards the itinerant community—seasonal workers who came and went, some from southern and west Texas and others from Louisiana and Oklahoma—never fulltime residents who tried to embed themselves in the community. And part was distrust of the town by the people who worked the land, who came into Larissa in the backs of pickup trucks in sweat-stained clothing only to be ignored by the residents who tended to view the workers as suspect. That divide had caused Buddy to not take their reports seriously at first, and it had only been Marjorie Kent's disappearance—and Bet's discovery of potential correlation—that brought renewed attention to the girls whose families lived outside of town.

"Well, honey," Bet finally said. "Those girls' families live out on that big farm."

"What farm?" Will asked.

This was not a conversation Bet wanted to have at the moment. She hadn't the patience, or the energy, to explain that there was an entire community of people down the road that Larissa was very good at pretending wasn't there.

"You've never seen it," Bet tried to explain.

"Why not?"

Bet slapped a mosquito that pricked her arm, seeing the rusty streak of blood on her skin. She tried to wipe it away, but still, there was a trace of it.

"We haven't had a reason to go out that way," Bet replied.

Her short response wasn't going to keep Will from asking questions. He had a tell when he was on a streak: the way his eyes opened wide to cause a small wrinkle on his forehead to appear.

"It's complicated, Will. Okay?" She continued. "This is all too much to think about, and I really don't want to keep talking about it."

"I know, but there's girls—"

"Will." Bet let his name sound like a small rebuke.

Keys jangling against each other. Car doors slamming shut. The rumble of the engine.

Will was silent on the way home, and when Bet looked over at him she noticed he no longer had the flowers, and she wondered where they were.

•

Bet hated grocery shopping, but she hadn't always. Used to be, when she and Norman were first married, that she loved it. The freedom to decide what she wanted to eat, the new recipes swapped with other women at church, each attempting to improve upon the others. She loved the checkbook too, signing her name Mrs. Norman Donald, and doing the lines of math to make sure she stayed within her budget.

Now it was a chore, and she sped through the aisles with her cart, no list in hand, simply determining what meals could be made quickly each night and shopping for three to four days at a time.

She was going to turn into an aisle to get a new bottle of dish soap but saw Gracie Howard there, a box of who knew what in her hand. Bet turned her cart the next aisle over and stared blankly at some packages of cookies.

Gracie Howard. Again. Bet's dumb luck. That woman really hadn't aged a day. Came back to Larissa looking like she'd been gone a month, not over a decade. Life hadn't treated her rough like it had done to Bet.

She picked up a package of sugar wafers, thinking about how she lived in Gracie's old house. How different their lives could have been if Gracie and Norman had ended up together. Then it would be those two in the McCallin house, with two boys, and Gracie running the errands and making Jell-O desserts with canned peaches inside.

It might have been Bet who married George Howard, and moved to Oklahoma, and lived in a big house with a daughter.

No. It wouldn't be exactly like trading places, of course it wouldn't, and Bet felt guilty for wishing it, if even for a moment.

She put the cookies back and took a package of Oreos instead.

Thankfully, Gracie was gone by the time Bet got to the end of the aisle, and Bet pushed the cart down the linoleum floor, one wheel wobbling erratically.

•

The sky was on fire. Orange, then pink, and above, purple fading into blue.

"What's this about? Smoking again?" Norman came out the back door, waving his hand in front of his face to disperse the smelly cloud and fend off the swarm of gnats that were festering inside the wilted Indian Blankets. Will had called them firewheels when he planted them for his nature patch.

"Work," Bet explained, stubbing out the cigarette on the concrete and putting the butt in a flowerpot. The bluebonnets she'd tried to plant never did grow, so what was a little tobacco to take their place?

"That bad?"

"Norman. Four girls are missing. Of course it's that bad."

"I didn't mean it like that."

She sighed. Maybe he did. Maybe he didn't. What did it matter?

The colors were changing by the minute. Already the orange gone. Just the thinnest lid of pink over the treetops.

"I always wanted a girl," Bet said. "I wouldn't tell the boys that, but it's true. I used to dream of ruffled dresses and ribbons and frilly socks. Now I'm glad we don't have one. This world is not a nice place for women."

"What has gotten into you lately?" Norman plucked the charred end of the cigarette from the flowerpot and carried it over to the trash can. The metal made an awful clang when he put the top back on, and she cringed.

"I'm tired, Norman. Of all of it. I'm just so tired."

"Then quit. We don't need the money."

"It's not about the money. It's about doing something other than raising children, Norman."

"You act like having a family is the worst thing in the world."

"I do not act like that. And there's nothing wrong with wanting, needing, to be something more than a housewife."

"There's a camping trip coming up," Norman said. "For the Guides. I'm going to take the boys. Up to Wichita."

"That would be good."

He waited, stayed, she assumed, because he wanted her to say more. But she was done talking and pushed back in the rocking chair.

Only the memory of lantana colors now. The sky coming down. She put a hand on her stomach and closed her eyes.

4

This Time, Be Careful

—Candice—

Candice looked out the window at the backyard of Cedar house, feeling sorry for the wilted and dead shrubbery. How was anyone supposed to keep a home as big as Cedar House clean and functional? She reminded herself that no *one* person was supposed to, and that houses this large were why she had a job.

Privately, she found this absurd.

Privately, she knew that part of her thought had to do with her duplication of work: clean here, then go home and clean there. Everett helped, of course, but he kept long hours at the diner and didn't care much for cooking at home when he cooked all day at work.

Privately, she also knew that part of her general dislike of Cedar House was because of what had happened there. She didn't want to think that she was like her mother; Salida believed people who died unnatural deaths might stay around as spirits in certain places. Candice did not want to equate herself with her mother, but Candice could not shake the feeling that Cedar House was an affected place, somehow.

When she was debating interviewing for the job, she'd read the advertisement to Everett one evening as they sat out in the backyard, him tending to puny stalks of broccoli attempting to spring up. She'd walked over to him and said,"What do you think about this? Seeking: housekeeper, discrete, honest, good with children. Generous pay to qualified applicants. Apply in person. 212 Cedar Street."

"Isn't that the Cedar House?" Everett had asked, frowning at a recently dug hole: squirrels.

"Sure is."

"Some terrible things happened there. Makes me queasy thinking about it. Doesn't that bother you at all? The thought of working in there?"

Candice avoided the question, because at the time, she hadn't yet really worked out how she felt about it. "We could use the money," Candice said instead, and then added, "They could use the money too." Candice was referring to their daughters, both grown women, both in Chicago, both settled with husbands—brothers, oddly enough—and Candice and Everett's youngest with a rounded belly and her own daughter or son on the way.

"They're grown women, Candy," Everett said, bending down and testing the dryness of the soil by digging into it with his finger.

"And wouldn't it have been nice if when we'd come here, we had a little more help? I'm not saying to give them everything. Just something."

Everett grunted. She knew that *he* knew she was right, but he wasn't going to say so. Not because he didn't want to give her the satisfaction, but because who knew when it might come up in conversation, in front of Rose and June—and in front of their husbands, too—and Everett had told the girls when they married young that part of marriage was choosing a partner with the ability to provide. He wanted his advice to be good advice, and he didn't want to look like a hypocrite.

That promise—to provide—was what sealed the marriage for Candice and Everett. Candice would never forget the night Everett appeared on her doorstep and asked her mother for her hand in marriage. He'd said, *I will always provide for her,* and he did, scraping and working and learning trade after trade until they had enough money for him to open the diner, which he did, in this small town which was as close to Nacogdoches as Candice dared to get. It would have been easier on her if all those years ago they weren't constantly counting pennies, worrying about what bills would be paid, and when. Candice figured she'd have fewer grey hairs if they'd had a little help, though she knew that wouldn't have been possible coming from his family or hers.

"I just think about that house," Everett went on, "and that poor woman. Poor man, too. I can't even imagine what it takes for someone to do something like that. Kill his wife and then himself. And that house sitting empty for years. Probably infested with rodents."

"Lots to clean then," Candice joked, and leaned away when Everett playfully batted at her shoulder with the palm of his hand. "People have been talking about them already, the people who moved in. Wife with no husband, never come back from war, and that girl. You know they say the girl might be some part that isn't white. Everyone is talking about it."

Everett burst out laughing and turned to look at her. "Say what? A Howard that isn't white?"

"They say her hair is black black black and her skin is dark too. And not sun dark."

"Did I ever tell you about my great aunt Cora?" Everett stood up. Brushed his hands on his pants. Led Candice back to the chairs at the edge of the house and poured himself a glass of sweet tea from the pitcher on the small table.

"I know the name," Candice said. "That's about it."

"We don't talk about her much. Lost to the family is what Ma said. Cora was a working girl in New Orleans. Billed herself as an 'Octoroon.' She wasn't Black. We're as white as they come, but folks believed her anyway."

Candice was taken aback. A prostitute in Everett's family, and one he'd never mentioned. Everett wasn't an exceptionally conservative man, so there was really no reason to have hidden the information. She raised an eyebrow, unsure of if he was yanking her chain. "And why have you never mentioned this before?"

"Don't know. Well ..." he took a sip and then cocked his head back. "Actually, I kind of forgot about her. She and ma stopped talking before I was born. An embarrassment for some of the family, I think. Point being," Everett went on, "no one is 'maybe' anything. You are or you aren't. Regardless of what people think."

They sat in silence a few moments, and the cicadas hummed.

"You want to know about the girl, don't you?" Everett finally asked.

"That's not true. I'm thinking of our girls."

Now, standing at the non-doorway to the laundry room of Cedar House, Candice remembered what her husband said: *no one is "maybe" anything*. What bothered her now was that Emily Howard was clearly Indian, and no one, not even her mother, was acknowledging it.

She thought about this as Gracie pounded up the stairs from the basement, sweat at her brow, with another box. "More," she said, setting the box down on the table. "You wouldn't believe all the junk down there. I don't think it even all belonged to them. There's stuff down there that doesn't make any sense. I should have had Ronald clear it all out when I agreed to buy this place. No, he should have done some clearing out before he sold it. I don't know what I was thinking taking this all on. Wait, she said, I know what I was thinking. A treasure hunt. Something to keep Emily occupied. Stupid of me."

Emily couldn't go down into the basement. Either because of the doorway or because she, like Candice, felt that it was not a place anyone should be in.

"Emily!" Gracie called, and the girl came into the kitchen.

"Want to look through this one?" Gracie asked.

"Depends," the girl said, coming into the kitchen and depositing herself in a chair. "Is there anything good?"

"That's what you're supposed to tell me."

Emily opened the box. Glasses. "We need more glasses? Fancy wine glasses?"

"For all those dinner parties we host?" her mother replied, laughing. "Candice?"

Candice didn't like taking things out of Cedar House, though she did. Neither Gracie nor her daughter wanted the small, burlwood clock. Or the remnant velvet from curtains (that smelled musty but appeared fine). Or the train set. Candice had taken them all, begrudgingly, because she could sell them and send the extra money to her daughters. Still, it made her feel awkward taking these dead people's things.

"Glasses, why not?" Candice said, bowing her head and looking in the box. She'd have to call Everett and have him pick them up. She had no desire to carry them across town.

"I got five more for today," Gracie said, turning back towards the stairs.

"Do you drink a lot of wine?" Emily asked Candice, picking up one of the flutes.

"Not at all," Candice laughed.

"The people who lived here must have had a lot of parties." Emily counted the glasses in the box, moving paper and rattling the numbers off: 16. "Ugh. I can't imagine sixteen people in one room. It sounds awful."

Candice agreed. She liked that Emily was often blunt. If there was one thing Candice didn't have to worry about, it was reading between the lines with what Emily said. The girl was not confined by typical societal rules, and Candice enjoyed that.

"And can you even imagine," Emily went on, "they must have smelled!" She wrinkled her nose. "All those bodies in the middle of summer. I can't even stand the smell of myself when the day's over."

"Maybe they didn't have summer parties. Maybe they had winter parties."

Emily shrugged. "Does it really make a difference?"

"So we're agreed then that parties are an awful idea?"

Yes. Emily seemed to think, leaning back in the chair and resting her feet on the spindle between its legs. "Well, maybe it depends on the people. If you really like the guests, maybe it doesn't matter if they smell bad. Or maybe it just makes it worse. I don't know. I never want to host a party."

Candice wanted to enquire further, to find out if possible body odor was the only real deterrent. Could there also be the lack of friends and having to confront that? Was it the potential rudeness of guests? She'd heard the women of the Garden Club speaking in their veiled niceties.

"I found some pictures of them," Emily went on, "in one of the boxes. The people who lived here. Mr. Gladwell didn't look very pleasant. No wonder no one likes Cedar House if *that's* who lived here."

"What was wrong with him?" Candice asked, wondering what the Gladwells *did* look like, because she had never seen them when they were alive. The washer had stopped and she went to gather its contents to hang it on the line out back. A dryer was on order but she doubted she'd want to use it when the thing arrived. Clothes dried in the sun just smelled better. She wondered what Gracie would say if the dryer went to waste. She began pulling out dresses and shirts and depositing them into the basket.

"I think she was pretty, but he wasn't smiling," Emily added. "Not a single smile in any picture. I bet he was unpleasant."

"People don't always smile in photos."

"Well they should. Who wants to look at a bunch of grumpers? That's not a great way to remember someone."

"People don't have to be grumpers"—Candice stumbled over the unfamiliar word and then smiled at it—"just because they don't smile."

"Well, it's not his house anymore anyway. It's mine. And I'm going to smile in it. All. Day. Long." Emily performed her best grin, which looked a bit like a grimace.

"You just see how long you can hold that," Candice laughed.

•

"So, what's the deal with the Howard girl?"

Candice and Everett decided to go for a walk because at home the garden called, the dishes beckoned to be cleaned, the kitchen to be straightened. Neither of them felt like doing those things and so they set off as the sun was in its decline. A miraculous evening: the smell of rain in the air—which Lord knows they needed—and a slight breeze. Not cool, but not hot.

They walked towards the park. Normally it would have been full at this hour, children playing with the thrill of summer in their bodies. But Marjorie Kent's disappearance meant the young ones in their neighborhood were kept close.

Along the way they passed their neighbors: men and women on their porches, exchanging news, snacking on taffy and drinking tea. Candice and Everett waved. Neighbors waved back.

"She's Indian," Candice said. "I'd swear on it."

"Really?" Everett turned down his mouth the way he did when he was thinking seriously about something. "Curious."

"You're telling me. Her mother is white, Everett. I don't think Emily is her blood."

"Maybe. Maybe not. Can't always tell just by looking."

Candice thought that Everett might be referring to her. They didn't talk often about Candice's family, partly because it was a sore spot between Candice and her mother, and partly because even though they loved each other, discussing who she was seemed to put up a wall between husband and wife. Or at least it felt that way to Candice, even if Everett never seemed to feel that way. While he didn't *see* a difference between them, she was, at least, aware of one.

Candice prodded, willing him to say it not because she wanted to fight but because she wanted confirmation, recognition. "What about me?"

"Your mother looks white," Everett said. "Your pa *was* white. *You* look white."

Candice frowned, looking down at her arms and hands.

"But listen," he said, "what you look like doesn't matter."

Candice wanted to laugh. Wanted to ask him how after all these years of marriage he could say what she looked like didn't matter, when he should have known it did.

"Besides," Everett continued. "Maybe it would be good for her to have you around? Can't be easy for her in that neighborhood."

"That's the thing though," Candice pointed out. "She's sick or something. Never leaves the house. Doesn't play with any kids or anything. Honestly, she might not even think about it." Candice wished this was true. That Emily Howard didn't see herself as different. That she'd be able to go through life not having to think about it, unlike how Candice grew up. Unlike how Candice, for decades, had been privy to the conversations where terrible things were said because the people around her assumed she was just like them, and they felt confident enough to spill their hate in front of her.

"Still though, may be a comfort to the girl."

It might be, Candice thought. If she was willing to talk to Emily about it. Could be trouble too, since Mrs. Howard was playing make believe with her own daughter. Candice wouldn't want to be the one at fault, to cause rift between mother and child. Maybe it would be *right* to talk to Emily about it, but her relationship with her own mother was strained—had been for as long as she could remember—and she wasn't about to traumatize another young girl with that same burden.

A police car was coming slowly down the street towards them, the officer's arm hanging out the window. Up ahead at the Cooper house a few people were gathered. Candice and Everett nodded to the officer as he passed, and he waved back to them in acknowledgement.

"What do you think that's about?" Candice asked.

The answer to the question presented itself quickly. Millie, bright in a blue sundress and with her hair curled, intercepted them at the end of the Cooper's driveway, lacing her arm in Candice's and saying, "Mind if I walk with you a bit?"

Candice looked towards the porch where men had gathered. They were talking low, their faces fierce.

"Of course," Candice said, confused but knowing an explanation was on its way.

"I'm just going to ..." Everett trailed off, and Millie shooed him towards the house.

Candice wished she'd had the guts to go too, to not be dragged off by Millie, but she let herself be taken because no, she wasn't brave enough to talk to Katherine again.

When the two women had turned the corner, Millie dropped her facade. "It's Marlene."

"What about her?" Candice asked.

"You heard all that drama about her running off with Sam?"

Candice had heard about it, because Millie had been the one to call her when it happened. Marlene, at only 15 years old, had apparently run away with Sam, a no-good backyard gambler.

"Well," Millie continued. "Sam's back."

"And?" Candice asked, wondering what news was going to follow, and suspecting Marlene was pregnant.

"So they didn't get married. Sam came back alone ..."

"Without Marlene," Candice concluded.

"Without Marlene," Millie repeated. "He went to Dallas to try working for his uncle 'cause of all that debt. But Dallas didn't pan out. Police say they're going to talk to that man, the uncle."

Candice didn't know what to say. She felt a tightness in her chest. She looked towards where the Cooper house was and put a hand up to her heart. "Then where is she, Millie?"

Millie twined the ends of her plait into a thin rope around her finger. "That's what they're trying to find out. Because Katherine is all worked up. Katherine thinks Marlene has been taken, because some children from the farm have gone missing, too."

•

Candice lay in bed but could not sleep. She kept thinking about her girls when they were little. Brave, fearless, both of them—a blessing and a curse.

She finally got up, careful not to wake her gently snoring husband, and made her way through the darkness to the kitchen. She picked up the phone and placed her finger in the second divot. She stood like this for a minute or so, contemplating the action, and then finally dialed the operator to call June.

June's husband picked up. "Hello?" His voice was heavy with sleep.

"Tom, it's Candice. Is June there?"

"You know what time it is, Mom?"

"No, but it doesn't matter. I need to talk to her."

"Something wrong?"

"No. I just need to talk to her."

"Hold a minute."

The line went quiet, and in the background, Candice could hear low voices.

"Mama?"

June's voice was like a heavy quilt. It settled on Candice and forced her back against the door frame. She slid to the ground and began crying.

•

Candice often marveled at how motherhood had changed her. For a while, after Rose was born, she felt a gap open between her and Everett. It widened with June—Candice protective and scared, all that labor for one woman with Everett working. The gap closed over the years as the girls grew, but until it did, she felt like a window had been put up between her and her husband. They could see each other, hear each other's voices through glass, touch but not touch.

She knew he tried to understand, but words always failed to communicate who she was and how she felt. It was not what she expected from seeing other mothers and their new babies. She'd thought birth brought husbands and wives closer together, a new, shared responsibility. No one had told her how birth cleaves both body and relationship.

This is what she told June on the phone. She'd meant to call to make sure her daughter was safe, feeling fine—spurred to this by the simmering fear for Marlene Cooper. But what she ended up relaying was her own narrative of motherhood: what is held like an infant, close to one's heart, what she wished her own mother might have said to her as she approached the birth of her own child. Not a warning, but a foretelling of sorts, that what is going to be felt is normal and understandable.

"You'll feel alone," she'd told her daughter. "He might be there. Friends might be there with dishes of potatoes and soupy casseroles, giving help and advice, but you'll feel alone. No one will understand the fierceness of this new priority, how you'll ache when passing your child to someone else, even for a second. How exhausted you'll be from your rent body and lack of sleep, but still how you'll buzz with paranoia when you wake to crying."

She told her daughter about how when June's sister was born, she and Everett had fought. Not anything to destroy their marriage, of course, but she told her daughter the private lives of women. "I think, if she had been a boy, things might have been different."

With her back against the trim, Candice told her daughter how she believed it took time for Everett to understand the difference between loving a child and loving the idea of a child. How sure he'd been, touching her protruding stomach hanging low, that a boy was coming. How this surety, when disrupted with the sight of Rose's swollen genitals, turned into a kind of dream space in which Everett knew he had a daughter but couldn't reconcile the reality with the ideas he'd formed. He loved his child, to be sure, but he'd loved the idea of what she could have been more—for a time.

"Mama," June said, "I'm not worried."

"But you will be," Candice replied, looking at the floor, imagining her daughters playing there, sweeping crumbs and hairs into the dustpan with their pudgy fingers.

Candice marveled at how nothing, nothing, could prepare a woman for motherhood. Not even another mother's experience, blunt in its telling.

•

She began to sleep fitfully, and some days she woke up so late Everett had to drive her to work. That day, in the car and as they crossed the invisible boundary of Grand Avenue, two mothers pushed strollers together, side by side on the street, until they stopped in front of Scooter's bakery.

Candice thought about Katherine Cooper, and how maybe now she should call her old friend. They hadn't really talked for years, but now Marlene was missing, and Candice knew—the way mothers do—that Katherine must be devastated. But Candice also wasn't sure if her overture would be welcome. Not because Katherine was cruel and because there was some bad blood between them, but because maybe Katherine had enough people already asking her. Adding one more might tip the scales toward overwhelmed.

Candice was just at the precipice of understanding this was *not* about reaching out to Katherine, that she was afraid really, not for Katherine but for herself, when they pulled up in front of Cedar House.

Everett took the boxes Gracie had put by the front door and put them in the back of their car. Candice kissed him on the cheek, feeling his rough whiskers bristle against her lips, and said, "Tonight, then."

•

Candice looked at the shallow gash on her wrist. It was bleeding. She'd cut herself and hadn't even noticed.

In the bathroom of Cedar House she rinsed her hands. Rubbed soap onto her swelling skin. Looked through the sparse medicine cabinet and came up empty. Then she put the toilet lid down and sat with a wad of toilet paper pressed hard against her skin.

She'd never noticed it before—why would she? She didn't make a habit of lounging in her employer's bathroom, but sitting there, her hand throbbing uncomfortably, her heart beating through her veins—Emily's voice was coming down and out of the pipes.

Laying out the house in her head, she knew the girl's bathroom was directly above. Emily was in there, singing.

The words were wrapped in air, too opaque to make out, but it was a song somewhat familiar. It had an odd cadence, and it reminded Candice of her grandmother's singing. Candice barely remembered the woman. Could hardly put a face to her. But her voice, Enola's voice, low and hanging above the ground like smoke, was etched in Candice's memory. It carried through the gaps Candice had of Nacogdoches, of the earliest years of her childhood.

When she pried the toilet paper away from her skin, pieces of it ripping and sticking to dried blood and disturbing the clots trying to form, she knew she'd have to go to Emily.

Candice didn't spend much time upstairs. Mrs. Howard had told Candice not to bother with her bedroom—she preferred to do that herself. Emily's room, partitioned by heavy curtains instead of a doorway, felt theatric, as if when Candice crossed that threshold she were cleaning a stage, not a house, and the oddity of this feeling—like she was on display on that stage with people, darkened somewhere, watching—reduced her to entering the girl's space only once a week. Emily dropped her laundry down the chute, and then put it away herself. The other two bedrooms were bare bones of old guestrooms. Curtains that collected dust. Their doors stayed closed, and every once in a while, if Candice was bored, she might take the vacuum up and go at them.

Candice went up the stairs and knocked on the wall against Emily's room.

"Yes?" The girl called.

"You happen to know where the bandages are?" Candice said.

After a few moments, Emily pulled the curtains back. She had a towel wrapped around her small wet body, water droplets collecting on the wool rug beneath her feet.

"What's wrong?" Emily's eyes scanned Candice and then landed on the hand she put out.

"It's not that bad," Candice explained. "Just snagged myself on something."

The girl, looking at the wound and now satisfied that there was no real emergency, walked Candice into her bathroom. The tub was full of water, a measly covering of bubbles quickly popping. "I found some bath scents," Emily explained. "Eucalyptus. Can you smell it?"

Candice inhaled. She couldn't, and said so.

"Neither can I," Emily admitted, opening the cabinet under her sink. "I can if I sniff from the bottle though." She produced a roll of cotton and some bandage tape. "I used to get hurt a lot," she explained. "I mean, I'd hurt myself. By accident. I'm accident-prone, or I was, Mother says. Here, let me help you."

Emily had Candice sit on the bed and played a good doctor, murmuring to herself and wrapping Candice's wrist well enough that the joint could still bend, overdoing it, but so gently Candice didn't point out the excessive dressing.

Candice looked out the girl's window, the view obstructed by limbs of the large cedar tree out front. They needed to be trimmed back.

•

Candice liked *I Love Lucy*. She was sad that the season was over, her Monday nights free for other things, things she didn't want to do: more upkeep.

She imagined New York City to be like Chicago, where Rose and June were. Flashy, big bands, and nightclubs. She'd never been to one.

Her wrist ached. When she got home, she unwound the bandage and found her skin to be hot to the touch. Or maybe she was just hot. Hard to tell after walking home in the summer sun. She winced, pouring alcohol over it, wondering what was taking Everett so long because she wanted to ask him what he thought about it. She could call the diner, but he wouldn't talk to her if he was cooking.

Let it breathe, she told herself.

Candice didn't want to clean. She didn't want to cook either, so she had a dinner of brussels sprouts and lardons from the fridge, not caring if it was cold and a little congealed. She wanted to call Rose, but Rose's line was all tied up. She thought to call Millie and ask if there was any news, but then decided she didn't want to be on the phone at all. Millie could talk, and Candice didn't also need a crick in her neck.

She watered the poor broccoli and then stood in the middle of the yard watching the grackles lined up along the edge of her roof.

"Shoo!" she said, waving her hands, but they paid her no attention, the silly woman below them who could do no harm.

"I said shoo!" she said again, walking closer. They glared down at her and didn't even bother to ruffle their feathers.

When Everett came home, he said her wrist looked fine and wasn't infected. She was worried for no reason. But Candice couldn't shake the feeling that something *was* wrong.

The worry started like a fluttering in her chest. And then it pumped down into her arms and legs. Everett told her to stop waggling her foot—it was driving him crazy—and so she got up. She went and got the piece of cake Everett had brought home and ate it at the counter. Her teeth were singing with sugar. She pressed her wrist into her thigh, felt the dull throbbing spread. She didn't notice she'd torn the wound open, its edges raw and ragged, swollen with new damage, until Everett came in and asked her why her dress was bloody.

5

A Tapestry of Promises

—Rebekah—

Rebekah tried to lift the stack of folders and felt her shoulders give. Luckily, she hadn't taken even one step, and when the papers fell, they did so all over the desk where they stayed relatively sheathed. Only one pile fell onto the floor, scattered over the worn brown carpet she wished the Historical Society would replace.

She sighed. Bent with her knees protesting, she almost keeled over and was only saved by reaching out and righting herself on her chair. It took her half a minute to get down on the ground and when she did, she sat back on her heels and wondered when her body was going to decide to fail her. She'd seen it happen with her sister, the body rejecting itself as the cancer spread, and she'd seen it too before that with Lillian. Though that deterioration was something else completely.

Rebekah pushed the thoughts of dead women away. Focused instead on the present. This rebellion of limbs did not match up with her sharp mind and all the things she wanted to do. Already she was contemplating selling the house she'd shared with her husband. It would be a shame to leave it—the memories buried behind and under the belongings of someone else—but the daily climbs up and down from the bedroom were not agreeing with her. She could, of course, transform James' office into a room for sleeping, but what would she do with his belongings? How would she feel looking at different walls, being unable to walk the labyrinth of his room in darkness at night when she could not sleep, the pattern of his reading chair, tables, shelves, and desk?

She sighed and reached towards the papers, bent over on all fours and feeling rather unladylike.

The folder's spilled contents contained Thomas Gladwell's notes. They had come in a box, delivered by Gracie, with a plate of gingersnaps baked by Gracie's maid and daughter. "I think they're more appropriate for the town historical society than they are in that basement," Gracie had said about the contents of the box.

Rebekah had a history with Gladwell, both Gladwells actually, and when she'd received the box of his belongings she did so with a mix of emotions that translated into a flush through her chest and a spasm through her fingers. She didn't let Gracie know about all that. The poor woman had enough going on with her girl, and there was no use talking about Gladwell because to talk about Gladwell invoked all kinds of unresolved issues.

Gladwell's handwriting on the notes was thin and slanted. The papers were yellowing and years of dampness in the basement had affected the quality. They were crisp the way paper turns when exposed to water and then dried. The pages didn't stack neatly. They warped and billowed in odd places.

What had he been working on, Rebekah wondered, flipping pages, finding some that were typed. A novel, perhaps? A western by the looks of it, based in Larissa in the 1800s. She did the math; it would have taken place before Thomas was born, and it appeared as if he'd written his father into it, or maybe an alternate version of himself, for a Thomas was there in the pages, a homesteader with a fear of starving to death.

Rebekah shifted her legs out in front of her and continued to shuffle through the pages. A map of Larissa was included with arrows she could not decipher. She checked the page numbers written in the upper right-hand corners of those typed pages: 23-38. She was missing something before and after. On page 38 Gladwell's narrative was cut off mid-sentence, going on to page 39, which Rebekah did not have. That half sentence read, *She was not thinking about her husband just then, though she knew he was down below, in the distance. She was thinking of her daughter, and of men that might have taken her and she .....*

She what? Rebekah had no clue who the daughter was, or who the woman was looking for the girl, but she couldn't shake the feeling that she was teetering on the edge of a cliff. One step closer and she would look down to discover something she didn't want to see.

She got slowly to her feet with the folder in hand and then searched the others still mussed on the desk. Property records—which Rebekah had been copying—and there were legal contracts pertaining to old sales. None of the other folders seem to have anything related to Gladwell's book. Perhaps there was more in storage? She'd have to ask on Monday.

She straightened the mess and then turned off the lights, locking the door behind her and stepping out into the heat of the Texas evening. Purse over her shoulder, she began the walk home, to the house beginning to refuse her, thinking of how nice it would be when Fall came.

•

It was the nightly routine: rinse her face, tie up her greying hair, wash out her stockings and hang them over the rod above the bathtub. Heat milk in the pan, make a cup of it with a splash of bourbon. Turn the radio on and have a conversation with Petrol, the tortoiseshell cat that had previously lived under the cracked slab of concrete at the gas station. Walk the rooms of the house, checking windows, drawing curtains. Wash the pan. Sponge out the cup. Turn the porch light off, climb the stairs to the landing, pause for breath—to rub her lower back or to flex her feet—and then into the bedroom where she would read by lamplight until nine p.m.

Petrol mewed her way into the room and leapt up onto the bed, her aim slightly off so her nails were dragging at the quilt: it was fraying from too many of those occurrences. The cat settled on the vacant pillow beside Rebekah and purred.

Tonight, it was *The Lottery*. Rebekah didn't know what drew her to the book displayed at the library. It had come from Dallas. Their old library stamp was still inside the cover and Rebekah didn't know how or why it had made its way to Larissa. Maybe that's why she picked it up, and took it home, despite the librarian's warning.

"A lot of trouble with this one," Marian had said, writing the due date on the card. "A lot of people upset with it."

"With a story?" Rebekah had asked. "If you ask me, it's not stories we need to worry about. It's what really happens."

Marian had stiffened at Rebekah's response, and Rebekah realized too late that what she had said might have come off like an accusation. It wasn't Marian's fault about the Kent girl, but she must, in some way, feel like it was since she was the last person to have seen Marjorie.

Rebekah read until the clock hands made their angle and then turned off the light, falling asleep to the low rumbling emanating of Petrol's tiny body.

•

It was the nightly routine: wake sometime between 1 and 3 and be unable to fall asleep again. Lie in bed until her eyes adjust to the darkness. Fold the sheets back, careful not to cover the sleeping cat. Get out of bed, count the stairs on the slow descent. Walk the rooms, which all opened into each other. Stop, finally, in the office. Walk in circles, touch the leather, run fingers over spines of books. Look out the window.

It was not the nightly routine to see anyone on the street at such a late hour, but tonight, someone was.

Still weighted by silence and unable to completely cross that border between sleep and wake, Rebekah was convinced, at first, that she was seeing a ghost.

The apparition walked slowly, its white gown hanging loose to its ankles. Its hair was straight down its back, breaking in parts over stooped shoulders.

Rebekah rubbed her eyes and then cupped her hands against the glass.

The apparition was moving out of the ruddiness of streetlight. It was a she, and her head was swiveling. She tripped but righted herself. Rebekah saw dark house slippers.

What kind of a ghost wears house slippers, she asked herself, coming to an understanding that this was not a ghost at all.

Through the office to the living room. The porch light. The front door opening. Rebekah crossed the lawn in her dressing gown without a thought to who might see her indisposed.

The apparition was Mrs. Kent, and as Rebekah got closer the woman became clearer. Her hair was disheveled, and her eyes were wide—roving in their sockets—looking everywhere but at the old woman reaching for her shoulders.

"Debbie," Rebekah said, standing right in front of her, blocking the woman's path. "What in the world are you doing out here?"

Mrs. Kent seemed to register the woman and explained with perfect clarity, as if being in her nightgown and house shoes roaming the neighborhood in the dead of night made good sense, that she was looking for Marjorie.

"Oh dear," Rebekah said.

Not understanding the old woman's comment, Mrs. Kent went on to explain that Marjorie had not come home from the library, had not had dinner, and it was dark now and Marjorie needed to go to sleep. It was bedtime, she explained, and Marjorie knew better.

Rebekah felt awful for saying so, but she suggested, "Perhaps Marjorie is already home now? You've been out here for God knows how long. I suspect you simply passed each other. It is dark," she added, looking around as if just now noticing this herself. "Come inside," Rebekah said, "and we'll phone your husband."

Inside the house Rebekah put on a pan of milk to heat and then "called" Mrs. Kent's husband. She felt a fool with the receiver in her hand, making up one half of a conversation, but she did so nonetheless because Gladwell was at the corner of her mind—Lillian, not Thomas—because something of this behavior invoked Lillian, who came back from Dallas sedate and never the same after undergoing treatment for her "behavior."

Petrol eventually came down the stairs and padded under the chairs as the women sipped from their cups. Mrs. Kent's had more than a splash of bourbon and Rebekah supplied her with a sleeping pill as well.

Rebekah tried to steer the conversation away from Marjorie, whom Mrs. Kent was relieved about—at home, safe and sound, tucked in though not by her own hands—and grasped for anything else to mention. The new member of the Garden Club, Rebekah's niece, Gracie Howard, and the discovery of a novel written by ... she decided not to give the name, afraid with the kind of fear that comes in the night that saying *Gladwell* might conjure something unpleasant. There was the upcoming Fourth of July Parade. The news of the new monkey at the zoo. The charity drive at the Methodist church.

Eventually Mrs. Kent stopped responding and simply patted the cat who had made its way into her lap. She fell asleep in the chair like that, and Rebekah slid a pillow onto her shoulder, beneath her head, and then watched the poor woman softly snoring. Eventually, she rose and thumbed through the phonebook to call Mrs. Kent's husband, explaining how his wife had spent herself crying and fretting. "She's tuckered herself out," Rebekah added, "and it's best to let her recover her mind a bit." When Mr. Kent asked why his wife had snuck out to Rebekah's house so late, Rebekah tried to preserve the other woman's dignity by saying, "Sometimes a woman just needs another woman."

•

It was the morning routine: set the kettle on to boil, make one fried egg and one piece of toast, shoo the cat away from the butter, feed the cat, eat at the table with the sound of the television from the next room.

This morning, as Rebekah chewed her bread, she decided that she'd walk by Cedar House on her way to work and find out if there were any more boxes in the basement that might have additional files, hoping she'd be able to recover more of Gladwell's book. Once she'd dressed, locked her door, looked up at the sky, and measured the sun, she took off.

Cedar House was only a few blocks away, but Rebekah didn't take the direct route. She avoided that path and instead of walking by the grand houses on Bell Street—those built by rancher and oil families—she took the longer route through the neighborhoods of smaller houses with their post oaks and scrubby bushes, their neatly lined windows nestled in brick of various reds and oranges. This walk, this route, was one she used to take with James.

Thank God James had been a surveyor, because that job came with a nice pension that now kept eggs in her fridge, paid her property taxes, and covered incidentals she might want: an ice cream one evening walking home or a dress or two. Thinking of dresses made her think of her sister—gone for years now—with her store full of colorful bolts and forms to silhouette all sizes of woman. She'd never been able to go into that store while Maggie was managing it—Maggie's memory was long and unforgiving—and Rebekah had to buy her dresses from department stores. That was, until Maggie had died, and Rebekah had inherited her sister's dresses, one of which she wore now.

Rebekah smoothed the fabric of her dress across her thighs as she stood in front of Cedar House. She felt guilty for not bringing anything. She felt guilty that bringing so many things, getting Gracie and her daughter "settled," had been a pretense to come to Cedar House so often. It wasn't that she didn't care about this new family, because she did. It just also happened that Gracie and her daughter provided a window into the past as well.

But now that Cedar House was occupied again—with different people: the woman, the girl, the maid—she didn't feel as compelled to come at all. The house felt different, and she'd discovered she didn't like that feeling, but had come on days the Garden Club met because what else could she do? To abscond would be suspicious, and rude. Still, her hands felt like they should be holding something. They held each other then, and she walked up the sidewalk.

The maid, Candice, opened the door.

Rebekah wasn't sure what to make of the maid, and if Gracie's hiring of her had been an intentional move to give her daughter a friend. Rebekah also wasn't sure what to do with Emily, who Gracie claimed was her daughter. She'd wanted to understand, of course, what was going on. But she didn't know Gracie well enough to inquire. "Is Gracie here?" she asked, skipping the pleasantries of normal conversation.

"Not now. Gone right quick to the hardware store. Would you like to come in?"

Candice held the door open, and so Rebekah entered.

Part of her new dislike of Cedar House was also the changes Gracie had made. She understood something was wrong with Emily, that she had some abnormal fear of doorways that required her housing to have as few as possible, but the gaping walls with their maw-like openings made the house feel like it was going to gobble her up. In the foyer there used to be a painting, oils that depicted the harbor in New Orleans in a bustling scene that felt out of place among the wood and rich colors of Cedar House. Now there was no painting, no wall for the painting to hang on, just a gap from door to the living room with its damask covered chairs and gleaming, low tables.

Candice took it upon herself to make Rebekah coffee, which Rebekah didn't refuse, and then Emily brought the coffee, balancing the cup and saucer in one hand, the other arm behind her back.

"Like a maître d," Emily explained, placing the cup in front of Rebekah.

Rebekah felt saddened to know that the girl had probably never been in a restaurant, let alone a fancy one. An effect of her condition of confinement.

"I want to thank you for the book," Emily said, sitting across from Rebekah, her legs too short to reach the carpet. "It's the most interesting thing I've had to read."

Rebekah tried to remember what book she'd given the girl. Something from that row on the third shelf of James' study—books she bought in preparation for a child who never came. "I'm glad," she said. "It must be awfully boring being inside all day."

"Not so much," Emily countered. "I find things to keep myself occupied."

Rebekah supposed this was true. She knew children invented all sorts of entertainment when left to their own devices. "How have you liked Larissa?" She asked, making conversation and wondering how long Gracie might be. Dusty wouldn't care that she was late, but if she took too long he might drive to her house to check on her, and then, when she didn't answer the door because she was really at Cedar House, he might grow afraid and think to call the police, or jimmy her door open, and Petrol might escape.

Emily shrugged. "Mother showed me some pictures," she said. "It just looks like a town. Nothing special. Besides, I haven't really seen any of it. Pictures are not the same thing as seeing with your own eyes."

"There are lots of photos at the Historical Society," Rebekah heard herself saying. "Maybe I could borrow them and your mother could tell you what the town used to look like? We have photos of everything, even Statler Creek when it was full of water instead of bone dry. It's not the same, but it is more."

"That's okay," Emily said. "Perhaps it doesn't matter what I see of the past because that's not how one comes to know it."

Rebekah was struck by how odd this remark was, how grown up it sounded, but didn't follow up as the front door opened and Gracie Howard came in carrying a little bird house.

"Rebekah!" Gracie said, handing off the item to Candice. "What a surprise! What are you doing here?"

Emily disappeared somewhere into the house, Gracie taking the vacated chair, her adult form replacing her daughter's. Rebekah looked at Gracie, the ghost image of Emily still there somehow, and decided there was absolutely no resemblance between the two.

Rebekah explained the mystery with the Gladwell pages and Gracie frowned at her. "Well it's almost all cleared out," she finally said. "Emily has taken some things, John and Earl took what they wanted, and Candice took a few things, too. I don't think we're likely to find anything now."

Rebekah felt a desperation to know where the rest of the book was. She even volunteered to go into the basement with Gracie and to paw around in the mildew and mold. Gracie assented.

Rebekah had never been in the basement of Cedar House, not in all the years it stood. The steps were lighted by two sconces in the walls—not bare bulbs—and though the smell of damp earth entered her nose, the place didn't look as miserable as she imagined it would be. The stairs groaned under her feet; she took them slowly, putting her hand against the wall for balance, following Gracie.

The basement was a large room, as large as Cedar House itself, the foundation made of irregular, grey stone. The feel of it reminded Rebekah of the old storm cellar in the house she had grown up in, and she was suddenly assaulted by the memory of spending long hours in the dwelling as a child, the flat door thrown open for light, the coolness of it in the searing, Texas heat.

This room was far nicer, if a basement could be called nicer. Bigger at least. Taller. Room for storage, for rows of self-canned goods someone in this house would never produce again.

"This is the last of it all," Gracie said, leading Rebekah to a corner in which some crates were gathered, as well as some boxes freshly assembled and filled with items. Gracie bent down and began searching. "I can't believe this all just sat here for years. Mr. Toller told me there was some distant relative, a cousin, I think, still in England who the estate went to. Didn't care much about what happened to it. Only wanted money from the house. Had to wait years for that, even. Without you suggesting Cedar House, that cousin would still be waiting."

Rebekah came closer to the collection of goods and looked over Gracie's shoulder.

"How sad that no one took care of things when they died," Gracie went on. "I don't remember them at all. Maybe saw her in the grocery a few times. We traveled in different circles. Did you know her? Or him?"

"Oh no," Rebekah lied. "We didn't travel in the same circles either. They were very wealthy people."

"Irene knew *of* her," Gracie went on. "Was completely shocked when she learned about what happened. Said that even before we moved up north Lillian wasn't right, but that she never did anything to invite violence against her. Mostly just sat on her porch, watching the world go by. Terrible thing to have happened." She sat back on her heels and looked up at Rebekah. "I almost didn't buy the house because of it."

"But you did, finally. Because?"

"Because it was still the most expensive house in town and Irene can choke on it." Gracie surveyed the boxes again and shook her head. "I'm sorry. Nothing's here."

Rebekah looked around at the odds and ends of what remained of the Gladwells. The items could have belonged to anyone. There was nothing remarkable or personal about anything.

"You know I haven't been to my parents' graves since I've been back," Gracie said, getting to her feet and scooping one of the boxes up in her arms. "Maybe I should go."

"You should," Rebekah suggested, though she didn't really feel any which way about it. When people died, they were gone. She was so used to telling herself this that the phrase—what's gone is gone—welled up with no effort at all. No point in dredging up the past, she thought, and then chuckled. A fictional past was okay, she decided, still wondering where the rest of the novel was. If there was even a rest of it. Maybe she remembered incorrectly. She'd need to have another look at those pages at the office.

Upstairs the two women said goodbye. At the front door, Rebekah looked into the library, its lack of furniture, that fireplace. Gracie hadn't done a thing with it, and the marble mantle was still cracked, spiderwebbed and chipped from where the bullets had lodged.

PART II

PLYING TENDER TONGUES

We know that surviving is to make a whole out of parts. We know this now, since finding more women. Since seeing prairies desperate for forests desperate for mountains. But still, We say, *Remember. Remember the part of the whole that is whole. Remember your homes. Remember your faces, remember your long walk and the walks before.*

Do not stay still. Or, stay still if you are hiding. Do not stay still, even if you are hiding. Clench a fist. Wiggle a toe. The body carries memories. Remembers the becoming of the undoing of others. Remember, We say, and sometimes the girl seems to hear Us, even those who are not Us, because the whole is made of parts that are all different shapes but are the same shape when unraveled.

We are everywhere. We are waiting. We have been waiting.

We say, *Remember,* though We know it will be hard, that some memories are too painful to recall, that part of repairing is speaking about them, that speaking about them means they are real, that to be real means to have a history, that to have a history means to want to forget. Sometimes.

But We are impatient. We have been waiting a decade. Decades. Centuries. We say, to each other, *time is a circle.*

We draw circles in dust. Make circles in the dust with our feet. We leave footprints on the tile, the wood. We track dirt onto carpet and grind it into wool that was never meant to be here.

We say, *Remember,* and our eyes shudder. We tell the girl to remember. An imperative of bone. We are remembering.

6

Sight in the Sideways

—Emily—

They are standing there like They are waiting. The Women who came with Candice into Cedar House have gathered in my bedroom, lined up against the wall, silent and trembling in their skins.

At first, I think something is terribly wrong with Them.

At first, I am afraid.

But then the longer I stare at Them, the more solid They become.

The more solid They become, the more I *feel* Them.

The longer I feel Them, the stranger their faces appear. Or maybe it is the light. Or maybe it is my eyes adjusting to the lack of light, because we are all in darkness.

And then I see that They are wearing masks. One looks like a bear. Another a wolf. One has antlers, and I think it is a deer. The others I cannot decipher.

"Hello," I say, and one of Them cocks her head.

"Are you lost?" I ask. "Are you real?"

I know I am fevering because sweat is dripping off my chin.

They do not answer.

"Okay," I tell Them. "I need to sleep now. I don't feel too good. You can stay. Or go."

When I close my eyes, I can hear the sound of feet stomping, though when I crack my lids, none of Them are moving. I can hear the thumping of drums, the shuffling sounds of moving through time.

When I look again, the Woman in the front moves toward me. I cannot tell if her hair is hers or if it belongs to the mask she wears. The closer she gets, the more the hair moves. It is long and swaying.

She smells like wood and blood and campfire and I do not know how I recognize these smells.

She says, *Osiyo. We have been looking for you.*

•

My mother is lugging box after box up from the basement, remnants of the Gladwell couple left behind because one of two things happen when a family line runs out and they leave behind possessions: they get thrown out or given away.

Mrs. Gladwell had lots of nice things. Etched perfume pots and silver combs and lots of jewelry (that I am not supposed to keep if I find it) and dresses that are too large for me but still very pretty. And she had all sorts of colored, glass figurines in the shapes of animals. There is a picture of her, too. Lillian Gladwell. In it she stands in the back garden. Her dark hair is piled on her head, and in one hand she holds a trowel. Her other hand is hidden behind her back, and she is laughing at something out of view.

While looking at her belongings, I find wrapped inside a heavy, wool scarf, a folder. All the scarves contain folders. Some of them have letters and postcards. Inside this one is a book, of sorts. Part of a book. Something that wants to be a book. It is about girls that disappear. Well, it is about a few girls that disappear, and it is also about a lot of other people who disappear. It is about this town, Larissa, a long time ago.

At night I read this story. I open the window and say the words aloud. The Women do not care too much for this tale. When I read from it, They become boulders and hunch into themselves, Women hunched like stones all around my room.

"What's wrong," I ask Them. Some of the Women have their hands over their ears.

They say the story remembers wrong. That part of remembering is searching, but that the story is not looking for anything. They say remembering means hunting, but to recover.

I ask, "You mean not forgetting?"

They say, *no*. Their lips do not move. They say through lips that do not move, *We mean this is part of remembering.*

And so, I'm trying to remember.

But it's hard to remember something you've never known, and it's hard to remember what you're not even sure you should be remembering.

•

When I wake, my pillow thumps against my cheek. No, it is my blood in my skin, pressing outward in the time of my heart, feverish and overpowering.

I stumble to the bathroom, wipe my face with a damp towel. I swish with cold water that makes my teeth hurt. I plug the sink. Fill it. Purse my lips into the liquid and drink it all down.

When I return to my bed someone has been in it. They have been in it for years. For lifetimes. The mattress sags in the middle, nestles me into its groove. I pull the sheet over my head. The light hurts my eyes.

•

I hear my mother and Candice talking. They come and go. Appear and disappear. But They are always here.

Sometimes They tell me stories. They say, *remember.* They say, *the work of recovering, of uncovering, is difficult for small bodies unfurling into new skin. Old skin made new. New skin like a skinned deer, shining with wounds and the dark stain of blood.* They tell me stories about women and men who mold girls like wet clay. Who beat them with hands and wood and good words. They say that when They are done telling stories, I must begin to tell stories. They are hungry for stories, They say. So hungry.

I try to tell Them stories, too. Sometimes I say things the way I want to, and sometimes I do not.

I am talking to them, my tongue fumbling over misremembered words when Candice peeks into my room.

"What do you need, Emily?" Candice asks.

I repeat myself.

"I can't understand what you're trying to get at," she says.

They are giddy. They are chattering too. They do not mind Candice, and so when she asks, "Emily, is that even English?" They wave their arms in large circles to capture all the old words I give them.

•

It is easier at night. Everything is quiet, and so I can hear better. The sun does not yell, and so my head does not hurt.

I open the window. The Little People call the owl and the owl comes. The Little People tell me to climb onto its back, and I say, *but I'm too big*, and they tell me I am not what I seem, even to myself, and so I slide out the window, sneak-thief, and anchor myself in feathers.

•

"Sweetie?"

My mother stands over me. She holds a glass in one hand, the other made into a fist. There is something hidden there.

She tries to offer it to me and I turn my head, say, ——————— ——————————————.

Her eyes go wide. "What?"

I prod each syllable through my lips, my tongue working a slur. "I don't want it."

She sits on the side of my bed. "I used to suffer like this too."

"No you didn't."

"Just take it? It will make you feel better."

•

Sometimes I am not sure if I am dreaming or if I am awake. Candice moors me to reality, and so if I see her, I know I am not asleep. Candice is never hiding between trees or oiling a bow. She does not let the scales of fish rainbow her hands and she does not sprinkle tobacco in these new places where I find myself.

Sometimes my eyes are too swollen to open and I call for her. Sometimes she says, "Emily, I'm here," and takes my hand. Sometimes she does not appear, and in my open palm I receive small gifts to help me on my journey: a scrap of red fabric, a pebble, a bead.

Sometimes when I am sleep traveling, They are there. When We are together in meadows or woods We build on each other's stories. They say, *it is all one long story*. They say, *what wounds can be passed on in blood*. They say that in the curves of my veins I carry memories, and not just my own. But when I try to cut myself open to hear these stories, They stop me. They tell me, *no more blood*.

And so I wake and call for Candice, and she comes to gently stroke my face. She puts a hand on my forehead. I can hear her smile. She says she thinks my fever has broken.

•

The boy coming down the street looks familiar, and it takes me a few minutes of trying to remember—it is so hard, makes me so tired—before I recognize him. He's one of the bike boys, I recall, who rode around in front of the house. The ones who didn't know mother and I were watching them.

He looks so miserable, white shirt sticking to him with sweat, back tire flat and rolling dumbly along the pavement. I call out my window. "Hey!"

The boy stops and looks around, trying to figure out where the voice is coming from.

"Up here," I call, waving my arms. "I got something for that."

The boy hesitates, and then crosses the street, pushing his bike up to the house.

I meet him at the door, proud that I've been able to call something from outside inside. "Hi," I say. "I have a tire pump." What I mean is, I have a memory of a tire pump. I hope I actually do have one.

The boy stands at the bottom of the steps, shading his eyes with one hand, the other steadying his bike. "I don't think a pump is going to work," he says. "The whole thing's come loose. I can see the innertube."

I don't know anything about bikes, really, and I'm certainly not an innertube expert. "Oh. Then I guess I can't help."

"It'd be nice to have some water though," the boy says.

I'm probably not supposed to invite people in—especially right now since girls are going missing—but he's just a boy, and Candice will be back soon with the flour so I don't see any potential harm in it. "I've got a faucet," I say, and the boy leans his bike against the bushes.

"Will," he says, extending his hand.

I put my arm through the doorway. It is a current, a storm, a pyre. I shake his hand. Its damp and warm. "Emily."

Will is clearly impressed by Cedar House. He looks up more than he looks down, studying the high ceilings and big furniture. "It's all imported from England," I say, leading him back to the kitchen, even though I'm not sure that it's true. I know some things were imported—but I don't know exactly what all was.

"I've always wondered what it looked like in here," he says, hand running along the top of the sofa as we pass. "It's different from my house."

It's not a very smart thing to say. Every house is different. But I don't hold this against him.

"Actually," he goes on, "I've never been in any of these houses."

"What houses?" I open the cabinet and pull down a glass.

"The big ones on Bell Street."

I fill the glass and then he swallows the water down in seven long gulps. I fill it again. "Want to see something really neat?" I ask, crossing to the wall with the basement door. I flip open the little square panel and point inside. "It's a vacuum."

"No way." Will abandons his glass on the counter and squats down to look.

"It runs the whole house, but our maid won't use it. She just sweeps and uses the portable one."

"Where does it all go?"

"To the laundry room."

"You must be rich."

"My grandma is. But she's not very nice."

"Who's your grandma?" Will puts a finger into the hole. Wiggles it around.

"Irene Howard. The library is named after us."

"Can we try it?" Will asks, standing up and examining his hand.

The laundry room. It has a door. I show him where the hose is and let him retrieve it. He fiddles with the sockets and then finally, a click. I push the button on the wall and the hose fills with life, crinkling and twisting in Will's hands. He laughs. Puts the nozzle to the floor. Nothing gets sucked up because the house is already clean.

Then a thunking begins to pound the wall. I hear it traveling along pipes. It ends in the laundry room, the clanging louder. I press the switch again. "Uh oh."

I watch Will replace the hose and open the compartment to the dust receptacle. "Do you have a flashlight?" he asks, and I point to the bucket on the shelf above the washer and dryer. He switches it on. His head and one arm disappear into the contraption.

When he emerges, his sandy hair is grey with dust. His shirt is streaked with a dark line of it where he leaned in, pressing chest against the metal lip of the door. "Here's the culprit," he says, holding the object out to me.

I do not reach through the doorway to take it. Once already is enough for today. I go get my own water glass, luring him out. "What is it?" I ask.

He comes from the laundry room, still proffering the object. "It looks like beads," he says.

I turn around and look into the cup of his hand. I poke the round things. Pluck one between my thumb and pointer finger. "They're not beads. They're pearls."

"Pearls," he says in almost-wonder. "You're so rich you have pearls in your walls."

I laugh.

"Can I have them?" he asks sheepishly. "I can maybe get a patch for this."

"Sure," I say. "What kind of patch?"

"A Guide's patch. We get them for doing Indian things. I figure I can use these to get my trading patch. Wampum."

"What's wampum?"

"Like Indian money."

"How much do you know about Indians?" I ask.

Will slides the white orbs into his pocket. "Not a whole lot. I'm learning."

"I got a whole book about Indians," I say, pointing to the ceiling towards my room on the second floor. "I think it was written by Mr.

Gladwell. He owned this house before us. He wrote about how Indians are pretty violent. Or could be. They killed the people who originally tried to settle Larissa."

"Oh, no, *I'm* not violent," Will says, distress showing in the shake of his head.

"I didn't say *you* were. You're not a real Indian after all. I'm saying the ones who lived in Larissa were. It says so in the book."

Candice picks this terrible moment to come home, and she isn't happy to find Will in our kitchen. Neither of us mentions the wampum, and she makes him leave, but not before he gives me his phone number so I can call him about Indian things.

•

Candice makes me sit at the table and then she lectures me from across the room, her hands pounding out a crust. I can't tell if she's angry or if this is just the way she makes pie.

"So I'm not going to tell your mother about this," she continues, "but under no circumstances are you to let anyone in this house, answer the door even, if one of us isn't here."

"What if the mailman has a package?" I ask.

"No. Not even of the mailman has a package. Not even if you look out the window and see him with a box in his hand and you know something wonderful is inside. Don't you know what's happening right now?"

I do know. Girls are going missing. But girls are not going missing from their homes, especially homes like Cedar House. "Yes," I say, instead of arguing.

"Lord, and of all children. A boy. You had a boy in this house without any supervision."

"I don't see what the problem with him is," I say. "He was disgusting anyway, and I would never kiss a boy who smelled."

"I'm not worried about you," Candice clarifies. "Who's his family, huh?"

"I don't know."

"That's right. You don't. You don't know nothing about that boy."

"I would think you'd be happy I have a friend," I say, pouting the best I can.

"Emily, I can see right through that face."

I smile.

"I am very happy you have a friend,"Candice says."I wish you'll have many friends in your lifetime."

"Who are *your* friends?" I ask.

They have come into the kitchen and stand around us. One of Them sits on the table beside me. A few of Them are looking into the glass cabinets. The one with the very long hair is watching Candice closely.

"Well," Candice says."My best friends are my family. My daughters, you know about them. And even Everett, I guess." At that she laughs." But there's also Millie, and Katherine Cooper. I used to be close to Katherine, but then ..." Candice reaches over to retrieve the rolling pin from the other side of the sink. Her hands pass through two Women who are sitting on the counter and they dissipate."It was a long time ago. We both just got so busy with life."

"Well, I have a friend now. And he's not violent. He said so."

"Did he? That's an odd thing to say."

"No it isn't. I was telling him how violent Indians can be."

Candice stops working and turns to look at me, leaning back against the counter."Indians are violent? What would make you say such a thing?"

"I read it in a book."

She shakes her head."I don't think that's true at all. Indians are just like everyone else. Some of us can be violent, but just like any white person can."

"Oh!" I say."Are you Indian? You don't look like it."

Candice looks down at herself."What *does* an Indian look like?"

I don't answer, because I don't know, I guess. They are chittering amongst themselves. Agitated. The one with the long hair is almost right in Candice's face, and Candice doesn't even see her.

"Come help with these apples," Candice tells me.

I stand beside Candice and try to mimic what she's doing, paring the skin away from the fruit. I am not very good at it and the skin I peel away is thick and uneven.

"The thing about Indians," she begins,"is that they don't have to look a certain way. Sometimes they have light skin, like me. And sometimes they have blue eyes, and light hair. There isn't a way to look like an Indian. Some people think we should look like old-timey pictures. Standing outside teepees and smoking pipes and wearing feathers. But that's just a myth, she says. Not many Indians ever lived in teepees. And I live in a house."

The Women in yellow hum, coming to form a semi-circle around us.

"How would you know someone is an Indian, then?" I ask.

"You wouldn't. Not necessarily. Look at your own skin. Are *you* an Indian?"

Candice seems to really be asking the question, not just joking. I look down at my arm, at the dark hairs, at my color.

They sigh. They sit on the linoleum floor and sway their bodies. They wait for me to answer.

"Why do you ask?"

"I'm just making a point, Emily. That you can't always tell who someone is just by looking at them."

They are rocking, heaving, saying, *Indian, Indian, Indian.*

"Am I Indian?" I ask Them, but no one answers.

•

In my bathroom mirror I look at my reflection. Behind me, They stand. One is sitting in the bathtub, and another is looking out the small, hexagonal window.

I know I don't look like my mother. Where she is fair, I am dark. I've always thought this was because of my father. In the photos of him, I can see a resemblance. Or I thought I could.

Remember, They urge, and my stomach turns to knots.

"I don't know what you're asking of me! I don't understand why you're here. Or what you want."

Remember.

"I'm trying," I tell Them. The Woman with the long hair comes to stand beside me. She pushes up her mask, puts her face close to mine, and then turns to look in the mirror.

We look nothing alike. Where her nose is wide, her eyebrows thick and straight, my nose is pointed, my brows arched.

She traces her jawline, and it looks like she's making a cutthroat motion.

But when I mimic her, finger running along my cheek, and chin, our hands make the same movements.

•

Mother comes home with some paper-clipped folders and says, "We're in business. And Mrs. Habbermire is coming over to help us celebrate!"

Candice has everything already done and when she leaves, she bends down and whispers to me, "Remember what I said. Don't let anyone in this house!"

Grownup talk is awfully boring sometimes, which is why I don't listen to mother and Mrs. Habbermire. Instead, I watch.

They go on and on about ordering fabric and tables and sewing machines, and how mother is going to have to go to Dallas and in Dallas there are entire blocks of businesses selling dresses and fabric and it would just be easier if Candice would agree to stay with me one night while she goes. And she keeps talking.

I say I wasn't listening, but that is a lie. What I mean is I don't care about what is being said. I am more concerned with how these two women look. Not only do I not resemble my mother, I look *nothing* like her or her aunt. I know that now, after spending hours in front of the mirror, comparing myself to the picture of her and my father before he went away to war. The color of my skin does not have a complement in either parent. My cheekbones are not as prominent. My nose has devised a whole new shape. None of this makes an argument for lineage.

Mrs. Habbermire compliments my mother on the food: roast chicken and green beans and biscuits, and my mother says she can't take any credit for it. It was all Candice. Mrs. Habbermire says that mother's mother loved roast chicken. Or used to, *before*.

Personally, I don't care for chicken. I think you could take any cooked chicken in the world and bury it in the ground and it would kill all the trees in a ten foot radius. But that's not something I could have told Candice when I'd already done something to put her off. Luckily, I do like ketchup, which I drown my forkfuls in.

After dinner, mother and Mrs. Habbermire take glasses full of cold coffee out onto the back patio and I don't care too much to watch them any longer and so I go upstairs to organize my things. My room is a mess, I know, and if Will is ever going to come talk to me about Indians, I wouldn't want him to think me a slob.

There isn't really enough space for all the things I've discovered in the Gladwell boxes. Rather, there is enough space but not enough shelves or places to put the knick-knacks on. I've put the collection of painted porcelain snuff boxes on the top shelf of my bureau. The floor around it is jumbled with my finds: an empty picture frame, a lace shawl, a record that is scratched, but scratched in a way that makes it look as if many small rodent paws were digging to uncover something.

I turn my radio on, sitting down on the rug and separating the items I've lugged up into two piles: keep and give to Candice.

When I am done, the sun is almost all the way down, and mother and Mrs. Habbermire are *still* on the back patio. I wonder if they are talking about the woman between them, Mrs. Habbermire's sister. My grandmother.

Try to remember, They say.

And something does come back then. It is only a wisp, a fragment, a piece of cloth on a body left to scavengers.

The back of my mother's head is not right. Her hair is the wrong color. I know this, and it feels like someone has slapped me. There is something unlocking in my head. A picture that moves like a carousel. A woman who appears, and disappears, her dark hair flying in the wind.

I turn to look at the long-haired Woman behind me. I reach my hands to her face. She smiles but does not smile. She takes off her mask and gives it to me. It is not wooden. It is warm and soft like old leather, and I put it on.

•

I move the lamp from the bed stand over to the window, the cord catching on the dining room chair I've lugged up, toppling it over. I stand breathless, my hands clamped around the brass, and wait to hear my mother's door creak open. Nothing. Nothing for a long time.

Tippy-toe across the carpet. Tippy-toe through the layer of dust I've been coughing up, settled now on the floor. I dance words into the dust. Here I write —- with my toe. Here I write —— with my heel. I set the lamp on the inside window ledge, and they come, the moths. They flutter against the glass and thrust their bodies toward the light.

•

Little girls disappear. That is what I learn from the book Mr. Gladwell was writing. Sometimes little girls are taken by Indians. Sometimes they are taken by the government.

•

I *would* like to have a library, but I wouldn't know where to begin. I have two books. Or, I have one book and one collection of pages. The Gladwell book is bothersome. I am missing some of it. When I told my mother I might be a writer, what I meant was, *I need to fill the gaps.*

•

There is music everywhere. It is in the wood, in my feet, in the beating of many hearts.

I *stomp stomp stomp* around the house when mother is not home and Candice is running errands.

I fill tin cans with hard beans and shake them as I dance.

I never dance alone.

•

I listen to what They say. Learn how to let their words sink through my skin and enter my blood, my heart, my brain. They are teaching me about the past. My past.

Remembering is hard. I know I've said this before, but I say it again.

Just like there is more than one way to disappear, there is more than one way to remember.

Sometimes remembering is like building a house: you can imagine what you want, but all you have are pieces that must be fit together, and that takes work, and tools, and time.

Sometimes remembering comes on all at once, like opening a door and learning just how cold it is outside.

Sometimes remembering is like setting a fire: you need to burn away the brush in order to help the roots grow back, better than before, new growth sprouting from the ground now perfect for weaving baskets, in which to carry more memories.

•

"Why aren't we going to celebrate the 4th of July?" I ask.

"To be honest, it doesn't feel right." My mother is painting her nails, the red varnish a garish cardinal's wing.

"Why not?"

"Because we lost your father in a war and wars are terrible things and I don't want to think about them."

"Hmm. I agree."

"Do you?"

"Yes, I agree that wars are terrible."

My mother looks surprised, but I don't know why.

"Even the war that made our country?" she asks. "That one was terrible too?"

"Even that war," I say. "Especially that war, because it wasn't our country to begin with."

My mother's mouth drops open. She makes a sound like she is choking, but she is not.

•

Sometimes remembering is like writing a story. There is always some part of it that cannot be told, because to try to tell it all at the same time would be impossible.

Thomas Gladwell writes about the settlers in Larissa, but he is not writing about the owls that hoot at night and the other birds they kill for food. He is not writing about the fish in the river or all the trees being cut down. He is not writing about the people who lived here before.

He cannot tell it all. To tell it all would make a mess of a story. Too many things. Not enough space.

I tell this to Them, and They know it is true. *Something is always lost to time,* They say. *But not all. Not all is lost. Remember. Remember. Remember.*

•

"You take care now," I say, and my mother laughs.

"I'm going to be careful, I promise. I'm going to try to be home later, but I want you in bed young woman. You're still not entirely up to snuff."

I watch her car pull away from the curb and wonder what goodies she'll come back from Dallas with.

Candice is cleaning up the leftover breakfast in the kitchen, and so I take to my room to read. I've completed Mr. Gladwell's book. I've read all of it I have to Them, and they have not come to like it any better, though they no longer cover their ears. Honestly, I don't think I care for it either. It's not especially good.

We all sit in a circle and read aloud from Mrs. Habbermire's book. They don't seem bothered by the stories, but neither do They seem to enjoy them. Instead, They seem to be waiting.

"I could tell you a story," I say, producing the HELP ME paper from where I've hidden it in my dresser.

They nod. Find more comfortable positions.

"I can't promise it will be good, though."

Remember. Remember.

I can't remember something I've never known, but I can use it for inspiration.

"Once, there was a lady," I begin. "She lived in a grand house made of hard wood and she loved flowers. The problem was that she was locked in the house. She couldn't get out. But she learned about the world outside from the flowers. That's why she loved them so much. The flowers were her teachers. She would watch them from the window and by their growth, or death, she knew what season it was. And depending on what insects came to land on the petals, she knew what the weather would be like. They would follow the movement of her around the house, turning their blooms in the direction of her body: the kitchen, the bedroom, the attic."

There is a knock on the wall, and They turn their faces sharply.

"Emily? Who are you talking to?" The curtain parts and Candice looks into my room. "That boy isn't hiding in here, is he?"

"There's no boy," I say, smiling at Them.

"What have you got there?" Candice asks. I hide the HELP ME paper in my skirt and hold up the book in my lap. But I know she isn't really interested in what I have. She's using it as a pretext to search out Will, who really is not here.

"They're just stories," I say, showing to her the illustration of the Forever Girl.

"Where did you get this?" Candice reaches for the book, and I hand it over to her. "I thought you were stuck on that Gladwell thing."

"Mrs. Habbermire gave me this book, and it's better. It's full of endings."

"Well I'll be damned." Candice puts a hand up to her mouth, her eyes going wide. And then we both laugh.

"Pardon my language. I'm just surprised ..."

"At what?"

"This here," she says, grunting as she sits on the floor beside me, "is a story I know. It's a story from *my* childhood."

They nod. The Woman with the long hair puts a hand to her breast.

"What do you mean," I ask.

"Well, the story is one I've heard. Maybe not this version," Candice says, flipping through the pages, "but I know about Forever Girl. And I know about the Little People, too."

"You do?"

"I do."

"How do you know about the Little People?" I ask, suspicious of her.

"Well...." Candice makes a face as if she is pained. As if something has happened in the time between words. "I haven't met any Little People, but I think, yes, my grandmother did. Or she says she did. I'm trying to remember ..."

They are buzzing. Pushing closer. Turning their ears to catch what Candice is saying.

"I ... hmmm," Candice huffs. "It will come back to me. My grandmother ..."

Candice seems to be having trouble talking. I want to ask her if she's okay, but then she smiles and pats the open page of the book. "My grandmother was Cherokee," Candice says, "and she's the one who told me this story."

"So you're Cherokee too?" I ask.

"That's what I've been told. But honestly, where I came from, we're all mixed up." Candice laughs. "I probably have some Choctaw or Chickasaw in me even. Maybe it doesn't matter, I'm Indian, aren't I?"

"Are you?" I ask, because I don't understand what it means to be Indian. They are trying to tell me, to get me to remember, but remembering is not the same thing as being.

Candice looks confused and says, "Of course I am."

I want to ask Candice more questions, but I am not ready. I think I must remember more before I know what to ask.

"Emily," she says, closing the book gently and resting it on one knee. "I've been meaning to talk to you about something. I've been avoiding it because I wasn't sure if it was my place, but sometimes you are more grown up than I think."

"Okay."

"Do you remember, when you were really sick, some of the things you said?"

They shift, lean in.

"What do you mean?"

"Do you remember what you were saying?"

Remember. Remember. Remember. Remember.

"I'm trying", I say, both to Them and Candice.

"It sounded like ooh-ne-chi," Candice says.

A dam. A sunrise. A deer with an arrow in its heart.

"It's u-ni-tsi," I correct her, the syllables like honey on my tongue.

They are smiling. They are standing and dancing through us. *Remember. Remember. Remember.*

"You know what it means," Candice asks.

"It means 'mother.'"

•

It is full dark and They have woken me from sleep. I have been dreaming of birds roosting in the tops of cedar trees. I am one of these birds, watching myself through a plume of smoke. Watching my body resign, becoming still. Watching Them line up alongside the road as people come to take me.

My cheeks are wet and They say, *We know. It is time. Remember.*

They are herding me down the stairs. Their dresses are different now. Not yellow, but all prints and colors, high-necked and long-sleeved. There is a new woman among Them, tall and unsure. Her hair pinned up in the memory of who she was. She is Lillian Gladwell, the woman in the picture I found. They are holding her hands, pulling her too, though she keeps looking back at me, uncertain.

Candice is asleep on the sofa, waiting for mother to come home.

I tip-toe through the kitchen, and I open the door. They dance through it. They try to take the new woman with them, but she staggers at the door frame, looking down and at her own body as if she can't believe she's here.

"It's okay," I tell her. "I know remembering is hard."

She frowns, watching Them through the glass.

They are in the yard, their feet shuffling, their dresses billowing. They are plucking the white roses off the back fence. They are putting flowers in their hair, behind their ears. Their hands are bloody. There is so much blood.

Remember. Remember. Remember.

They are trying to tell me a story, but I put my fingers in my ears.

"I'm not ready," I say.

They lie down in brown grass, arms askew, legs akimbo.

Remember.

I want to, but remembering is hard.

Remember, Remember, Remember.

Lillian Gladwell gasps and then is not there.

I smell the scent of fried bread. Remember hands holding food out to me, wrapped in coarse cloth. A woman I know is my mother, my real mother, taking me into her arms as a car rumbles behind me. She is crying, and I am crying, and she is saying, "Daw-nv-da-go-hv-ee. Until we meet again."

7

Crosshatch

—Bet—

Bet didn't want to look, but she felt like she had to. The photos were right there on Marcil's desk, stacked neatly near the corner.

She peered back through the open door and into the station at the men working with their heads bent, not one of them paying her any attention. She stepped closer to the pictures with her eyes still on the officers.

The first photo was of Marjorie Kent's arm. Somehow, it wasn't as gruesome as Bet thought it might be. Maybe because it wasn't attached to a body. Maybe she felt disconnected the way the arm was: just some thing to be puzzled over.

The flesh was ragged at what would have been the elbow, darkened with dried blood and dirt. Bone was lighter than skin. This, the boundary point at which body became nothing—this *did* bother her. Still, she made herself look through the stack, thinking that as a mother, she had to. The witnesses should not all be men, even if some of them were fathers.

The second photo was of the charm bracelet. Removed from Marjorie's wrist, it lay against whole wood, draped over a log perhaps, splayed out for the camera at the scene. The bracelet was cluttered with hearts and little locks. That was all. Hearts of all sizes, some engraved with designs and some sterile and flat, others bulbous and round. The locks were fewer and farther between, and Bet wondered why there were no keys.

No, wait, there. One other charm, partially hidden behind one of the hearts. But it was not a key. It was a music note. A little quarter note, its stem bent.

Marcil cleared his voice at the doorway. Bet backed away from the desk.

"Don't know why you'd want to see that," he said.

Bet didn't have an explanation she could give, or that she wanted to give, and felt embarrassed.

"All this is turning out to be some mess, isn't it?" he continued.

Realizing that she was blocking access to his chair, that she was standing in his spot, Bet shook her head—silly her—and rounded the other side of the desk, making a path for Marcil to where he belonged.

She thought *mess* was an understatement, but bit her tongue.

"Four girls," Marcil sighed. "Three girls," he corrected. "Three missing girls and one dead one. This doesn't look good, Bet."

What was she to say to that? Any commentary she could offer would say it for what it was, not just what it looked like. Something that was violent, uncontrollable, unfixable.

"Are you learning anything at least?" She asked instead.

Marcil rubbed his eyes. Pushed his chair back and pulled the shades down. "Nothing other than what you see here. Which doesn't tell us anything."

Bet couldn't understand what the problem was. In the movies she saw, in the books she read, police investigations never got stumped. There was always some clue. Some path worth pursuing.

"I can't believe there's nothing," she said, trying to frame her tone in a way that really made it sound like disbelief and not a rebuke.

"There's not nothing," he said. "We just haven't found whatever it is yet."

"Did you go out to the farm?" Bet asked, easing herself into the chair across from her boss, hoping that Marcil was in a mood to talk, and if not that, maybe he at least wasn't going to push her out.

"We went out there," he confirmed. "I don't know if they were happy to see us or angry. Felt like I was kicking a hornet's nest. One minute they won't say anything and the next I can't shut them up."

"Did they say anything useful?"

"Who knows. We found out that the girls disappeared in the middle of the day. Not taken from those shacks Mrs. White calls houses. The older one, Georgia, she just up and vanished while playing with some other kids. Never came back out of the woods from some hide-and-seek. Rita had gone with some of the women to the five and dime and she just disappeared from the store."

"In Larissa?" Bet asked.

Marcil nodded. "Right under their noses. That's why they came up here that day. Right to the police station. They were already in town."

"But didn't anyone go looking for her?" Bet asked, and this time, she couldn't keep from sounding accusatory.

"Buddy said he'd send someone out there," Marcil said.

"And did he?"

Marcil didn't answer.

"Well ..." Bet didn't know what to say. Marcil knew Buddy had dropped the ball, and he'd already fired Buddy for it. "That means two girls were taken in town. Three, I mean," Bet corrected herself. "Marjorie, Rita, and Marlene."

"I don't know about Marlene," Marcil said. "Honestly, I don't think she just disappeared. If you ask me, that beau she had is involved somehow. We're going to look into it, but these other girls, they come first."

Bet cocked her head to the side and wondered how Marcil determined which was more important, how he weighed the disappearance of girls to determine who was of greater value and urgency.

"I think," she said, "that I need a cigarette. Marcil, is there anything I can get you from the gas station?"

•

Bet stood outside Pete's Gas-N-Go, and she was thinking about the girls. Hating herself a bit because every time she thought of them, she started with Marjorie. She was always the first to come to mind. But Marjorie had been the fourth to go missing, and Bet knew she was embodying a true Larissian: relegating the workers of Mrs. White's farm to a far corner of her mind, even if she knew it wasn't right.

She bought another pack of Lucky Strikes, the brand her father had smoked, and coughed on the first inhale. Then she leaned against the glass and watched people come and go from the ice cream parlor across the street. Finally, she stamped down the glowing stub with the ball of her foot, grinding it into the oil-covered ground of the gas station.

The cigarette had made her pleasantly light-headed.

She'd quit seven years before, when she was pregnant with Alton. The smoke had made her nauseous. She could smell it on the furniture and in the curtains, permeating the plaster. When she tried to light up, her own body rebelled, sending her gagging into the bathroom.

Now smoking felt like a homecoming, and she was falling easily back into the habit. And what was wrong with a little comfort right now, she asked herself. What was wrong with looking for something to make the world seem a little more tolerable?

•

When Bet got back to the courthouse with Marcil's soda, he tried to send her right back out again. She'd offered to do him one favor, so she guessed he thought it was fine to do him another: go pick up his wife's wedding ring from Pearlman Jewelers because her diamond had come loose and she had sent it there to be fixed. Marcil would not be back before Pearlman's closed because there was a fight at the new shoe factory and he was on his way down there to straighten things out. "Better not be Buddy," he said, "causing problems up there because he's angry with me."

As she was getting her purse, she noticed a slip of paper on her desk. An attached note asked her to copy edit an advert looking for a new police officer. The city was hiring *two* new officers to help with its growing population, fueled by the uptick in industry and the calls coming more often about parts of town she never went, areas filling up with temporary housing and shanty bars. She sighed and typed up what had been messily written, correcting some misspellings and grammar errors.

Bet walked down to the town square and along the way, wondered what might happen if she applied. There wasn't anything in the language she'd just edited to suggest only men could be hired, and Bet *had* been the one to put the pieces connecting the missing girls together. No, she thought, they didn't know for sure yet that everything was connected, but without her close attention, they might have permanently overlooked a potential link. What she'd done was still good work. And what had Calvin said? Maybe Bet could take Buddy's place. The comment had been made in jest, but really, why not?

Bet was surprised that she began to actually picture the possibility, and more surprised to find that she actually wanted to make it happen. She was intelligent, a hard-worker, and persistent. She wanted to contribute to a greater good, and that's why she looked for a public service job to begin with. And Bet wasn't afraid of the kinds of situations she might encounter as a police officer. She'd already been dealing with them second-hand for years, and being married to Norman reinforced the understanding that life could be mean and bloody. She'd be prepared. *Tough as nails,* Bet whispered to herself, dropping the envelope into the postbox.

When she returned from her errand, she went and asked Lt. Brown for an application. He handed it over without a second thought, and she carried it back to her own desk where she completed it with impeccable penmanship.

She was giggly, bubbly. She put the ring box on Marcil's desk, right on top of her application to become a police officer for Larissa, and she walked home, no longer bothered by the slight of a personal errand. She smoked two cigarettes along the way.

•

The boys swept into the house like a tornado, bringing with them slips of grass and the smell of chlorine. They left their still-wet swimsuits draped over the rim of the tub in the downstairs bath and then disappeared out the backdoor to join their father where in his hands, he was turning over instructions for the tent.

It would be a fight, she knew, if Marcil even considered her. Norman would take it as a challenge to his manhood—his wife a police officer. He'd had a chip on his shoulder for any kind of government work since he was refused for service.

Maybe Bet was itching for a fight. Maybe she wanted to punish him in more than just small ways. She felt a glee when she imagined driving the cruiser, dressing in that blue uniform in the morning, draping one of those uniforms over the ironing board and asking if he could take care of it; her new schedule—*police,* she would say, *don't have the weekends off*—and then kissing him on the cheek, leaving her husband to stare wide-eyed at her out the door.

If Marcil would consider her, she imagined he'd even give her the weekends for work. No one complained about working Saturday, or even Sunday, but no one really enjoyed it either.

After dinner they all played a game of Chutes and Ladders. Will had wanted to play Clue, but the game was too complicated for his younger brother and he sulkily agreed to the *baby game,* as he called it, an insult that stuck with Alton and caused the younger boy to scream when he thought he wasn't winning, wiping all the pieces from the board and storming from the kitchen.

"No dessert for you if you're going to behave that way!" Norman called, at which point Alton came back, shoulders hunched, and apologized to the ground.

If she had threatened him, Bet thought, it would have ended with a door slamming and him wailing into his pillow.

When Alton hesitantly asked her later to read a story to him, she agreed, but she said Will got to pick it out.

"I'm too old for bedtime stories," Will told her, but she said no one was ever too old for stories, and he picked *The Secret of Skull Mountain,* an entire book and not a story, and Alton fell asleep not too long after the Hardy boys discovered the low water level.

•

"Mom?"

Bet was in the front yard, watering the geraniums and trying not to get her cigarette wet. When she turned towards Will's voice, she saw her older son sitting on the porch steps. She hadn't even heard him come out.

"What's happening doodle bug?"

"Mom," Will whined. "Don't call me that. I'm too old to be 'doodle bug.'" He chastised her, but still, he was smiling.

"That's fine, *Will.*"

"I was wondering if we could talk?"

Bet went to turn off the hose and then crushed her cigarette out on the pavers. "Come over here, out of the sun," she said, waving him into the shade of the wisteria tree. Bet sat on the ground and patted the grass. Will came to her, swinging his arms a bit like he did when he was younger and had an ask he knew she'd say no to.

"I've been thinking," he began, "that maybe I can help you with the missing girls."

Bet frowned, not because it was a ridiculous thought, though it was that, too. She made a face because it made her sad to think that Will was that good of a person, to *think* he should help even though he was still a child.

"See," he went on, his voice betraying his excitement. "I'm getting my tracker badge, and I'm learning some skills. It says in the Guide's book that Indians were really good at tracking things. Animals they hunted for food. Other tribes, you know, that attacked them and so they go attack them back. So I'm learning to track like them. Maybe I can help the detectives."

"I see. I think that's really kind of you to offer, Will. But this is a very grown-up situation and I don't think it's appropriate for you to help."

"See, I knew you would say that. So I've already been practicing."

"Oh have you? How?" Bet found herself curious now.

"I re-read a bunch of the Hardy Boys books. I was thinking I could learn something from them because they're really good at figuring out mysteries."

"But it's a tracker badge, right? And tracking doesn't necessarily mean mystery."

"I know." Will gave her a look as if she was silly to think he didn't know the difference. "But they do find things, too. Which is why I thought I might be able to help Andrew."

Bet nodded in concession.

"He'd lost his dad's pocket watch. Actually, he wasn't supposed to have it at all. That was the real problem. If his dad found out he took it, and lost it, he'd be in big trouble."

"That he would be," Bet said, thinking that if either Will or Alton lost something of Norman's he'd whoop them.

"But we were out near Stadler Creek," Will went on, getting even more excited now, leaning forward and ripping the scalloped leaves of a weed from the ground. "And you know what it's like out there. All trees and stuff and really woody. So we couldn't remember exactly where we'd been. But then I was thinking about the Hardy Boys, and I was thinking about the Guide's book, and guess what?"

"What?"

"I remembered that when you're tracking animals, or people even, you can look to see if bushes and trees have branches broken off. And you can look at the grass too—if it's tall grass—to see where it's been flattened down by people walking. And I did it, Mom. I was able to find out where the teepee was! I mean, he amended, it wasn't really a teepee. We were just pretending it was, and I found the watch!"

Bet could tell that Will was proud of himself, and she was too—Will was smarter, maybe, than she gave him credit for. But what was sitting in the back of her mind was the teepee. "What do you mean teepee, Will? What were you pretending was a teepee out in the woods?"

"Oh," Will said, like it didn't matter. "There are all kinds of old tents back there. I don't think anyone lives in them anymore. Patrick said all the people who used to sleep in the woods live at his dad's motel now. They got factory jobs so they can sleep in beds."

Bet didn't know what disturbed her more, that Will seemed to take no notice of the possible danger he had been in, playing make believe in a vagrant camp, or that the vagrant camp was there at all.

"Will, I think you did a really good job finding that watch, I really do. I'm impressed with you. But that's not at all like trying to find the girls. I hope you can understand that."

Will hung his head, but nodded.

Bet patted his knee and told him, "But you know what? You'd make a really good Indian."

He looked up at her and brightened a bit. "You see? That's what *I* was thinking. I make a good Indian, so maybe I can help find the girls. Because they're Indians too."

"What?"

"Yeah." Will looked confused. "Andrew's uncle is the one who buys the cotton off Mrs. White. He says the girls out there are Indian. The ones who disappeared. Didn't you know that?"

"No, Will. I didn't. No one told me."

Bet didn't think it would help, but it couldn't hurt either. She called Marcil at home to tell him the rest of the missing girls were Indian. Rita and Georgia, at least.

8

Talking with Shadows

—Candice—

Candice was in the middle of pressing one of Gracie's dresses when the phone rang. She sat the iron upright on the board and went to the alcove near the basement door. "Howard residence," she answered.

Laughter greeted her. Then mocked her. "Howard residence," the voice repeated.

Stunned to silence, Candice didn't respond.

"Is Gracie home?" the voice asked, drawing out the long A in the name.

"Just a moment. May I ask who is calling?"

"Mrs. Howard is calling."

Irene Howard, Candice thought. Now the rudeness made sense. She'd never met the woman, but she'd heard stories. And Gracie didn't say much directly, but when she did, Irene's name was almost hissed through gritted teeth.

In the backyard, Gracie was on her hands and knees, a watering can at her side. Candice walked across the uneven pavers that had pushed up and become disjointed by grass.

Gracie looked up when Candice told her that her mother-in-law was on the phone, wide eyes going wider under the brim of her hat. "This can't be good."

Candice went back to the sheets and tried to be discreet with her eavesdropping.

"Irene. Good to hear from you." Gracie looked at Candice and rolled her eyes. "Yes, I know," she went on. "Yes, there's going to be a parade. There's always a parade, Irene, on the Fourth of July."

Gracie fell quiet and there was an extended silence.

Candice moved the hot iron over cotton.

"I see." Gracie's voice sounded strained. "Well ... yes. Alright then." And then she hung up.

Gracie just stood in the kitchen, still holding the receiver, but down at her side.

Candice came and pried it from her fingers. Replaced it where it belonged. "Everything alright?"

"My husband. George. His tags have finally been found."

•

Candice went home full of stories, but she couldn't find the strength to want to relay any of them. Not the one about Irene Howard and the dog tags or the one about the settlers of Larissa, written in the hand of Thomas Gladwell, the narrative about hard, home-steading life and Indian attacks Emily seemed so interested in. The girl was hoarding papers in her bedroom, musty smelling things she'd discovered in boxes brought up from the basement, and one stack of them was a rather badly written narrative of a Larissa long past.

Emily herself, combined with Gladwell's story in Emily's hands, had made Candice think about her own history. Hearing the girl reading the tale of the town's deceased early residents, and thinking about where Emily might have come from, opened a door into dwelling.

"Do you think this was one of his relatives," Emily had asked about the main character. "The name is the same. Thomas."

Candice sat in a chair next to Emily's bed. The girl's fever was off and on, and with the touch and go sleepiness, Emily had constructed a type of nest for herself out of narrative. Parts of Gladwell's book and sections of newspaper lay spread out in a circle with Emily sitting cross-legged in the center.

"I wouldn't know," Candice admitted.

"I just hate not knowing things," Emily replied, huffing and setting down the papers she held.

Candice was, at just that moment, wondering if Emily's words were doing double work. Was the girl really just talking about the Thomas Gladwell they were reading about? Or was her mind turning over other unknowns as well? Perhaps her own history?

"Well the world is too large to know everything," Candice finally said.

"If you say so." Emily sounded skeptical, turning to a section of the newspaper. "I wish I could know about this," she went on, tapping a finger on the article about the missing girls. The paper was beginning to slowly report on all of them, not just Marjorie Kent. The particular piece was also about Rita Randall and Georgia Stock, girls, Candice found out, who disappeared from the farm. But there was nothing about Marlene.

"These girls are all so … unfinished," Emily huffed.

Emily's wording struck Candice as odd, scary even, but that word—*unfinished*—lodged in Candice's thoughts and followed her home.

When Everett came home from work, he found his wife at the dining room table with a piece of paper in front of her.

"Look at this," she said. "I never thought to put it all down before."

Everett draped his apron over the back of the chair next to the one she was sitting in and put his hands on the table, leaning over to see what she'd written.

"A family tree?" He asked.

She nodded. Pointed to the fourth row up to a blank line where her great-grandmother's information should have been listed. "I should know more about her," she said. "But I don't. Why don't I?"

It bothered her that she couldn't trace where she'd come from. Her name, up to her mother's—Salida—with notations of place and years. Her mother's up to her grandmother's—Enola—with notations of place and years. Her grandmother's up to her great-grandmothers, Ida Rose. A single notation about possible birthplace. And then a question mark.

Candice knew Ida Rose had been removed from Texas with her family in 1838 when the Cherokee were forced to move again, this time up into Oklahoma. But she only knew that much because before her grandmother died, Candice's mother would still talk about being Indian. Once Enola passed, and Candice's mother left Nacogdoches to become white, taking Candice with her, she stopped with any disclosure of who the family had been before her.

"I look at this," Candice said, "and I think I should know. I don't mean someone should have told me. I do mean that, too. But what I really mean is that there isn't a reason under the sun that anyone shouldn't know where they come from. It isn't right."

"Maybe you should call your mother?" Everett suggested. "If you press her, she might tell you."

Candice didn't want to call her mother. If she called her mother, her mother would ask what was new, and if her mother asked what was new, Candice would feel compelled to tell her about Marlene. And if she brought up Marlene, then she would bring up the other missing girls, which meant she would have to bring up Mrs. White's farm, because nearby they'd found part of Marjorie, which didn't bode well for Georgia and Rita. And if she brought up the farm, and how Georgia and Rita's families were there, toiling away on land that used to be theirs and now wasn't, her mother would talk about "those people" as if she had no allegiance to them. As if the Indians there were strangers to be ignored. As if everyone who worked there was there by choice, not by circumstance. And Candice didn't want to talk about those things because it would end in a fight, like it always did.

Candice thought there had to be records somewhere. She hoped there were records, because she'd rather get the information herself than quarrel with her mother about it. If she went back home—not forever, she thought, just for a trip—she might be able to find people who still remembered. Lots of families never left Nacogdoches, and their memories were long.

"Could work," Candice told her husband, though it was just to placate him, to end a conversation she now regretted starting.

"What's got you into all this?"

"I was just thinking about history. How it changes but stays the same. Seems I should do something to keep it from looping back on itself. Straighten out all the forgetting and not knowing."

•

That Sunday, Everett made sweet potato pie and Candice made what she now called "wormy rolls."

"That doesn't sound very appetizing," Everett said, taking them from her as she locked the door.

"I think it's fun," she said. "Inventive. A new way of calling things." That's what Emily had called them, the small, dough crescents Candice made for her.

The church service was somber, the minister's sermon one on hope. Candice sang a hymn along with the congregation, but the song didn't sound right. Flat. No one putting their heart into it besides Lulu, which was understandable since church was the best part of the old woman's week. No one would begrudge her the joy of song, even if Marjorie Kent had been murdered. Since no one else could put effort into it, Lulu seemed to carry them all.

In the basement of the building, Candice found Katherine Cooper, who looked like she'd aged a decade since Candice really looked at her last.

The women had bonded years ago when Katherine and her husband Daniel had first moved to Larissa, and only a few blocks away from Candice at that, because they'd recognized in each other a familiar soul but a person not yet known. However, over the years they'd drifted apart, and it was more Candice's fault than Katherine's.

Katherine's weekend trips to and from Rusk County to help care for her own aging mother became a fence between the two women. Katherine still had her attachment to her ancestry, could still come and go from the place she'd grown up in. Could sing her people's songs and go to the pow wows. Could still ride back into town at any moment and feel she belonged. And Candice felt like she could not.

When Candice had confided to Katherine that she felt like her mother had stolen something from her, had locked the door to her past, Katherine had said it was never too late to go back to Nacogdoches. To know. When Candice explained to Katherine that she was only *part* Indian, and was worried she'd be seen as an outsider, Katherine asked what *part* of her *was* Indian.

Candice hadn't been able to discern if Katherine was trying to help her, or if Katherine was admonishing her. It had terrified her—this possible confrontation, Candice's own friend telling her she wasn't Indian enough—and afterward, they'd drifted apart. It was easy to do that with two young girls: give all of what she had to them as a way to ignore what she didn't want to deal with.

Now Candice thought Katherine must be feeling utterly alone, surrounded by people who were subdued, and grieving, but for Marjorie. Where was her husband even? Katherine was so marked by her skin, a dark door in a white wall of faces. Was so out of place, Candice thought. Maybe Candice wasn't Indian enough, but she *was* Indian—Candice told herself this, nodding—and Katherine, she knew now, had been forgotten in the wake of Marjorie. Katherine, and her daughter Marlene, swept under the rug not just by Larissa, but by their own congregation as well.

Candice now looked Katherine over. She was sitting with a few women Candice knew, wives of her husband's friends, though Katherine didn't really seem to be talking with them. Putting aside her fear of rejection, telling herself that if *anyone* was an outsider, it was *those* women—who couldn't possibly begin to understand the entirety that was Katherine—Candice made Katherine a plate, pulled up a chair, and joined the women.

Allison Nyquist was prattling on about the new animals at the Zoo on the west side of town, and Candice spoke in a whisper so soft she could barely hear herself.

"Katherine," she said sliding the plate over, "I'm so sorry. If there's anything I can do ..."

Katherine's dark eyes turned toward Candice. "I am so tired of people telling me they're sorry," Katherine told her. "Sorry for what, is what I want to know. People talking like they're sorry she's dead. But she's not. We don't know she's dead."

The other women at the table quieted, and Candice looked between them, hoping one of them would come to her rescue.

"Everybody's talking like she's past-tense," Katherine went on, her fork spearing the sweet potato pie.

"Oh no, honey, no we're not." Rosemary Mackie was shaking her head, leaning towards Katherine.

"Y'all don't even know," Katherine continued. "You don't even know."

"Know what?" Rosemary asked.

Katherine looked at each of the women in turn, no one daring to speak until she'd finished her thought.

Finally Katherine locked eyes with Candice. "Those girls, "she began. "Those girls out from Mrs. White's farm? They're Indian. Those girls? Rita and Georgia? They're Indian."

"Oh, honey. That's not a fair comparison," Rosemary responded. "Just because you're," and Rosemary paused as if stumbling towards her next word, "Indian ... it doesn't mean anything."

"Maybe not. Doesn't stop the wondering. You know what I found last night? Marlene's baby doll. She held that thing so much when she was little the arm fell off. I had to help Marlene sew it back on. I remember, I remember telling Marlene her girl was lucky to have a mother like her. A mother that could sew her up. Marlene wasn't very good at sewing. I never wanted to make her do it because I didn't even like it, and her doll's shoulder was all crossed with ugly knots."

Candice wasn't sure what she should do. If she should keep quiet, and listen, or if she should try to redirect the conversation.

"But she *wanted* to do better after that," Katherine went on. The woman was rubbing the handle of her fork between her fingers furiously. "She made little dresses for her doll. Made a little dollhouse for her too. And Marlene made her doll a bed out of sticks. A living room table out of sticks. A car, out of sticks. She's going to be such a good mother one day. One day. Yes, she's going to be a very good mother."

Katherine was getting a faraway look in her eyes. Her face was still trained on Candice, but Katherine was looking through her too.

None of the women knew what to say, or how to respond. And so no one did.

•

After church, Candice sat out on the back porch, absentmindedly picking at the scab on her wrist. The conversation with Katherine had unhinged her a bit—made her angry and guilty and desirous all at the same time.

She knew it was unfair to be jealous of Katherine, but that seed was still rooted in her gut, making her sick with her own emotions. Candice knew it wasn't fair either to compare herself to Katherine—that the comparison couldn't stand up to scrutiny, or logic, because neither had any control over how they were raised. But still, Katherine had ties to her tribe that Candice didn't have.

Now Candice was warring with herself, caught between the desire to find out more about her own family and being disturbed by what Katherine had said—that the two girls missing from the farm were Indian too—which meant three girls, three missing girls of four, were Indian. Candice was teetering between a desire for knowledge and a fear that the knowledge may be a curse. In shame, in secret, she was glad her own girls were grown. Were not in Larissa. Would not go missing because they were Indian.

•

Later that night, Candice confided in Everett. They'd set up some dominos on the kitchen table and Candice had brought up the new information to Everett—that Indian girls were going missing, and that she feared saying it all aloud made it true: they were taken because they were Indian.

"Candy," Everett said, "you know not *all* those girls are Indian. Marjorie Kent wasn't."

"But it's too much of a coincidence, isn't it? Everett, what are the chances?"

Everett agreed it was strange—a "statistical anomaly" is what he said. Odd indeed that in Larissa, in the "middle of nowhere east Texas," these specific girls had gone missing. "But still," he said, "it doesn't mean anything."

Candice was not so sure. She didn't know exactly what it meant, but it did mean *something*. Maybe it was meant as a sign. A sign to spur her into action. Into movement towards the past. Here she was confronted by two girls: Marlene with her physical absence and Emily with her emotional one. Two girls that were spaces, or holes, or mirrors with unknown reflections.

Maybe it was a sign that Candice should fill the gaps—something to push Candice into knowing.

Or maybe it was a different kind of sign. Maybe Marlene's disappearance was a warning. Maybe something in the universe was telling Candice to do her work before it was too late. Before the opportunity passed. She should find out now—before it was too late, before something happened to stop her—where she came from.

She shook her head, realizing the slippery slope her thoughts were taking her down. She told herself that there was no meaning in this. That she couldn't use the girls as an excuse to begin her own journey and that she was starting in the wrong place, looking for reason where there was none.

"You okay?" Everett asked, disrupting Candice's thoughts.

In the living room, applause and laughter erupted from the television set.

"I'm just wondering," Candice said. "If it even matters how—why—I get there."

"Get where?" Everett's brow was furrowed with concern.

"The beginning."

"What beginning?"

Candice shook her head, realizing she wasn't making any sense. That she wasn't communicating the leaps in her thinking. "Never mind," she said. "I'm just trying to work something out."

•

Candice asked if she might leave early, and Gracie waved her okay. The woman was going to *finish with the damn yard,* she swore. *Or at least those wicked things along the fence.*

And so Candice found herself looking through the large glass windows of the Historical Society and watching the man inside who was seeming to have a lot of trouble with his typewriter.

"I know you."

Candice spun to see the old woman related to Gracie Howard. Rebekah Habbermire.

"What are you doing here?" Mrs. Habbermire asked.

Candice risked an honest answer: "I'm trying to decide if I should go in."

"It ain't gonna bite. Come on, then," she added, shooing Candice in ahead of her.

Mrs. Habbermire opened the door and Candice followed her inside, taking stock of the ugly grey, metal desks and the walls cramped with wood-framed photos. The man bent over a table looked up, adjusted his glasses, and said good morning.

Mrs. Habbermire introduced him as Dusty, and then said to Candice, "You're in now. Impressed?"

It sounded like the woman might be joking, but not knowing if she should laugh, Candice said, "Mightily. Look at all this history."

"And us, its keepers," the woman responded. She dropped her purse on a desk and went to the coffee maker. "What can we do for you?"

Candice didn't feel comfortable sitting. She was all too aware that she was there to ask a favor, and she didn't want to seem presumptuous or overly comfortable in her asking. So she continued standing, looking from image to image hanging on the walls. "I'm interested in records," she said.

"For Cherokee County?" Dusty asked, now interested.

Candice cringed at the name, the home of Larissa, a town which had forgotten how it began itself.

Mrs. Habbermire clinked a spoon in her mug.

"No," Candice admitted. "But the problem is I don't know where to start. I've got some names. Birth places."

"Well let's have a look." Thankfully, the man came to her, taking the paper and opening it, scanning her handwriting. "Well this doesn't look too difficult, he said. Local by Texas standards. Just a hop, skip, and a jump away."

Um, Candice added, clearing her throat. "The problem is that this stuff here is what I know. I'm hoping to find out what came before."

Candice knew that Ida Rose had been born not far from Larissa, not far from Nacogdoches either, where her descendants would settle when they returned to Texas. Ida Rose had been born in Smith County, almost a decade before they'd been removed to the North. But for Candice, knowing what happened during Ida Rose's life, knowing what happened in Oklahoma, and before the removal—a mystery. Ida Rose was a shadow in what Candice knew of her family. From what she could gather, Ida Rose couldn't have talked much about what happened in her childhood, and the rest of her family—*her* mother, father, and siblings—remained shrouded.

Mrs. Habbermire looked over the man's shoulder at the paper Candice had given him. "So what do you need to know?"

"Well …" Candice cleared her throat. "I'm thinking of trying to build a family tree."

"A family tree? Well you've come to the right place!"

"Perhaps," Candice conceded, "But what I need might be hard to get? I don't know. My family aren't …" Candice faltered for words because she hadn't really planned what she was going to say, and now—in the moment—she wasn't sure what she *should* say.

"The thing is," Candice sighed, "I don't have a lot of information. And my family, we're Cherokee, you see …" It felt strange identifying herself aloud in this way to two people Candice had never said otherwise to, and she found herself wondering if *they* knew *their* family histories. "And I don't know how records are kept or where they're kept or …"

"Cherokee?" Dusty got a pencil and began to make a note on the paper. "I wonder," he mused, "if the Dawes Rolls might have something …"

"The Dawes Rolls?" Candice didn't know the term, and she felt her face flush red with asking a question she felt she should know the answer to.

"Oh, maybe," Mrs. Habbermire said. "The Dawes Rolls—names of people who lived in Indian territory. Some tribes, at least. Cherokee are there. People from the Five *Civilized* Tribes."

"Not everyone of course," the man corrected. "But lots of people. My ma used to say we were Cherokee too, but my great grandmother didn't want to be enrolled. Was afraid she'd be forced onto a reservation."

Candice flinched when the man said *were*, an echo of Katherine in her mind: the past tense.

"This name here," the man said, "this your great grandmother? No last name I see, but we can start here. See if she's there. See where that takes us. We can make some inquiries. Do you have anything else?"

Candice shook her head. Thought that if she'd only call her mother, then maybe she could give them more.

"That's fine. This is something. Can I keep this?" he asked, holding up the paper.

Candice nodded. "If you can find anything," she said, "I'd appreciate it."

Dusty took her number and said he'd investigate.

•

Candice stopped by the diner and made the obligatory rounds, greeting all the customers who knew her by name. She'd come to talk to Everett and tell him that she'd decided to try the Historical Society first, but he was flipping chicken on the flat-top stove, gave her an apologetic look—sorry, not right now—and sent her on her way back home.

She tried to remember what Enola had looked like. She pulled out the photo book that she kept on the top of her daughters' bedroom shelf and sat on one of the narrow beds the girls used to sleep in. They had refused to be given a specific place and switched beds whenever they wanted. Who was the last to sleep where Candice now rested?

The answer was Candice, who sometimes came into the room and laid down, imagining she was beside June or Rose, calming them back to sleep after a nightmare. She missed her girls.

In the album, there were very few photos from long ago. Most of the images were of her immediate family—Everett and June and Rose. But there were photos of Candice when she was a child—with Salida and her pop before he'd gotten crushed when a car slid off its blocks. After that, photos of little Candice, and of her family, became scarce.

At the end of the book were two photos of Enola. In one, taken right before Enola died, she was more movement than woman, a blur in a shaky camera, bending down at the firepit out back from her house. What Candice was interested in now was the photo on the last page—a photo she hadn't looked at in years because for so long, it hadn't felt relevant. Or maybe, it had been too relevant—too much to consider.

The oldest photo she had was of Enola when she was a child—decades before Candice's own mother was born. It was Enola herself that had given the photo to Candice before they'd left Nacogdoches for Dallas, something, she said, to remember her grandmother by, pressing it into Candice's hand while her parents weren't looking.

Looking back, Candice wondered if Enola knew her daughter was trying to separate Candice from her history, as if moving her away could erase her indigeneity.

In the photo, Enola was a girl in a high-necked, long-sleeved tear dress, and she smiled at the camera as if excited to be having her portrait taken. Candice recognized herself in her grandmother, parts of herself at least. In the wicker-framed mirror between the two beds, Candice studied her face, squinted until she was blurry, wondering, if through closely lidded eyes, someone might mistake her for her relative. They had the same oval face and long nose. same lopsided ears, the left a little lower down than the right. They might have had the same smile lines too, Candice thought, but in the photo, Enola was not smiling.

Candice wondered how much Enola had looked like her mother, Ida Rose. If Ida Rose had looked Indian, or looked white, like Candice. It was hard to tell with the photo—there was no color—and Candice couldn't discern, or remember, the tone of Enola's skin.

•

Candice put the leaf in the table and then covered it with the cloth discovered in the Cedar House basement. It had been too pretty to sell, or give away, white and embroidered with bluebonnets and Indian paintbrushes, a ring of flowers reaching for each other around the edge and then a whole bushel of them in the middle.

Friday night was poker night, when Everett and his friends would cause a ruckus in the kitchen and Candice and the wives would sit on the back porch trading stories and news. It rotated from house to house, and with the Tempers bowing out due to a nasty summer cold, the turn had fallen to the Washingtons. So Candice cut up fruit to mash into ice water and cursed the oven's heat when she opened the door to check the shoofly which was bubbling and browning. She should have made an ice cream Charlotte, something cold, but that would start melting the minute the women carried their plates out. Summer was a time for desserts, but not a time for them at all.

Fanny brought with her a book that the women passed around. It was Nabokov's *Lolita* and she tried to convince the other women to buy it too so that they could all read and talk about it.

"I know what y'all are thinking," Fanny said in response to the women's aversion. "But if you ask me, it's a look into men's minds. Appropriate reading for right now, I think."

"Lord, Fanny," Bethany said. "Now is not the time. This is disgusting. I don't think we should even be talking about it."

"Y'all know," Fanny went on, unwilling to be put off, "that whatever happened to Marjorie has happened at the hands of a man. Now I'm not saying this here is true." Fanny shook the novel as if to demonstrate. "But what I am saying is that there's a psychology at work. A pathology. We could learn something from a book like this. Give us some insight into the differences between men and women, differences the men won't even talk about."

Candice thought that part of what Fanny said had some merit. The sexes had their private lives, distinct from each other. She was not convinced though, that reading a book about a man who "falls in love" with a child would provide any answers applicable to their real lives.

"Fanny," Dorsett began, "really, this is just unseemly. I for one have no desire to read about ..." she trailed off, thinking what most of the women must be thinking: that the book might be too close to what was currently happening in Larissa.

"You don't understand though," Fanny protested. "It's not just about him." A brief look of disgust passed over her face. "It's about the *girl*, too. It's about Marjorie."

"I don't want to even think about it," Dorsett said, shaking her head.

"You don't get to *not* think about it." Fanny admonished her. "You think Larissa is a bubble all shiny with soap colors in the sun. That bubble's gonna pop soon, and you better be prepared. No one gets to go through life thinking bad won't happen to them. No one."

"You do know," Candice finally said, offering her first real comment of the evening, "that this isn't just about Marjorie."

All the women turned to her, and Candice looked at their faces—open, confused, waiting.

"There are four girls who are missing," Candice offered. "Three of them are Indian."

"What are you talking about?" Fanny asked.

"Weeks before Marjorie, two girls from the farm disappeared."

"Well I don't know," Fanny mused. "Who knows with them, right? Those people are always coming and going."

"I doubt they'd lose track of their own children," Candice muttered.

"How do you even know this?" Dorsett asked.

"Katherine Cooper said so."

"Who's Katherine Cooper?"

Candice's mouth dropped open. "She lives just a few blocks over," she told them. "Has lived there for years."

Fanny and Dorsett spoke at the same time, both women talking over the other.

"She doesn't go to my church," and, "Didn't her girl run off to get married?"

Candice realized then that these women had no clue what was happening in Larissa.

•

Candice found herself thinking about Katherine after the women had left, missing her old friend because the people on her back porch were most certainly not individuals she wanted to spend any more time with.

Now that she thought more about it, she realized that Katherine must know people out at Mrs. White's, either because she searched them out, or because they'd become her community away from Rusk County. How else would Katherine have known that the girls from the farm were Indian? Candice wondered now for the first time how Katherine must have felt living in Larissa, and if she'd been lonely the entire time she'd been here. Maybe that was part of the reason she went back to Rusk county so often: she missed her people.

Her people.

Candice thought about what she'd told Emily and how there wasn't a right way to look like an Indian. She'd said this in her own defense, but she couldn't help but feel she'd lied to the girl. Katherine looked Indian. Candice thought the people out at the farm must look Indian too, like the faces she remembered from childhood, Enola's friends and her own mother's, back in Nacogdoches, who'd fallen into obscurity for her with the time that had passed. She couldn't remember a single name, not even a single face, but she could collage a look, and she knew she didn't have it.

Everett was sweeping the floor, collecting the stray bits of pretzels and popcorn. "We lost Ed today," he said, drawing Candice's mind back into the kitchen, away from the memory of her childhood home, away from Enola, and Salida, and the farm.

"The new boy?"

Everett nodded.

"So soon. Why?"

"Why do you think," Everett asked. "Got a better paying job at that shoe factory. He was good, too. Fast, nice. Not so great with words but you don't have to be a dictionary to work in a diner. We'll miss him."

"Gonna put the sign back up then?"

Everett leaned the broom against the fridge, a movement that said this wasn't going to be a passing conversation. "I was thinking," he said, "about offering the boys partnership."

The boys meant their daughters' husbands.

"Now it wouldn't be as good as those jobs in Chicago," he added, "but it would be stable. We've been at this for years now. We know we're going to be just fine. And with the way they're all going there's gonna be more babies, and more stress, and they could use a community, a mother."

"It takes a village to raise a child," Candice agreed.

"It takes a village to raise children," Everett countered.

"And what's made you think all this?" Candice pulled a dishcloth from a drawer, draped it over the leftover food and tucked it under the plate.

"I just think it would be good," he said.

Candice raised an eyebrow.

"Ain't nobody stealing babies," Everett said, hurt by his wife's lack of enthusiasm.

•

On Sunday the church was buzzing with holiday plans. It would be a three-day weekend, the 4th falling on a Friday, and everyone was all excited because of it.

"It would have been better," Attie said to Candice as they scooped food onto plates, "if it was a Monday. I'll be up all night on Thursday cooking. Be too tired to enjoy anything come Friday. But God didn't see fit to make that happen, I guess."

The calendar didn't see fit to make that happen, Candice wanted to say, but didn't, murmuring in agreement and balancing a plate on one hand and another on her forearm.

But when she went to look for Katherine, she couldn't find the woman anywhere. She wasn't at her normal table, and she wasn't at any of the other tables either. Her husband was also missing.

With helpings for two, Candice finally found Rosemary and asked after the missing woman.

"I guess you didn't hear," she said, "that Katherine is too good for us now."

"What do you mean?"

"Her and her husband aren't coming here anymore. They go to a different church now, not that I would call it a church."

"What are you talking about, Rosemary?"

"They go out to the farm now," she said, lifting her chin up a bit. "On Sundays, they're going out there."

Candice just stood and took it in. Katherine had left them.

•

That night, Candice found herself in her girls' bedroom. She tried to imagine what Katherine must feel like, was paralleling the move of her own daughters to the disappearance of Marlene.

That day when June and Rose had asked her and Everett to meet Tom and RD, Candice had learned there had been a whole, secret side to her daughters' lives. How had she and Everett not known their girls were dating? How had they not known their daughters were already talking marriage? Had already picked out men, brothers no less, that they were going to abscond with?

And then they'd met those boys—Candice could hardly think of them as men at the time—in the restaurant on the first floor of the Lynch building. Named after the first mayor, a man who owned two gambling houses and a brothel back when Larissa was nothing more than a way stop for the expanding railroad, the Lynch building was one of the classier eateries in Larissa, and as Candice sat at the table and listened to her husband interrogate Tom and RD, all she could think about was how the building had once been a place where women, and girls, had sold their bodies. Or had been made to sell their bodies—Candice wasn't sure which. Legend had it Tillamock Lynch—Candice doubted this was the man's real name—was killed by one of his own women in Sibylline House for doing something too horrible for history to remember.

So she sat there, trying to be friendly, trying to support her two girls that had gone off from under her to find themselves husbands, and all she could think about was how she'd lost them without even knowing it. Something over the years had shifted, had moved, and she had not caught it. She had to fight back imagining her girls working in Sibylline house. Had to remind herself that her girls were laughing at Everett's jokes, not the jokes of men coming to purchase them.

When later that evening, she and Everett returned home, their girls still out with the boys that would become their husbands, Candice had told Everett that they had lost their daughters. He'd said no they hadn't, that this was a normal part of life and that Candice couldn't expect them to embrace spinsterhood. Everett hadn't understood what Candice really meant: that there was no going back now, only forward, and that there was a space of time that could never be revised, could never be fixed, and that she knew she'd missed her opportunity to learn how to keep them close.

9

The Betweens, Traversed

—Gracie—

The article said Mrs. White was having coffee on her porch when one of her hounds returned from roving with a limb in its mouth, a dress sleeve still attached. It had been brought by the dog from God knows where and attached to it was Marjorie's charm bracelet, the lace of her sleeve all twisted in it.

The article wasn't so explicit, of course, but the women of the Garden Club talked, and so Gracie learned about the details from Mrs. Daphne as they sat in the woman's living room, listening to her girl and her friends from the backyard where her maid kept watch over them.

"She is in such a state," Mrs. Daphne said, pouring herself more tea and taking more sugar than Gracie thought appropriate for a woman their age. "Mrs. Kent has damn near lost her mind."

"Can you blame her?" Mrs. Tandy's eye was twitching. It seemed to be a tick that grew worse with uncomfortable situations or conversations.

"I can't believe you left Emily at home," Mrs. Daphne continued, looking at Gracie. Baiting her, Gracie was sure of it. "I can't stand to have my girl out of my sight."

Gracie wanted to state that currently, Mrs. Daphne's daughter *was* out of her sight, technically, and that Emily wasn't alone but was with Candice, but she had no energy to pick a fight.

"Where's Mrs. Habbermire?" Gracie asked instead, trying to change the subject, or rather, fishing for different information, since Mrs. Habbermire knew the whole town's dealings and if she wasn't at a meeting of the Garden Club, she was sure to have at least told someone there what she knew.

Mrs. Bee brightened at finally being able to contribute something. "I don't think she's been feeling well, lately. We used to talk all the time, you girls know we're such good friends, but she's barely called me in the last week."

"Unwell?" Gracie asked, surprised.

"She's not unwell," Mrs. Daphne cut in. "She's working all those hours at the historical society. If you ask me, it's good that she's doing something, now that you're all settled in, Gracie."

Gracie wondered just how large a favor she had asked of Mrs. Habbermire all that time ago when, panicked, she'd called the operator and asked for the only living relative she had left. It had been an awkward moment when Mrs. Habbermire came on the line and learned who she was talking to, Mrs. Habbermire saying, "I'm so glad to finally talk to you again. All these years ..." And then Mrs. Habbermire began to cry, and Gracie was embarrassed that she didn't feel the same way.

Mrs. Habbermire had been glad to do it—to get the house ready—and Gracie had even offered to pay her (*as a temporary estate manager*, Gracie had joked), but Mrs. Habbermire said it was the least she could do. Gracie hadn't known what Mrs. Habbermire meant by that—the least she could do. It seemed like it should have been the other way around, what with Mrs. Habbermire being the one to take care of Gracie's mother in those last months. Gracie had wanted to come then, but couldn't have brought Emily, and she didn't trust Irene to be left with the girl.

"I don't know how she has the energy to do it all," Gracie admitted to the Garden Club, wondering if she should have insisted on paying her for helping to ready Cedar House. Maybe Mrs. Habbermire needed money and that's why she was working.

"It's the children," Mrs. Tandy said, "having children wears you down. Rebekah is lucky enough not to have any."

"Isn't that true," Mrs. Daphne added.

Seeing now that the conversation was shifting away from the Kents, Gracie began to explain the problem with the roses, hoping the Garden Club might, if presented with the opportunity to talk about gardening, actually pursue the conversation. She explained that everything else in her yard was dead or close to it but that the roses were replenishing themselves as fast as she could take them down.

"I don't know why you'd want to remove roses," Mrs. Worley scoffed.

"I'm not exactly sure they are roses," Gracie clarified, "but they have thorns." She proceeded to describe them, and Mrs. Bee was shaking her head up and down.

"Oh, my dear! They're Cherokee roses. They're invasive. You're doing the right thing."

"Cherokee?" Mrs. Daphne asked. "Didn't Marjorie have some book with her that went missing? One about Indians? I can't be the only one who is disturbed at the thought of that little girl reading about the Killough Massacre right before ... she ... went missing."

"Alice," Mrs. Tandy admonished, "what a thing to say!"

Gracie's head was beginning to hurt, and even though she knew Emily was fine at Cedar House with Candice, she still decided to take her leave. If the Garden Club was not going to talk about gardening, perhaps she wouldn't come back.

•

Gracie could not shake the feeling that something was wrong in Cedar House.

The thought was cloying. Someone had been there, was still there, always out of sight, and never heard. Sometimes the floors groaned when she was just sitting in her chair and Emily was abed. Sometimes she thought she heard a door closing. Other times, she could swear there was whispering.

She found herself searching rooms regularly, opening cabinets too small for anyone but a child to fit in, and going down, down, down to the basement, the place she imagined someone might hide it waiting until dark.

Emily didn't seem to think anything was amiss, and neither did Candice. But they were so caught up in each other—Candice fretting over Emily when she was sick, Emily asking for Candice even on the woman's days off—that Gracie was beginning to feel she was playing second fiddle. Perhaps this is where the uneasiness came from: an odd manifestation of wounded pride. Of worry.

She tried to smother her restlessness with the business—looking at storefronts with Ronald Toller and recalling her childhood when, in the summer, she would often spend entire afternoons in her mother's dress shop, helping her to cut patterns and stock fabric. Gracie was spending so much time with the real estate agent that Mrs. Daphne had even asked if there was something going on between them, and Gracie had almost sputtered out her tea because the idea was so ridiculous.

Gracie could not entertain Ronald as anything more than a friend, and he wasn't even that. Any ideas she had about dating—and there were a few, occasionally—had gone out the window with the call from Irene. Nasty woman that she was, she hadn't even sent Gracie the tags, or the letter that had come with them. She had xeroxed it and then penned a note to accompany it, stating that George might have been Gracie's husband, but he had been Irene's child.

She was caught in the liminality of closure. She'd thought she'd made peace with George's death years ago. And it *had* taken years. Years of thinking there would be a phone call, or a letter, or George showing up one day on the steps of the sprawling home in Oklahoma. It had been years of smothering sobs in the big bed she had shared with him. Years of rehearsing the act of hope with Irene over meals. Years of enduring Irene's darkening moods when both women began to accept George would not be back.

And then, there was Emily. The girl had started to suture a wound closed. Years of skin around a frayed heart drawing together again. Until now.

"Good God, Mrs. Howard, what are you doing in here?"

Gracie was standing in front of the library fireplace, the room filling with smoke, flames crackling the underbrush she'd collected, wilting and curling the petals of roses she'd thrown atop the letter Irene had sent enclosed with the photocopy of the letter Irene had received, but which *had* been addressed to Gracie, about George's confirmed death.

Candice came in and began opening windows, trying to fan out the room with her hands. "Have you even had someone look up that chimney?" She asked. "Smells like you're roasting some poor birds."

Gracie had not asked John or Earl to check the chimney. It was Texas, in summer, and lighting a fire had been the last thing on her mind when she moved into Cedar House. Christ, she said, rushing to the kitchen to fill a pitcher with water. Stupid woman, she muttered to herself. Candice was right behind her, grabbing the vase off the dining room table and throwing irises and water onto the fire that fizzed.

"Mother?" Emily called from upstairs.

"Just an accident," Gracie called back, shaking her head, knowing her excuse made no sense and that Emily wouldn't let the smell go—she'd ask about it later.

"Going to burn the house down because of that woman?" Candice asked, still waving her hands, pushing air around the room.

"Too bad it's in my name now, isn't it?" Gracie couldn't even see the letter she'd set alight. It was blackened to bits and the ash sludged with water.

•

She sat in a wicker chair on the patio, watching a rabbit loop around the yard, picking and choosing what it wanted to eat. Gracie watched it for a long time. Watched it noting her, and deciding she wasn't a threat. Watched the rabbit's white tail flashing as it hopped from bush to bush. Watched it sit on its hind legs and clean its face with its little paws.

The rabbit was slowly coming closer, and Gracie realized that it wasn't interested in her, but rather the bird feeder she'd bought from the hardware store and stocked with seed now scattered on the ground. The closer it got, the more Gracie marveled at its fur: brown from a distance, but up close, a mottle of white, grey, and brown, a black band running atop its head between its ears. And its ears were twitching every which way, both with a mind of their own, listening to every little sound. Gracie liked the way its little mouth moved from side to side, or in a circle.

The rabbit eventually lay down, stretching itself out, *asking for the spit*, Gracie thought.

"Hello, friend," Gracie said. "If it was morning, birds wouldn't even let you get so close."

Twenty minutes ago they were still at the bird feeder, but with the sun setting, they had retreated to the tops of trees, and though she could hear their calls, they were not close. The birds had fled the garden of Cedar House.

The light from the kitchen, cast out into the yard, twitched. A shadow moved out across the pavers. The rabbit bolted.

When Gracie turned to look, she saw her daughter in the kitchen. The girl's nightgown was mussed and she kept looking behind her. When her head turned, Gracie could see Emily's mouth moving. She was talking. To someone.

Gracie grabbed the trowel at her feet and ran to throw open the screen door. Emily dropped the cookie she was holding and it broke apart on the floor.

They looked at each other, mother and daughter, and then Emily cocked her head, bent to collect the bits of cookie in her hand, and proceeded to eat the largest ones.

"Who were you talking to?" Gracie asked, scanning the kitchen.

"No one."

"Emily, are you sure?"

Gracie's daughter just looked at her and shook her head.

•

"This looks very nice," Gracie said. She stood in the old Armstrong building, looking out the long windows onto Grand Avenue. It had once been a saloon, and then a bank, but was now parceled into different businesses with apartments on the second floor. "My good luck, I guess, that whatever was here went under."

Mr. Toller ran a hand along the wall and then rapped his fist against it. "Well, there is the upstairs."

"What's wrong with upstairs?" Gracie looked to the ceiling. It was a long way up.

"Transients," he admitted. "Problem is, people who own this building live in Dallas. Don't find their way over here much. They're in a bit of a pickle. Long-term lease with the people who run the boarding house—"

"I thought you said they were apartments?"

"They are, but run like a boarding house. Mostly factory workers, people that don't stay in the end. It's been affecting the, uh, street value of these spaces on the ground floor."

"Something wrong with them? The people up there?"

"Men, mostly. Well, all of them. Nothing wrong with them, not that I know about. It just doesn't look good. People don't feel good having others they don't know around. There's a separate entrance for them in the back—you'd probably never come into contact with them, not with your business hours—but they can look, rough. Unsavory."

"I don't know," Gracie mused. "I like this place."

She did not say that part of the appeal was that from where she was standing, she could see her mother's old dress shop. It was now a florist, but if she squinted, and her vision blurred, she could pretend the business, as she remembered it, was still there.

"You do know how to sew, right?"

Gracie rolled her eyes at him.

"And you know that most women buy their dresses from department stores now?"

"I know that."

"Then you're not doing this for money."

"I'm not doing it for money. I'm doing it for myself."

•

Gracie had said it around Emily many times: forgetting is a blessing. But Gracie wasn't sure if this was true. She'd told Emily that forgetting can be the brain's way of healing itself, and that if Emily couldn't remember parts of her life, it was okay.

Something was wrong with Emily, though. *That* was true. But all the doctors brought into the house in Oklahoma could not exactly identify what was going on. One went so far as to theorize brain damage—perhaps the umbilical cord had been wrapped around her neck, depriving her of oxygen at birth.

Gracie didn't like to admit it, but something mentally wrong was the most plausible answer. Another doctor said that sometimes mental issues manifested in a more severe fashion as puberty set in, and Emily wasn't that far away now. The girl was going to need love and patience. And that doctor had said it was a good thing Gracie was the girl's mother because he didn't know many women who would be so understanding.

Gracie couldn't imagine *Irene* as a young mother. Irene loved George fiercely, maybe more so because his birth had almost killed her. There was no second child. George had said she'd been very loving, if a tad overprotective, as he was growing up.

But somewhere—with Beatrice, perhaps—something in Irene had slipped.

Gracie remembered the first night she'd met the Howards. George had been talking about her for weeks, and Irene and Adelbert wanted to know what all the fuss was about. Gracie had been nervous to the point of wanting to vomit, and went over the story with George three times on the car ride to his house.

"But did you ever notice me when you were in school," she'd tested him.

"For real? Or for the story?" George smiled and Gracie slapped his thigh lightly.

"Both," she said.

"Yes, I noticed you. But you were always so busy. Cheerleading and violin or with some book in your hands."

They had parked in front of George's house and Gracie had turned her back to the car door and studied him, his dark hair, the nose with a slight bump. "And the first time you talked to me was ..."

"At the zoo."

"The zoo, right. And where was I?"

"You were trying to feed popcorn to the zebra."

"George, you're going to make me sound stupid."

"Fine, *I* was trying to feed popcorn to a zebra and you came up to me and kindly, but firmly, informed me that zebras were not supposed to eat popcorn."

"And then?"

"And then I looked into your eyes and fell down a well and asked if you'd like to have an ice cream with me."

Gracie did not like the part about the ice cream. It was too close to the truth and in the shadow of that night with Norman. But she didn't complain or suggest a correction. She didn't want to talk about that, and technically, George *had* asked her if she wanted to go for ice cream, but that was after. Days after.

Once dinner with George's parents was done, after pie, Gracie had heard Irene whisper to George that Gracie seemed like a nice girl.

•

"We need to make a decision," Gracie said.

"Just one?"

Emily stood outside the library looking in and Gracie was studying the empty shelves.

"Do we want a library?" Gracie asked.

"Is there a point in having a library if I can't go in it?"

"Do you want a library? Knowing that is the first step."

Emily looked around the empty room. "I like that window," she said, pointing to the stained-glass that overlooked Bell Street. "I bet the sun comes through in all sorts of pretty colors."

"The sun never comes directly through that window," Gracie pointed out. "This part of the house faces north."

"I wonder," Emily continued, "if the window was made to reflect the garden or if the window inspired the garden."

There were flowers made of glass: yellow and red and blue and purple. They didn't seem to be of any variety Gracie knew, but then again, the stained glass was not incredibly detailed.

"Do you think that came from England, too?" Emily asked.

"Possibly. Probably." Now Gracie also wondered about the garden and the window, but what was planted had not thrived in the years of drought and with not being kept up, they'd likely never know. "But do you want a library?" She asked again.

"Do *you* want one?"

"Emily."

"Fine, yes, I would like a library. And I would like a red chair to sit in and read. And I would like to pick out my own books. Maybe I'll even start writing a book. I'll need a desk."

"That's right. You're going to be an authoress."

"I have ideas."

"Well ..." Gracie had not yet broached the subject of school with Emily. They still had a few months before deciding what to do. Most likely, it would be private tutoring again, and Gracie was glad for George's insurance money now because she could talk to Irene even less.

"Mother?"

"Yes?" Gracie looked at her daughter.

"What is that?"

"What is what?" Gracie tried to follow her daughter's line of sight and arrived at the fireplace. "It's chipped is all."

"No, down by the baseboard."

There was something there, something brassy in color, probably dislodged from when Gracie had cleaned out the fireplace. She walked over and bent down, prying the object from the small gap between the baseboard and the floor. It was a bullet casing.

"What is it?" Emily asked again.

"How did you even see this?" Gracie could almost feel her daughter shrugging. "It's just an old button."

"Is it?" Emily asked.

When Gracie turned her head around, Emily was walking away.

•

That night, Gracie had an odd dream. Or rather, it was odd that she remembered the dream, because she almost never did. She forgot them as soon as she woke up. They were only fleeting feelings and impressions of narratives that made no sense.

That night, Gracie dreamed that she was on a camping trip with the mysterious Lillian Gladwell. But Lillian was a little girl who dressed like a boy, and they were camping at the top of a mountain that was also a jungle.

There was a house on the mountain that was also a jungle, and inside there were animals in cages. All the cages were made of stained-glass windows so that Gracie could barely make out what they were: a silhouetted lion, elephant, and bear.

Lillian wanted to set the animals free, but Gracie was trying to convince her not to because she was worried about being eaten.

Lillian wouldn't listen, though, and she took off her belt and began to slap at the glass with the buckle, and when it shattered, Gracie was the little girl and Lillian was Gracie, but Gracie as a teenager.

They were in the bathtub together in the house on Woodlee—the one in Oklahoma—and Lillian was hysterical. She was rubbing her skin off with a washcloth and the bath water was turning bright red.

Gracie had tried to stop herself, to grasp her own arms, and Lillian, who was Gracie, grabbed back, struggling, fighting, until Gracie's head was under water.

She woke up crying, her chest swelling with sobs she could barely stifle with her blanket, and then she could not go back to sleep. Instead of insisting on the futile effort, she went downstairs and made coffee. She carried it out into the pre-dawn and sat in her chair, listening to the birds awaken. Once it was light enough, she continued staring, because the roses were back. Again.

•

The word *invasive* rolled around her head all day. That's what Mrs. Worley had called the flowers. Invasive meant overwhelming, overpowering, non-native. She thought about herself, and Emily, in Cedar House: invasive. She thought about the thing, the presence, in Cedar House: invasive. Gracie thought about the Germans in the second world war: invasive. She thought about the troops—like her George—going to Europe: invasive. She thought about the authorities going into Emily's first home: invasive. She thought about herself, in Irene's house, with Emily: invasive. She thought about the night she really met George: invasive.

Later, when she heard the word coming softly from the library, she screamed. No one was there, but most certainly, someone had just whispered, *invasive*.

•

Emily was upstairs with Candice, and Gracie said she was going to the grocery, which she was, only afterwards.

The ice cream parlor—Archie's—was still there. From inside her car, the store appeared to be exactly the same: from the checkered floor to the pink walls to the tables and chairs and the counter itself. But it wasn't the store she was interested in.

Gracie got out of the car, clutching her purse to her side. She walked around Archie's to the back and saw the alley gap. In the daylight, it didn't look so long, but that night, in the dark, not even starlight could reach down into it.

She walked to the entrance and peered down it. Red brick, metal doors. She told herself that it didn't look so bad. She told herself that the past was the past. She told herself that there was nothing to be afraid of now. She was convinced that if she could face this place, and what happened here, maybe the *thing* that was shadowing her would stop. Go away. Once she could put the demon to rest, Larissa would welcome her back again, and her mind would quiet.

Gracie made herself enter the alley and walk its whole length. She looked straight ahead and didn't blink once. When she emerged on the other side, out onto Finley Street, she finally took a breath, turned around, and walked it again.

Gracie stopped at the indentation where she had been pinned. That night, it would have been completely shrouded. She did not know what business it opened into. Not then, not now. She saw rust at the bottom of the door, the iron flaking away in orange sheets. She put her hand against the brick wall. She leaned into it, feeling dizzy.

Somehow, in all the time she'd been back in Larissa, she'd managed not to run into Norman. At some point, she knew she would, but not yet. Not yet.

What would she do when she was finally confronted with him? Would she spit at him? Curse at him? Do nothing at all?

She thought of Norman's wife, Bettye. Wondered if that woman endured the same kind of violence Gracie had in the alley, when, excited for the first date she had ever agreed to, she didn't think twice about the dark cut through to get back to the square. She wondered about a different life in which it was Bettye who first tore at George's shirt, him saying *it's over, it's over,* until she knew it really was over, and Norman was laying on the ground with blood at his mouth. Bettye could have been the woman who took a long time to accept another embrace, but finally did so, escaping into it, running away from Larissa. It could have been Bettye that married George, and Gracie that married Norman, learning only too late what kind of man he was.

Gracie was shivering, and she kicked the wall. Mortar crumbled out and fell to the ground.

When she got back to the parking lot behind the ice cream parlor, she looked down into the alley again.

It was the same, but it was not the same. And she was glad for that.

10

The Point Where Further Stretching is Impossible

—Rebekah—

Dusty *had* gone through the Gladwell boxes, and he told Rebekah they were in the back room. Would she like him to get them for her?

Of course I would, she wanted to snap. She had a terrible headache that was just starting to abate, and she'd been fighting a fogginess all morning. She just didn't feel right, and it was making her grumpy. But instead of being rude she said, "Does it look like I can lug boxes around?" making a joke out of her age.

The front door to the Historical Society was held open with a brick, the back door too, creating a wishful causeway for breeze. Above her, ceiling fans moved hot air.

She wanted to be alone. There was nothing *wrong* with Dusty. The retired mailman never said anything wayward. But that was just it. He was too good.

When Rebekah had arrived there this morning, he'd made coffee and remembered to bring more sugar—from his own house!—because Rebekah liked it but every morning lamented her forgetfulness. He'd vacuumed, and cleaned the windows, inside and out. The waist-high handprints of children walking by were gone. He'd brought lunch for her as well, turkey sandwiches made with his wife's cornbread. She would like them, he said, but Rebekah didn't care much for cornbread.

Rebekah found herself wondering about Dusty at home. She imagined he might drink too much at night (that would explain why his face was always red). She imagined he picked his nose and wiped the gross green globs on the underside of his nightstand. She imagined he might have a penchant for pornography, and she was still thinking about the lewd images he probably collected when Dusty gently placed the Gladwell boxes on the empty table behind her desk. She buried her face in them immediately, hoping to hide her blushing cheeks.

While Dusty clacked at his own typewriter on the other side of the room, Rebekah began to remove items and lay them out. These included the architectural plans for Cedar House, which, she noted, had been revised numerous times, rooms appearing and disappearing, getting larger and smaller. There was also a thick, detailed log of the expenses incurred while building the house and wrapped stacks of receipts: from builders, the hardware store, from furniture makers overseas in cities Rebekah had never heard of.

There was a loose pen and a blank notebook. The folders beneath these items contained various papers with faded inks. She went through them one by one, hoping this was a mistake, that the rest of Gladwell's book was hidden between them, but nothing.

She tipped the box toward herself to look in the bottom. A few hard candies and a photo.

The photo was of Thomas and Lillian, and Rebekah's breath hitched in her throat.

It had been what? At least fifty years since it was taken?

It was their wedding photo. Thomas was tall and straight-backed in a suit, that awful beard of his reaching almost to his collarbone. Lillian was seated in front of him in a high-necked dress, her hair rolled up and pinned away from her face.

"Oh, Lillian," she said.

"What was that?" Dusty asked. She heard his chair push away from his desk.

"Nothing," Rebekah said, holding the tarnished frame in both hands.

•

At noon she told Dusty she wasn't feeling well. He asked if she wanted him to drive her home, but she refused the ride, claiming fresh air might do her some good.

Her purse was heavier than normal with the silver frame inside it, already aching her right shoulder. She saw Gracie coming out of Bartlebees and waited until her niece was gone before crossing the street and opening the glass door to be accosted by the lunch rush. She did find a space at the bar, which is not what she preferred, and she had some trouble getting up into the high chair. Then she ordered a tuna fish sandwich and a slice of cherry pie.

She ate the pie first, trying to track all the din around her. The two men to her right were talking about some oil leasing deal. Rebekah spun, wobbling on the rounded seat, and looked at the patrons. She didn't recognize a single one.

How could that be? She was seventy-two years old and had lived in Larissa all her life. She remembered when there was nothing but land on the sides of Highway 52. She remembered when the ballpark was built, when trees were felled for it. She remembered the courthouse, even before it was remodeled and fitted with white stone. She remembered when there were more people on horses than in cars, and she remembered when Bartlett Park didn't even have a name, back before the circus set up, bringing its acrobats and animals, becoming its own little zoo along the river. She remembered when it *was* a river.

She suddenly felt very sad and lonely. She didn't feel like she had any real friends, and then there was Maggie McCallin, Gracie's mother and her own sister, whose breasts had swelled and lumped with tumors. Rebekah listed all the people in town that she knew: a good number, close to forty. But none were in Bartlebees holding forks and dabbing their mouths with thin paper.

She asked for her sandwich to be wrapped up and vacated the seat, a man in painter's overalls quick to take it once she'd gathered her things.

•

"I'm an old woman in a new world," she complained to Petrol. The cat sat on the wide ledge of the front window, her tail swishing the gauzy curtain, her head jerking, neck lengthening. She was following some insect buzzing on the other side of the glass.

Rebekah didn't recognize any of the actors on the TV, and she tried to remember the last time she even saw a movie. It was *His Girl Friday*, over a decade ago. Where *did* the time go?

The time, she figured, was swept out from under her like dirt through the back door. Soon, she'd be gone with it, a withered husk all dried and light and turning to dust and blowing in the wind.

Across the street, two children she didn't recognize, brothers probably—one much smaller than the other—were snaking through the Davison's yard toward the back gate. The fence there was covered in the wild fingers of honeysuckle, and she watched the children pulling apart the flowers, stamen invisible at this distance, but disappearing, she knew, into mouths.

Honeysuckle ran wild on the farm she grew up on. She'd thought when she was small that there was actually honey in the flowers. The business of bees was unknown to her, and so she'd spent an entire afternoon plucking bloom after bloom, piling a basket full of them, thinking to take them home to her mother who would be so proud of her girl's inventiveness. Rebekah had imagined toast laden with golden syrup she had collected, how her father would say *this is much better than molasses,* and Rebekah would start her own business even, filling canning jars with her special honey, Cabeca's she'd called it, her dreams stacking on top of each other. Better she not use her real name or people would be coming for miles, knocking on her door, looking for the girl and her prize-winning honey that would make the family a fortune.

And then her mother explained that all Rebekah's work was worthless. *They are pretty, though,* she'd said at her daughter's downturned lips while Maggie laughed. Rebekah had let all those flowers wilt into oblivion until the mass of them was flat and starting to smell. At that point, her mother made her turn the basket out in the bushes.

Oh, stop being so grim, she told herself, turning the television off. She stood next to the cat, ran her fingers through its fur.

"You don't care about time, do you?" she asked it. "Nope. You don't even know today is not yesterday."

•

Clocks, and the keeping of time, or being unable to, was a problem. Time was being kept all across Rebekah's house. In James' study, a carriage clock on the topmost shelf. A new Westclox Moonbeam in the bedroom with false daylight and unruly clicking. The Baxter mantle clock in the living room. A mint green, rounded wall clock in the kitchen, and its twin that she'd bought to hang in the Historical Society. These she needed like a towline in order to scaffold the progression of a day. It was easy, living alone, to daydream away the hours. To close her eyes for a short rest and wake up to a disappeared sun. Rebekah couldn't mark when these changes had started—her inability, at times, to understand how time had passed without her knowing—but she did know it was starting to happen more and more.

There were no clocks in the Gladwell story. The Killough family, homesteading unsure land, measured their days by the sun's movement across the sky. Rebekah sat in the study, in the chair James used to sit in, and arranged Thomas Gladwell's novel excerpt in front of her. Starting on a random page was not ideal, but Thomas was not an expert writer, and she told herself that what she didn't have wasn't a complete loss. There was obviously some plot that she was not privy to, but she knew what story it tracked—the Killough Massacre—and she already knew the general outline of how that had transpired. That was well before Larissa was a proper town, back when it was wilderness and Indians.

She hadn't read many Westerns, because Westerns were for people who didn't live in the West. Or the South. Because they were really the same thing: all grassland and cow patties and oil and people trying to manifest their destinies. She suspected the Killough family woke with their roosters crying, no alarm clocks for them. No sundials even, in that garden where the wife was trying to bring up herbs. When the children, spent with hoeing and bending, still had enough life in them to run off into the woods—there were woods back then, Rebekah surmised—they came in when the sun was going down, eating bland food and falling asleep on hay pallets to rise again to the sound of the world commanding work.

James had bought most of the clocks in their house, even though that man could tell time through only some wicked intuition. Rebekah remembered when they were driving back from Vicksburg, from the battleground where Confederate General Pemberton was driven into the defensive by Ulysses S. Grant. That was only a month before the accident, and Rebekah had been worried about money. They'd just bought the house—outright—and she didn't want to spend a dime on another motel room. James had craned over the steering wheel looking up at the sky and claimed they'd be home just before sundown, and they were, six hours later, just as the sky was turning magnificent shades of pink.

James' old glasses were dusty next to the carriage clock. Rebekah slid them on her face and watched the world through weird vision, the room blurry and making her so dizzy she almost fell over. This must have been right for him, she thought, marveling at all the ways people could see the same thing, but differently.

She removed the metal frames and then squeezed her eyes shut, pressing her fingers into the soft places that wanted to give way.

Rebekah's life hadn't amounted to much. When she died, there'd be so little left of her to make a mark. No one would care, or remember, that she'd copied documents for the Historical Society. She'd made no real contribution with the Garden Club, though the idea in joining it was to beautify Larissa. She had no children, either, so no one would even talk about her. She had a house. And a cat. That was it.

It felt like she had only really lived when she was younger. Back then, she'd even fancied becoming a writer. If a teenage girl could write *Frankenstein,* Rebekah could surely write something too. She'd tried, of course, but in the end she was embarrassed at her attempts at narrative, and those pages she'd written were long gone.

When she looked at the Gladwell papers again, she saw them anew. If she couldn't begin a story, maybe she could finish one. In Gladwell's story, she saw Thomas Killough as a young man, telling his son who was playing Indian—hoping to see some war chiefs, find a scalp fallen from some brave's belt out there in all the trees—that Indians were nothing to fool with. Thomas Killough, in the few pages Rebekah had, managed somehow to never have a conversation with his wife or daughter. There were two Thomases—the one in the story and the one writing it—both with a willful oblivion to what was happening right in front of him.

•

Rebekah had really come to like the ease of frozen dinners and at times had even begun sharing them with Petrol. Tonight it was a Mexican-style dinner. Rebekah had no idea what Mexican food tasted like. Though some cities in Texas had Mexicans, all sorts of people south from the border, somehow Larissa had not attracted any, and Rebekah was curious about the box: the triangle of rolled something in the entrée portion of the tray, the way all the colors were the same but different things: yellow cheese and rice, brown beans and sauce. She wasn't sure what the little red portion was, but everyone needed a little mystery.

When she bent to open the oven, lightning shot through one of her knees and she lamented to Petrol that her aching bones were just ratchets, laughing at herself when she understood what she'd said was not what she had been thinking. "My aching bones are just wretched," she corrected, but the cat didn't care about her wrong words and hopped up onto the counter to sniff at the hot food. Rebekah ushered him down as phone rang, and bless her heart, it was Gracie Howard, inviting her to dinner. It was short notice, Gracie apologized, but Mrs. Candice was cooking for more than two people and the fridge was filling up too fast. "I thought," Gracie added, "that I might ask you about a few things, too."

Rebekah left the Mexican-style dinner on the counter, knowing full well Petrol would have her tongue in it the minute the woman was out the door, and she wished Petrol might tell her what the red stuff was. If only cats could talk.

•

Rebekah commented on the lack of décor. "You're a Bell Street woman," she said. "Decoration is expected of you." The Bolou family across the street from Cedar House—heirs to some fishing lure company making a million dollars—had a flagpole. Rebekah had heard they even had a water fountain—in their *house*. Who needs a water fountain when there are perfectly good sinks?

Gracie held the door open and rolled her eyes at Rebekah's claim she needed to be more festive. "All that expense, and for what? To compete with folks I don't even know."

"As if you're worried about money."

"Fine, then," Gracie said, not unkindly, "I just don't feel like celebrating the 4th. Let them come with their pitchforks and torches."

Rebekah laughed at the image of the women of Bell Street with wild hair and eyes, chanting and waving their weapons.

Dinner was a hodgepodge of food. All leftovers, which any woman besides Gracie Howard would be embarrassed to offer a dinner guest, but Rebekah was coming to understand that Gracie Howard didn't care much what people thought about her.

"Where's Emily?" Rebekah asked. The little girl was nowhere to be seen.

"The fever again," Gracie told her. "Laid up in bed with it. You know it used to beat me up every year. Sneezing. Ears itching. Never happened in the summer, though. Something's wrong with these trees. Not the right time of year for this."

"Could be the drought," Rebekah offered. "Excess pollen or some such thing."

"Mayhap," Gracie said, looking unconvinced.

Rebekah sat at the table in the dining room sandwiched between the kitchen and living room, her chair angled so she could see Gracie at the oven and counter. "How's she working out? The maid?"

"Candice? Great. Emily seems to like her. That's important."

"You know I've always wanted to try her food," Rebekah admitted. "Her husband works over at the diner near one of those new factories and I reckon that to cook food for a living means you're good at it."

"Well, that is Candice's husband. Not Candice."

"Are you saying her food is bad? You invited me over here for a sub-par dinner?"

"Rebekah! No! I would only do that to someone I don't like. And you've been a gem."

Gracie brought all the food to the table: leftover meatloaf and green beans and mashed potatoes and chicken and dumplings and buttery corn cut from the cob. "You want something to drink? Besides water? I don't have a lot. I can make something with rum." Gracie began to survey the inside of the sideboard. "I've never been much of a drinker, and Irene forbade it in the house. You know I bought a bottle when we moved here thinking I'd sit out in the backyard, having women over. I've never had the chance to be a hostess. And now I don't even really want to be one. I'm going to have to kill that bottle by myself or leave it for Emily in my will."

In the end both women sat with rum runners, laughing at the terrible pairing of food and beverage, and recounting the days of Larissa, long gone.

Gracie sat back, swirling the shards of melting ice in her glass.

"When your mother and I were little," Rebekah said, "must have been right round 1910, I was all feet that summer, scraped up so bad with all my falling, people thought my daddy was beating me, and that square was just full up with horses and buggies. Oh lord, Gracie, all the shit. All the flies. Your mother couldn't stand it, and she was worried to death I was going to trip over my own two legs and step in it, bringing the flies home with us."

Gracie tried not to laugh, but humor beat out her efforts and she started giggling, some of her drink slipping out of her mouth and dribbling down her chin. "You know, I drive around sometimes, just looking at what's changed. Larissa feels like a city now compared to when I lived here before. The canning corporation, that manufacturer out there by the highway for all those oil and gas parts. A shoe factory. Where did all of it come from? Feels like it just sprung up overnight."

"It's been over a decade, Gracie. A lot can change overnight, even. You know, I was eating lunch today at that place on the square—the one with the green awnings—and I didn't know a single person in there, Gracie, not a one. People coming in from all over now to work in these factories. All those little motels down south along the highway are full up with people moving here for work. There aren't enough houses for them all! Can't build them fast enough."

"I would hate that," Gracie admitted, "living in a motel."

"I can't even imagine."

"Listen, Rebekah." Gracie said slowly, her eyes glancing to the ceiling. "I've been meaning to ask you about my mother."

Rebekah nodded, holding up her glass. Gracie refilled it from the pitcher. After the first two drinks when the women were feeling loose and giggling, they made finishing the rum their goal, and Gracie had dumped it all into a pretty glass pitcher.

"I've been wondering," Gracie admitted, "what things were like, at the end. If she was happy, at least."

If Gracie really cared, Rebekah thought, she could have visited her mother. Maggie had been terribly ill, and in her last weeks, was throwing up everything she ate. She was a skeleton with too big eyes, and when she was awake and not drugged with painkillers, she cried often.

"I think she was happy," Rebekah said, her mouth turning down to contradict her words. "She'd made peace with it at least."

Gracie let out a sigh. "That's what I was hoping. She always told me not to come, but I didn't know if she was trying to keep me from seeing her or if she just understood about Emily, or ..."

Maggie did want her daughter. She'd said as much to Rebekah before things got terrible. Rebekah would always remember what her sister had said when she first went into the hospital: "I can't ask her to sacrifice for me, but I can ask you to atone."

Rebekah didn't want to keep talking about this. The past was the past. There was no fixing what happened, and it was better to not think about it than to revisit old wounds. It might have been cruel, but Rebekah was desperate for a way out of the conversation, and so she asked about Ronald Toller and how much time Gracie was spending with him.

"Rebekah," Gracie replied, "I haven't dated any men since George. Irene wouldn't have had it. I didn't want it. Maybe one day, sure, but not right now. You remember, don't you? When your husband died?"

Rebekah did remember, and it had been sad, but she'd gotten over it. Maybe that was Gracie's problem: she was in love with her husband when Rebekah had simply loved hers.

"Did you ever read *The Odyssey?*" Rebekah finally asked.

Gracie shook her head.

"James did. He loved the classics. We've an entire library of Loeb, green and red, Greek and Latin. You know those?"

Gracie shook her head again.

"No matter. Point is. Odysseus is lost for all those years. Ten, I think, sailing, trying to get home. And when he finally gets back to that blasted little island he finds all these men courting his wife. And she'd put them off, over and over for ten years."

"So you're saying maybe waiting's a good thing?" Gracie's fork scraped along her plate pushing food around.

"Oh, Gracie, I'm so sorry. No girl, I wasn't saying waiting is right. I was saying that I don't believe for one minute Penelope spent ten years alone. If that story had been written by a woman, it would have admitted all sorts of improprieties."

•

While Gracie was in the bathroom, Rebekah went to the library. She placed her hands along the edges of shelves and walked its perimeter, coming to stand before the stained glass. She was with Lillian when the other woman picked it out. The wood frame had rotted almost off the glass in that antique store that was now gone. Lillian had taken Rebekah's hand and said they would make a garden just like it. A secret garden.

Rebekah had said something about the book, something about hoping they wouldn't invite a plague, and Lillian had laughed and responded that she wasn't thinking about the book. She was thinking about other secrets, and then she winked.

When Gracie came into the library, she went to the few standing photos on a shelf and moved them around. "Look at this," she said, and dropped a small object into Rebekah's hand.

It was a bullet casing, and Rebekah screamed and dropped it.

Gracie took a step back, startled by Rebekah's reaction. "It's not live," she said, stooping to pick it up.

Her head swimming, Rebekah tried to think of a response. But she was overtaken with story, one told again and again in the newspapers: Thomas Gladwell shooting Lillian, right here in this room, and then shooting himself.

Rebekah was shaking, and she suddenly felt very nauseous. "It just ... it just gave me a fright. I think all the alcohol has gone to my head."

Rebekah was inebriated. Gracie said she was worried about leaving Emily to drive Rebekah home, but by the time the women were ready to leave, Emily had wandered downstairs in search of a snack, her thin summer nightgown heavy with sweat, looking like she'd had a few too many herself. The girl hummed, seemed to flit around the dinner table, grabbing at food with her hands, not bothering with a plate. To Rebekah, the girl looked like a fairy. Looked "fine," she said to Gracie, and Emily said she'd be okay on her own for a few minutes.

In the car, Rebekah slumped in her seat and then had to muster all the effort she could to climb out of the car once they got to her house. She stood for too long at the base of her porch steps, waving to Gracie Howard until there was nothing but dim red taillights. Then she tripped going up, landing on her blasted knees, but laughing.

She abandoned her normal nightly routine and fell asleep on the sofa with Petrol half on her chest and half on her right arm, smiling at what a good time she'd had. She mumbled to the cat about it but didn't notice how only half her words came out, slurred and incomprehensible. She was proud of herself. How she'd given Gracie Howard good advice. Or she thought she had, because she couldn't remember exactly what she'd said.

When she tried to get up, just once, to use the bathroom—her bladder straining—she found herself unable to move, and not caring much about it.

PART III

•

SICKLE OF MENDING

We weave shadows into new birth. We meld, and swell, and hover in the corners of rooms, behind doors, in doorways.

Sometimes We see her, the woman who hovers. Sometimes We are telling the girl, *Remember*, and the woman falls to her knees and says, *I am trying*, and then looks at where her body is lying, looks at the cold marble so far from home, and says, *I think I died there, but I can't remember.*

Sometimes, We want to help her, but it is hard enough helping each other.

Sometimes We leave the house. Nestle in roses that are ours. Sometimes We dance through town and blur the greedy eyes of outlaws. Sometimes We travel slowly in low waters and look for bodies. Sometimes We find them, but they are not the ones We were looking for.

When We return, We tell the girl to take off her skin. We say she's spent too much time indoors. We tell her to flay herself with a knife, to put on feathers, to travel to other homes, or, what were homes.

Remember. Remember. Remember.

The woman appears. She is in the doorway. She says to keep quiet. That he might hear the remembering of women.

We say, *Remember*.

She says, *I need to forget*.

The girl is grasslands. She is down caught in a spider's web. She is a spider carrying an ember to light a fire that will burn, but not bright, just enough to make smoke in which she will hide.

Sometimes the woman crosses her arms. Listens to our stories. Sometimes she opens her mouth as if to speak and then wraps her jaw in fine silk. We think she has a story. We are worried there is not enough space to share. There are so many stories to tell, and not enough people who will listen to them.

11

Uncover the Dead

—Gracie—

Gracie tried to call Mrs. Habbermire, but the woman wasn't picking up. Running errands, Gracie assumed. She felt bad that she hadn't seen the other woman as much as she wanted to, and the dinner they'd had was fun. More enjoyable than anything Gracie had done in a long time. And it was that dinner, and the relief she'd felt afterwards, that helped Gracie reflect on what was and wasn't productively contributing to her life.

She would not be returning to the Garden Club. Gracie didn't feel like she fit in, and besides, she was getting busy preparing to open the dress shop. There was only so much time in the day, and Gracie wanted to spend it in ways that made her happy. Getting to know the aunt she hadn't been around when she was young made her happy. Time with Rebekah allowed Gracie to conjure up the Larissa she had known as a child.

But Mrs. Habbermire was still a mystery. They could talk all day about Larissa, long gone, but they rarely talked about their own family. Whatever had split her mother from her own sister had happened years before Gracie was born, and now, Mrs. Habbermire didn't seem so bad. When Gracie's mother was sick, Mrs. Habbermire would call up north and update Gracie with all the things her mother wouldn't, or couldn't say. Then she just took care of everything.

Now that Gracie was back, Mrs. Habbermire was giving her even more room. From that first conversation where Gracie had called and asked for help in finding a place to live—Mrs. Habbermire stifling sobs and saying she'd been so lonely—things had changed. Gracie expected Mrs. Habbermire to become a fixture in her life, but the woman hadn't been around all that much, only coming by invitation and stopping by unannounced once. Gracie wondered if her presence was a reminder of Maggie. If Gracie looked too much like her mother. Maybe this was why the older woman hadn't turned up as often as Gracie thought she would, and why she seemed to avoid talking about Maggie.

Gracie drove to the florist and bought tulips. Then she drove to the graveyard.

There had been a long line of McCallins in Larissa, all the way back to the city's founding in the mythical time of Tillamock Lynch. And all of them, Gracie's parents included, had been buried in what people called the East Lot, which was not a lot at all but rather an older cemetery, not as flashy as the one south of town.

She parked and looked through the diamond-shaped fence at the tombstones. Most of the graves must have had flat plaques, because the adornments above ground were few and far between. The graveyard was not that large, but it still felt daunting trying to find where her family lay.

She walked down the rows, her white shoes coating with ginger-colored dust. She didn't mean to, but she kicked it all up into the air until a small, low cloud of it followed her every step.

When she found her parents, she felt guilty that she didn't *feel* more, felt guilty that she'd only brought flowers for her mother. Her father was one memory of a man in a cowboy hat, half in shade. He died of pneumonia before Gracie's fifth birthday. So she divided the flowers up, laying them across the headstones. She thought she should say something but didn't know what. It felt awkward to address the dead, and if such a thing as ghosts did exist, she doubted they would stay to inhabit rarely visited cemeteries. If she was lucky, her mother was haunting what was now the Donald house.

"You're not here," Gracie began, feeling foolish and looking around to make sure she was indeed alone, "but I'm sorry. Sorry I wasn't there. I hope you can understand that I had to stay away for Emily. It's unfair, I know, that the young always take priority over the old—you weren't even old—that daughters come before mothers. But life isn't fair, I suppose."

If her mother had been there—had been listening from below ground—Gracie knew she would understand. Did understand. Why else would she have lied to Gracie? Claiming she was better than she was? Daughters always come first.

The air beside her rushed into her ear and she ducked, seeing a grackle swooping low and then rising up to land in a scraggly tree on the other side of the fence. The tree—a cedar, Gracie saw—was shadowing a thin, stone obelisk.

She exited the graveyard and walked the whole perimeter, arriving at the cedar tree and watching for the bird, lest it dive-bomb her.

The obelisk was darkened with thin, patchy mold, and compared to the cemetery, had not been kept up.

Gracie got on her knees and tried to read the inscription. The only word she could make out read *Killough*.

Gracie knew about the Killough Massacre. She'd learned about it in school when she was young. She'd even written a paper on it once. She'd gone around town to collect oral histories and had come away with a story full of holes. It was all the Indians' fault, she had been told. But blame, she knew, was rarely applicable to only one place. She had wished there were Indians for her to talk to then, not just the ancestors of white settlers. But the original inhabitants of Larissa had been removed, or moved up north, leaving behind nothing but one half of the story.

The shadow of the obelisk loomed long. Something in its darkness was welling up, and Gracie didn't feel like she could go home just that moment. But there was nowhere really, for her to go.

She found herself parked along the square, sitting in her hot car, picking at memories she thought she'd put to rest: Irene's friend in Oklahoma discussing the native children at the state school. The conditions of the children there when this woman had gone to do her charity work. The bruises that peeked out of sleeves. Their silence. "I don't know how to feel about them," the woman had said. "I don't think they're savages, but neither are they civilized."

The sun was sparkling on the windshield and Gracie's eyes were watering. She told herself the day was too bright.

•

She didn't want to go home. And so she didn't.

Gracie found herself in a diner eating a slice of hummingbird cake and listening to the conversations of the other patrons. If it looked odd that she was at a table alone, it wasn't made obvious to her. Everyone was too caught up in discussing the imminent holiday and parade.

Chewing slowly, Gracie strained to make out the words of the women at the closest table. Plates clattered and somewhere in the kitchen a dish was dropped and shattered.

"I don't like it one bit," one woman was saying. "Too many people coming in, changing Larissa. You know they drive around in those loud trucks at night and I can hear them all the way down the street with the tailpipes spitting. Where do they come from? What are they doing?"

The other woman responded, "They're making those shoes you're wearing!"

"Well I know that. I don't mean *work*. Too many men for such a small town. If Mr. Lynch was still alive, I bet"—the woman lowered her voice—"I bet his brothel would be busy as a beaver."

Her friend laughed.

"And poor Leo," the woman went on. "I saw him driving just yesterday. I know his car. Saw him through the window. His face just looks awful. Got beat up in that big fight at the factory. I don't like the way these men act. Like savages."

There, that word again: savages. Gracie shook her head. She tried not to think of its presence—twice within a span of a day—as an omen.

•

When Gracie woke on the morning of the 4th of July, she found her collection of lipsticks all turned over on the vanity. And downstairs, in the dining room, every single chair was pulled away from the table. She checked the house again. Found Emily asleep and undisturbed in bed. Searched each room, and every cabinet. Ran her hands along the walls down there, just to make sure Cedar House had no unknown doors. Went down into the basement and then retreated upstairs to make sure all the windows were fastened closed.

She'd had the locks changed when they moved in. But what if one of those men who'd said such cruel things about Emily had a key? What if everything that was going on was a sick joke? Or something worse?

Even with the knowledge that she and Emily were alone, at the moment, she didn't want to even be *in* Cedar House. So she fled to the backyard, furious and anxious.

The clouds could not be distinguished from each other. The sky was a grey sheet, and it hung over Gracie as she worked, shears in her hand, at the roses that had seemed to take over the back fence in its entirety overnight.

Cherokee Roses. Gracie had gone to the library to find out more about them, compelled to do so because it was too much of a coincidence. And it was too uncomfortable that they were the only plant thriving in the garden, that they would not be erased, that they bore a name she couldn't bring herself to say aloud, a name that even when she said it silently, stuck in the throat of her mind.

She learned that the Cherokee Rose *was* invasive, and it wasn't native to North America at all. It gained its English name sometime in the 18th century, and its blooming season was long past, which didn't seem to affect what was growing in her yard, the shrub blatantly disregarding the rules of seasons. She read that the flower had been planted by Indians, by Cherokee among others, and that when the tribe had been removed in the early- to mid-1800s, and forced to embark upon the Trail of Tears, wherever a woman's teardrop fell, one of these flowers would spring up.

Gracie now wondered how the legend came to be. When reading, she could not discern the identity, or ethnicity, of the story's source. The author of the botany guide she'd read made no mention of how, or where, he collected his information.

Now, as she stood at the fence, surveying the flowers, she was trapped between thoughts: one part of her wished to tear it all down, to dig up roots, to salt the earth. But another part of her was recalling what she'd read, that the plant could grow up to twenty feet tall. That the thorns were to protect it from those who sought to remove it, that the flower would protect itself the way the Cherokee had been unable to. That the women who cried along the Trail of Tears, who lost their parents, and siblings, and sons, and daughters, looked behind them as they walked, and saw the rose, and were reminded that they would endure.

It was a story meant to comfort, but it did the opposite to Gracie. She couldn't put a word to what she felt at that moment, recalling the tale. Imagining all those dead Indians left along the way.

•

"Emily!"

When her daughter didn't appear, Gracie went up the stairs and peeked in her room.

Emily was napping in her bed, snoring and surrounded by books and papers.

A shadow along the wall moved and gave Gracie a start. When she studied where it had been, and the angle of the sun coming in, she realized there shouldn't be any shadows at all.

•

Mother and daughter sat at the dining room table. Because of Gracie's avoidance of the holiday, she hadn't asked Candice to prepare anything special, and so she and Emily ate ham sandwiches and cold barbeque beans.

Emily was unusually quiet. She chewed like the rabbit from the garden. At times she tilted her head, tapped the balls of her feet against the hardwood, seemed to track movement in the room that Gracie couldn't see. Gracie's attempts at conversation were falling flat, and the silence made her even more nervous. She'd been on edge all day, and she exhaled a breath she didn't know she was holding when Emily said, "Do you believe in ghosts?"

Gracie chewed the food in her mouth and swallowed the hard lump. "Why do you ask?"

"Just wondering."

"I don't really know," Gracie replied. "I guess it depends on what you think a ghost is." She was remembering the shadow. Combating the feelings that something had been moving around Cedar House. "I've never really given it much thought," she lied.

"That's surprising."

"Is it?"

Gracie was beginning to become uncomfortable. Emily's odd mood was palpable, changing even the air in the room.

"I've been reading about them. About how this town is haunted by them. It says so in my book, all the people who were killed back when Larissa wasn't even Larissa yet. A whole town full of vengeful people, waiting."

"Waiting for what?" Gracie asked, recalling the obelisk in the graveyard, thinking of the Trail of Tears.

"I don't rightly know. That's why I was asking about ghosts."

"Don't be silly, Emily. There's no such thing as ghosts the way you're talking about them." Even as Gracie said it, she didn't believe it herself. Ghosts, she thought, didn't have to be white sheets, rattling chains. Oh no, they could be memories too, haunting the living, dragging them into a dark abyss.

"I think there are probably ghosts," Emily went on. "I think some things are too terrible to forget, even in death. And that we have to stay here until our stories find an end."

Gracie shivered, unable to reroute her morbid thoughts, the mental images of bodies rotting in coffins, people trapped under the earth, their minds churning thoughts into the roots of flowers, flowers sending pollen up into the air, pollen breathed in by all the people in Larissa, an infection. "People die every day," she told her daughter. "And death *is* an end, Emily."

"People die every day," Emily agreed. "And it's why they die that needs to be said. That's what bothers me," Emily followed up. "All the stories left unfinished."

"What do you mean?" Gracie was appraising her daughter now, noticing the way Emily's body was held, the way the girl's shoulders were slumped, as if in resignation, or as if she'd been bowed over by the weight of time. "You think knowing people's stories will stop the ghosts?" Gracie asked.

"No," Emily laughed, the sound echoing off the walls. "I mean, there's a gap. It needs to be filled."

Gracie told herself that she was not disturbed by her daughter. Emily had never been one to explain herself, but more and more, what she said felt cryptic. Gracie wondered if a kind of distance was growing between them, becoming increasingly convinced that something was wrong with Cedar House, and that it was affecting Emily in ways she didn't understand. Had Emily too been seeing the shadows? Had she been feeling the presence of something that was other? "Emily, has something happened to make you think all this?"

Emily had disassembled her sandwich and was pinching off small pieces of meat and dropping them back onto her plate." In the book I'm reading, those murdered settlers come back. They come back to warn others that Larissa is a dead town, a trap. But I don't think that's right at all. Places don't die, do they? No, but the people in them do. Like the Indians in the story. They died. Or were moved. Or were removed. But the book doesn't tell their story." Emily looked right at Gracie and said, "I'm remembering."

Gracie sat back, all the air in her lungs useless for speech, wondering what exactly Emily was remembering, afraid to ask, and unable to respond.

Here was her daughter, *her* daughter, she told herself, and she was remembering ... what? Emily couldn't possibly be recalling her earliest years. Children don't remember that. Even Gracie only had scant memories of anything before she was five. Not memories, even, but snippets of memories. The drapes in the church. A lamp beside her bed. Her mother, standing in front of the stove, doubled over in pain.

"I want to show you something," Gracie said, hoping to steer Emily away from whatever path she was trying to get Gracie to travel down.

Emily stayed at the table as Gracie climbed the stairs. When Gracie looked over the railing, she could see her daughter with her head cocked to the side, whispering to herself.

In her bedroom she opened the chest. Inside, among photo albums and old papers, her wedding dress, a dried bouquet of flowers, were two boxes. One was small, embedded with abalone and lacquered.

The other was long and slim, made of unfinished wood, and locked. They were the boxes of her daughters, both girls reduced to containers.

She took out the little box, and when she returned to the dining room, Emily had removed the plates. Brought glasses of sweet tea to the table. Outside, rain was coming down in sheets. The 4th of July was ruined for the people of Larissa, Gracie was sure of it.

The chair she pulled out next to Emily shrieked along the wood, and the girl leaned forward to see what Gracie had. She produced the three photos and put them side by side in front of Emily. "This was Beatrice," she said. "She was born a few years before you."

Emily picked up the middle photo with her right hand, and with the fingers on her left, traced the edges of the picture.

"Sometimes I wonder if I was meant to be a mother," Gracie said. Thunder boomed outside, but there was no lightning. "I was so afraid after Beatrice," Gracie found herself saying. You can't see, but here, on the back of her skull"—Gracie touched the back of her own head to demonstrate—"it didn't close properly. After Beatrice, I was afraid to try again, because what if it happened a second time?"

"You would have blamed yourself."

Gracie nodded. She was trying not to cry. "And then I couldn't try, because your father, he went off to war and never came home."

"He wasn't really my father, was he?"

Gracie covered her face with her hands, but even that wasn't enough, and she shut her eyes. Emily knew. Of course she knew. Was it only Gracie then, all this time, who pretended that Emily had always been only hers? No matter which way Gracie went, she was always going to arrive at this moment, here, right now. The walls she erected and told herself were dead ends could not weather the test of time, and now she'd have to come clean from her lies. Oh she'd been a fool. So stupid to think her daughter would never ask about her life before Gracie. "You know he wasn't your father," she whispered to Emily.

Emily put the picture down and craned her neck to look into the box, to the small lock of hair tied with a thin, purple ribbon. "There's a story," she began, "about a girl who disappeared. I read about it in the book Mrs. Habbermire gave me." Emily took a sip of her tea, and when a little spilled onto the table, she mopped it up with the sleeve of her dress. "It's about a baby girl, and how she was taken from her crib and replaced with something else. She was a changeling."

"Sweetie," Gracie said, "Beatrice was not a changeling."

"The thing is," Emily went on, "the girl, the baby, she disappears. But the story isn't really about her. It's about her mother. And I think I understand the book better now. All those stories of missing girls. The book was never for children. It's for the mothers who lose them."

Gracie bent her head and began to cry. There had been so much loss in her life, and she'd never given herself the space to feel it. Her mother, her husband, and then her daughter, born and unable to survive. For decades Gracie had ploughed onwards with blinders on, learning that the business of day-to-day living was easier when one felt less, or refused to feel at all. When she thought a child would complete her. When she thought she could erase one family in favor of building another. Now, Gracie was coming to understand that the world she'd built was even more unsustainable than the lies she told herself.

Emily got up and stood behind Gracie, rubbing her back in large circles circling smaller. "I've been remembering," she said.

"Emily, please don't." If only she had more time, Gracie thought. More time to plan and to be ready for this conversation.

"It was going to happen sooner or later, wasn't it?"

"Oh, Emily."

Emily stood up and walked into the kitchen. Gracie could hear the screen door screeching open. She got up, lunging into the other room.

Emily stood in the doorway, turning to look towards Gracie when her feet thumped onto the tile, and then she crossed, slipping out into the yard.

"Emily!" Gracie rushed to where her daughter was, expecting to find her on the pavers, thrashing, her eyes rolling back into her head.

But Emily was out in the rain. She was spinning, her dress soaked to her body, showing her skinny legs. Lightning arced across the sky, and Gracie shrank into herself.

"Mother," Emily called.

Her daughter was asking for her. Her daughter had gone through a doorway, was not cast down because of it. Was dancing in the water, framed by the roses on the back fence.

Gracie stepped outside, cold then, drenched within a minute. Her ankle turned on one of the pavers, and she went down hard on her knees. When she looked up, it appeared as if Emily were being pulled along, dancing with people Gracie couldn't see. Emily's arms were taut, her hands holding the invisible hands of others.

Gracie scrambled back, shaking her head, whispering *no no no*, calling to Emily—"Do you see that?"—because there was something in the yard, a figure wreathed in rain, an absence of water moving towards Emily.

She wanted to scream, to run to her daughter, to snatch her away. To bring the girl to her.

But Emily was laughing. The roses were laughing. Thunder boomed. Gracie sat alone.

12

Anchoring the Other Side

—Emily—

In Mr. Gladwell's book, Patience Killough disappears.

It took me some time to understand because I am missing part of what he wrote, but now I've been able to put it together. He thinks Patience Killough was taken by Indians.

They tell me it is wrong, all wrong, and at night, the Little People in the tree share with me what really happened. They saw it all. They are still seeing.

"But why would he write this then," I ask.

They say, *Because he is a man, an invader, though he wouldn't use that word.*

They tell me that stories have power, and that We need to tell them to remember.

"But there are so many stories," I lament. "How do I know which ones to tell? Which ones are right?"

They say none of my stories are wrong. They say there are only different stories, told by different people, but I am the one who *needs* to tell them. Some people are simply not heard, because no one is telling *their* stories. It cannot be listened to if it is not said.

Listen, They say. *We will tell you stories to nourish you. Here is a story …*

I do not like the story They tell, one about a little girl whose mother gives her up. Who is forced to give her up. Who doesn't want to give her up because it is a final, terrible loss, in a life, in the lives, of losing.

They tell me this was *my* mother. They tell me that They were watching, had always been watching, until I was taken and They could not find me. They tell me They collected many women on their way to finding me. They tell me some of Them have gone now to find other girls. That the sickle of mending is threshing through time.

Lillian Gladwell stands near the curtain. She does not talk, but she listens. I think she is trying to remember. I think Our stories are helping her remember.

I tiptoe to my mother's room. I open her door—just a peek. I see her head, the blonde hair. I see myself in the big mirror on the far wall. I am a shadow, an echo of another woman. I am remembering.

Beside me, Lillian is fretting. Shaking her head. She goes to the vanity in the room and sits down. She watches me through the mirror.

•

I wonder what the stories of the Gladwells are. Even They could not tell me because They were not here, and to tell a story, someone has to hear it first. Or see it and then tell it. Lillian still does not want to talk. Mayhap, when she's ready, she'll talk to Us.

Right now, she watches people walking by Cedar House. All morning I have been making up stories for them. I mean, about them. I think they are confused lemmings. They have forgotten they are animals and thought dressing in pants and shoes and skirts would save them. But here they are, the herd of them scurrying to the cliff. The water will strip them of their costumes, and they will emerge sodden and wilted into remembering what they are. They are leaving their homes, the settlers of Larissa. They are leaving their crops in the field and looking left and right for Indians. They are hurrying to safer places, but they do not know that nowhere is safe. They are birds who have forgotten how to fly. They are stones rolling towards the forests that used to be here. They are all girls on their way to disappearing.

"Emily!"

I hear my mother, but she sounds very far away, like she is in a cave.

"Emily? Come see. I have something for you."

She pokes her head out of the kitchen, beckoning me.

At the end of the tunnel I see her, and she is holding something. "What is it?" I ask, turning back to the window, uninterested in gifts. More interested in stories.

"I made you something," she says.

A voice whispers in my ear, *Remember.*

When I turn to look at my mother again, she is framed by two Women. They are growing and shrinking and trembling.

"Lunch is ready," my mother says.

When I blink, They are gone.

My mother is not as good a cook as Candice, and I do not like ham sandwiches, but I am hungry and thinking about holes, and so I eat to fill me up.

Outside, there is a dark line above the horizon—a wall of rain is there, and I know it is coming for us.

I watch. I wait. Nothing seems to change, but everything is changing. The wind begins to pick up, and in the yard, I see a small branch fall from the cedar tree.

I cannot remember the last time I saw a storm.

"People die every day," my mother is saying. "And death *is* an end, Emily."

"People die every day," I repeat, because it's true. The earth yawns to take back what it gave us, but it is patient too, not overly eager to gobble us up. No, it's people who move too quickly, forget too soon. Death is not an end, it's the beginning of a story. "It's why they die that needs to be said," I tell her, thinking of all the stories buried in coffins. Of all the stories smothered by soil, made quiet by hands that so lovingly covered mouths. "That's what bothers me," I admit. "All the stories left unfinished."

"What do you mean? You think knowing people's stories will stop the ghosts?"

There is a spider at the corner of the table, lazing circles. Turning. Turning. My mother does not seem to notice it, but it is loud, each tap of a leg, again and again, like a door slamming closed.

"No," I tell her. She does not understand. This is not about ghosts. This is about Them, the Women who have come to collect me, to take me into the fold, into the memories of me, and Us, splintered, separated, sewn back together through stories. "I mean, there's a gap. It needs to be filled." Stories must find themselves to find their end. Or beginning.

"Emily, has something happened to make you think all this?"

"In the book I'm reading," I tell her, "those dead settlers come back. They come back to warn others that Larissa is a dead town, a trap. But I don't think that's right at all. Places don't die, do they? No, but the people in them do. Like the Indians in the story. They died. Or were moved. Or were removed. But the book doesn't tell their story." Doesn't even bother, I think. Thomas Gladwell, like my mother, a muzzle. Only she is capable of change. "I'm remembering," I tell her, because I am. I am remembering who I am.

"I want to show you something," she says, and gets up.

She is gone a long time, and while she is away, the rain comes. I stand and go to the window. Press my palm to it. I open it just a little and gulp down air singed with storm. I go to the table, cup the spider in my hands, remembering a story of another spider, in another time, who weathered water in order to save what was left of life. I release the spider outside and it tiptoes away through the rain drops as if they are not thousands of tiny fists battering a small body.

In the kitchen I can see the words on Lillian's table—*help me help me help me help me.* Somewhere in the house, she is crying.

I pour a glass of tea and drink it. Then I pour another. I wait.

When my mother does not come back, I clean the table in the dining room and from where I stand, I can see into the library. Can see Lillian at her stained-glass window, tracing the spiderweb of metal with a finger. Some of the Women stand with her, talking softly. Lillian is nodding her head, shaking her head, saying, *I don't want to remember.*

When my mother returns, she looks like she's transformed into an old woman, stooped and shuffling. It almost looks like she's dancing, tapping a small drum, but it is a small box, and her fingers work nervously.

When she sits down next to me she sighs, and then opens the box, taking out some pictures.

"This was Beatrice," she says. "She was born a few years before you."

I am buzzing. She is going to tell a story.

A door opens.

"Sometimes I wonder if I was meant to be a mother, she admits. I was so afraid after Beatrice. You can't see, but here, on the back of her skull, it didn't close properly. After Beatrice, I was afraid to try again, because what if it happened a second time?"

There was a girl before me. In the picture, she is so small. I cannot believe I ever would have been so tiny.

"You would have blamed yourself," I tell her. You do blame yourself, I want to say.

"And then I couldn't try, because your father, he went off to war and never came home."

I am remembering, even though I already knew. "He wasn't really my father, was he?"

"You know he wasn't really your father."

And I do know this. My father, who is not here. Who has not shown himself to me. Who is somewhere, another town. A state. Another time, maybe. A man who cannot, or will not, break through the Women who came to find me.

"There's a story," I begin, and by the time I am done telling my mother that I *know*, she is crying.

"I've been remembering," I tell her.

"Emily, please don't."

"It was going to happen sooner or later, wasn't it?"

"Oh, Emily."

They are here, and They are crying too. Crying for all the disappeared girls, for the mothers who lost them, crying too, for my mother, who is not one of Us, but who understands loss.

I get up and reach my hand to the long-haired Woman. I take her into the kitchen where I open the door, see all those roses up at the fence, specks of white out in the storm. They are telling me a story, all Their voices talking, about how the flower means nothing. How it means remembering. That it all depends on who is telling the story.

•

There are many ways to cross, like there are many ways to disappear, and not all crossings are towards something. Some crossings are away from something, which can be the same thing as towards, depending on where you are standing.

I remember a doorway.

Away. Towards.

I remember many doorways.

Once, when I was much smaller, I was pulled through a doorway. And then I was pulled through another. And another.

I am beginning to remember them, the crossings.

The first doorway did not have a door. It was roughhewn logs smoothed by hands over time. When I grabbed at it, I touched a rough patch, splinters lodging in my fingers.

The second doorway was painted white, and the smell inside was stale, and the room beyond was full of crying, and though I could not understand the words, I knew they were calling for help.

The third was the same doorway, but from the other side. I was pulled, out, out, out, by my mother's hand, and for a long time, I was quiet.

•

"Mother." I open my mouth and feel the rain on my tongue, hitting my teeth like small pellets. I drink it down. "Mother."

She looks at me, but We are spinning.

I cannot tell if she is still crying. She is looking, her eyes blinking, her lashes clotting into spikes of dark hairs.

"Do you see that?" she asks, yelling almost. I can barely hear her.

The long-haired Woman takes my hand. Yes, I see it. I can see Them dancing together. All of Them. The yard full of Women shuffling and stomping their feet, causing thunder. It is so loud, and beautiful.

13

The Only Color You See

—Candice—

She timed the attempted phone call so she could honestly say she had to go or else the store would close. Candice did intend to go, right after she hung up, and already had her purse on the counter next to her. The line rang nine times and Candice was thankfully about to give up when her mother, Salida, answered, her voice deep and slow.

"Hello, Mama," Candice said, feeling like a little girl again.

"Candy!" Her mother's voice went up an octave, the telling of surprise. "Oh sweet girl, how are you doing?"

Candice pictured her mother sitting in one of the metal chairs in her kitchen, the phone carried over to the table, its long cord stretched across the linoleum. "Sweet girl" is what Salida always called her, even when Candice wasn't so sweet, refusing, as children do, to live up to the pet names bestowed upon them. When she was little, the wallops for failing to sweep, or scrub, or clean the windows were paired with that name—Candy—and created a kind of dissonance. Getting slapped and being called Candy at the same time was more effective than any hand by itself.

"How are you, Mama. How's your arthritis?"

"Making life hard, but nothing I can't survive. Been taking some concoction, and maybe it helps some."

Candice didn't know how her mother managed, getting up at 3:30 in the morning, walking three blocks to the bakery in the dark, then using her gnarled, cypress-like hands, joints swollen, knobby, her two pinkie fingers facing outwards, to knead and roll and pound. She'd asked her mother to quit, to retire, and the woman had said, "And what then? Wait for y'all to send me a check you can't afford every month? Sit around the house by my lonesome with your girls run off up north?"

Salida had a point: work was a place to see people, talk to people, to keep the woman's mind sharp, even if it was a detriment to her body.

"That's good," Candice replied.

"How are my babies?"

June and Rose. Candice knew they talked to their grandmother. More than she talked to Salida. Candice had been careful not to color their perception of their grandmother as they grew up. Maybe this is why she found herself telling fewer and fewer stories as the girls aged. It was hard, in the moment, to remember to cut certain parts from the narratives, and when she found herself recalling the time she'd used some of pa's reclaimed wood to try to make herself a tree house, hitting the nails at wrong angles, bending them into all sorts of shapes, she'd been so caught up in the memory that she launched right into how her pa had found her ruining his belongings and reddened her hands with his belt strap, him saying her hands were not suited to building and that a woman should welcome the softer arts of cooking and cleaning.

"Girls are good," Candice said, relaying how June was due by the end of summer. She did not mention Everett's idea, and she did not mention the missing girls. She preemptively squashed those conversations by asking about the cake they used to eat at Christmas.

"You got acorn flour?"

"No." Candice didn't think she'd ever seen such a thing, even at the grocery.

"That's how we used to make it, when I was little," Salida went on. "Acorns are bitter, and Lord, it was so much work to get it all ready. So I changed it to chestnut. You can use regular flour, too, and grind up oh ... maybe half a cup worth of chestnuts and throw those in too. If y'all don't have acorn flour, you probably don't have chestnut flour either. We got everything in Dallas," she said, giving Candice the recipe from memory. "You making it for some party?" she asked.

"4th of July, Mama. That big ol' picnic every year." She imagined her mother nodding. "And if I'm going to get all these things, I need to head to the grocer right quick."

"A well-stocked kitchen has all those things," Salida told her daughter. "All the time. Pantry staples."

"Everett does most of the cooking now, Mama. I can't keep track of everything while"— She cut off, about to say "while working, too," but she hadn't told her mother about the Howards or Cedar House and instead finished with, "all I have to do," a phrase with no meaning, just something to say to fill the gap that could have contained admissions and confrontations and entirely different conversations.

"Y'all going up north for the birth?" Salida asked. "June said she might want some help up there."

Crafty June, Candice thought, scheming to offer her grandmother a different job. She wondered then if June had meant the invitation or if she'd said it out of kindness, not seriously expecting her grandmother to get on a bus for days. If the girls were to move back, would Salida see that as a reason to come to Larissa? Could Candice stand being in the same house with her mother again?

"We haven't talked about it yet, Candice said. Everett would be working so it would be just me, I suppose."

"Or just us. You and me."

Candice winced and hoped the squeak of her voice didn't make it to the other end of the line. She thanked her mother and said she needed to get going. What she needed to do was get to the store and then over to Cedar House. She did not tell her mother that she was going to stay with Emily while Mrs. Howard went to Dallas. When Candice hung up the phone, she thought about how neither woman said *I love you*. It just wasn't their way.

•

Candice imagined the specter of Ida Rose following her. She even looked back a few times to make sure the woman wasn't there. But Candice didn't need to see her ancestor to know she was walking within her shadow.

She was feeling guilty about her mother. Worried not just about Salida possibly packing up and moving to Larissa if their girls came back—she'd make an argument, Candice knew, for working with Everett at the diner if he did indeed offer their sons-in-law a partnership—but also about the unspoken feeling between them, at least on Candice's part. She was unnerved, wondering about if her daughters harbored resentments, had their own untellings that had pushed them north to Chicago, and that might keep them there.

Candice believed she'd been a good mother. She'd asked this every night for months after her girls moved, lying in bed and mopping up tears with the hem of the sheet. "I was a good mother, wasn't I?" she'd ask Everett, and bless that man, every night he'd given her a new reason to think so, recalling events so small and insignificant Candice hadn't committed them to memory.

She thought about Ida Rose, following along behind her, and how that woman had probably been separated from her family by disease, or malnutrition, or by financial strain or bad health. Candice knew the difference, now, from folk *choosing* to go different ways, but she also knew those choices were often governed by an unseen system that made the choices for them—Rose and June's husbands for example, seeking the North because the South didn't provide enough for them.

Ida Rose had probably been separated from her mother, or else there would have been some story, passed down, about Candice's great, great-grandmother. Instead, that woman, or the idea of her, was a hole. And that hole was filled with the possibility of blood: of cousins, generations removed, all connected by the women who'd been cast far and wide across time and distance.

"Phooey," she said, wanting to spit and then thinking how crude that would make her look to the passing motorists. "Ida Rose," she said, "I feel you back there, patient and watching. I only wish you could say something." Then, correcting what she said and reminding herself that spirits didn't exist, said, in the past tense, "Had said something. I wish you had said something."

•

The next day, Everett left early in the morning to help set up the cooking for the picnic, and Candice tried her hand at Salida's chestnut cake, which turned out okay, she thought, but could have looked better. To dress it up, she made a glaze of water and powdered sugar and drizzled it on top.

If she had gone outside, if there had been any laundry to take down, or if she'd felt the urge to water the still-struggling broccoli, she would have seen the grackles, again, lined up at the cap of the roof. But she didn't, and went about singing along to the radio and transferring the cake to a nice plate.

By the time they arrived for the 4th of July celebration, however, Candice's mood was starting to darken. First it was the sheer number of bodies, and the way they divided themselves. For years Candice has simply accepted that Larissa had patterns that weren't worth disrupting, and the way the town split itself at the center was one of them. The courthouse lawn and square were only so big, could only accommodate so many people. Historically, on the 4th, this meant there wasn't enough room for everyone, so many of Larissa's residents were relegated further down Grand Avenue to Yamini Park, and this was where Everett set up, along with the rest of their church congregation. This meant that when the parade came, Candice and everyone else at the park were passed by, not arrived at. It meant *hearing* hooting and clapping and the big band from the courthouse lawn instead of seeing it. It meant the parade each year ending not with horns and fanfare and smiling faces from the courthouse steps, but with the backs of people's heads disappearing down the street: musicians, veterans, all the children in the bike parade.

Candice was also thinking deeply about the reason for the celebration, dwelling in a space that was beginning to cast a long shadow over the day. What did it mean that she was here? That Candice, *part* Indian, was participating in festivities celebrating the formation of a country whose government had caused so much damage? She was very much aware, as she walked through the park with a cake in her hands, that the land she was on was American but not American. Was used first by Indians before Americans took it away. When Millie found her, Candice was standing at a table heaped with food, looking around at all of Larissa's people and wondering if she was the only one trapped in the bottom of a well.

"Happy Fourth!" the woman said, and Candice, surprised with her own violence, had a phantom reaction of reaching out and slapping Millie.

"If you say so," Candice said, finally setting down her plate. She wiped her hands against her dress, the fabric pulling against the callouses on her palms.

"What's got you in such a foul mood?"

"Nothing. Ignore me." Candice didn't want to talk about it with Millie. She was becoming more aware that the phone call to her mother had been the beginning of something that unsettled her.

The two women stood in silence for a moment, and when Candice didn't offer up any more comment, Millie looked from side to side, and then slipped away, mumbling something as she went.

Candice didn't want to be celebrating. All around her was laughter and the sound of people talking loudly. The smell of beer wafted from people's mouths, and she began to obsess over looking at lips, of ignoring the words rushing past them and trying to match the shapes of English to shapes of Tsalagi, to dive deep through the shallow waters of these people's speech and to find, in the depths, some memory of Enola.

It had happened once with Emily, when the girl was in her fever uttering familiar but forgotten words. An arrow in Candice's brain, lodged in the center of language unused for so long it had formed a carapace to protect itself. A soft shell made hard over the years. A barrier to preserve a vulnerable interior.

Emily had said *unitsi*, and now Candice looked for the shapes of a syllabary as she strolled through Yamini Park. Here, a man's mouth formed *wo*, and here, a child's tongue slipping out *sa*. Candice stopped hearing words all together and instead searched for the components of words: *ne, tlo, yv, la. Ha, gu, de.* She tried to pick up these pieces and assemble them, but when she whispered a composite, it never sounded right. The way she'd always spoken, the way she'd been taught to speak, guided the unfolding of syllables and put stress in the wrong places.

Everett waved to her from his post at the grill, and Candice made her way over to him, feigning smiles to Larissians as she walked. When she reached her husband, the smoke was blowing in the wrong direction and her eyes stung with it. Candice came up behind him, burying her face in his back, feeling the sweat through the fabric of his shirt.

"This storm is coming in," he said. "Another few hours and we'll all be running for the hills. Good thing we start early."

"Good thing," she parroted back, not really thinking one way or the other that it was or wasn't fortunate.

"You remember," Everett began, his tongs scraping the grill grate, "that one year Rose fell out of the tree?"

Candice did remember. Of course she did. Mothers do not forget the injuries of their children.

"Look at that now," Everett continued, nodding with his head across the park.

Candice stepped back from her husband and found the live oak Rose had slipped from, that had snapped her wrist and left her crying in the dirt with her dress hitched up her waist, in too much pain to comprehend how much of her body was on display. Someone had groomed the live oak. Had lopped off all the branches closest to the ground, had created a clearance that would keep any child off the tree.

"That's odd," Candice said. "Why do you think they did that?"

"Beats me. But they're all like that. Look around."

Candice did look, and every mature tree in the park had been trimmed. It looked like a river had come through and taken all the low hanging branches from every single one of them. She tried to remember the word for tree but wasn't sure if she even ever knew it. She tried to remember climbing trees in her own childhood. Tried to remember what Enola's property in Nacogdoches looked like.

"They better hurry up with that damn parade," Everett said.

Candice realized he wasn't talking to her, but to Era Davis who had come up with his plate, asking for a burger off the grill.

•

They came down the street. First the sound of the marching band, which drew people in Yamini Park to the broad avenue. They came down the street, the high school band, in their dark pants and blue bow ties, behind them young cheerleaders waving poms and tossing hair-sprayed hair. They came, grown men holding flags: the American flag, the Confederate flag, the Texas flag, men wearing jodhpurs and resting the poles against their shoulders like rifles. They came on horses, and in the backs of trucks decorated with balloons and signs and tossing confetti into the street behind them. They came too, little boys on bicycles, corralled by fathers and mothers who occasionally picked up a child fallen from their seat, a procession so slow it interfered with their riding. They came, the men who had fought in the war, in the back of the mayor's convertible, or sitting in chairs on a slow-moving flatbed decorated with hay bales and bunting and large, cardboard replicas of the medals they wore on their uniforms.

All of these people came, and Candice fixated on watching them leave, had turned her body at a forty-five-degree angle from everyone else in the park, was looking towards the square down the road where the front of the parade was jamming up, fanning out, backing up everyone else trying to make it to the destination. Candice was watching the destination, and was tuning everyone out, which is why she didn't see what was happening at the end of the procession, the addendum to the parade no one had anticipated.

"What in the world?" Everett put his hand on Candice's shoulder and when she turned to look at her husband, she saw what everyone else was already staring at.

The end of the parade was passing and people from Yamini park were already flowing out into the street to follow it to the square. But now that mass of bodies was opening back up. People were stopping to look behind them, and then moving out of the way.

Katherine Cooper was walking along Grand Avenue. She was wearing a yellow dress and her hair was loose and unstyled down her back, a straight and shining length moving like a wave in the wind that was pulling too at her hem, that was billowing her skirt as she moved. Behind her there were two other women that Candice didn't recognize, but she knew who they were. She didn't know their names, but she knew their look, their bone structure, the toughness of their faces. They were the mothers of the other missing girls. The mothers of Georgia Stock and Rita Randall. The first two girls to go missing from Mrs. White's farm.

Each woman had over her heart a terrible, bright, arterial wetness: red paint slick and still dripping down their breasts. Candice could see too that the right hand of Georgia's or Rita's (she wasn't sure) mother was stained, and that as the woman walked and flexed it, she carried with her a threat, a warning, a reminder.

"Oh lord, she's gone off her rocker."

Candice wasn't sure who said it, but someone was giving voice to what most people were thinking. Most people besides Candice. She understood not with words, but with silence, and image.

"Where is—" Everett broke off and disappeared into the crowd.

Candice watched the women walk on. Watched as people parted for them. She wanted to run out into the street. To join the other women. But before she could even really bring her body to move, Charles Cooper emerged from the crowd and was rushing to his wife, Rosemary and Alice behind him, and with them, other people from their church.

Katherine was intercepted by her husband, but she walked around him. He stepped in front of her again; it didn't seem as if he was trying to stop her but rather to get her attention. He wasn't putting his hands up or pulling at her body. Candice watched his mouth move but couldn't make out the words.

The mothers of Rita and Georgia were ahead and on either side of Katherine now, and Katherine was stopped in the street, shaking her head and refusing to answer her husband.

And then the rain began. Candice felt it first hit her forehead, and then a drop pelted her cheek.

The people of Larissa were caught between the spectacle of the missing girls' mothers and the impending storm, beginning to slowly move their bodies out of the street, towards the shelter of trees, or towards their cars on the other side of the park.

Candice was glued in place, and by the time Everett came to take her by the arm, she was becoming soaked, water running down her nose and lips, dripping quickly from her earlobes.

Katherine Cooper and her husband were still in the street. The water was running the paint down her body and her dress was soaked with it.

"Come on, Candice, come on." Everett was tugging Candice, and she let herself be taken. She could not see the other mothers, did not know where they had gone, but as Everett guided her to the car, she could see the end of the road: the town square where the mothers would have been arriving, the people there fleeing the rain, emptying out, leaving the celebration.

•

Candice was surprised to see the article in the paper, but in hindsight, it made sense. It was a profile, not only of Marlene, but of the girls from the farm: Georgia and Rita. There were even pictures of the girls, all of them, though Marlene's was larger.

Marlene was a Larissa girl, featured front and center, and Candice figured then that someone other than the mothers knew what had been planned; Katherine, probably, had talked to a reporter. Had gotten someone to care, and that person had timed this article in the 4th of July edition of the paper to coincide with the mothers' walk. If only, Candice thought, the whole town had been forced to witness it.

Candice didn't know Marlene all that well now. She talked to the teenager at church, and that was about it. She found herself wishing she had made more of an effort, but no one could have guessed a thing like this would happen: that Marlene would go missing.

Marlene was twelve years old and what the newspaper reporter called "a bright student." In addition to playing the flute, Marlene was teaching herself Latin with books provided to her by the high school principal, Mr. Richardson. Marlene wanted to attend college and eventually, she wanted to be a nurse. Teachers of Marlene's had been interviewed and remarks about her had been quoted: "smarter than a whip-stitch" and "not even a mean dog would bite her." An older girl who used to babysit Marlene even said, "I know I shouldn't reduce her to her beauty, but she really was something." There was even a poem Marlene had written for English class, done in iambic pentameter, a wild revision of history wherein José Maria found himself in a more modern Larissa, marveling at all the change.

Candice now had the paper folded in her lap—she was going to save it—and she and Everett sat under the roof of their back porch, watching the rain and lightning, listening to the far-off booms of thunder, until the water crept to their feet. Then they returned inside to the dampness of the house pressing down on them, and stripped off their clothes, piece by piece, until they ended in bed. When the lights snapped out, they touched each other in the dark.

Afterward, Candice lit candles. She'd had to dig them out of the back of the pantry and didn't have enough holders for all of them. Everett rigged up some more bases for them by dripping wax into the bottom of coffee cups, and they stood together by the front window watching the dark river of water pouring down the street.

"Did I ever tell you about my cousin Lou?" he asked.

"The one you tricked into planting 'magic beans'?"

"Her," he agreed, chuckling.

"She had this little dog when we were young. A mutt. Little brown and white thing that was always yapping at the door when we came knocking. Dixie, I think, was its name. Or maybe Tricksy. I can't remember. Anyway, there was a massive rain one day in March. I wasn't at her house for it—I was at home wishing it would stop raining—but lightning hit the ancient live oak in their front yard. That was the last of the tire swing. The tree fell down, missing the house, somehow, but it hit the fence, knocking it down, and Dixie, Tricksy, found a hole. Shot straight out in the gap with Lou watching—her pa couldn't stand its whimpering and barking anymore and had put the poor thing outside. Anyway, Lou saw her dog escaping through the branches and wanted to take off after him, but her parents wouldn't let her. She never got the dog back. Don't know what happened to it. It just up and disappeared."

"That's a sad story."

"She looked for that dog for weeks. Months, maybe. Her pa wouldn't let her get another one after that. Said it was a sign that dogs and that family weren't meant to be."

"Convenient."

"Did I ever tell you about great-granduncle Jim?"

"Everett," Candice said," please, no more stories."

"You okay?"

Candice was not okay, and she said so. "You've got all these tales," she told him. "And what do I have? I've got so little. I can't tell you about Uncle so-and-so or Aunt whatever-her-name is. I can't hear any more tonight. It's too much."

"I'm sorry. Sometimes I forget."

It wasn't his fault, Candice thought. She talked about her own anger and sadness so little that of course he wouldn't be thinking about it. If she never pointed out the gaps, how would he see them?

By way of her own apology to Everett for shutting him down, she reached for his hand.

•

Candice woke with a light in her face, the power back on and her having forgotten to turn the lamp off because the house had already been dark. The radio came on too, quiet from the kitchen. She didn't remember leaving it on.

She got out of bed, turning the knob and leaving Everett in the dark, and went into the kitchen. The radio was playing "Someday You'll be Sorry." The clock read 10:23.

With a mother's intuition she knew something was wrong. It sang in her body like a current and she couldn't calm herself down. Her hand was already on the phone when it rang.

"Candice?"

She recognized Tom's voice, June's husband.

"What's happened?"

The man started to cry, and Candice was shushing him, trying to coax out his words. "Just take a breath," she said. "Deep breath. One after the next. Tell me what's happened."

The man was hiccupping like a child, but he managed to eventually get out what he was trying to say. June had gone into labor early. "She's gone," he said. And the grandbaby. The grandbaby was sickly, but alive.

14

Scream for the Loss

—Bet—

The frame of Alton's bike was decorated with crepe paper. Silver stars hung with fishing line from the handles. He wanted an American flag to flow behind him, fluttering in the wind as he peddled in the parade, but when Norman saw the fabric loose on the ground, Alton trying to affix a corner of it with glue to the back of his seat, the boy almost got another slap. Instead, he got a lecture on American pride, and bravery, and respect.

Even with that, Alton was too excited to eat the eggs, bacon, or cantaloupe, and bounced in his chair singing "You're a Grand Old Flag" while Norman smiled, mistaking a child's excitement for any holiday as patriotism. Bet felt her nerves fraying. She was glad Norman would be there today helping Alton while she spent her time with Will.

The cobbler was cooling on the stove. Norman had given their five dollars to Richie for the barbecue. They were to leave the house at 1pm. The only problem was the weather.

That morning, sitting outside with her cigarette, absentmindedly ashing into the cup of coffee at her feet, Bet couldn't help but chuckle at the sky. It had roared up in her—the absurdity of it—most of Texas withering in drought and now, on the 4th of July no less, the promise of something torrential brewing.

Bet remembered a story her friend Annie had once written to her of, about Mother's Day 1946, back when the woman still lived in Durant, Oklahoma, at the southern tip of Tornado Alley.

Fischer's market had set out the world's supply of potted geraniums. Pink and red and pots stacked up to peaks on bleachers in the parking lot.

Annie was at home with her newborn watching the sky turn green, wondering where her husband was.

And then the funnel hit.

Annie watched it come together over the tops of little houses. She knew she should get inside, but something kept her fixed in the front yard, babe to her chest, not even calling for the dog.

That tornado hit Fisher's, tearing all the plants and flowers up into its column, a mass of a pink pallet looming closer until the spell broke and Annie ran for the house.

"That's what finally sent me in," she'd written. "A *pink* tornado. Never heard of a pink tornado and I figured it must be extra dangerous."

Only later would she learn the color had nothing to do with danger and had everything to do with geraniums.

Bet wondered if the rain would hold off. She wondered if there would be time to suck on watermelon and savor the sauce Al made from scratch every year, the chicken tender and falling off the bone, making people laugh because they always forgot how perfectly cooked it was, chuckling at themselves because the plop of meat back onto paper plates sent sauce scattering onto shirts, sometimes onto the ground where ants would appear as if summoned by a magician.

Inside now, at the table and lost in her own thoughts, Bet tried to listen for the sound of rain over Alton's voice. She partly hoped it would hit soon and wasn't sure why she wanted the day to be ruined for everyone.

•

Norman put Alton's bike into the trunk of the car and he and Alton went north, where the parade would start, and Bet and Will went west, on foot, to the square. They became part of a loose column of people, a lazy exodus of residents, all heading the same direction, all complaining about the sky.

"At least we're not burning up," Will said conspiratorially to his mother. Bet thought he sensed her mood. He'd been especially accommodating all morning, careful not to be under her feet, offering to help whenever he could, shushing his own brother whose voice echoed through the house. Bet didn't know if she should feel guilty for her son's hypervigilance or grateful that he wanted to take care of others.

Will carried the dish of cobbler. Bet thought how funny it would be if he tripped. Not him of course, with scraped knees, but that fruit and butter and crumble topping on the ground, all gone to waste except for the bugs and birds who would find it.

To get to the square, the long line of residents had to pass along Bell Street. Or, they didn't have to, but they chose to, a tradition since the families there always decorated. They even had their own private competition for it.

The porches were draped with bunting. Blue and white and red flowers grew in flowerpots. One house even had a flag high on a pole, though it hung droopily.

Cedar House had nothing.

Bet stopped in the street before the mansion and commented on it. "That's brave," she said, wondering how Gracie Howard had the nerve to be so bold.

"Well, they're new," Will said. "Maybe Emily and her mom haven't had time."

"Emily Howard? You know her?"

"I know Emily. We talk about Indians."

"Have you been in that house? Why haven't you told me?"

"Mom, I don't have to tell you *everything*, do I?"

The words wounded Bet, but she didn't say so. She kept walking, Will at her side. "What's she like?" Bet asked about the girl. "I hear she's got something and can't leave the house."

"Does she? I think she's right nice. Smart, and funny."

"You like her Will?"

"I said she's smart and funny. Of course I like her."

That's not what I mean, Bet wanted to say, but she didn't. She'd already been reprimanded—her son was *entitled* to his own business.

She was frustrated, or hurt, that Gracie Howard had been Norman's first pick, and now Gracie's daughter had caught her own son's eye. She wanted to tell him that he couldn't see Emily, but she couldn't come up with a good reason on the spot.

•

Bet floated through the crowds. Hello. How are you. Good to see you. How is that person that I'm only asking about because it's polite?

She was growing annoyed at the good times, the forgetting of the missing girls, the probability that their bodies were somewhere, flies at their skin, in their eyes.

Bet didn't know until that moment—standing there on the courthouse lawn with a plate of potato salad in her hands—that she believed all the girls were dead.

She didn't know until that moment, when her stomach rebelled, that they had again become *the girls*, all four of them somehow the same person, despite her efforts to name them. To keep them separate.

She tossed the plate into a nearby barrel. Bees buzzed around the top of it.

Mothers kept sharp eyes on daughters. The only children running, weaving between adults, were boys. The girls kept to small circles, wistfully watching the games they had been forbidden.

The humidity had become worse than the heat, and with it, Bet smelled herself. Not her body, but her clothes, which she knew she'd left in the washer too long. She smelled like mildew, and, embarrassed, she tried not to stay too long in any one conversation, worried that the small breezes would carry her scent to whomever had captured her.

The clock tower struck two shortly before the sound of the parade could be heard coming down Lynch Street. The band: horns, drums, and flutes. The people in the square shifted its shape, becoming an arrow towards the sound. Soon, she was the only one still standing near the dessert table. She watched the backs of others with her arms crossed. Knowing she looked glum, she climbed the courthouse steps. She sat at the top, fanning herself with a paper plate as if overheated.

Here came the townsfolk in their proper places: the high school band, followed by the Women's League, followed by people in costume from the Civil War, antique guns resting on shoulders, a Confederate flag carried by a man in a shell gray jacket. When the boys on their decorated bikes came, she looked for Alton, but he was lost below the tops of heads. Other boys had done a better job with their creativity, and Bet felt guilty knowing Alton would win no ribbon. If she had helped him, he might have stood a chance.

Last, but not least, came the veterans. Calvin sat beside Andrew Marshall, the oldest veteran of World War I in Larissa, on the back of the mayor's own convertible, the mayor himself at the wheel, sunglasses on and grinning.

They came slowly down Lynch Street, waving, nodding. The mayor pulled the Mercedes as close to the curb as he could, people parting, but not well enough, to let him do it without some difficulty.

Bet leaned her head back and felt the first drop of water on her face. She looked and saw Will with his Guide friends, but his brother was missing. She searched through the crowd, pushing past people emptying out of the square, to find her husband talking with a man she didn't recognize.

"Norman," Bet said, breaking in with a smile, "have you seen Alton? The heavens are about to break open. Your car still up at the grocery?"

Norman nodded. "You didn't see him?" he asked.

"No, I didn't see him." Bet tried to keep the irritability out of her voice. She still smiled.

Norman took off in one direction, Bet another, both calling for their youngest son. Soon Will too was combing through the crowd, looking for his brother.

"Alton!" Bet was asking people if they'd seen him, found herself unable to recall what he was wearing that day, unable to give details that would make him identifiable. People shook their heads, said, "I'm sure he's around here somewhere."

What they meant, Bet knew, was that Alton was fine. He wasn't a girl.

When the rain really started to come down, ruining what was left of the celebration, Bet was still yelling for her boy. She felt like something had come loose in her throat. The name—*Alton*—rattled around not in her mouth but behind the thin skin she kept touching, her hand pressed to her neck.

"Bettye!" Jo Tandy caught the back of Bet's shirt and pulled her up short. "Bettye! Stop!"

"I have to find Alton," Bet said, pulling away. She called his name again.

"Bettye! Stop! He's fine, he's fine. They found him. Calm down, Bettye, look at yourself!"

•

At home, Bet sat and looked out the living room window. The rain was pooling in ditches, creating small ponds across the yards and where the streets dipped low.

She'd fought with Norman when he arrived back with Alton, their youngest son drenched and refusing to meet her gaze. Norman said Alton had gone with two other boys in search of the fireworks, the big canisters of explosive powder and chemical colors. They'd had it on good authority that the "fireworks weren't well guarded," though Norman wasn't sure what the boys had planned to do with them even if they had found them, which they didn't, because the fireworks, before they were destroyed by rain, weren't set-up anywhere near the market.

There was anger there, and also relief, but anger again, this time making Bet's eyes throb and her hands shake when Norman said he'd already punished Alton, told the boy he would no longer be attending the Guide's camping trip. "Oh, he was howling, Bet. Begging. Pulling on my pant leg, tears for days."

Bet was angry because Norman hadn't consulted her about revoking the trip for Alton, and she was angrier still that Norman's decision to mete out the punishment meant she would not have the weekend alone, to herself, which is what she wanted. Needed.

"You're taking him," Bet said, her voice raised.

"I can't go back on my word," Norman said, aghast. "What sort of example is that to set?"

What sort of example is that to set? Bet's head swam with colors. The words were out of her mouth before she could stop herself. "Who are you punishing, Norman? Me or him?"

"What's that supposed to mean?"

The rain was still coming down.

"Nothing," Bet said. "It means nothing. Don't listen to me. You never have before."

Norman grunted. "You think he should still go?"

"Yes, I think he should still go. Find something else to threaten him with. Don't pin him on me."

"Are you afraid of him, Bet?"

Bet couldn't imagine what her face looked like, what she gave away in her mouth, the wrinkles of her forehead, her eyes. Everything was numb.

•

Bet was reading the Saturday paper, already wrinkled and half ruined with Norman's careless handling of it. Of course he hadn't folded it neatly. Who cared if Bet also wanted to read the paper? She wondered where Norman and the boys were—the house was quiet for a weekend morning—but at the same time she didn't care where they'd gone off to. The headline on the front page read "Elephant Stranded in Tree Saved by Trunk." A stupid play on words, Bet realized, once she'd gotten deep enough into the reading to understand it.

The unexpected summer storm had caused Statler Creek to swell and become a river. It ripped up over its embankment, flooding the small zoo, carrying with it animals who had no escape. Poor Aldie Marks, who owned that stretch of property and the animals on it, had tried to save them from the rapidly rising water. Panicked, he simply opened their cages, letting loose the monkeys, flamingos, and sheep to escape their confines and fend for themselves. Frannie, the solitary elephant, had been trapped in her large enclosure, but instead of drowning, managed to wrap her trunk around a tree, her big body buoyant through the night, until the water receded enough for her to bring the whole thing down with her. Despite being uprooted, Frannie would not stop hugging the trunk, dragging it along in the grey appendage swinging from her face.

Bet was imagining the beast, her heart rending for it—more so for the scar it would bear in its mind than for the night spent trunk on trunk, when the phone rang.

When she picked up the receiver it was Marcil, and he had news.

The rain had swollen Statler Creek, and there, among the carcasses of animals trapped by the drainage grate, was the rest of Marjorie Kent. Aldie Marks had found her, the man already crying for his peacock whose wet feathers draped the girl, plastered to her skin.

"I know it's Saturday," Marcil apologized, "but now's your chance. We need someone to step up. This is going to be a shit storm and we're all out in the field. You want to prove yourself? Help me."

Bet tried to tamp down the rush she felt pulling on a pair of slacks and flat shoes instead of a dress. She left a note for Norman, then wadded the note up and tossed it into the kitchen trash.

The sun shining on still-wet pavement mocked her, implied it was going to be a lovely day, sending green shoots up out of the ground, new growth for the parched summer. Pools of stagnant water made reflective surfaces in the low spots of lawns. Birds were pulling water-logged insects and worms out of the grass. The mosquitos were going to take over in a day or two.

The police station was mostly empty. Marcil, in his hurry, left his jacket on the coat rack and was out the door, only pausing long enough for Bet to confirm that she did know how to operate the radio. The phones rang more than Bet thought they would, a combination of both the storm's wreckage and it being the weekend. She took messages about downed trees and washouts. About a missing cat. About a stolen car. A roof of one of the motels some of the new factory workers lived in had fallen through and their power was still out. Some man, drunk at ten in the morning, called to say he was out of beer and that he needed some delivered. Bet politely told him the police could not deliver him beer, and he called her a bitch and hung up.

When Marcil came back he was accompanied by the mayor. They closeted themselves in the conference room and Bet watched them through the open shades, shaking heads and trading papers. Calvin arrived later, in his hand a brown package the size of photos. Bet wondered who had developed them, and what promise he'd made not to talk.

When Mrs. White appeared in her mud-caked cowboy boots, Bet knew it was worse than she thought. And Mrs. White didn't even bother to stop to talk to say hello to Bet. She went straight back to where all the men were, threw the door open with a force to rattle the frame, and then shut it with the same amount of will.

Bet wished she was a fly on that wall, because Marcil wasn't happy at being interrupted. He was pointing back towards the door and

Mrs. White was shaking her head, jamming her finger into the table, at something Bet couldn't see.

•

Mrs. White's phone hadn't been working on account of the storm. She didn't want to risk using the party line because she didn't want to "wade that deep into what was happenin.'"

What was happening, Bet learned, was that the storm had washed away shallow graves. Uncovered the body of not just Marjorie, but of Georgia Stock. The Stocks and the Randalls—all the people out at the farm—were in an uproar, though it took hours before Mrs. White even knew what was going on. Hours before anyone bothered to come up to her house, knock on her door, and tell her that a body was found on her property.

Bet was caught between a mother's grief and her own private joy, because even though the situation was dreadful, she was riding in the car with Marcil with a promise of new employment. He'd even said it would be useful having a woman in sensitive situations, and she bit down on her impulse to respond to him, listening to him instead as he filled her in.

Georgia had been found in a manner similar to Marjorie—in waters wished for by all of Texas—but her body was trapped against a tree slumped into the tributary to Bartlett Creek when its roots, barely anchored in arid soil, had become water-logged, the water rushing, taking topsoil, sending the already half-dead giant across Pleaman's Stream.

Some of the farm children had found Georgia while imagining the fallen tree a great bridge to somewhere, anywhere, other than the fields their parents worked in.

Bet didn't want to think about how what they'd seen was going to stay with those children. How for their entire lives they were going to remember that storm on the 4th of July and what it brought.

Pleaman's Stream ran on the west side of the farm, the boundary line between Mrs. White's property and the large tract of land leased by S&G Drilling. Bet tried to think of where Georgia might have come from, where her and Marjorie's bodies had been hidden, or buried, but she'd never been this far north of town and didn't have knowledge of the area necessary for imagining.

As Marcil slowed the car, driving through the area of the farm with the cabins, Bet suddenly felt very aware of her life with all its comforts. The cabins were small and depressing, built up on brick stilts. No windows in front. No chimneys she could see. Sloping metal roofs that must have caused a racket in the rain and wooden siding warped with age. Bet thought it should be criminal to make people live in such places.

The workers of the farm watched as the police car rolled on, faces impassive. They were gathered in groups on porches, and the ones who were alone, walking in the muddy paths, were quick to join others.

Bet wondered at the faces, at the people who came and worked here. Some people, she assumed, were white—destitute with few resources. But many of the workers seemed to look different. Darker skin, darker hair, darker eyes. Before Will had told her, Bet had never known that many of Mrs. White's workers were Indians, and she wondered where they went when the planting and harvesting seasons were over. What homes they went back to, and if they were better than what they had here. She imagined them getting on horses and riding away. Imagined them with bows and arrows and tomahawks on the plains. Imagined mothers with babies strapped to their backs, leaving the farm and realizing too late that their burdens were too light, their daughters gone, missing, left somewhere along the way.

She knew this thinking was wrong. That the people here had not been transported across time from some serial narrative from the 19th century, but she didn't know enough about Indians to imagine anything else. She put her head down to avoid looking at them. To avoid them seeing her. Because she wasn't sure what tells might be written across her face.

When they got to their destination, Bet's shoes sank into the ground, and she jumped when she heard dogs barking. Marcil offered his arm when they had to make their way down a steep slope of the creek's embankment, apologizing to her for his lack of foresight and promising they'd find her something more appropriate to wear from then on out.

Quickly, Bet also became aware that she was the only woman, the police officers nodding to her, calling her Mrs. Donald instead of Bet.

As Marcil listened to one man, Bet saw through the trees the stooped forms of people, and she knew then that the families of the missing girls were there, perhaps unwilling to abandon Georgia's body but refusing to do so because at least, at last, they had her back.

There was a tall man sitting hunched on a log, elbows on his knees, watching a woman who had waded into Pleaman's Creek, her dress soaked up to her breast, clutching the body of a child. Bet knew this must be Georgia's parents, their names unknown to her because though they had been there, on the report, she had not committed them to memory.

The police were trying to bring Georgia out of the water, but her mother was protesting.

Bet felt she might vomit and forced the acid back down her throat, her swallowing audible and wet. She'd never seen a body take on water before, and it disgusted her.

"Bet," Marcil said, coming up beside the man. "Jean has to let go." He motioned to the Stock woman with a quick nod of his head.

Has to let go—what stupid words, Bet thought. Man didn't even understand what he was saying.

Bet removed her shoes and set them on the ground. Her toes squished into the earth.

Everyone had gone still, eyes moving between the two women.

Bet stepped into the water.

Between her sobs Jean was saying, "oh lord, oh lord," a chant, a prayer.

"Jean?"

The woman did not look up. Everything was too quiet then.

"Jean." Bet's movement through the water was like someone banging pots. It hurt even her own ears.

"She was so good," Jean said, her eyes closed and rocking her daughter. "So good."

"I know she was." Bet waded closer to the other woman.

"Oh lord, she was so good. Wouldn't hurt a fly. My baby. My baby."

Bet reached out her arm and put her hand on Jean's shoulder. Jean paid no notice.

"Jean," Bet whispered, hating herself for what she was about to say. "You have to let go."

15

Choiring of Memories

—Rebekah—

For the past week, Rebekah had been unable to remember the duties of her evening checklist, so she invented a new nightly routine, relatively unaware of some of its absurdity. Rinse her face, tie up her greying hair, and throw away her stockings because washing them felt like too much of a chore. Salute the radio for its loyal service as she leaves the kitchen with a cup of warm milk and bourbon. Provide each houseplant with an affirmation to give it strength to grow. Turn off the lights downstairs, open the front door, survey the street and the yard and nod gravely when all is quiet. Have a one-sided conversation with Petrol as the cat meows incessantly, letting the little beast know *she* is the master. Master of the cat. Master of the universe.

At the bottom of the stairs Rebekah paused. *What if*, she wondered.

She went back into the study and flipped the light switch. The cat followed, mewling as if to say, "This isn't right. Come back. Climb the stairs."

Rebekah peeked out the window, the last vestiges of daylight darkening. Then she sat at the desk.

The two wedding photos were anchors at the far corners. On the left, the portrait of her and James, and on the right, the picture of Lillian and Thomas.

Rebekah took one picture in each hand and laughed. She worked the photos out of their frames. She flipped the photos over, lined them up. She could not shake the feeling that it wasn't a coincidence:

both brides sitting in chairs slightly in front and to the right of their husbands. Same height, even. While Thomas' hands hung to his sides, one hidden by Lillian's body, James' hand was on Rebekah's shoulder.

"This will do," she said to the cat who watched from the floor.

She opened the desk drawer and took out the scissors. She smiled as she trimmed the photos, cutting out background, cutting out husbands. When she was done, she picked the Gladwell frame and arranged the two figures she'd kept side by side. Then she fixed the velvet-covered backing, turned the little screws in place, and flipped it over. Lillian sat in her chair, and Rebekah, with a bodyless hand on her shoulder, sat beside her in another.

Rebekah pulled a pen from one of the drawers and looked at the cat. "And so we work backwards," she said. Petrol jumped up onto the desk, sniffed the contents of her glass, and then quickly retreated to stand in the doorway, her tail swishing, unsure of if she should stay or go.

Rebekah counted the seven pages she had of Gladwell's novel, chuckling at how each time she saw the letter "I" it appeared misaligned with the rest of the text. She thought it was fitting that they were skewed, because I's were inherently confused—*people* were inherently confused about who they were. It was absurd the way people used the pronoun with such confidence. How had a typewriter known to comment on that? She re-read his story, an old anger welling up in her chest. Thomas might have been gifted at business, but he was not gifted with narrative. His story was slow, boring, and completely devoid of interesting characters or language.

"Ugh," she said to Petrol. "Just listen to this. 'And because it had been agreed upon that they would be allowed to return to gather their crops, they did. But harvesting is hard work, long work, and like God did not create the world in one day, neither could the food needed to nourish his flock be gathered in such a short time. When Thomas returned to the house, dusty and dirty and tired, he found little rest. There were three families in the small space. The Killoughs, the Williams, and the Woods. The children were fussing and would not calm under their mothers' admonishments, and the mothers themselves were lacking patience.'"

Petrol seemed completely unmoved by the excerpt, which did not surprise Rebekah.

Spreading the papers out before her, she told the cat, "I will write a better history than this."

Rebekah took her pen and struck through every single line of Thomas Gladwell's type. Then, in the space between his lines, she started writing to fill in the gaps.

•

When Rebekah decided she was done for the night, her hand cramped something fierce. She wondered if ice cream would be good on toast. If lightbulbs knew they were on. If the moon—even if wasn't really made of cheese—might still taste like cheese.

The clock above the bookcase read 3:35. She couldn't remember the last time she'd wound it and got up to do so now. When it started ticking again, she adjusted the hour and minute hands. She didn't know what time it was, but she set them to 9 and 12. *Time to go to bed,* she thought.

Upstairs, Petrol was already curled on the spare pillow, and from her deep breathing, looked like she'd been there a while. Rebekah got into bed and reached for the nightstand.

Tonight it was *I, Robot.*

"Can you see this?" Rebekah asked the sleeping cat, angling the book as if it might actually look. "I've never heard of anything like it. I'm glad I'll be dying soon. I don't think I want to see the future."

•

"Do you know what I just can't stand?" Rebekah asked Dusty as she came in. She set her purse on her desk and removed her shoes.

Dusty looked quizzically at her.

"Double first names," Rebekah declared. "Like Mary-Lee or Margaret-Sue. It's like people can't make up their minds and want both instead of one."

"Well," Dusty said, scratching his chin, "in *their* defense, it's the parents' doing. The double naming."

"That's who I was talking about," Rebekah said, as if Dusty hadn't a clue what she was saying. "The parents."

"Of course." Dusty looked to the floor and at Rebekah's discarded flats.

"You know what else I can't stand?" Rebekah added.

"I haven't a clue."

"Carrots. I just realized it this morning. I've been eating them my whole life and I've never liked them. Not raw. Not steamed. Not with brown sugar glaze."

"Oh. I suppose that *is* odd."

"How does someone go their whole life eating something they don't really like?"

"I would think—"

"My gosh!" Rebekah was so astonished that she sat down. "And I just realized something else!"

"Mrs. Habbermire, are you okay? You're looking a bit pale."

"Dusty. I don't think I like working here."

"What?" Dusty took a step back.

"Really, Dusty. Really. I just realized it! I think I need a change. All kinds of changes. How does a woman just wake up one day and realize everything is wrong? Am I in the wrong life? On the wrong planet?" Rebekah began nodding to herself. "My lord. My lord! Dusty! This is it! A revelation. I've got other places I need to be!"

"Mrs. Habbermire, you're acting quite … concerning."

"Dusty! What am I doing here, wasting all my time? And it's not just this," she went on, motioning to all the things in the room. "I need to sell my house! I just can't do it anymore. Soon I'll need to move on," she said, imagining a future she saw theorized once on a television program, one in which she might drive a flying car all the way from Texas to Florida.

Dusty opened his mouth to speak but Rebekah cut him off again. "I think I need to leave right now. There's just so much to do, now that I know what needs doing."

"You're going now?" Dusty got up and moved towards Rebekah, but then seemed to realize he had no real plan and had gotten up without a reason for doing so. "But there isn't a hurry, is there?" Dusty asked.

"Tomorrow's the Fourth, and we were going to dress the windows. I could really use your help. I hadn't planned to do it alone ..."

Rebekah thought that Dusty was sounding a tad whiny. "I really don't know what you think I could do that you can't do by yourself. I'm in no condition to climb a ladder."

"A ladder?"

"No ladders! No more stairs, either. And I'll tell you something. I may be too old for robots but I'm not too old to know when my body just isn't having it anymore."

"Robots?"

"Oh, I know all about the robots," Rebekah said. "They're going to kill us all."

"Mrs. Habbermire," Dusty said, almost pleading with her.

Rebekah shook her head. "I'm sorry, Dusty." But she wasn't really. Apologizing was a formality, and she tried not to smile as she slipped her toes back into her shoes. She'd rather not have to put them back on, but she couldn't very well walk home barefoot. Fine, then, she said, standing up. "Toodles, Dusty. I'll see you soon."

When Rebekah stepped back out into the day, closing the door behind her and disappearing Dusty with it, she felt pounds lighter. And at home, Rebekah began cleaning out her kitchen, wondering how she had amassed so many dishes and utensils, piling everything she didn't want into the old vacuum box she'd never thrown away and now found a use for.

•

It was the nightly routine. Put the dirty dishes in the downstairs bathtub to soak. Close the curtains so the children down the street can't spy on her. Turn the armchairs in the living room around so they'd stop staring.

Then she went into James' old study and began to work. She had Thomas Gladwell's papers in front of her, a cat near her feet, and a fine glass of bourbon.

Despite her earlier failed attempts at writing, Rebekah Habbermire decided that she had always been a storyteller. Knowing this—that she had the ability of imagination—made her feel a bit closer to Lillian

Gladwell, who was a natural at telling tales, both her own, and the ones she fabricated.

The women used to play a game during those times when Thomas was out of town, where Rebekah would open a dictionary at random and choose three words of which Lillian would have to make a story. Rebekah would choose the strangest words she could find—words so archaic or exotic Lillian couldn't possibly know their definitions. Lillian was smart though and often guessed something close to the actual meaning of words.

Wight. Purfle. Fizgig. Rebekah wasn't sure if these were words she had once spoken into the dining room of Cedar House, on cold nights when fires crackled, the two chimneys sending plumes of black smoke out into the sky. She wasn't even sure if they were real words or something she'd just made up. She wondered what would happen if she used these words in her own story. A part of her liked this idea—a code of sorts—something to keep burglars or nosy neighbors from being able to decipher the manuscript she was authoring. She didn't want anyone ever reading what she was writing. It was only for her and Lillian, a kind of excavation, or private conjuration of what had been. It would embarrass her even in death and sully the Habbermire name if anyone found out what had happened between them. There was no saving the Gladwell name, which was already ruined, shot through with two bullets from Thomas' revolver, that gun he'd so proudly worn, passed down by the men in his family with its gold scrollwork and carved whalebone handle.

She wrote without thinking, marveling at how the story told itself. She didn't even need to try. A memory told Rebekah what would happen, a woman's hand on a poker stoking the fire, another watching the bent frame of her friend, thinking of the marvelous shapes of bodies when they curled in on themselves, or around others.

•

The next day, Rebekah almost forgot it was the 4th of July. If she hadn't turned on the radio, she could have gone the entire day without knowing. When she looked out the front window, sure enough, people were walking in small groups towards the square. So she put on a Sunday dress and left her house.

She walked alongside a family she did not know, pretending she was the grandmother. She wanted to admonish the children who were running wild, up into yards, pulling leaves off bushes and almost trampling into an ant hill. "Remember that time you got poison oak," she wanted to say to the boy whose fingers were green with shredded leaves. "Remember how you got it, just pulling leaves off things all willy nilly."

Rebekah did not remember it was she who'd had poison oak, pulling vines off the fence of Cedar House before Lillian had been taken to Dallas. The maid had worked alongside them, her mouth sealed with a promise not to tell Thomas the two women were together again. The yard had grown up, manic with the spring rains. Lillian had fired the gardeners for gossiping. "I'm tired of men," she'd said, "and all their demands. Rebekah, you're right not to be married again. Brings nothing but trouble."

The maid had said, "yes ma'am," and Rebekah had wondered at the time if it was agreement or acquiescence.

All these memories, though, were inaccessible to Rebekah now. They might as well have occurred to someone else, because Rebekah was already planning for grand-grand babies, impatient for Joseph to grow up already.

Even after her family dropped away, blending into the crowd growing in the square, Rebekah kept walking. She passed by where her sister's old dress shop had been, and the jewelers, the old antique store, and the pub. Soon, she was walking in front of houses she'd never seen before.

A car pulled up beside her and parked. A man got out, and he asked if Rebekah knew where she was.

"Of course," she said.

In that moment, the fog cleared. Maybe it was the sudden confrontation with the other bodies around her, people on the other side of the street, on porches. All unfamiliar.

"It's about to come down bad," the man said.

Now that Rebekah studied him, she understood that he was a police officer. And because Rebekah was a storyteller, what she said to Officer Peters sounded like it could be true. She needed her maid, she said.

The woman had no phone and Rebekah was just furious with her for not showing up to work. "You know how it is," Rebekah said, "when you get a bee in your bonnet."

Officer Peters drove Rebekah to her house, and she thanked him for dropping her off, promising that she'd let her husband handle those matters from now on.

She didn't know what time it was, and the cat was practically screeching. She was so tired after all that walking and her brain was buzzing. She put the cat outside and closed the back door. She drank two glasses of water and then let the cat back in because its howling at being drenched was worse than the howling of it being hungry.

•

It was the nightly routine, but it was not night, merely dark with day rain. Make a sour cream and wheat bread sandwich and then sit at James' old desk and work on her story. Tonight, the window was open, and Rebekah could smell the petrichor. It reminded her of spring nights in Cedar House, sitting in the back yard after a storm, her and Lillian keeping their voices low so Nora couldn't hear them.

It was hard, the remembering, but so was the telling. It was difficult to tell two stories at once: hers and Lillian's and Lillian's and Cora's. Difficult to separate truth from lie and reality from fiction. But she was trying. She was trying because she knew now that to tell a good story meant she was going to have to tell everything.

•

Rebekah found herself more excited by the taking of her things than the getting rid of them. It began with the issue of the cluttered living room. All the things Rebekah decided she didn't need were getting piled up there, and not only did it annoy her to walk through the mess, but it was starting to stress her out as well. It was one thing when all the junk was stored away in closets and cupboards, and quite another when it was spread out all in one room of the house.

She carried a green lamp to the curb and set it down. Technically, it wasn't her trash day, but she didn't care. She'd rather leave it on the lawn than leave it in her house. When someone just took it, she thought she could bring out other items she decided were rubbish: a decorative pillow, old glasses, a bunch of kitchen utensils she'd tied up with her robe's sash. Once she'd made enough trips to get rid of all the small things, she tried to haul out one of the living room chairs, but it wouldn't fit through the doorway. It was light enough to scoot along the carpet, but too heavy for her to actually lift, so she abandoned that project in favor of searching the rest of her house for more, smaller items.

•

Rebekah was feeling like a new woman. Not only had she cleaned out the junk, but she'd also cleaned out her closet. And she'd cleaned out the pantry. She'd accidentally cleaned out Petrol's cat food, which she knew she needed to replace, but it was late, and it was time for the nightly routine.

She settled in at the desk and the cat followed her, meowing a little too much for Rebekah's liking. She wondered if she'd have to lock it out of her bedroom that night.

"Come here you little grumpy bumpkin," she said, patting the edge of the desk.

Petrol leaped up and nosed her face into Rebekah's fist, looking for food that wasn't there.

"Enough of that," Rebekah scolded her. "Tell me what you think. We're almost there. We're almost done."

Petrol was licking her paws, extending her claws. She wasn't listening, but then, Rebekah thought, the story wasn't for the cat anyway.

•

Rebekah woke to the cat's throaty growl. Petrol was sitting on the window ledge, looking across the dark yard.

"What is it," she murmured, pulling her face up from the papers, ink etched along her cheek.

The cat hissed and fled the room.

Rebekah got up and went to the window. She couldn't make out a single thing in the darkness, nothing that would have spooked the cat. Still, she stayed. Looked out in the night. Wondered what was occurring that she was unaware of. Thought that she should go investigate because once, long ago, she'd seen a woman in the middle of the night. A woman in her nightgown, roaming the neighborhood. Rebekah couldn't remember what had happened to the woman. Couldn't remember who the woman was. But she was becoming increasingly sure that there was someone out there. Someone who needed her. Someone calling her name, a familiar rhythm, a beacon.

PART IV

•

STELLATE MYSTERY, THE NEW THAT CALLS

We hear a woman say, *you have to let go.* But there are many kinds of letting go, just as there are many ways to cross, or disappear. We do not think this woman knows all the shades of what she says.

We call to each other and say, *Look. This is where We died. This is where We were killed. This is where We shed blood on the ground through birth and wound and here is where We were forgotten.*

Look, We say to each other.

We look.

We look and listen.

We look and listen at this town that was once our home, that still is.

Come now, We call, and the girl comes. We sit in a circle in the grass wet with new water. We tell her stories. We say, *Remember.* Her tongue is unpracticed. But she is trying.

This is how to tell a story, We say, and We show her our scars white in moonlight. We dig nails into wood. Tear up what was built over. We eat berries made of glass. We tell her to throw off her thin skin because what is underneath is starting to shine.

Sometimes, she leans into Us. Leans into the memories, and our bodies. We laugh. She is remembering.

Remember, We say. *Remember cold nights, and ice, and the pit that is your stomach and your heart and the absence of drums.*

Remember, We say, and the woman who follows Us, who is another woman disappeared, and found, begins to talk.

She says, *the girl is a bird. She has long arms made of feathers. She is a bird. I am a bird.*

Her voice is just a chirp, warbling through silk.

We confer amongst ourselves, ask if We are willing to share this space. Understand the many stories that have not been told. Understand We must find a way to tell them all. We say to her, *you are wearing a mask,* and she knows this is why her talking is difficult.

Remember, We say.

Remember, the girl says. To herself. To Us. To the woman who follows.

16

Crave True Stories

—Emily—

My mother and I sit at the kitchen table, both of us drinking coffee, though she will only give me a little. It is bitter and bold and feels like a fitting drink for the conversation we are going to have.

I am not sure if she believed me when I told her about Them. I'm not sure she believes me now. I think I could convince her if I told her all the things They've told me. If I spoke to her all the stories of Us that I am learning. But I don't want to give that to her, even if it is proof. Some things are so sacred they cannot be shared, and They tell me this is my decision, and if I don't want someone to know, I don't have to say anything.

"I can't see them," she says, wide-eyed with her hair unkempt. She hasn't bothered to brush it yet this morning.

"Of course not," I say." But They're here."

My ancestors are all around the house. They sit in the living room. Walk the library. Are gathered at the dining room table. They are talking constantly, to each other, to me. We speak two languages, all of our tongues loose with remembering. With creating, and recreating.

"I've thought, once or twice ..." My mother drops off, staring down into her cup."I've thought, a few times, I've seen someone ..."

"That was probably Lillian," I say, and I think she looks disappointed.

I am caught between feeling sorry for her and being angry at her. She seems so vulnerable now, my mother, that I don't want to tell her that They will never show Themselves to her. And at the same time, I *do* want to tell her. And I want to tell her why. I want to say, "You have taken away so much. What makes you think you deserve to share now?"

But I do not say something I know will wound her. I do not want to be an architect of pain, even if a castle of it has been built for me. Anger, I think, does not mean one has to be cruel.

"Lillian Gladwell?" she asks. "Her ghost?"

I do not believe Lillian is a ghost, and I do not believe They are ghosts either. I cannot pretend to understand, because I don't, but I do not have to understand to accept. "She comes and goes," I say about Lillian. "I think she's remembering too."

My mother sighs. Shakes her head. Mutters "ghosts," and asks herself, softly, "What is a ghost? "

I do not respond.

Then she says, "Emily, I don't know where to start. It's been so long. I've spent so long pretending ..." She is going to say more. Wants to, I think. But she does not continue.

They say, *Sometimes blood calls to blood, and sometimes, blood answers. It screams its remembering from the inside of small mosquitos. It burrows into the safe soil and cocoons a larva until it awakens, soft-tongued and uncertain, because of new blood.*

My poor mother. It must be so hard for her to remember.

"I will tell you a story first," I say. "A true story. And then you can tell me my story."

She nods.

"A long time ago, there was a girl. Her name was Patience Killough. Her father was a homesteader, and they were one of the families that had settled Our land. There was a treaty that was supposed to protect Us, but it didn't, and some of Us were angry because white people were coming and taking what was not theirs. Continued to come and take what wasn't theirs. We agreed to let the Killoughs come to harvest their crops. But not all of Us were happy about it. And so they were killed, the Killoughs, and others too, all of them, but Patience. It is impossible to tell the entire story, but this is what I learned from Thomas Gladwell. He left out so many important things. Like the love Patience had for Ocona, and how she'd left the farm for him. Left her family for him. See, this is what I will tell you. This is the story. It is every story. Someone is lost, which means someone loses."

"That's not what I expected you were going to say," my mother responds.

I think my mother is stalling for time. Afraid to confront the story *she* must tell *me*.

The Woman with the long hair comes into the kitchen. She stands behind me and puts her hands on my shoulders. They steel me for what I am about to hear.

"It was happening a lot," my mother begins. "You have to understand that they thought they were doing the right thing."

They are whispering, *you do* not *have to understand, because "understanding" invites acceptance. "They" means so many people other than Us.*

"I was so lost then. Irene and I both were. Your father ..." she stumbles and corrects herself, "George had been missing for years. And I wanted to be a mother so badly. And when I saw you, sitting outside with your knees pulled up to your chest, back against the wall of the schoolroom, looking up at the sky like you wanted to conquer it, oh Emily. It was always you. I had been waiting for you, and I didn't even know it. It's like that sometimes, recognizing someone before you even know them. And until you, I didn't know that I could love again."

They say, *Always you. Always you. Always you.*

"It was terrible, that place. That home and school. None of the children looked happy. Hardly any of them spoke. And you, alone. Emily, you were the only Cherokee child there. Doubly alone. Like me."

They whisper, *Alike, not alike, akin, a shadow, a mirror painted red.*

My mother goes on. "They thought it would be better if you could grow up with me. Learn English. Not live in poverty."

They are angry hearing this—*not poverty*—but they still listen, and all of Us sit in silence with this information. Sit in the feeling of being taken through doorways, because yes, there was a place that has been buried in my mind. A building cobbled together of many buildings. And there a stone that was placed in my mouth which stole my words. A cave that We entered, and came out of, but never came out of. An oubliette where We left Our stories. My mouth is sour with the almost memory of the place.

"You have to understand," my mother continues, "they said that your mother could barely feed you."

They say, *You do not have to understand.*

"Oh, Emily. Say something."

I do not know what to say. I wonder where my birth mother is. I wonder how my mother thought she'd be able to hide this from me forever. Or maybe she didn't intend to.

"I think," I begin, "that it is good we came here. I'm not sure They would have found me if you hadn't brought me to Larissa."

She sobs.

"It is not a bad thing," I tell her. "Knowing. Remembering. We are telling a true story now."

•

In the book Mrs. Habbermire gave me, there is a story about a girl who went missing. In the story, the girl goes to sleep, and each night she disappears.

When I read it to my mother, both of us in her small bed, she says, "I don't know how you can stand to be near me."

When she tells me this, I sigh. Look at the two of us through the mirror on the other side of the room. Do not understand my own desire to forgive, which comes like working clay. A shape, nothing, slowly becoming recognizable.

They ask me how I can be so kind, even though They know.

It is not my mother's fault, and she did not take me. I was taken before she ever knew me. She was simply the next person to receive me.

She didn't just take you, They say. *She took what you are.*

This, I know is true, and I grunt, my mother mistaking the sound for that of a physical discomfort.

She shifts so that I have more room to turn pages, and her foot slips out the bottom of the sheet. "I used to think like the woman in the story when you were little, smaller than you are now. There were nights when I would wake up in a panic, knowing something terrible had happened to you. But there you were, asleep, in the house, nothing amiss."

I know there are many ways to disappear, and my mother, she does too. But she does not know *all* the ways to disappear.

At night, I have been climbing out of my window onto the big branch where the Little People sit. They tell me that there are ways to disappear, even when you are sleeping. They say the stories they hear people tell have it all wrong—that it's not like a magician with a hat, or cape, or cage. But then, We know now that just like there are many ways to disappear, there are many ways to tell a story.

•

Dreaming is a way of remembering.

Sometimes I dream that I am a bird, and I fly through storms.

One night, I dreamt of this house before it was a house. I saw a grove of trees being cut down, and I saw the rabbits fleeing through the underbrush, the grackles watching their nests tumble down into dust, their eggs cracking, little bodies broken in leaves.

Another time I dreamt of a different house, but this one was not really a house. Maybe it was just a different kind of house.

There were no walls, and the beds were high, so high that my mother had to lift me up, up, up until she set me on the bed beside her and tried to cuddle me. She pulled me close against her, but she was bending my wing, and I tried to turn and look because I knew she was not my mother, but her face was nothing but clouds.

And then I dreamed of Patience Killough. Dreamed of her calling out for *her* mother, and Patience's daughter calling out for her. I tried to help them, flying above, going very far away until I could not even hear them anymore.

And then I found bodies of battered women and women dead from childbirth. Women who died in their sleep and women who were shot in the head. Women who were not women when they died, but the idea of women, or made into women by men who tell themselves stories. And I realized, from high above, that everything I was looking at was a graveyard. The entire world was a grave, full of people who had been forgotten.

•

Will is showing me his new patches, the awards he's gotten for being a good Indian. I want to tell him that he is not an Indian at all. He is just a YMCA "Indian Guide," a boy wearing a mask that does not fit. But I also don't want to risk the only friend I have, so I let him talk and do not tell him he is being stupid.

"This one," he says, "is for building a teepee."

"That's great," I say, running my finger over the embroidery, wishing for the world's smallest pair of scissors to snip the threads.

"It wasn't *quite* a teepee," he amends. "It was more of a tent. But I think it was close enough."

"Did you get a wampum patch?" I ask. "For the pearls?"

"No." Will frowns. "Pearls aren't wampum, I guess. Wampum needs to be shells."

"What's this for?" I ask, pointing to a patch in the shape of a drum.

"That one is for storytelling. I told a good story."

I am interested in this—his story—but he goes on to tell me how his story was better than his brother's.

"Father got really upset at him," Will says. "Because of all ..." Will drops off. "My father said it was too violent."

"Why? It was just a story," I say, because I have seen worse things, I'm sure, than what his brother made up.

"It was a *true* story," Will says, "and a mean one. We were supposed to be *making up* stories. That's what storytellers do."

"Do they?" I ask.

Will frowns.

"What story did *you* tell?" I ask.

Will is proud of his story, one about a sly fox who thinks he is smarter than everybody else until he is tricked by an otter who is much cleverer. It isn't very original, but I understand why his story got him a patch when his brother's story did not get *him* one. Will says his brother's story was about murdered girls and vengeful Indians.

"Where did your brother even get that idea?" I ask.

I hear the back door close and then my mother in the kitchen, the water running.

Will shrugs. "Everyone's talking about it."

"About what?"

"The girl," Will says. "Who got killed. The whole town is talking about it."

"I didn't think anyone cared," I say.

"No, they do," Will protested. "Because there's a murderer, Emily!"

"So that's what people care about? A murderer?"

Will looks confused.

"Are they talking about a murderer," I ask, "or are they talking about the girls?"

"A murderer, I guess," Will says. "But there was a big article in the paper about the girls. On the Fourth of July."

"I wish I could have read that," I say, wondering where our paper went, and why I haven't seen it. "I'd like to know more about the girls. Someone needs to tell their stories."

But Will seems to think there's something more interesting about the murderer, and something more interesting about Marjorie than there is about Georgia, or Rita, or Marlene. He says he wonders if Marjorie disappeared because of the curse.

I don't believe in curses, but I don't say so because I want him to go on.

"We read about it around the fire," Will says. "There's a book of Indian stories we read from at the Guide meetings. And in this story, there was a medicine man who was upset that his tribe's land got stolen and he cursed all the white people. And then the Indians killed them."

"If the white people were already cursed, what was the point in killing them, too?"

Will hadn't thought that through I assume, and he doesn't respond.

"Well, I guess it was *a* story," I relent, "and stories don't always make sense. I bet I could get a storytelling patch," I say, wondering about if I could be a Guide. Since I'm Indian, I'd think they'd have to let me be one.

"It's harder than you think."

My mother peers around the corner. She makes a motion with her hands—space, please, more space between me and Will. She wants a gap. That's what she said: an arm's length away from each other. Really, I think she only let Will come over because she is feeling guilty. If it was up to her, I'd have no friends.

"Well," I begin. "There was once a little girl, and she disappeared." I wait for Will to say something, to critique how I start, but he doesn't. "There was a bird who saw it all, but because she couldn't talk—not like people—she couldn't tell anyone what was happening. She saw the girl sneaking out of her house to meet a man who arrived in a car with all its lights turned off. The bird saw the girl put her small hand in the man's large one. Saw the man put a finger to his lips. Quiet, quiet. The bird battered her wings against the windows of the little girl's house, trying to wake her parents, but her parents said "oh it is storming outside" and thought the noise was thunder. So then the bird—"

"What kind of bird was it?" Will asked.

"Does it matter?"

"Maybe. It's hard to imagine without knowing what type of bird."

"An owl. It was an owl."

Will nods, as if everything is okay now, so I continue.

"Then the owl went to the dog who was sleeping on the porch. They had a dog, the girl's parents, and it had to sleep outside because it had fleas. The owl went to the dog and tried to tell him to bark to wake up the parents but the dog couldn't understand the owl and so he ignored her. The owl was desperate now for someone to listen to her—she had a story that was being told right then, at that minute, that was important for someone to hear. So the owl went to her friends and said 'we must follow the girl' and they listened, because they all spoke the same language, and they all went."

"Went where?"

"Stop asking questions or you're going to ruin it!"

"Okay, sorry."

"So the owls found the car. The little girl was inside the trunk, and she was asleep because she was hurt. She was dreaming of a story, but the owls didn't know that. The car was driving down dark roads and it turned off into the grass, and though the trees were in the way, the owls could follow because the car's headlights were as bright as the moon."

Will is looking uncertain, but he needs to hear this. Someone does.

"They came to a river. What used to be a river. The remnants of a river. The little girl was still asleep inside the trunk, so she didn't feel it open, didn't feel the man lifting her out, slamming the trunk closed with his elbow. The owls saw it, and they started making a raucous. They were hooting and screaming—"

"Owls don't scream."

"Yes they do! Quiet now, or you won't know how it ends!"

I notice that Will is farther away from me now, two arms apart, at least.

"So the owls were screaming because they knew something terrible was going to happen. The one owl—the first owl—swooped down low and tried to grab at the man's eyes. He said 'fuck' and swatted at the owl. Hit it hard and broke its wing. The other owls saw this and then knew that they could not intervene. That if they did, they might get hurt, too. The first owl could do nothing but watch then, and the others, they stopped making noise because what was the point? Anyway, the owl watched as the man started doing what men do. The owl watched as the man removed his belt. The owl watched as the man put his belt around the girl's neck, like a noose, and pulled tighter and tighter."

"Emily ..."

"And then the owl watched the man as he carried the girl to a place of earth between two trees whose branches had grown into each other. And the owl couldn't see him very well because it was on the ground with a broken wing, and the grass was too high, but it knew there were only two bodies breathing—itself and the man—and that the disappeared girl was dead."

"Emily, I don't—"

"That's not the end, yet. The owl couldn't fly, and so it had to stay there, on the ground. The others dropped it mice, but the owl had no water. She was so close to the river—what used to be the river. She tried to make her way over to it, to get something to drink, to quench her thirst. It took days. Weeks even. The owl knew she was dying but what could she do? She was delirious by then, so much so that when the man came again with another girl, and then another, she wasn't sure if it was real or if it was a dream. She was so close now, to the water. And then something miraculous happened. It started to rain. It started to rain! And she opened her beak and drank and drank and drank."

Will is very quiet.

"Is it worse than Alton's story? Mine *did* have talking animals."

"It is worse than Alton's."

"Why? Because it's true?"

"Because it's awful, Emily. It's gruesome. It's sad. It's just ... awful."

I'm not really hurt by this because They are behind him, nodding their heads, proud that I've said something worth hearing.

•

In a dream, my mother disappears. She pulls her shirt up over her face, and every time she pulls it down, she looks different. Not that she's a different person, just making different faces.

I squawk at her and fly away.

When I see the owl, I circle, unsure of what to do. I am only a little bird, not strong enough to carry all the weight she calls to me. She is speaking a language I understand a little of, enough to make out *help me help me help me*.

When I land, she waddles to me, her broken wing trailing behind her. She is my mother, and the longer she talks, the more I understand.

She is telling me—in a cadence that drawls, loose with rhythm—everything that has disappeared. She tells me everything that has been forgotten. It comes in pieces, like a broken window. I can see it, but it is shattered, and it wants to cut me. And so it does.

•

"That," I say, "is burnt."

"It's not burnt. It's ... crisp."

"I don't know how we're going to survive without her," I say, eying the cornbread that is, indeed, burnt.

"It's only for a little while," my mother says, hopeful.

Candice will not be returning for some time, and we don't know how long it will be. I miss her and sometimes find myself wanting to cry even though it's her daughter who has died, not mine. I want to call her, but my mother says we should wait because we don't want to "overdo" it. I don't think she understands what I am offering, but maybe she does and thinks it isn't needed.

"Maybe someday soon, she says, we can drop off something nice for Candice and her family to eat and while we're out, go to the library. You must have gone through everything you have now."

"Maybe," I say. Even though I want to go to the library, the grocery store, to Candice's diner and certainly her house, I'm not sure if I'm really ready to stray too far from home. For the moment, it's enough for me to just imagine going, taking a pencil with me to write down all the titles of the books I want to read. One day I even want to go buy them, maybe from a store in Dallas, and put them in my library here in Cedar House so I can read them in the red chair I'm going to have. But I am nervous. I don't know, really, what's outside, and what it's like to move in Larissa.

My mother is checking the back door. Turning the deadbolt. She is gathering her purse.

"Wait, "I say. "Before you go. Will mentioned a newspaper story. From the fourth of July. Where is our paper?"

She rubs her forehead. "It's probably still on the porch. I was so upset that day already ..."

I walk with her to the front door, and she opens it, stepping back to let me pass.

Outside, the sun is breaking through clouds and a car rumbles down the street. I see the paper, folded and under one of the wicker chairs.

"I hope it's not wet," my mother says.

I bend down and reach to retrieve it. "A little bit," I say. "Maybe I can still read it."

"I'm going to lock the door behind me, my mother says. Remember, don't open it for anyone."

In the Cedar House library, I spread out the paper. It is still wet, but not ruined, and if I unfold it, maybe it will dry faster. While I wait, I listen to Them sing. They are everywhere and nowhere, content to wander the house, sleep on the sofa, converse with Lillian in the garden.

I am remembering, and now, I remember Irene.

But the remembering is incomplete. I know this because of the way my not-grandmother's face keeps changing: different colored lipsticks and sometimes her mouth turns down, sometimes up.

In the memory, or maybe it is many memories, Irene is showing me a photo album full of grey women.

"And that," she says, pointing to a picture of my mother outside a low, brick building, "is where we found you."

I am thinking about the building. The school. Or maybe it was a house. Is a house a house simply because people live there?

Anyway, I've been thinking about the building because I recognize the door. And I've been trying, very hard, to remember, or forget, what was on the other side.

17

Until You Can No Longer Make Believe

—Gracie—

Gracie lay in bed, shivering under the covers even though it was hot in the house. The fan turning above her cast weird shadows along the walls, and she closed her eyes to keep from seeing them. She thought she might be delusional, that all the rain she'd sat in, watching, watching, had caught up to her with a nasty cold. She was hallucinating shadows as Lillian Gladwell, who, just moments ago, seemed to slide along the wall.

It was easier to say she was sick. Being sick meant she was not crazy. Being sick meant the world had not overturned its own laws for living.

What Emily had said afterwards, what Emily had said to her later that night on the 4th of July, it stuck to her. Found entrance into her body through her mouth, her nose, her ears, her tear ducts. "The world is full of women," Emily had said, "that you refuse to see."

But now that she was seeing *something*, had been forced to, she was less unnerved by the ghost of Lillian Gladwell—it was actually a relief that she hadn't imagined all those things—and more unnerved by the guilt she felt. She'd seen herself as a caretaker for so long that to confront her complicity in an action that really harmed Emily made her gut twist up. She had refused to see so many things, her own daughter, and what she'd done to her, among them. It was uncomfortable to sit in a space where every day, every hour, she was reminded that she'd taken something from Emily. There were moments when she wished she could go back in time, to correct her horrible mistake by never hiding anything from Emily. And there were also moments where she wished she could go back in time and pick a new place for them to move to, never bringing her daughter to Larrissa. She remembered what her own mother had told her once, one of the few pieces of advice that survived all these years: you can do anything for a short amount of time that you can't do forever. Gracie tried to take that to heart, hoping one day they'd all feel better.

•

That evening, Emily went up to her room and then refused dinner. She told her mother she was fine, just tired. "Tired, and tired of thinking," Emily had said with a sad smile. Gracie had eaten by herself and then tried to watch TV. That didn't entertain her, so she began to read the Gladwell book Emily had let her borrow. When the themes of history and identity started to overwhelm her, Gracie tried to go to bed but could not sleep.

Now she sat on her bed with the wooden box of Emily's adoption paperwork in her lap. The hairpin she'd bent back and mangled trying to pick the lock was in her right hand, and in a fit of frustration, she threw it at the wall. When Emily had first come home with her and Irene, she'd thrown away the key, thinking she could literally lock away the past. She'd been a fool to think so. Now she had a locked box that she wanted to open and couldn't.

Gracie had asked her daughter why she thought her illness had resolved itself, why Emily could "cross" now, and Emily had said that she'd never been ill. She'd been erased, she said, and that if something isn't there, it can't move.

It had been a puzzling statement, another one of Emily's cryptic insights. It said something, but *what* it said, Gracie was unsure. Gracie wondered how much damage she'd done. How much of that erasure Emily mentioned was achieved through her actions, or inaction. Maybe she should just give Emily the box? Let her decide what she wanted to do with it? Gracie wasn't sure.

She got up and put the box back in the chest. Looked out the window into the dark yard and the tops of other houses. She felt alien in her own life. She felt detached, an observer, not Gracie Howard at all, but an unnamed woman in another town, in another time.

•

She knew exactly how she'd gotten to this point, could map her life with all its timelines to explain how she was here, in Larissa, at this exact moment. But at the same time, knowing *how* did not explain *why.*

Gracie did not like to ask *why*. Had avoided asking *why* her entire life. What was the point? Why speculate when the speculation just led to more unanswerable questions? Now she found herself asking *why* and rationalizing some answers while becoming increasingly angry at others.

Why had Norman Donald tried to rape her all those years ago? Because he was entitled? Because he had no feelings? Because that was how she was meant to meet George, a savior, and then her husband?

Why had she never come to see her mother when she was dying? Was it really because she was afraid to leave Emily with Irene? Or was it because death felt too threatening to face? Because it was easier to not be affected if not forced to confront death directly? Was it because she didn't care enough about her mother?

Why had her mother not asked for her? Was it because she didn't want to burden her daughter? Was it because of something more unsettling? That it didn't matter to her if she saw her daughter or not? The daughter who had abandoned her first, after all, moving to Oklahoma and never visiting, rarely calling?

Why had she lost Beatrice? What had she done to be punished in that way? Punished with no sense of time, she thought, because maybe fate had been looking forward, to Emily.

And why *had* she adopted Emily? Was it because she wanted to replace Beatrice? Was it because she wanted to replace George? Or was it because truly, when she saw Emily on the lawn of the school, she realized her capacity to love had not been destroyed after all?

Gracie rubbed her forehead and closed her eyes. Her thoughts were a loop, a terrible ouroboros, constantly devouring itself.

Now she'd been sitting on the porch for hours, in the full dark, and Gracie was thinking about Irene. Wondering if the woman had changed at all since Gracie and Emily had left. Wondering if that last letter Irene had sent would be the end. Would she ever talk to Irene again? Did she even want to? No, she knew. She didn't want anything to do with Irene Howard ever again. The woman was better left to be a memory. Not even that.

Looking down Bell Street, at first, when Gracie saw the figure, she thought she was seeing another ghost. The apparition walked slowly, its white gown hanging loose to its ankles. Its hair was straight down the back, breaking in parts over stooped shoulders. But then Gracie thought that the ghost she knew of was in Cedar House, not out on Bell Street, and she knew she was seeing a woman.

Gracie got up out of the wicker chair and went down off the steps. Looked at her watch to see the time was almost midnight.

"Are you okay?" Gracie called. The woman was coming straight for her, calling out to her, her voice slicing the night.

"Lillian?" the woman called, stumbling.

Gracie began to run, and she caught Mrs. Habbermire under the armpits as the older woman was going down onto her knees.

"What are you doing?" Gracie asked, trying to get Mrs. Habbermire back to her feet. "Oh my God. Look at you."

"We have to help her," Mrs. Habbermire was saying. "Help her. Help her. Help her."

Gracie slung one of her aunt's arms across her shoulders and was trying to get her to the front yard of Cedar House. From the sidewalk Gracie saw the light in Emily's room come on, and then the girl's figure in the window.

Emily met them at the door, holding it open as Gracie got Mrs. Habbermire over the threshold and into the foyer.

"Let me go!" Mrs. Habbermire said, wresting her body from Gracie's. "Lillian! Lillian!"

"Stop it," Gracie was saying. "Just calm down."

"Lillian!" Mrs. Habbermire had thrown open the double doors to the library.

"She's coming," Emily said.

Gracie felt something. A stir of air. She would have missed it if Emily had not just said what she did.

And then Mrs. Habbermire was holding an invisible body, saying, "I thought I'd lost you. Lillian. Lillian."

Mrs. Habbermire began to cry hysterically, and nothing Gracie or Emily did could calm her. She was talking rubbish, words that were not words, and sentences that made no sense.

When Gracie tried to touch her shoulder, to bring the woman into the living room to sit down, Mrs. Habbermire lashed out and scratched her face.

Gracie backed up, hand to her cheek, shocked at her aunt's behavior. Mrs. Habbermire rushed towards her, slipping on the newspaper sheets Emily had left on the floor, sliding into Gracie, and taking her down. Mrs. Habbermire's balled fists found purchase with Gracie's chest, and her face, and her arms, until Gracie was able to roll the other woman over, screaming all the while for Emily to call the police.

By the time they arrived, Mrs. Habbermire had curled up on herself and was lying by the fireplace.

•

The next morning, Emily was in the kitchen. She'd made Gracie's coffee and was now making scrambled eggs.

"How are you doing?" she asked. "You look awful."

"Thanks," Gracie said flatly, stepping into the downstairs bathroom to look at her face. There were three ragged scratches down one cheek, and a bruise had formed on her forehead.

"I hope she's okay," Emily said when her mother returned. "Can we call the hospital later? And ask after her?"

That's where the police had taken Mrs. Habbermire. Gracie worried if she'd had a mental breakdown, but for the life of her, she couldn't understand what had brought it on, and she said as much to Emily.

Her daughter didn't answer, but seemed to be listening, again, to someone Gracie couldn't see.

"Do you know something?" Gracie asked, filling a mug and sitting down at the table.

"I know all sorts of things."

"About Mrs. Habbermire. Don't be coy." Gracie said this sharper than she meant to and then apologized. "It's just ..." she started. "It's just, there's something missing. She knew Lillian. Must have. Something's happened to make her fixate on the Gladwells, or break down, or ... I don't know," Gracie sighed. "I just want to know what happened. I look back at everything now. Her suggesting the house, her getting it ready, all the stuff I donated to the Historical Society, and there's a part of the story I don't have yet. I don't understand."

Emily did not say anything to Gracie. No insight. No revelation. As she listened to the spatula scrape against the bottom of the pan, Gracie thought of what Emily had said about Lillian Gladwell's death: *It's a gap. It needs to be filled.*

•

The doctor called Gracie and told her he thought it was very possible her aunt had a series of strokes. He said Rebekah wasn't seeing anything now—no delusion—and Gracie had bitten her tongue at the word, *delusion.* She knew Lillian was there, somewhere, thought that it hadn't been a delusion at all, but rather something she simply wasn't allowed to see. Mrs. Habbermire, he told her, could go home in a few days, but she couldn't be left alone. Could Gracie stay with her? Or could Mrs. Habbermire stay with *her?*

It wouldn't be ideal, Gracie knew, to live with Rebekah. She'd have to have Rebekah live with her, here, in Cedar House, where everything was a mess, a torturous, confused mess with Emily. But it would only be for a short time, she told herself, and she owed it to Rebekah, for everything the woman had done.

Gracie called the police station to request help getting into Mrs. Habbermire's home to collect some things.

By the time Gracie got to the house, the police had sent over a locksmith, and he was escorted by a woman Gracie recognized. It was the woman she'd seen outside the hardware store not that long ago.

"Hello," Gracie said slowly, looking between the woman and locksmith. Inside Mrs. Habbermire's house, she could hear a cat meowing. "I'm Gracie. Rebekah's niece."

"You have some identification, ma'am? I can't—"

"It's Gracie Howard," she told him. "I can vouch for her."

"And you are ..." Gracie asked.

"Bet. Bettye Donald."

"As in ... Norman Donald?" Gracie asked, and the woman nodded.

Gracie wasn't sure how to respond. How to react. This was the woman who married Norman? Did she know what kind of man she lived with? Gracie hoped—for this woman's sake—that Norman had righted himself in the years she was away.

"Our children know each other," Bet finally said, filling the silence that had opened between them. "My son is Will."

"Yes, they do know each other, don't they?" Gracie eked out. Lord, it couldn't get worse, but it had. Emily's only friend, Norman's child. She wanted to scream, but instead said, "Will, he seems like a really nice boy."

"He is. He is."

While the locksmith worked, Gracie tried to look at Bet without being too obvious, and she suspected that Bet was trying to do the same with her.

It was too awkward, and it was obvious—the studying of each other—so to break the silence, Gracie asked, "I don't want to seem rude. Forgive me if it's rude to ask. But what exactly are you doing here?"

"I work for Marcil," Bet said, and when Gracie didn't reply, she added, "I work for the police."

Gracie couldn't believe it. Norman's wife worked for the very people who could have put him in jail all those years ago. What was she then? A woman stronger than Gracie? Weaker? Complicit? How could any woman marry Norman Donald?

"Alright!" The locksmith stood up, turned the doorknob, and smiled. "In you go."

Gracie stepped up onto the porch and over the open bag of tools.

"Whoops. Sorry." The man bent down to collect his bag. "While you're in there I'll just switch this out right quick. That way you can have a key."

Gracie nodded and cracked the door open. She was immediately accosted by a small, tortoiseshell cat that squeezed through the opening. "Shit," she said.

"I got it." Gracie turned to see Bettye holding the cat.

"I guess bring it in here," Gracie relented, pushing at the front door that seemed to be partially blocked on the other side.

When both women were in Mrs. Habbermire's home, Gracie closed the door and sighed. "What in the world is this?"

Mrs. Habbermire's house was a catastrophe. None of the furniture made sense. The sofa was in the middle of the room and the carpet had been folded in half but was still on the floor. One chair was turned on its side, and the other had been put on top of the coffee table.

"I wouldn't think she was strong enough to even do this," Gracie mused.

Bettye stooped to put the cat on the ground, and it took off into the kitchen.

Gracie moved through the room, following the cat. In the kitchen, there were boxes on the floor, on the counter, on the table. The cat's water and food bowls were empty.

"Was she moving?" Bettye asked, picking up one of the cat's small, plastic dishes and filling it from the sink. The cat jumped up on the counter and purred loudly.

"Not that I know of," Gracie admitted. "And I just can't make sense of ... this."

"It's a mess," Bettye said. The woman was opening cabinet doors.

"What are you doing?" Gracie asked her, taken aback by the way the woman was going through Mrs. Habbermire's things.

"Looking for cat food. Poor thing is starving."

Gracie watched Bettye look for the food, but when Bettye turned up empty, Gracie opened the fridge to see if she could find anything. The only cat appropriate food was milk, which Gracie thought she remembered cats liking, and so she filled the other dish with that. The cat went to it immediately.

"Look," Bettye began. "I don't have to be in here. I can wait outside."

"No, no, it's fine. It's fine. I just need to get her some clothes. I think the bedroom is upstairs. Just give me a minute," she said, fleeing Norman's wife.

Up in Mrs. Habbermire's bedroom, Gracie opened the small closet and began to choose items. She recognized one of the hanging dresses, one her mother used to wear, and when she pulled it out, the scent of lilac tickled her nose. Gracie wondered how many things of her mother's Rebekah had kept. If maybe, after all, it wasn't too late to recover something for herself.

But she didn't want to dawdle in Rebekah's house now, not with Bettye Donald roaming around.

When Gracie finally came back down with the bag of clothes, she was wondering how she was going to transport the cat to Cedar House when Bettye called for her. It was strange to hear her name coming from the woman's mouth, and it sent chills up Gracie's arms.

"Bettye?" She asked tentatively at the bottom of the stairs.

"In here."

Gracie set the luggage down and went into the room to the left of the living room, what looked to be an office.

The cat was sitting on a large wooden desk, and Bettye was in the desk chair. Gracie stepped into the room and looked around. "I'm ready," she said. "I just have to figure out how to get the cat—"

"Gracie. Come look at this."

Gracie walked through the room and took what Bettye had in her hands, a silver picture frame. At first she didn't quite comprehend what she was seeing. It was a picture of Rebekah when she was much younger, but the other woman in the photo was too small, was a slightly different shade of grey.

"It's not one photo," Bettye said. "It's two. She put them together."

"Why would she do that?" Gracie asked, scrutinizing the picture. It looked like Rebekah was in a wedding dress.

"There's this too," Bettye added, tapping the papers on the desk. "It makes sense now."

"What makes sense now," Gracie asked, beginning to get angry that Bettye was not speaking plainly.

"Read it," Bettye said.

"I don't have time," Gracie told her. "I need to figure out how to get the cat over to the house and then I need to start putting a room together and—"

"They were lovers," Bettye observed. "Your aunt and Lillian Gladwell." The woman stated it like a fact or mundane piece of information. Like she's just said the sky was blue or her shoes were ready to be picked up from the cobbler.

Gracie felt her face flush, and she reached for the papers. "You had no right to read these," she said. Gracie didn't know exactly what the papers were, but they clearly said something that made Bettye think what she just said.

"I'm sorry. I know I didn't. I didn't know what they were until ... I'll go now," Bettye said. "My recommendation is to just empty one of the boxes and put the cat in it. It might complain, but it'll keep it out of the floorboard of the car."

Once the other woman had left, Gracie sat at the desk and looked down at the stack of papers. Mrs. Habbermire had struck through all the existing type with a dark blue pen and had written in cramped hand between the lines. The script was so tiny Gracie had to squint to read it.

"There are many kinds of love," Rebekah had written. "The Greeks had four words for love. My husband taught me that. And even though philia meant brotherly love, there was no such word meant only for women. One might say that philia could apply to either sex, but we know this is not true. I know this is not true, because utility and pleasure are not true friendships. Real friendship cannot be expressed in words. Only in action, in thought, and in the body."

•

When she was done her eyes were aching and her head was pounding. She didn't know what to do with the information, whether she should treat it as fact or fiction. But if it was true, it would explain many things: the rift between Rebekah and Gracie's mother and perhaps why Thomas Gladwell had killed his wife. But the more Gracie thought on this, the more holes appeared.

For the affair to have caused the problem between sisters, it meant Mrs. Habbermire would have told Gracie's mother about the whole thing. But maybe Gracie was underestimating the closeness they used to have. Afterall, she never knew them together before the gulf had opened between the two women. And for the Gladwells—Thomas Gladwell hadn't shot Lillian until much later in life. But what had Rebekah said? She'd claimed Thomas Gladwell had been sick with syphilis. Maybe his brain truly had rotted, was stuck in the past, where Rebekah and Lillian loved each other.

Gracie didn't know what to do with the papers. She wanted to pretend she hadn't found them, but that felt impossible because Bettye Donald had seen them too. Even if she burned them, Mrs. Habbermire's narrative couldn't be completely untold.

She went to open the desk drawer, prepared to put them away—to hide them—until she could think through how to handle the situation. But when she tugged on the knob, it stuck. She jiggled it, but it wouldn't come undone.

Maybe this was the world's way of telling her to take them? To find a safe place for the story Rebekah had told?

"Why does it matter?" she asked the cat that was brushing up alongside her thigh.

But it did matter, she knew, because as she looked back down, her eyes began to discern what had been struck through. As she read what Rebekah had tried to erase, she discovered this was not just Rebekah's story, but Thomas Gladwell's story as well. The one about Larissa that Emily had been reading.

18

Restless Scaffolding

—Bet—

Bet was laughing so hard Norman called her crazy.

"What the hell is wrong with you?" he asked, which made Bet double over, one hand on the counter to keep herself upright, tears in her eyes, nose snotting an ugly bubble. "You can't be a cop!"

It had been a long time since Norman had hit her, and the lunacy of the situation, that he had assaulted a police officer without even thinking about it—because she was a woman, still, just his wife—was the world's way of making dark humor.

"See," she said, voice low, finally catching her breath. "I knew you were still the same man I married."

"Don't let being right go to your head." Norman was out of the kitchen then, going to the car. Going somewhere, anywhere, that Bet was not.

In the bathroom, Bet examined her cheek in the mirror, three lines of red fingers against her white skin.

She'd hoped by the time she was out of the shower, they would have paled enough that she could cover them with makeup.

•

She knew Marcil was, as most of the men were, out at the farm. Working around the clock, talking to every living soul up at Mrs. White's and some besides, remote neighbors who were coming out of the woodwork. Marcil had said finding Georgia was a blessing in disguise. That Marjorie could have been washed down from any of the tributaries, but that Georgia told them exactly which one it was. Pleaman's Creek, running right through the farm, indicated whoever had taken the girls, and probably Rita too, had known the property well enough to not only snatch a girl right from it, but to dispose of her there too.

Bet had balked at his words, "a blessing in disguise." She doubted Georgia's parents felt that way. *She* didn't feel that way, even if it meant the police had their first lead, which, she reminded herself, didn't seem much like a lead at all.

Marcil said it pointed to someone at the farm. Someone in the workers' own community. Even the newspaper had picked up on it, some reporter suggesting that one of Mrs. White's workers could be a culprit, starting at the farm and expanding into Larissa. But Bet had seen their faces, and she doubted the culprit was one of their own. Not only that, but Marcil and the whole town it seemed like was forgetting that Rita hadn't even been at the farm when she was taken. When she disappeared. She was *in* Larissa, shopping with women. And there was Marlene Cooper, too. Bet didn't know how the older girl fit into all of it, but when Marcil had handed her the Friday paper, the 4th of July paper she'd never read because the day had been too busy with her own family misery, she'd learned Marlene was also Indian. Three girls out of four. It was too much to be coincidence.

Bet couldn't stand being in the kitchen, so she sat on the floor in the living room with the atlas in front of her, a pencil in her left hand. She felt all this was up to her somehow. That she needed to prove herself to both the men in Larissa, and to Jean Stock too, who was going to bury her daughter this very day, leaving her body in a town the family would abandon in a few months. She needed to prove herself to Katherine Cooper and Patty Randall as well, because their daughters were still missing. And Bet felt like even though people were looking for the girls, they were looking more for the man who took them.

Most conversations in the police station were about a killer, and what he might be like: a possible pedophile, a vagrant, maybe someone who had been in Larissa long enough to understand where easy prey played, but surely not a longtime resident. When she was out and about, catching snippets of gossip, the people of Larissa were reporting what they'd done to ensure their *own* safety: new locks on doors and windows, children restricted to fenced backyards, no more evening bike rides or weekend campouts. Sometimes, if a resident noticed Bet nearby, they'd avert their eyes as if ashamed they weren't somehow doing more to help find the missing girls. The mother of one of Alton's classmates at least had the decency to apologize when Bet walked into the beauty parlor one day and heard the woman speculating about what *unholy impulses* drove *the murderer* to seek out and extinguish the youth.

Her eyes drifted away from the area on the map around the farm and to the southeast side of town, where she had grown up. She'd only ever lived in two houses: this one, bought the week she was married, and the squat, one-story ranch her parents owned before moving, which butted up against the Feverview Farm with its chickens and the two donkeys, Hazel and Butter, to protect them. She used to walk to the fence line and call for them when she was little, trying to feed them cornsilk and apple cores. Their lips and teeth had frightened her—moving all over the place, faux-snarls chomping at her refuse.

Bet looked at Tally Street now, tracing a finger along the line, trying to remember how she'd ridden her bike to school. At the intersection of Tally and Dixon she stopped, tapping the paper. Dixon used to dead-end there, a T of roads. Beyond the split rail fence was pastureland with its lonely peach tree. The fruit there had been free game, since no one used the land or the rundown shack. No, not a shack. A depot. Nothing but coarse wood planks and an opening for a doorway. A little piece of nothing between Larissa and Huntsville, part of the old Missouri—Kansas—Texas railroad that had been abandoned in the late 1800s when a new line was extended. Bet remembered some boys in her youth claiming that depot was haunted by the souls of slaves who died on their journey.

Now it looked like all that land had been bought up and developed. Bet didn't recognize any of the street names, but she knew the houses there would be small and similar, built fast over the years to accommodate Larissa's booming population.

She leaned back against Norman's armchair and drew a big circle around the new neighborhoods, thinking about whatever parts of

Larissa had been lost over the years. What other spaces had been paved over or forgotten about.

•

Bet changed into her dungarees and boots. Then she begged her neighbor's car and drove slowly down back roads north of town, sometimes with her head all the way out the window so she could see where dirt gave way to grass. She looked at the foliage too, looking for pathways that might have been overgrown and neglected. She was about a quarter mile from where FM 2236 hit Highway 86 when she spotted what she wanted and stopped the car.

There were no fences here, not west of the farm where Mrs. White's property met the oil company, separated by a small county road. To her right was a gap. Not a very noticeable one, not like the one off Dixon, only recently abandoned. The gap here was only there if one wanted to see it: the way the plants had too much space between them, the way if you looked just right, not straight on but at a 45-degree angle, they curved the perfect, narrow path. The trees were not so many that one would see what had been there, but now Bet knew what she was looking for: a road fallen off maps, forgotten in its disuse. Found, or remembered, by someone murdering little girls.

She parked, got out, crossed the road, and started trudging through the underbrush. "Like a Guide," she thought, "going to get my tracker patch."

Bet walked for close to twenty minutes, eyes surveying the ground. She didn't need to be an Indian to understand the branch snapped off at door height or to comprehend the meaning of flattened grass made by tire tracks.

When she arrived at Pleaman's Creek, she was stopped by what could have been a bridge, at some point in time, if it hadn't been so mangled and rotten. Nothing was left of the wood that should have been over the water, just broken planks jutting over one side, the weeds growing up between them, yellow dandelion flowers sprouting with the recent rain.

She found Lone Star beer cans, some crushed by booted feet and some just dented and full of rainwater. Bet poked through the underbrush with a stick she'd snapped off a tree, moving grass and jabbing at mud. She finally waded into the creek bed, her boots sucking into the earth and making it hard to walk.

Finally, her stick caught on something, and as Bet squinted, she could see whatever she'd found was right at the surface, sticking half out of the clay and colored like the sediment around it.

It was a shoe, though it hardly looked like one all covered in muck. Bet discarded her stick and dunked the shoe into the water, swishing it around, clearing off the mud that crusted it.

Small and well-worn, it was a child's shoe, a little red half boot made of leather. Bet couldn't tell if it was a girl's or boy's boot, but maybe it didn't matter for the people at Mrs. White's farm. Maybe they wore whatever they had.

Bet set the shoe on the ledge of the riverbank, the sharp edge where earth had broken off and been carried away with the rains. She got on her hands and knees, slopping through the mud, digging her hands into its wetness and coming up with great globs of it that she spread on the ground, looking for the shoe's lost mate. As the sludge was coming apart in her hands, another item was revealing itself, and Bet knew right away it was fabric. She held it up, shaking it, little droplets of muck splattering her shirt and arms.

At first she thought it might be a glove, but as she unfolded the item, she realized it was a pair of girl's underwear. Bet could see the thick edge of strained stitching, a bit of ragged lace around the leg holes.

•

The men were interested in the mystery of the underwear, which girl they had belonged to. Bet was the one who told them it had to be Rita's, and she did so trying to hide her disdain. "They're too small for Georgia," she said. The panties were laying on a plastic bag on the conference room table.

There was a tension strung between the police officers in the room, some congratulating Bet on what she'd found, like she'd just won a heavy hand of poker, and some who put their chins up at her, refusing to admit she'd done anything to help. And to be fair, Bet told herself, she hadn't actually done anything, yet. It's not like she'd found Rita, or had saved her.

They were talking now about who might have known about that old road. Someone at the farm, certainly. Or someone who worked for the oil company. Bet couldn't understand why they were here at all, talking about maybes when there was a small girl still out there, waiting to be found. She wanted to yell at them, to pull them up out of their chairs by the backs of their shirts and demand they get back to the stream, but Marcil hadn't even told them he'd hired her yet, and Bet knew the hierarchy of the boy's club. Better not overstep now, lest she risk their wrath later on.

While they debated the likelihood of someone from the farm being the abductor, while they wondered how many of the people "out there" had cars, or a criminal history in their hometown, Bet was unnerved that she'd spent her whole life in Larissa and now its history was yawning up in front of her, a history she felt like she should know, but didn't. Some parts of the town were disappearing, and others were rising from the dead. Bet was thinking about the book Marjorie had on her when she was taken. The one about the Killough Massacre where the local Cherokee had cut down pioneers. She was thinking about seemingly endless cycles of violence that transcend time, about how now it was Indian girls who were dying, and for the first time in a long time, she found herself praying to God.

She'd given that up a long time ago. Given up church, too. Given up any pretense of belief. All the asking she used to do of the almighty had gone unanswered. But here she was again, pleading to the unseen. Asking Him to intervene. To keep the circle of history from coming back round again.

•

Bet had just stomped down her cigarette when she heard the phone ringing inside. For a minute she thought she wouldn't answer. She was tired and hot from doing the laundry and wanted nothing more than to lie on her bed with the fan whirling above her, perhaps, even, in just her underwear.

But then she picked it up, and it was Marcil. He wanted her to do something for him. He wanted her to meet a locksmith and verify that the person going to Mrs. Habbermire's home was indeed a relative. "Didn't even know she had anyone left," Marcil said. "Thought when her sister died that was it."

"Mrs. Habbermire?" Bet asked. "What happened to her?" She didn't know the old woman well, but they had been friendly back when Bet was in the Garden Club, and Bet always waved to the woman when she walked by the Historical Society.

"Had some kind of attack," Marcil said. "Was half out of her mind last night and is now up at the hospital."

Bet hoped the woman was okay, and agreed to go to her house.

But when she arrived and was waiting with the man who would let them in, Mrs. Habbermire's cat sitting just inside the house and screeching through the window at them, Bet was shocked when she saw who it was walking up the sidewalk. It was Gracie Howard. She'd forgotten about who Mrs. Habbermire's niece should have been. Bet looked skyward and thought, *you bastard.* As if it wasn't bad enough that Will was friendly with Gracie's daughter. Now she had to be friendly with the girl's mother.

Bet had banned Gracie's name. Norman was always comparing her to the woman early in the marriage, in sly ways, subtle ways, that told Bet Norman had been slighted and still felt cold about it. Gracie McCallin, because that's who she was before she married George. She was a prize for sure, and one Norman lost. Always dressed in the best clothes, her mother making her custom dresses that fell just right, accentuated her small waist and ample chest. It had taken Bet many years to stop hating the idea of Gracie, and that only started to happen once Gracie married George and the whole family had gone to Oklahoma.

Now that Gracie was back, Bet couldn't seem to escape the woman.

•

It was evening by the time she arrived home, and she was lost in thought about Mrs. Habbermire, about Cedar House and Lillian Gladwell.

Mrs. Habbermire had written, "There are many kinds of love. The Greeks had four words for love. My husband taught me that. And even though philia meant brotherly love, there was no such word for women."

Bet felt tears forming and she stood looking at her front door, trying to compose herself before walking in. She didn't want her boys to see her crying. Didn't want Norman to either, because she'd made a decision right then to never show weakness to him again. She didn't know how lonely she'd felt until she'd read Rebekah's story.

When she came into the house, the TV was on, but no one was watching it. She turned off the set and walked down the hallway to the boys' room. Empty. Her own bedroom was empty as well.

"Will?" She called. "Alton?"

In the kitchen, Bet looked out the windows and saw her children around the fire pit with their father. They were all decked out in their Guides attire and had hotdogs over the flame. Norman had taken away their campout in Wichita, but here they were, having their own.

Alton was talking and gesturing with his hands, his skewer waving around wildly. The hotdog flew off the end and landed a few feet from him, and Norman laughed hard, throwing his head back. Will didn't seem to find it funny at all and somberly sat in his camp chair while looking down at his hands.

Norman hadn't been able to keep good on his threat. Maybe they weren't with the rest of the troop, but here they were, pretending something similar. Maybe he did it to get back at Bet. To stick it to her in some way because she was asserting her independence. Or maybe he'd forgiven Alton for the boy's adventure. But forgiveness wasn't something to be given; it was something to be earned. Or maybe it was both. Either way, she had more than her fair share of marks against the Donald men—*men*—she realized, her boys were nothing but men in disguises, and she was getting all rustled up inside thinking about this.

It's a trap, Bet thought suddenly. She felt her face heating up and she clamped her jaw down tight. For the first time she found herself wondering what life without Norman would be like. If her new job would provide enough income for her to live without him. How Will and Alton would react to not having their father around all the time.

If it would make them hate her, and if they might turn out to be better people because of it.

19

Wilderness Dirge

—Candice—

There had never been so many funerals in such a short period of time, not in all of Candice's life. Marjorie Kent, Georgia Stock, and her own girl, June.

And then it was happening quick, all while Candice was sitting on the back porch, unable to move because her body was so heavy with loss. Tom was coming with the baby, Della, as soon as the infant could travel. Rose coming, too, and her husband RD. Candice's mother even, Salida. All coming to Larissa.

Everett had talked to her, and Candice had listened but could not bring herself to respond. All week, every time she wanted to say something, she felt her throat seizing up. And being unable to speak, she'd shake or nod her head instead.

Everett said this was the family's way of repairing itself. That sometimes a death was also a healing. Candice knew that he wanted to believe this, that he was starting to believe it with every repetition he uttered.

But all she could think about was her own baby being buried up north, that lonely body in a cemetery no one would ever visit, not after Tom was gone.

"She's beautiful," Rose said over the phone Candice cradled to her face. "Thin as a rail but she'll plump up." And then, "oh, mama, I miss her. I miss her so much," and both women were crying, matching their gasps into the phone.

Candice and Everett spent their nights in the girls' bedroom, facing each other across the small gap between the single beds. They'd talked about it, having Tom and Della move in with them. Everett would build another bedroom onto the back of the house, and in the meantime, Tom would share this room with Della, and they'd put the rest of their money into the Cooper house just a few blocks over. All of that money Candice had been saving working for the Howards, and continuing to work for them, she'd said, would go towards a home for Rose, RD, and Salida. It would be tight for a long time, she knew, but they'd done it before—the stretching, the planning. And they'd do it again.

Katherine and her husband were moving. Even Everett didn't know if they were leaving town or just leaving the house. "Maybe," he said, "it's just too much being there."

Everett closed the diner the day of Georgia's funeral. Candice didn't ask him too, but he did anyway, putting up a sign on the door with the newspaper article taped to it, the one which said how Georgia had been found, a blip of writing on the third page. All day they worked in their house, cleaning it up to get it ready for their family. Everett washed bedding that had been stored away and then clipped the billowing sheets to the line out back. Candice swept and mopped floors, wiped out sinks and cleaned the toilet. They said little, but labored in sync. Everett noticed when the dirty water in Candice's bucket needed to be changed and took care of it for her. Candice saw Everett pulling washcloths from the closet and made the lemon and vinegar cleaner for the windows. When Candice collapsed on the floor, unable to keep herself from crying, Everett mirrored her.

•

The husbands put in their notice and used their last paychecks, selling off the little furniture they had, even the crib June had bought, to buy a jalopy that all four of them could fit in for the drive back down south. Tom kept the Moses basket, though, saying June put too much of herself into the embroidery.

Everett offered the phone to Candice and she shook her head. He mouthed, *it's Rose,* and Candice mouthed back, *not right now.* She'd decided it was time to see Katherine Cooper. She'd been a coward for far too long and only realized it now that both mothers were lost in loss.

On the way over, Candice wondered how Katherine would react to her. She hadn't seen Marlene's mother since the Fourth of July, and even though she and Everett had driven by the Cooper house many times since then, she'd never seen anyone coming or going. The house had been shut up tight, though Everett assured her they still lived there; he'd seen Charles just the other day at the bank.

When she arrived, she took a moment to straighten her dress and then adjusted her hat. When Katherine opened the door, the home's interior smelled like winter, like wood recently burned. And warm spices: vanilla, cinnamon.

"Hello, Katherine," Candice said.

"Candy, it's good to see you."

Katherine wore no makeup, and there were dark circles under her eyes. She didn't smile, but she did reach out for Candice, and both women stood in the doorway, holding each other.

•

Katherine Cooper knew about June, and said that she didn't believe Marlene was gone, but that she understood, in part at least, what it felt like to lose a daughter. Candice was quick to reply that she didn't think Marlene had passed either, that she still had hope, and Katherine said, "But she's not here, is she? It feels like a loss right now, even when I tell myself it's not. You see all this," she said, motioning to the mess of house around her—boxes and packing paper and various household objects all lined up against the wall—"We have to sell the place. It's the only way to afford a private detective. The new place is ... We're moving in with my sister, and her husband, for the time being. We have to leave Larissa."

"What if she comes back here?" Candice worried aloud.

Katherine sighed. "We just can't afford to stay. It's taking all we have and more to get our campaign mounted. Besides, your family will be here. If Marlene comes back, I know you'll call me right away."

Candice felt like Katherine was saying something but not saying it. Maybe suggesting she was glad it was Candice's family, because they were Indian, too. But Katherine didn't know Salida. She knew Salida was Candice's mother. She did not know Salida didn't see herself as Cherokee.

"I hate it, though," Katherine admitted, touching the rag she had tied up around her hair and sitting down in one of the living room chairs. It was an invitation, maybe, to continue talking, and Candice grasped at it.

"We miss you at church," she said.

"It's nice to know *someone* does. Once Sam came back without Marlene, I started to feel like I didn't know any of those people anymore. All smiles and white teeth, wishing us well, but when they weren't talking to me, they never talked about Marlene. If Marlene wasn't being talked about right then, she wasn't there at all. Like dogs in a thunderstorm, those women. Putting their heads under the bed with their rumps sticking out, thinking just because they're not looking at something it isn't there."

Candice couldn't help but laugh at the image, and Katherine smiled weakly.

"I'm thinking all the best things I can," Katherine continued. "But it's hard. And sometimes I almost lose faith. With Georgia, and Rita ..." Katherine didn't finish her thought.

"You've been up there? At the farm? Talking with their mothers?"

Katherine nodded. "It's good," she said. "Not to be alone. Sometimes I don't know who is helping who. If it's me helping them, or them helping me."

"Does Charles go with you?"

Katherine nodded. "He does. We've been spending more and more time up there. And every time we drive by Mrs. White's house, it's a punch to the gut. I don't know how much money she has—I think it's a lot—and she pays them almost nothing, Candice. But they come out each year anyway. You know why?"

"Why?"

"I always thought it was because they just, I don't know. Didn't have options. I mean, some don't. Not everyone out there is Indian, anyway. But the ones who are, they come back every year because so many of them were *born* there."

"At the farm?" Candice was shocked, never once thinking of the farm as anything more than a waystop.

"A dozen people, Candice. Born in those ugly little cabins. All within a few years of each other. Back when that land was being cleared for planting, a whole bunch of people lived there, full time. Choctaw, Cherokee, Chickasaw, and Creek, too. Mrs. White's daddy lured them all out, telling them they could one day buy those piece of shit houses and make a home here."

Candice's heart sank, knowing exactly what had happened. That they'd never been able to afford the land, or the houses on it, and had probably moved on eventually to other local places where they might be able to survive.

"A part of me thought it was odd, Katherine said. Them coming back here. But I talked to one of the elders one Sunday, and she told me that it didn't matter to her who her family worked for, whether it was some white lady in Larissa or if it was some white man in Fort Worth. It was still gonna be a white person, because white people were never going to give up what they took. Not just land, but the ability to make a living. She said that at least, out on the farm, she could show her grandchildren how to live. That far from the city, she could pretend, for a time, that the way of her ancestors wasn't disappearing. They still make kanuchi out there. Pound the hickory nuts into paste in pestles made of logs. Still hunt too, in those woods along the creek."

This made sense. Candice craved the past as well, even if it was for other reasons.

"But," Katherine said, "Rita and Georgia change everything. It's not the same to them anymore, with the girls gone. And Marlene. Everywhere I look I see Marlene. She's a phantom I can't shake, and I, some days, I can't imagine staying in Larissa anyway, watching her never grow up, just a child even when I'm grey and hobbled."

•

Later, after Everett came home and together they were packing up the girls' room, folding sheets, putting belongings into boxes that would be stored, Candice told him what Katherine had said, and wondered aloud about Ida Rose, and if it was possible that she herself might have long lost family out at the farm.

"Did you want to name Rose after her?" Everett asked, pulling a pillow out of its case. "I never did ask. Didn't really think about it until recently. Rose is a popular name."

Candice had asked herself this question many times over the years, and truthfully, she did not know the answer. Maybe some part of her had channeled Ida Rose when she was pregnant, because it was that winter that Salida had brought out *her* photo album and taken her daughter on a trip through the past in a rare moment of vulnerability, showing her the photos Candice's father had taken with the Simplex he was so proud of. He'd run a good business then, a mechanic by trade with his own rented garage he worked in until the year Candice turned nineteen—the year a car crushed him.

"This is the house you were born in," her mother had said, showing Candice a photo of an impossibly leaning home, added onto in odd places, the wood siding matching up horizontally along one side and then, in the front, a haphazard crisscross. "It wasn't so bad when we lived there," Salida said. "You see that porch? Perfect for avoiding the sun. Used to sit out there and talk with the neighborhood women until after the sun went down. We left when you were five, because your daddy was tired of living in the middle of nowhere. But he took this picture a few years later, when he bought the camera and we went back for my mother's funeral. He wanted to remember it. The house where we had you. I think we were the last tenants there. Went to hell in a handbasket with no one living in it."

Candice had mentioned Enola then, and begun to ask questions. Her mother had opened a door to telling, and with the opportunity, with Salida finally saying something of the past, Candice wanted to reach out into it. When Candice asked her mother about Ida Rose, Salida had said she never knew the woman.

Ida Rose.

Candice now knew, with the certainty one has in sudden moments of epiphany while grieving, that Ida Rose had been with her for a long time, even if she hadn't been able to see her.

•

"I'm not calling to beg you back. Take all the time you need. I was just hoping you were doing alright."

It was Gracie Howard on the other end of the line.

"Let me talk to her!" Candice heard Emily say, and then Gracie added, "Emily wants to say hello."

"Hello!"

The girl practically yelled into the phone and Candice pulled the receiver away from her face. "Hello, Emily. Are you feeling alright?"

"Right as rain. But it's you I'm worried about. I had a dream about you and when I got up, I made mother call. I didn't have your phone number."

Candice thought of Emily at the kitchen table, swinging her legs, Gracie across from her, leaning on her elbows.

"Sounds like it might have been a bad dream."

"Oh, it was. I don't need to tell you everything because that would be upsetting and I'd rather not repeat it, but oh, Candice, you were so sad and I thought your heart would break and I just needed to tell you that she's not gone. She'll never be gone. She'll always be with you."

"Emily!" Gracie admonished her daughter, and then Candice heard them whispering, too quiet to make out the words but loud enough to know Gracie wasn't happy with her daughter. "I'm sorry, Candice. I didn't know she'd bring it up," Gracie said, coming back on the line.

"No, Mrs. Howard. It's just fine. Children have a different way of processing things like this, and really, it does make me feel better," she lied.

•

Rose called from a motel that morning, and Candice accepted the charges. "Late tomorrow," her daughter said, sounding exhausted, Della screaming somewhere in the distance.

Tomorrow. Tomorrow, Tom, Della, Rose, and RD would come. Today, Salida would. She no longer drove, but the owner of the bakery had offered to bring her, and now Candice was waiting for her mother.

Candice had been watching for her, pacing the house so fiercely Everett threatened to make her go outside—"that heat will wear you out," he'd said. He was cooking in the kitchen and he slapped at her hands each time she tried to help. He wasn't being mean, Candice knew. They just both needed their space.

When she saw the car slow in front of the house, then park, then Salida step out, at first, Candice was frozen. She didn't know why. She just watched as the man who brought Salida got her bags out of the trunk. Salida had three of them.

"Is that her?" Everett called from the kitchen, squinting towards the window. Candice couldn't speak. "Candy?" Everett came into the living room and saw Candice staring through the glass. "Aren't you even going to help?"

Everett opened the front door, still in his apron, leaving grease smeared on the knob. It caught the light and shone.

When Salida came into the house she looked around and nodded. Then she saw Candice by the window and came to her.

•

"This is nice," Salida said when Candice came out onto the back porch.

Candice didn't know if her mother meant the day was nice, the yard was nice, or if being with her daughter was nice. Maybe all of it. Maybe none. She didn't feel like asking for clarification because that man from the Historical Society had just called and said his search had been a dead end. He'd said that it was possible her ancestors never registered, and that a lot of people didn't end up on the Dawes Rolls. Then he'd suggested Candice 'talk to her family,' which felt like foreboding advice on the day Salida arrived.

What options did she have left, though? And if she was going to do it, maybe now *was* the time to ask. Salida was staying here in *her* house, *her* town. And when Rose came with Della, Candice was going to bring them into the fold. She wasn't going to do to them what Salida had done to her: obliterate their history. If Candice didn't do something now, their knowing would be lost.

"I'm thinking of making a trip back to Nacogdoches," she blurted out. "I hardly remember it these days."

Salida harumphed. "You'd be wasting your time. Better to stay here and take care of your family."

"Why can't I do both? Take care of our family and make a trip back. Maybe we'll all go back. Rose hasn't ever been to begin with."

"That's a nowhere place, Candy. Stop talking nonsense."

"No it's not. It's where we come from. And I want to know more about it. About us. I ... sometimes I feel like a massive part of me is missing," she admitted. "Other people know their pasts."

Salida was small, but her voice was big. "What more do you need to know?"

"Our history. What it means to be Cherokee. What I've lost. It's almost like you don't care about any of it," Candice replied.

Salida shrugged. "I made peace a long time ago about not knowing. Besides, I don't know why you'd want to look back to that. It was a terrible time."

"Sometimes backwards is forwards, Mama."

"Don't speak to me in riddles."

"I mean we have to understand the past if we're going to understand now, and the future. Rose is coming home, Mama, and it's not going to be too late for her. It's too late for June, but not for Rose and Della. And I want them to know."

"Know *what*, Candice?" Salida used her daughter's full name. "You want to tell them about how our family used to starve? About how they never had a home? About how being Indian marked them for the rest of their lives? They'll never be successful, Candice, if they can't integrate."

Salida had never been so blunt before, and Candice was taken a bit back.

"It's best to move on," Salida said, nodding.

"Move on from what?" Candice raised her voice. "You know not ten miles from here, there are Indians, *Cherokee* Indians, who haven't had to "move on"? That haven't been whitewashed like you did to me? Like I did to my daughters? I want to understand where we come from!"

"Sounds like you paid more attention in school than I thought. Do you mean 'understand' or 'know,' because those are two different things, and one comes with a whole lot of baggage. Besides," Salida continued, "if you really want to move forward, and make progress, you got to imagine something different. Something entirely new and not influenced by what happened."

Candice wasn't sure how that would ever be possible. How anyone could say the past didn't matter and that it didn't affect the unfolding of things to come. "You want to forget it all happened?" She asked, realizing that's exactly what Salida had done.

"I'm just saying, some people live in the past, and that it's not right."

Candice began to wonder then what the root of all this was—her mother wanting to forget. What had happened over the course of her life to make her feel this way? If Candice desired her history because it had been withheld, then what did knowing it do to her mother?

The two women sat in silence for a while, Everett banging in the kitchen.

"Here's the thing, Mama," Candice said after she'd thought a while. "I don't think we can do either. I don't think we live in a time where the past doesn't matter, and I don't think we can pretend it didn't. But I can *understand* what you're saying, that there has to be a place where that's not all we are."

"And there will be," Salida said. "Maybe not tomorrow, or in a week, or if you go back to Nacogdoches. Maybe not in a year from now, or when Della is grown. Maybe not when her children are grown. But slowly, slowly, it will happen."

"So you think we *will* forget?"

"Oh, child, have you not been listening? We're *never* going to forget. That's not what I'm saying. I'm saying the past can't be the only thing for us."

Salida was a contradiction in words.

"Forwards, backwards, maybe it's irrelevant," Salida suggested. "It's going to be the same thing, no matter what. It's the same and it's different."

"Now *you're* talking utter nonsense," Candice said.

20

Home Song

—Rebekah—

The feel of the hospital bedsheets was awful. Like sandpaper, Rebekah thought, rumpling them in a huff. Her legs were covered in hives. Red bumps and splotches of pink skin. The sheets were scratchy and smelled of bleach.

Even knowing she shouldn't itch them, her hands disappeared beneath the white linen and she ran her palms over the spots. *Not scratching,* she told herself. *I'm not scratching.*

Beside her, the hospital food was still untouched. A little metal tray with a slice of meatloaf and scant portions of mashed potatoes and peas. Rebekah eyed the food again, but still, she had no desire to eat. What she *did* want was to go home, but the doctor had told her that she "wasn't ready yet," whatever that meant. Rebekah felt fine. A little fuzzy perhaps, but she knew that was only because of the drugs they'd given her. It wasn't *her* fault if she felt a bit off.

"You're awake!"

A woman Rebekah didn't know came into the room, a clipboard in her hand. She wore a white uniform that looked as if it could have been made out of the same fabric Rebekah was lying on, and she didn't know how the woman appeared so at ease.

"I've *been* awake," Rebekah told her, leaning back because the woman had a stethoscope in her hands.

"That's good! That's very good!"

The nurse was talking to Rebekah like she was a child, and she frowned. Everyone was acting as if she was an idiot, and she wished they'd show her some respect.

"When can I leave?"

The woman didn't respond right away and shook her head slightly to indicate she was trying to listen to Rebekah's heart.

"I'm as healthy as a horse. Can you stop? That thing is cold." Rebekah put her hands on the little metal drum and pulled it away from her skin.

"Mrs. Habbermire. If you can't behave then—"

"Stop talking to me like I don't know what's going on!"

The nurse put her shoulders back and lifted one eyebrow. "Do you know?" She asked. "Do you know what's going on? What brought you here?"

Rebekah opened her mouth, but she didn't have anything to say. She knew she was *at* the hospital, but she couldn't remember why. She'd been working on her manuscript. She'd completed it. She knew that. Maybe she'd had too much to drink? She wanted to ask the woman if that was true—that she'd consumed too much whiskey and perhaps fallen or had an accident. But asking would prove she didn't know why she was laid up in the bed she was in now, so she didn't.

The nurse's face softened and she patted Rebekah's leg. "The doctor is going to come talk to you soon. Why don't we just get you comfortable?" She collected the wadded sheets from the bottom of the bed and pulled them back up over Rebekah. "See? Isn't that much better?"

•

Just on the other side of the window, an ash tree had lost a branch. The heavy limb had ripped away from the trunk enough to crash into the grass, but it was still attached at the bottom of its gash, a thin sheet of wood bowing like a bridge to nowhere. The nurse had said it came down in the storm, but it looked fine outside, and Rebekah didn't know if it was a test of some kind—how she might respond—so she didn't say anything.

Now there were three grackles on the downed arm, and they were all standing in a line, each just a little lower down than the one before it.

Monkey see, monkey do, Rebekah thought, remembering three little figurines she'd seen once at a flea market, carved and painted, crouched down low, one covering its eyes, one its ears, and the final one, its mouth.

One of the birds turned towards her and opened its beak. She could not hear what it said.

The door to her room opened again. It had been opening all day, and no one ever knocked. They just barged right in. This time it was the doctor with his round wire glasses and beady little eyes. He was followed by that same nurse Rebekah didn't like.

The man didn't even sit. He stood at the foot of the bed and stared down at the folder he had with him, reading silently, his lips forming words he wasn't making audible. Finally, he grunted—what a disgusting sound—and said, "How are you feeling?"

"I'm feeling just fine. Healthy as a horse."

"If you were a horse," the nurse said, "you wouldn't be in the hospital."

If it was a joke, it was a bad one. Rebekah didn't laugh, thinking the woman might actually be making fun of her.

"I'm afraid you're not as healthy as you may think." The man came around the side of the bed, took Rebekah's arm, and pointed with the fingers of his other hand at the small, purple bruises like pennies under her skin. "Do you remember how you came by these?"

Rebekah did not. "I assume you did it, with the way you're handling me." She yanked her arm away and held it close to her chest.

Unfazed, the doctor shook his head. "Those," he said, "are from the police. From three nights ago. Do you remember what happened three nights ago?"

Rebekah was beginning to get angry.

"I'm afraid you've had an episode," he went on. "After talking to your co-worker, and your niece—"

"You did what?"

"After talking to them," he continued, not unkindly, "I've determined you have senile psychosis."

"Senile?" Rebekah raised her voice. "I do not have senile, whatever it is. What is wrong with you?"

"Mrs. Habbermire, if you could just calm down ..." The nurse was coming around the other side of the bed.

"I don't know what makes you think that, but I'm as healthy as a horse!"

The doctor looked at the nurse and neither spoke for a moment. Finally, he asked, "Do you know what day it is?"

"I don't ... I don't have a calendar in here," Rebekah said in disbelief.

"Can you tell me what year it is?"

"I ..." Rebekah thought hard, and she wanted to say 1952. "With all the drugs you've given me, you've gone and confused me!"

"Can you remember the name of your niece?"

"That's Maggie's daughter. She's my niece." Rebekah was suddenly thrown back into another hospital room, not unlike the one she was in now. That room had been in Dallas, at the big hospital Maggie had spent her last days in. Maggie, so skinny at the end, too tired to even talk properly.

"I want to go home," she said, trying not to cry because she didn't want these people she didn't know to see her do so.

•

When Gracie appeared in the doorway of her room, at first Rebekah thought it was Maggie. They looked so alike, mother and daughter. But Maggie would never be caught dead in pants. She owned a dress shop, and she made the most beautiful clothes.

"They won't let me go home," Rebekah told her.

"I've brought you something," Gracie said, setting down a little suitcase and pulling a table with a tray of half-eaten food over to the bed. Gracie took the tray and removed it to the nightstand. "Blueberry scones, from Scooter's." Gracie reached into her purse and pulled out a paper bag. "I used to eat these all the time. And Larissa has changed, but Scooter's is still here."

Scooter was the man who owned the bakery just off the square, but Rebekah hadn't been in it in years. "Can I go home?" She asked again.

Gracie sat on the stool no one ever bothered with and held the bag in her lap. "The doctor says you can leave," she began, "but that you need to stay with us for a while. Until you're better."

"Everyone keeps acting like I'm sick!"

"Well, you gave us quite a fright. Don't you remember anything that happened? I found you on the street, Rebekah. You were right in front of Cedar House. You were looking for Lillian Gladwell. And then you attacked me. Don't you remember?"

Gracie was making up horrible stories, and Rebekah couldn't understand why her niece was lying to her. She started to shake a bit, to curl her lips around the edges of her teeth.

"Rebekah … I know. I know, and it's okay," Gracie said, taking her aunt's hand.

"Clearly nothing is 'okay.'"

"Rebekah, I found your story. Your book. What you were writing. I know—"

Rebekah felt like Gracie had slapped her across the face.

"You went into my house," she whispered.

"To get some things for you. And to take care of your cat. I didn't go through your belongings. Not really. It was just … there."

She'd read Rebekah's story, and if she'd read the story, she knew everything. It meant she knew about Lillian. And not just their affair, but she knew Lillian. All the things Rebekah promised not to tell. All the things Lillian left behind when Thomas moved her to Larissa. Cora, New Orleans, the swamp city and its ports with the smell of fish, entire city blocks made of women. Women leaning off balconies, women in bedrooms, women made of stone and wood and made into something they were not at all because they were all made by men.

Rebekah felt her face flush, and she looked away. "You had no right to go snooping through my things."

"I wasn't snooping. I was trying to help! Because the doctor told me you couldn't go home and—"

"What do you mean I 'can't go home'?"

Gracie sighed. "Rebekah, it's not safe for you to live alone right now. We'll get it all straightened out, but for the time being, you need to come stay with us. At Cedar House. We'll have it all ready for you tomorrow, when you get discharged."

Cedar House. Rebekah didn't want to relive what had happened there. She might not know what day it was, but she knew she didn't want to go back to Cedar House. She did begin to cry then, and Gracie leaned forward to hug her, the soft thump of the scones hitting the floor.

"I brought you some things to wear," Gracie said against her face. "Do you want to get dressed instead of wearing that robe? Put something else on? Maybe you'll feel better if you do?"

Rebekah didn't think putting on clothes would change anything, but she nodded anyway.

•

After a dinner Rebekah didn't want to eat but did so because her stomach was cramping, she lay in the darkness of the hospital room until the pills they gave her finally infiltrated her blood stream. Her thoughts loosened and Lillian entered them, memories of the two of them together during better days in Cedar House. Listening to jazz records and dancing by candlelight in the parlor. Roleplaying women from history and tearing apart Lillian's bureaus, fashioning costumes so they could be Cleopatra or Marie Antoinette. Using an old gramophone horn to speak out silly and absurd radio "broadcasts."

That was the version of Lillian that Rebekah wanted to remember. Not her friend and lover incapacitated by gunshot, drooling on her front porch, wrapped in shawls and blankets. She'd been able to endure Cedar House because, up until now, she'd also been able to decide how much time she spent there. What would happen to her when she couldn't leave? When she was forced to relive and confront the damage done there.

"I don't want to go back," she cried softy, before sleep took her.

•

That night she dreamed of Lillian.

The two women were in the turret bedroom of Cedar House, but it was also a brothel, and the walls were rough plank wood and the candles with their long flames were filling the space with greasy smoke.

Lillian was telling Rebekah a story about a forever girl who refused to grow up because she did not want to become a woman. Rebekah was lying back against Lillian, watching their feet as they wrestled their toes together.

"I wish I had never become a woman," Lillian said, and her voice was like an oil fire.

Rebekah sat up and turned around to tell Lillian that if *she* had never grown up, then *they* would have never met. But Lillian was not the young woman of their youth. She was old, the way she looked sitting out on the porch decades after Thomas had split them up. There was a thin pick, a metal rod, sticking out from her eye near the tear duct, and blood was starting to drip down towards the right side of her nose.

Rebekah scrambled back, falling off the bed and landing on the floor where her hands slipped on a mass of shining, black feathers.

Lillian was talking now, but the words were the thrush of bird song. She reached up for the metal and pulled it loose, and when she did, her skin started to come with it. Rebekah didn't want to see what was happening, but she couldn't look away. The room was smokier now, and she hoped what she was seeing was *wrong*. That it wasn't happening. That Lillian was not becoming undone and that it was all a trick of the light, a shadow self of Lillian appearing because of the smoke.

Lillian was singing, and as she sang, she unstitched herself. Pulled and pushed that giant needle through her body, so that what was beneath started to show through.

Her skin was like Spanish moss, hanging from a tree, and all around them was the music of birds, a chorus singing Lillian into a new shape, a bird with bright blood blooming in its flight feathers.

PART V

STONE-STEMMED END

Hear, We say, calling to disappeared girls. Pleading with them to come home to no home, to find Us through the dark, the soil, the muddy waters.

At night We crowd doorways and streets. Slip through cracks and travel on winds. When We find them, the girls, Us, We rest our foreheads against unsung wood and listen to the other side, all the ragged breathing of displacement.

Here, We say, knowing they have come a long way from home, been brought a long way from home, to this place of remembering.

Hear, We say, and We sing. And stomp our feet. And reach our arms out to all those who have disappeared, all those who have been taken.

We cry. We pick up our skirts and walk, again. We have known many trails, and none have been kind. We go out to look for girls. We look for them in caves and streams and houses. We look for them through doorways and between open car doors and in the faces of other girls who are close to disappearing.

Some of these girls, they hear Us. They do not know our words but blood calls to blood and they turn their heads, looking for voices that have no bodies. We want to take them all. We want to put sweet fat into their mouths, to scent their hair with smoke, to fringe their arms with the skins of animals.

Remember, We call to them.

Listen, We call to them.

And they come to Us.

21

The Point of First Departure

—Emily—

When my mother leaves for the dress shop, she locks the door behind her. Through the library windows I watch her walk down the sidewalk and get into her car. She sits there for a long time. Her hands are on the steering wheel, but she doesn't go anywhere.

"What is she doing," I ask Them.

Remembering, the long-haired Woman says. *She has been hunted down by it. She is paralyzed with memory. She is trying to learn how to fit into its skin.*

I wish I could crawl into my mother's brain. Be a worm and inch my way into her memories while she is sleeping. Explore her maze-mind and go in all the rooms, make all the crossings, let everything out that's been locked away.

The long-haired Woman shakes her head, says, *It is not for you to decide when she tells her stories.*

•

After I clean up breakfast, I go into the backyard. I lay in the scratchy grass and pick the small wild strawberries. They are bland, but they are new, and unexpected, so I enjoy them. I watch the birds wheeling overhead. Hear them chirrup and squawk at each other over the bird feeder. I find a cicada shell anchored to a short stick and can see through the skin that it has shed. The roses on the back fence are impossibly large.

When I come back in, Lillian is still in the library, though the Women are gone, hiding in the house, out looking for girls, or dancing across time. I tip toe into the room, trying not to disturb her. She is looking for Mrs. Habbermire, I know, but I have nothing I can tell her, so I am quiet, doing my best to make as little noise as possible as I collect the newspaper Mrs. Habbermire tore with her feet.

I do not blame her for destroying it, and I fight against metaphor, trying not to think of the ripped paper as Mrs. Habbermire's own thoughts. I want to fight off the feeling that to Mrs. Habbermire, it didn't matter what happened to the story because Marlene and Georgia and Rita mean so little to her. I don't think that it's true. It's just hard not to feel that way since she was the one who ruined it all.

I take the wad of ripped and brittle paper into the parlor and then close the library door to give Lillian some privacy. I try to order the pages, but some are torn beyond repair. I sigh at all the damaged stories in my hands.

I find a triangle of photo, black and white dots that make part of a face. I search through the other pages to find the rest of this person, to assemble them back to whole. But when I find the sheet I am looking for, my world sways, shimmers, and I am inside Their vibrations, on the other side of the veil, looking through.

In my hands are two halves of a girl. She is Rita Randall, the newspaper says, and this is not the first time I've seen her. I have seen her many times, in my dreams. In the story I told Will. Rita Randall is not missing. It's just that no one has found her.

A sound comes from my throat, calls Them into the room. I show Them the picture. I tell Them I know where Rita is, and that we need to tell someone. I rush to the phone, but I do not have my mother's number at the dress shop. I do not know if the dress shop even has a phone.

"What should I do?" I ask Them. "What do I do?"

I do not want to call the police. I do not want her found, recovered, by people that did not know her. Even *I* did not know her, Rita Randall, but I saw her, have seen her, during the dark night of my dream, of many dreams. It was the story I told Will, the story of a girl who disappeared, and the story has a place, a name.

I am standing in the kitchen with the phone in my hand. I am thinking of calling Will, but what would he say? I've already upset him once.

Caught between urgency and reflection, I dial his number anyway.

"Hello?"

A woman answers the phone, and for a second, I don't say anything.

"Is Will available?" I ask.

"I'm sorry, he's not home." She pauses, then asks, "Who is this?"

"This is Emily Howard," I say. "I just ..." I can't go on, because I don't know how to say what I need to.

"Emily? Are you still there Emily?"

When I try to speak next, my voice comes out as a squeak, high-pitched and shrill, the words difficult to unwind from my mouth.

"Emily," the woman asks. "Is something wrong?"

And I tell her.

•

In the living room, I open a window. Put my hands on the rail and push up. And it does open. But not all the way. I try the window next to it, and again I am stopped. I try all the windows on the first level of the house. They are all stalled by nails. They can open enough to let the air in, to funnel in the sounds of the outside world, but a body—mine, a girl's, a man's—cannot fit through.

Lillian Gladwell is still at her window. Lillian Gladwell is picking at the nail that keeps her stained glass immobilized.

"Have these always been here?" I ask her. The nails' flat heads are speckled with paint, and I do not know if the brothers made these windows into half-things at my mother's request, or if they've been like this since before we moved into Cedar House.

Lillian Gladwell looks at me, and opens her mouth, but says nothing.

I try the front door again, and then the back. I can see through the space between doors and frames to the small piece of metal fastening them closed. This house is made of bars, but I have been dreaming, and know I am not locked inside Cedar House.

They line the stairs to the story. They are weeping for the girls and women We have lost, and I do not know if the hands They offer me are to pull me back or encourage me onwards. They are lost in Their own grief. Their own remembering.

In my room I push up the window, wondering now if this is the only way out of Cedar House. If this was Lillian's room, and if she too listened to the Little People in the tree. The Little People are not here now, but they have worn the bark off the branches they sit on. Left the presence of their bodies on the wood. I look back to see Them crowding through the doorway, coming to see what I will do.

I climb out the window onto the ledge of the porch roof. I am walking carefully to the tree when I hear someone yell, "What are you doing?"

I look towards the street, careful to lean my weight back so it doesn't carry me forward and into the yard. It must be Will's mother, standing down there, shading her eyes against the sun and staring up at me.

"The front door is locked," I call to her, and shift my feet forward, baby steps, towards the trunk of the tree.

"Emily," she yells. "Stop, just—"

I don't know what she thinks is the alternative. And besides, I am not completely incapable. I may be young, but I am not stupid.

When I reach the tree, I hold on to an upper branch and step onto a lower one. Like a tight rope walker, I make my way to the trunk and begin to shimmy down it. I'm hugging the wood and begin to slide, my dress riding up and my feet finding ledges as I make my way down. I look below me and see the branches near the bottom of the tree have been cut away, and I either have to jump, which I'd rather not do because it seems a tad far, or I need to lower myself down onto the porch railing.

It's a bit of a stretch—I'm a little too short—and as I lower one leg, reaching out for the rail, my balance tips and I start to slip.

For a moment, less than a second, my body is weightless, and then I reach forward and grab the gutter, the tips of my fingers crunching old leaves, and the leg that's hanging down makes contact.

Well, I mutter, staying there for a few seconds until I feel secure. When I know I'm stable, I grab the column and bring my other leg down, the awkwardness of it pitching me forward onto my hands and knees below the overhang.

"I'm okay," I yell, standing up and looking down at myself. The dress is going to need to be mended.

When I begin walking, my right knee hurts, but it doesn't feel like anything is broken. My hands are a bit scraped up, and stinging, but I'll be fine.

In the yard, Will's mother is standing with her mouth hanging open. Maybe she saw my underwear. I hope it wasn't too scandalous.

22

Erasure Until

—Bet—

Bet lay awake in bed, the moonlight streaming through the window, the breeze coming through every now and then, lifting the thin curtains.

The missing girls. The dead girls. She saw all of them in the shadows that played on the wall, the four of them—Marjorie, Georgia, Rita, and Marlene—bumping into each other, separating, joining hands, melding into each other.

When she closed her eyes, she saw the parts that were left behind: the shoe, the muddy underwear, Marjorie's bracelet, her arm. Marjorie's arm, still a mystery. Either an animal, or animals, taking it at the joint, or something more heinous. Marcil said whoever did this graduated to Marjorie, started with the Indian girls they hadn't paid much attention to. The police hadn't acted in time.

They had the farm doctor come in and look at the arm to see if he could understand the measure of the break. Before death, after death, what might have severed it from the body. But the chewing of the bone kept him from definitive clarity on if that had happened before or after. Marcil said it was possible the man was still escalating, moving from molestation to dismemberment. She remembered the way he said *moving*, as if it was still ongoing, as if Marjorie Kent was not the last girl.

She got out of bed and went into the kitchen, drinking a glass of water and staring down the short hallway into the dark bathroom.

She went there and touched the metal faucet, drew her hand along the shower curtain. She opened the medicine cabinet and then closed it. And then she went into the boys' room.

Alton was sleeping in his feather headdress, facing the wall, his thin shoulder a perfect right angle to the ceiling.

"Mom." Will was watching her. Knew she was there though she hadn't made a sound. She came and bent down beside him.

"I wake you?"

"Nah. I'm having trouble going to sleep."

"You want to eat something with me?"

In the kitchen, Will explained that he was thinking about the dead girls, too, and what Emily Howard had to say about them.

"You saw Emily today?"

He blushed. He said, "She knows all kinds of things, really smart things. She knows things people shouldn't know either, like about the girls."

"Like what?"

"She says she's seen them at night. Like mice through an owl's eyes. She sees them through car windows and she follows them."

"She's dreaming about them?"

Will shrugged. "She doesn't talk about it like dreams. Mama, what she says ..."

"What does she say, Will?"

Will began to cry then, softly, and his face screwed up an awful way.

"Oh, baby." Bet got up and came around the table, taking the top half of his body into a hug. "Why are y'all even talking about it? It's awful, not something you need to be worrying about."

"I can't stop imagining it," Will sobbed, and he told his mother the story.

•

The next day, the violence of Emily's story still in the front of her mind, Bet called a lawyer. She wasn't sure exactly what she was going to say, but the time had come—she knew. There was too much violence in her life. The girls. The history with Norman. No, not a history, Bet thought. History implied something was done. Over. Ended. And it would never end with him.

Now there was Alton, too. Still a child, though it was hard to see him as such.

It might not be too late for him. Bet wondered if perhaps she'd had it all wrong. Maybe Alton was not irretrievable and becoming his father. The problem could be that Norman spent too much time with him. And what had Alton heard, and seen, of his father's rages? Alton could be learning by example.

So maybe he *was* just a child, still in the liminal space of becoming. Bet might still be able to shape the man he would grow into. If she intervened.

On the other end of the line, a woman answered the phone, but said Mr. Hofer was out of the office, and asked for Bet's number. She was loathe to give it, worrying that if the lawyer called her back, and someone else answered, her secret would be given away. But she did give it, assured that when he called back, he knew how to be discreet. "You're not the first woman looking to leave her husband," the receptionist said. "And if we didn't know how to handle the situation, we wouldn't be in business."

Bet found it hard to be away from the phone. She cleaned the kitchen counters and organized the cabinets. Arranged all the dishes in neat, stacked rows. Then she went to work in the bathroom, polishing the faucet covered in filmy toothpaste-water and scrubbing out the tub. When finally, the phone rang, she slipped on the tile in her rush to answer it before someone else did.

•

Bet hung up the phone and for a moment, didn't know what to do with herself. She'd just talked to Emily Howard. Gracie's daughter. And the girl claimed she knew where Rita's body was. Frozen in place, Bet screamed when Alton tugged on her skirt.

Her youngest son staggered back, clutching his hand as if he'd been burned.

"I'm sorry. Alton. I'm sorry." Bet bent down and put her arms out, but Alton did not come into her embrace.

"I'm hungry," he said instead. "When's lunch?"

"Lunch is going to be late today, okay? Mom has something that she needs to do. Do you know where your father is?"

Alton shook his head.

"Listen," Bet said, standing up. "If I leave you here, by yourself, are you going to behave? Can you be a big boy? Can you promise me you won't get into trouble?"

Alton bit his lower lip and nodded. "I won't get into any trouble."

She stood, with her hands on her hips, and studied his face.

In the moment, it was hard to *not* see Alton as just a child. His chubby cheeks, his button nose. The way his hair was mussed, still, because he hadn't combed it yet. He was wearing his Guide's vest, and his moccasins. A child playing dress-up. A child, still a child.

Bet made a noise that vibrated in her throat. *No, no,* she said to herself. "Come on. You need to come with me."

•

"What is that girl doing?"

When Bet pulled up to the curb, she didn't understand what Alton was asking. "Who is doing what?" she asked, unbuckling her seatbelt.

"Her," Alton said.

Bet turned to see her son pointing out the window. When she looked towards Cedar House, she saw Emily Howard climbing through a second story window, stepping out onto the first-floor roof above the porch.

"Goddammit," Bet cursed, throwing the car door open. "Emily!" She called. "What are you doing?"

The girl looked down at Bet, who was running through the lawn. "The front door is locked!" she yelled.

Bet realized what Emily was saying. She didn't have a key to her own house. Her mother had gone to her shop, and in an effort to keep her daughter safe, had made sure no one could get in, which also meant Emily had no way out.

"Emily, stop. Just— "

But Emily wasn't listening to Bet. She'd already stepped into the branches of the tree, was making her way down, the yellow of her dress a blur between the foliage.

Bet didn't realize she was holding her breath until Emily almost fell. She stepped forward, but the girl's feet made contact with the porch railing and she reached for the gutter, sliding down from the branch and then, jumping down the last few feet, landing but falling forward, catching herself on stick arms on the other side of the baluster.

"I'm okay," Emily called, standing up and dusting herself off.

Bet couldn't help but stare when the girl stood. Emily didn't look a thing like her mother. Bet had assumed, of course, that Emily was Gracie and George's daughter, but she clearly wasn't.

The girl walked towards Bet and then took her hand, leading the woman to her own car.

•

In the backseat, Alton wouldn't leave Emily alone. Will hadn't said anything to his brother about his new friend, and Bet's son wanted to know all about Emily. What it was like to live in a mansion. Why her skin was so dark. If her mom would be angry that she ripped her dress.

Emily didn't respond to his questions, but she did ask him what he was wearing.

The car rolled to a stop at an intersection and Bet looked both ways.

"They're my Indian clothes," Alton said to Emily, and the girl laughed.

Bet turned to glance at them and saw Alton looking confusedly at Emily.

"Emily," Bet began, not quite knowing how to ask what she wanted to. Not knowing how to talk about what Emily had seen without being too graphic in front of Alton. "How do you know how to get there?" she asked. "Do you need a map, or—"

"No, the girl said. "I can explain it to Gracie. She used to live here. She'll understand."

Bet thought it odd that Emily referred to her mother as Gracie, but she didn't inquire after it. "I wish I had known," she said instead. "What Will told me ... I thought it was just a story." Even as Bet spoke, she knew she still didn't really believe Emily Howard. It was hope that drove her to Cedar House, not logic. Hope that was taking her now to Gracie's dress shop. It was hope—not belief—because they were very different things.

"If you had listened better—that is always the problem, the lack of patience, or listening but not listening, or not listening for long enough," Emily said, "you might have heard the owl's words. You might not have known you could understand them. Many people don't. Not because they don't have the patience to listen—but because they don't understand how memory sings itself back to life."

Bet felt chilled. She didn't understand exactly what Emily was saying, but she understood the strangeness of the statement, and her inability to access it was less disturbing than Emily saying it.

When they arrived at the dress shop, Bet made the children get out of the car. She wasn't comfortable leaving them alone.

Bet peered through the frosted glass of the building but couldn't see anything inside. Behind her, Alton stood looking at the street, and Emily was mumbling to herself.

She was just about to knock when Gracie opened the door, purse on her shoulder. She startled back a few steps when confronted with a person she didn't expect to be there.

Gracie looked terrible. Bet recognized the look of a woman who was losing herself because she'd seen that face in the mirror dozens of times.

"Emily?" Gracie asked, wiping tears away. "What are you doing here?"

23

All Bodies, Small Bodies

—Gracie—

Inside the dress shop, Gracie was sure she was losing her mind. She couldn't stop the onslaught of thoughts, was crumpling under the weight of the wrongness her life had become. She sat on the floor at the back wall, wiping her tears away with her sleeve like a child. Every time she stopped crying, an echo of her pain resounded. Another woman crying. An alternate Gracie. Another version of herself, somewhere else, crying as well.

There was no other way it could have been, she knew. Every version of Gracie that existed, every one would have found herself *here*.

It was lonely, the terrible realization that she'd never really made her own choices in life, never had control over how her life unfolded. But here she was, back in Larissa, with the ghost of her other self, crying even as *she* had finally stopped, showing her that there was a plan she had not been privy to. That something greater than herself had been involved in the construction of her life. That all roads would have led to what was happening now, no matter what she had done.

Gracie pounded the floor and yelled, "Shut up!" But the ghost that was her didn't listen. Or didn't care. And continued on, unrelenting.

Finally, she couldn't stand it anymore. She got up, retrieved her purse, keys, and hat, and went to the door.

When she opened it, Bettye Donald was there, and Gracie instinctively stepped back, her heart hammering in her chest with the suddenness of someone unexpected standing right in front of her. And then from behind Bettye, Emily stepped out, and beside her was a small boy.

"Emily, what are you doing here?"

Gracie was shocked to see her daughter. Emily had said she wasn't ready to leave Cedar House yet, and now she was here, with Bettye Donald. For a moment, jealousy reared up and Gracie found herself angry at both her daughter and Bettye. *She* was supposed to be the one that Emily shared this moment with.

"How—" Gracie began, coming out and closing the door behind her.

"You locked me in," Emily said. "And I couldn't call."

The surprise of seeing her daughter, standing in the sun in downtown Larissa, gave way to a sudden worry. "What happened?" Gracie asked, bending down to look at her daughter, seeing now that her dress had torn at the waistline, taking in the fresh scrapes on Emily's hands.

"I know where Rita Randall is," Emily told her.

"What do you mean you know where Rita Randall is?"

A car came quickly down the street, and Bettye moved to pull the boy closer to the building.

"I've seen her," Emily told her mother. "And we need to go find her."

"You've seen her? One of the missing ..." Gracie trailed off, and her daughter nodded.

"We should call the police," Gracie said.

"I *am* the police," Bet told her.

"But you're not—"

"No." Emily cut Gracie off. "We are the ones who need to find her."

Gracie wasn't sure exactly what Emily meant. This was too much. This was not supposed to be how things went. Things were supposed to get easier now that the truth was out, not more complicated.

"What do you mean 'find her,'" Gracie asked, paying more attention now to the boy, who she realized was dressed in some mock Indian attire.

"She's in tall grass," Emily said. "Being watched over."

Gracie didn't know how to have this conversation in front of Bettye Donald, and she didn't want to. Bettye wouldn't be able to understand what was happening with Emily, and rendering Emily so visible—not just what she was, but *who* she was—was enough to make her want to cry all over again. She'd wanted to protect Emily, and she was failing, still.

"Oh, sweetie," Gracie said. "I don't think this is a good idea at all. Maybe we can—"

"I think we should go and see if we can find her," Bet said. "I wouldn't want … I wouldn't want anyone else to either. You understand?"

Gracie thought that Bet was saying she didn't want the police to find Rita. The men to find her. Maybe, because they were women, and mothers, the responsibility was with them. But Gracie didn't want that obligation. She didn't want another thing that was her responsibility, not when she was already cracking.

"We shouldn't take him," Gracie said, nodding to the boy. "If we find something …"

"I know," Bet said. "I know."

Emily looked so small, standing on the cement in her ruined dress, arms hanging limply by her sides, one sock pulled up, the other rolled down on itself. Though she *looked* like a child, there was something about her face, the hardness of it, the tight jaw, the way her eyes were opened wide, and big, and taking in everything.

Gracie felt like Emily was sizing her up. Was saying, without words, that Gracie owed her this.

•

They took Bettye's car. Her son was quiet in the backseat, picking up on the tension. He'd started to say a dozen things, but each time was interrupted by Emily who had been trying to explain how to get to where Rita Randall was. Gracie's daughter was trying to describe the area from a bird's eye perspective, and Gracie felt they were going around in circles, despite her best efforts to translate Emily's words into some kind of map. "There were trees far back from a field," Emily said, and they drove slowly along the open pastures Bet could easily remember. "No, no," Emily corrected. "It's less … clean. Like no one takes care of it." This took them farther out of town where the land of old farms had been allowed to partially reclaim themselves. "Ugh," Emily complained. "None of this is right. It's a forgotten place. Or a secret place. A place people used to use, but not for crops or animals."

Bettye took them out into county territory and eventually turned down a hard packed dirt road and when they passed by a live oak long split by lightning, Emily gasped and said, "this is it," sitting up straighter in her seat and turning her whole body to the window.

Gracie knew where they were. Recognized the back country lane. It took them through clear-cut land, past black oil rigs moving their heavy limbs. This land had once been owned by George's family, and it was leased now to this new company. Gracie recognized the dogwoods on either side of the road, planted by Irene before Gracie knew George. This was the road that would take them to the old Howard house.

But the sign they passed read *G&D Drilling*, and under Emily's direction, they did not turn off towards where the Howard residence used to be, hidden by a bend on the road and wax myrtles and hickory trees. Emily told Bettye to follow a small path, not a road even—just two ruts for tires—back towards empty fields.

"There's a stream somewhere," Gracie heard herself saying. "If we go far enough. George used to fish it in when he was little. On the other side is Mrs. White's farm."

"I know," Bettye said.

In the backseat, her son asked when they were going to eat lunch.

"In just a little, okay?" Bettye told him. "If you want, we can go get sandwiches and ice cream."

Gracie didn't know what was going to happen, but she doubted very much that Bettye was going to want to do either of those things once they were done.

"Stop here," Emily commanded, and Bettye slammed on the breaks.

Gracie put her hands out and caught herself on the dash.

Emily was already opening her door.

"What about him?" Gracie asked. "Shouldn't he stay here?"

"Keep him close by," Bettye said. "If you see anything, let me know."

Outside the car, Bettye was walking quickly after Emily, and Gracie was left with the boy. She put her hand out to him, and he took it, walking beside her, both of them slower than Emily and his mother.

"What are we doing out here?" he asked.

"Well, we're looking for something," Gracie told him.

"We're looking for Rita? I wish Will was here. If we find her, can I get my tracker badge?"

Gracie didn't know what a tracker badge was, and said, "I don't know. Maybe."

There was more distance between them now, and as Emily approached the tree line, from behind, with her hair blowing as she ran, Gracie couldn't help but feel her daughter was rushing away from her. Bettye trailed behind, a stick in hand, parting tall grasses like a divining rod for the dead.

"Do you hear that?"

Gracie stopped when the boy tugged on her hand.

"Hear what?" she asked.

"Listen, "he said.

And she did. Gracie strained her ears, and she could hear something, low and keening. "What is that?" she asked, more to herself than to the boy.

He let go of her and began to walk into the grass.

"Wait," Gracie began to say, realizing that she didn't even know the boy's name.

But he was away from her now, looking at the ground. Bending down.

Oh god, Gracie thought, rushing after him. He was going to find Rita. The boy was going to find her.

"Look at this!" he called, and from the excitement in his voice.

When she came up next to him, Gracie saw something small and brown humped up in the green grass. A doll, perhaps? She approached slowly, trying to make sense of what she was seeing. The thing unfolded into an animal, an owl, the tufts of feathers at either side of its head like wilted horns.

She looked at the owl and the owl looked back. The noise had stopped.

The boy bent down again, crouch-walking closer to the bird. The owl hunched down lower into the ground. Its wing was cocked open and Gracie thought the feathers were ruffling in the breeze. Then she bent down next to the boy and she saw it was ants on the broken appendage, moving in the plumage.

"Poor thing," she said. "It's really hurt, isn't it?"

"We need to help it," the boy said, taking off his vest.

"Don't touch it," Gracie told him. "It's wild."

"It's okay. You do it like this," he said, draping the suede over the animal. "And then you hold it like this, so it can't bite you."

The boy collected the bird, keeping the fabric up over its head, his hand against its neck in a way that immobilized it.

It was only once the boy lifted the bird up, cradling it against his chest, ants up and down his arm, that Gracie saw what the owl had been sitting on. A book.

She knew when she bent down and looked at the title that it was Marjorie's book, the one about the Indians, about the Killough massacre. Gracie was picking it up when, in the distance, from somewhere beyond the field, and through the trees, she heard Emily wail. Heard her daughter scream, and the sound was a spike to her heart.

The boy swiveled his head and began to walk that way with the owl, but Gracie put her hand on his shoulder. "Wait here, okay?"

"But what if they're hurt? What if—"

Bettye came out from the foliage. She was running towards them, huffing and puffing by the time she got to them. She was crying—Gracie could tell that much.

"You need to go to her," she told Gracie. "Go to her. Stay with her. I'm getting the police. Alton—"

Bettye looked at her son, at the bird in his arms. For a brief moment, something flashed across her face, and then she said, "Alton, come with me. Come with me. Bring it. Hurry."

"Where is she?" Gracie asked.

"Just there," Bettye said, pointing. "Go to her."

And then they were gone, Bettye and her son's footsteps thudding away, leaving Gracie with the book clutched to her chest, staggering towards the brush beyond.

•

She went and found her daughter sitting in the undergrowth. Emily was on her knees, and Gracie moved closer, she came to understand her daughter was holding the dark and dirty hand of a dead girl.

"Emily," she said quietly, "come with me now."

"I can't leave her! "Emily turned to look at Gracie. Her face was red, and she closed her eyes. Took deep breaths to try to quiet herself.

"She's gone, Emily."

"She's right here!"

"I mean—"

"I know what you mean." Emily sobbed, and Gracie didn't know what to say in response.

Emily turned back to Rita Randall, to the body of the girl hidden by leaves and small plants. As Gracie stepped closer, she could make out the girl's yellow dress, a dirt-streaked Mary Jane. Emily was wailing now, bowing her head into the girl's hand and turning her face into it.

Gracie was stunned, and the longer she stood there, and watched, the clearer Rita Randall became. And Emily's slow actions—her lowering herself down to the ground, moving closer to Rita, curling up beside her and moaning—ripped through Gracie.

"Oh, Emily". Gracie collapsed next to her daughter, laying a soft palm against the girl's back, wishing this could have been different.

24

Reclamation, A Solitary Act

—Rebekah—

Gracie didn't talk much in the hospital, and Rebekah thought she looked awful: puffy eyes, swollen face. Even her hair was frizzy. And then Gracie barely talked on the car ride to Cedar House. Now, they stood at the bottom of the porch steps, Gracie with Rebekah's little suitcase in one hand, Rebekah's hand in the other.

"Do you want some help?" Gracie asked, going to set the bag down so that Mrs. Habbermire would have support climbing up.

Rebekah shook her head, putting her hand against the wall of the house and going up by herself. She stopped behind Gracie, who had her keys out now and was unlocking the door.

"All the bedrooms are upstairs," Gracie was saying. "If that won't work, I mean, if you don't want to go up and down, we can do something for the time being in the living room. Or the dining room." Gracie sighed. "We hardly ever eat in there," Gracie went on, turning the doorknob. "Most of the time we're in the kitchen. I can have the table moved out and we can put a door in. There's not a full bathroom but—"

When the door opened, Rebekah saw Petrol fleeing from the woman standing just inside Cedar House. Lillian was there, but not there. A shadow self. Enough body to be recognizable, not enough to hold. Rebekah began crying, and then Gracie was rubbing her back, apologizing for nothing in particular.

•

Clearly the girl could see Lillian too, and her eyes flicked to the woman every time Lillian moved. Gracie didn't seem to be as aware, but Rebekah noted that sometimes Gracie seemed to move around the spaces Lillian occupied, like she sensed that space was already full.

Rebekah hadn't said a single word since coming into the house. She was afraid that if she spoke, the spell might break. Lillian might go away again. That by vocalizing the other woman's existence, or anything for that matter, Lillian would disappear.

The Lillian that now moved around the rooms of Cedar House seemed nervous, which was not the way Rebekah thought ghosts behaved. In all the movies and television shows she'd seen, in all the stories she'd read or listened to on the radio, ghosts were spirits that carried grudges. Or wanted revenge. They were angry souls bent on havoc or, if not that, disturbance.

Lillian wasn't disturbing anything except Rebekah, who wasn't even disturbed exactly, more confused, and saddened. Sometimes Lillian sat in the chair across from Rebekah and smiled. Sometimes she was at the window looking out into the street. Sometimes she just walked around, glancing back at Rebekah, as if waiting for her to speak and say something.

But no one in Cedar House was saying anything. Gracie had given up on conversation with Rebekah since Rebekah was too stunned to talk. Emily and her mother hadn't said a word to each other, and though they acknowledged the other's presence, there was an obvious tension between the two. Gracie was in the kitchen cooking dinner with the radio on, and Emily was sitting on the floor with her back against the sofa, writing in a notebook and looking up every now and then when Lillian passed close by her.

Rebekah thought, *I must be crazy. The doctor was right. I'm losing my marbles.*

She kept looking to Emily, who nodded as if to encourage Rebekah.

Rebekah was wringing her hands. Maybe Lillian had come back from the grave because of Cedar House. Maybe she was angry at Rebekah for bringing Gracie into it. And then Gracie had ruined it. Made it into an entirely different place.

It was *an* answer, but Rebekah also didn't think it was *the* answer. Rebekah imagined that if she were Lillian, she wouldn't have wanted to come back to the house the way it was. It would have been too much a reminder of what happened here. Maybe she came back because it was a *different* place now.

Rebekah had never seen Lillian here when she was readying Cedar House for Gracie. And she'd spent days in the home, dusting, and polishing wood. Collecting the sheets laid out over the furniture. Shopping for new linens, and towels. Washing dishes that hadn't been used in years. Cleaning windows until they were clear again.

During that time, she hadn't felt anything even close to a presence. She'd only felt a deep regret and longing. Many days she would just suddenly start crying until she could sit down and compose herself. She'd thought then it was a mistake to try to make this place Gracie's home, but she'd been wrong.

The library's pocket doors were drawn closed, but Lillian kept going there and standing in front of them.

If Lillian was a ghost, then maybe she couldn't open doors. Maybe she couldn't touch anything. Affect anything around her. Did Lillian want to go in there?

Rebekah looked at Emily and gave a small cough. The girl looked at her and then at Lillian.

"Oh," she said, putting the journal aside and standing up. From where Rebekah sat, she could see the girl was using a newspaper clipping as some sort of bookmark, and a stranger's papered face looked up at nothing.

Emily walked on the balls of her feet to the library where she moved the heavy wood panels. And then she stood there with her back against the wall, waiting.

Finally, only once Lillian had gone in and was out of sight behind the wall, Rebekah stood.

•

"Well she can't sleep in there."

Gracie and Emily were not as quiet as they thought they were now that they were speaking to each other.

"I think she can do whatever she wants," Rebekah heard Emily say, and she smiled because it was funny to her to hear a child speak that way to her mother. There was something of herself in the girl, even if she wasn't blood.

There was a pause and then Gracie said, "There's nothing to sleep on. If she sleeps in that chair she's going to get a crick in her neck."

"So she gets a crick in her neck," Emily retorted. "It won't be the end of the world."

The end of the world. Rebekah used to think the end of the world was when you died, and now she wasn't so sure. What if the whole world was filled with ghosts? What if they were everywhere? All the time? Only no one could see them?

Lillian wasn't in the library at the moment. She'd just stood at the stained glass until the sun had started to set, and then she'd disappeared. When Gracie came to get Rebekah for supper, Rebekah was too afraid to move. But Lillian had gone anyway. One moment she was there, and then she wasn't.

Now Rebekah was back at her post, hoping Lillian would return. If she came back, this time Rebekah told herself she would say something.

"I think we should move the sofa in there."

Rebekah heard Emily walking in the living room and then there was a screeching noise, something heavy pushed across the floor.

"Emily, hold on. You're going to scratch the wood."

Rebekah didn't even turn around when they came in. She could hear them moving, Gracie's panting and Emily's tiny grunts. She stared at the window.

"I'll go get some blankets and a pillow." It took a moment for Gracie to leave, but she finally did.

"Mrs. Habbermire," Emily said. "I can bring a lamp in. Do you want a light? Or something to read?"

When Rebekah didn't answer her, Emily left anyway, to get the things she thought Rebekah needed.

•

In her story, Rebekah had written, "The old West allowed for all kinds of bending and it wasn't that uncommon for women to be with women and even men to be with men. We're all full of holes," she'd claimed, surprised at her own brusqueness, "and mayhap it doesn't matter who fills them."

She was looking at the hole in the mantle, at the place one of Thomas' bullets had split the marble. Rebekah never understood what happened that night. It had been decades since she'd seen Lillian, and by then, Thomas had brought her back from Dallas, "fixed" there by a doctor who put a spike in her brain. Rebekah had only seen her sitting on the front porch, rocking in her chair, staring at nothing—not even recognizing Rebekah on the few occasions she'd dared walk by.

She'd always just assumed Thomas finally went sideways. Succumbed to his own baser self when the syphilis did enough damage to finally let the real Thomas loose.

Now she wondered what really happened, and if Lillian could, or would, tell her.

Emily scratched at the door and then came into the room. She was holding a plate of cookies in one hand and a glass of milk in the other. Under one arm was a book.

"Hi," she said, looking around. When she didn't see Lillian and went to sit on the sofa, Rebekah assumed she figured it was fine to stay. Rebekah wanted to ask her to leave but didn't. She was lonely, she realized, and confused. And she was so tired of being alone.

"This is the book you brought me," Emily said. "I don't think, when you gave it to me, you had any idea what would happen. How this book makes sense right now. You know that girls went missing? Most of them died. Rita, and Georgia, and Marjorie. They disappeared, and then ... Then they were found. This book is full of girls that disappear, Mrs. Habbermire. All the girls in this book disappear."

She held the book up for Rebekah to see, but the volume looked nondescript. It could have been any book.

"But the neat thing about the book," Emily said, opening it and turning to a page marked by a thin ribbon, "is that because of the book, they're not forgotten. I know they're not real. I know these girls are made up, but they're always going to be here now, as long as someone is reading the book. Do you understand what I'm saying?"

Rebekah was listening now, actually paying attention to the girl, because Emily seemed to be trying to tell her something important.

"Writing something down," Emily said, "and telling the story, even if it's not real. That's important. I've been thinking about what's real and what's not. I've been trying to figure out the difference between the two. And I know the difference. A part of me does. But then, a part of me doesn't. A part of me wonders if maybe there *isn't* a difference sometimes, and if that's okay. Anyway, I wanted to tell you I'm glad you're here. Maybe you'd rather be at your own house. I don't know. But I'm glad you're here."

When Rebekah didn't respond, Emily sighed. "I'll leave the book for you. In case you want to read it."

•

Rebekah awoke to a sound she recognized from long ago. In the dark, she was bewildered at first, because the room was not her bedroom, and what she was sleeping on was not her bed. Then she remembered she was in Cedar House.

The sound she heard was Lillian's voice, saying her name, like someone whispering into uncertain darkness, unable to discern who, or what, might be waiting.

"Lillian?" Rebekah said the word, and then clasped her hand over her mouth, holding her breath.

Rebekah.

Rebekah sat up, slowly letting her breath out.

Lillian was sitting in the chair Rebekah had finally vacated, and she was leaning forward, hands outstretched in supplication.

Rebekah went to her then. Down onto her already bruised knees, putting her cheek against the memory of silk.

•

Gracie and Emily were in the backyard, their chairs angled awkwardly. They weren't facing each other, but rather sat like two points on a triangle, and the third corner, Rebekah saw, was Petrol.

Her cat was splayed out on the lawn of the garden, arcing on its back and twisting its body, batting at a flying insect too small for Rebekah to see.

"Go on," Lillian said, "I'll be here."

But Rebekah didn't step out, because Gracie and her daughter were talking and she didn't want to disturb them.

"I keep saying I'm sorry. I don't know what else I can do." Gracie leaned forward, putting her head in her hands.

Emily looked over at the cat and took a long time to respond. "I don't think you understand what you're apologizing for," she finally said.

"Of course I do!"

"Then you're apologizing for the wrong thing. I'm not even angry. I'm just hurt. Doubly so because you don't understand."

"Then you have to tell me," Gracie moaned, and Rebekah took a step back from the screen door.

Lillian clucked her tongue. "Oh, They don't like that one bit."

"I guess I can't expect you to come to it on your own, then. I'm hurt," Emily explained, "because of what you took away. Not that *you* raised me, but that you erased me while doing so."

"I didn't erase you, Emily. You were so sick. All the time. I didn't know what to do."

"No, you didn't know what to do. And I'm not angry at you for that either. Maybe if you had told me, it would have been different. Maybe it would have been the same. But I can't pretend things haven't changed now."

Gracie leaned forward again, her elbows resting on her knees. "I just hope that one day you can forgive me."

Rebekah didn't understand what was happening, but something had transpired between mother and daughter and she didn't want to come into the middle of it. She was feeling a bit peaceful, and she wanted to linger there.

Petrol chose that moment to snap to attention, her body tensing, her entertainment over. She meowed, and when she saw Rebekah through the door, she jumped up and bounded towards her, giving Gracie and her daughter a wide berth and running along the edge of the pavers to where Rebekah stood, inside the house, just out of the cat's reach.

Mother and daughter both turned to look, and Rebekah found herself discovered.

Gracie warily got up and scratched her forehead. "How are you feeling? Hungry? I guess it's time for breakfast."

Rebekah opened the door, and Petrol came to rub against her legs. When she tried to reach down to pick up the cat, it fled back into the yard.

"She'll come around," Lillian told her. "She's just not used to Us yet."

25

Scar Where the Puncture Was

—Candice—

The beat-up old station wagon arrived at the house in a cloud of exhaust. Rose was practically out of the car before it started moving and was up the steps of the house before Candice could open the door. And then they were all together, the women of Candice's family.

Della wouldn't stop squalling until Salida took her and rocked her, and Candice tried to fight back jealousy. It was unfair that the infant took to her great-grandmother more than she took to Candice. But she was just a baby, so maybe there was nothing to read into.

The house was cramped with so many people in it, and at dinner, there wasn't even room for RD, who volunteered to sit at an awkward corner spot with his placemat falling off the edges of the table.

It was a homecoming, but it didn't feel right. Not only was June not with them, but the conversation steered towards the diner, and the Cooper house, and within a few hours, they weren't talking about June at all. Candice couldn't stand it and began collecting the empty plates.

In the kitchen, Rose came to find her. "How are you doing?" she asked.

Candice's daughter had lost all her cushion, had leaned up out in Chicago. Her face was narrower than Candice remembered it being, but when she tied her hair up, reaching then into the soapy water to help her mother with the dishes, Candice saw Rose had her ears. How had she never noticed that before?

"Honestly," Candice said, "I don't know how y'all can talk about anything other than June."

Rose nodded but replied, "We can't talk about her all the time. Haven't you been doing other things too? Living life despite it?"

She had, but she also hadn't thought that June would go from them so quickly. She was the reason they were all here, and now the family was in the other room discussing paint colors.

"We can't sit in her memory all the time," Rose said. "At some point, we have to move on, a little."

"You sound like your grandmother."

Rose pursed her lips and turned the sink on. "What I mean is that we can't dwell in that grief all the time. Life makes that impossible—we have other things that demand our attention—and we can't do it either. If I were to make every thought about her … "

Candice understood what Rose was thinking and elbowed her softly. "I know," she said. "I didn't mean to say we should, or that we can. I just don't know how to deal with it all. With them in there talking about the Cooper house like it's something to be excited about."

"Why can't we be happy about it? It allows us to be here, doesn't it?"

Candice dropped the cup she was holding, and it broke against the divider between the two sink basins. She realized she had never even told Rose about the missing girls, and about Marlene.

•

They were sleeping when the phone rang, and Everett mumbled something, turning over and taking the sheet with him. Not wanting to wake the baby, Candice sprung from the bed. In the girls' room, Rose slept in one bed, the Moses basket beside her, and Salida was in the other. In the living room, she tiptoed over RD, who was curled up on the floor next to the sofa where his brother slept.

In the kitchen, she cupped the phone and said, "Hello?"

"Candice, is that you?"

Who else would it be, Candice thought, wondering who the hell would call in the middle of the night. "Who is this?" she asked.

"It's Charles. Charles Cooper. I thought you should know. They found Rita."

•

"I'm going, too," Rose said. She was already slipping on her shoes.

"Someone has to stay and watch Della," Candice whispered fiercely.

"They can do that," Rose said, screwing up her face like her mother was being ridiculous. "That's her pa in there. He knows how to take care of her."

Candice knew that, but she couldn't bring herself to say what she was really thinking, that she didn't *want* Rose to come.

Everett's head appeared through the doorway. "Are you going or what?"

Candice said, "no," and Rose said, "yes."

"Whichever one it is," he said, "y'all need to get gone. You've taken too long as it is."

"I'm going," Rose said, in that tone of voice that said she'd argue till the cows came home.

"They don't even know you," Candice protested.

"They don't know you either," Rose countered. "Besides, I do know Katherine. Maybe not well. But I care about her. God, after everything ..."

"Fine. Fine. Just hurry."

Everett was waiting by the door with the keys in his hands. Candice was sitting with Della, and Tom and RD both stood, looking like they wanted to come too.

"No," Candice told them.

"It'll be okay," Everett said to the brothers.

They clearly wanted to say something, but Candice cut them off with a look.

"If I can care for a baby I can care for two grown men," Salida said. "Boys, come sit down here."

Rose went to kiss her husband, and then she was out the door with Candice.

•

Candice wasn't sure what was happening. It had been Charles again, not even Katherine, who called that morning. He told Candice his wife had been out at the farm all night, ever since they learned about Rita, and that she was still there, and the folks were going to do something.

"I just got back," he said. "She wants you to go out there, Candice. She said by seven. It's important that you're out there by seven."

"What do you think is going on?" Rose asked. "What are they planning?"

Candice shook her head. "I don't know," she said curtly. She wasn't used to driving. She didn't do it a lot and it made her nervous, being in control of such heavy machinery. It didn't help that the roads this far out were pockmarked with ruts and it felt like the wheel was going to jump right out of her hand.

When they turned and passed Mrs. White's house, Rose said, "I've never been out here." "God, look at that place. It's like a mansion."

And it was, three stories tall with a porch that wrapped the entire home. Candice wondered if Mrs. White was looking out her window, watching her car as they traveled down the long drive towards the cabins.

When Candice and Rose pulled up to the place where the seasonal workers stayed, the people at Mrs. White's farm had already gathered outside.

"Here goes nothing," Rose said, getting out of the car.

Standing on one of the sunken porches was Katherine. She was talking with the two women who had walked with her on the Fourth of July, the mothers of missing girls, all holding council. When Katherine saw Candice she said something and started to make her way towards her.

As Candice looked around, she saw that the few trucks and cars were packed to capacity, some of them even with belongings stacked up on their roofs, tied down with blankets and rope.

"Are they leaving?" Rose whispered to her mother.

"Looks like it."

When Katherine got to them, she hugged both Candice and her daughter, holding Rose at arm's length afterward, saying, "You sure have grown up."

When Katherine dropped her arms, Rose leaned in and took the woman back into another hug. Candice saw her daughter's lips moving against Katherine's hair, and the woman nodded.

"I know," Katherine said. "I know."

"What are y'all doing out here?" Candice asked.

"Well," Katherine said, nodding to a man walking by, "we're burning down the farm."

"Come again?"

"Not the whole farm. But this. All this." Katherine gestured to the shanty homes on either side of the dirt lane.

"You can't do that. This is someone's property!"

"Keep your voice down if you're going to say something like that here," Katherine admonished Candice. "Besides, whose property is it, anyway? Really think about it."

"Oh, my," Rose said. "There's going to be trouble."

"Trouble for Mrs. White, maybe. Everyone here is leaving. Going back home. They'll be gone before Mrs. White even knows what's happening.

"Everyone?" Candice asked.

"Everyone," Kathrine repeated. "Every single person here has agreed it needs to go. It's been the cause of too much grief. For the girls' families. For the whole community. Even for the people who've only been out here for a few seasons. Goodbye, and good riddance."

Candice didn't know if she wanted to be a part of this. It was a crime, what these people were about to do, and she didn't want to end up in jail.

"I can tell you don't know about all this," Katherine said. People were carrying wood, split logs of cedar, into the small houses. "But let me tell you something. Fire cleanses, Candice."

Candice looked to her daughter, who didn't tell her any which way—with words, or her body—what they should do. "How are *you* doing?" she asked.

"I think, if Rita and Georgia went missing because this place is here, maybe it shouldn't be here. If it's gone, maybe this won't happen again."

Candice didn't think burning down the cabins would stop other girls from being taken. Setting fire here wouldn't prevent other girls, in other places, from going missing. But, she thought, it couldn't be about all girls. It was about *these* girls.

"We'll help," Candice said.

•

Candice didn't talk to the mothers of Rita and Georgia, but she talked to a few other individuals, in passing. She felt shame that she'd thought the people out here might be dressed in animal skins or pioneer style dresses. That the people at the farm would have been scooped up out of the past and dropped on the outskirts of Larissa. No, instead they wore jeans, and T-shirts. Tennis shoes, too, even on the feet of an ancient woman who sat on a log, her rheumy eyes watching everyone move about.

In a strange way, the whole place reminded her of Nacogdoches. It looked different, but there was a palpable sense of solidarity. Candice watched her daughter helping to pack up a car and thought that there was no longer any time to waste. The farm was going to go up in flames, and no one outside of the community knew it. What if Nacogdoches was lost too? What if Candice took too long, and by the time she really made an effort, there was nothing to find?

She would go back. She would take Rose with her. They would discover what they could, and Candice would do her best to remember what was lost.

It was hard work carrying the wood, setting up great stacks of it in the cabins. Some people were still bringing their belongings out.

By the time they were done, the sun was starting to go down. A large bonfire was set up in the middle of the lane, waiting to be lit.

"Your shoes are ruined," Katherine told Rose, but Candice's daughter shrugged. "I have others."

Candice's hair was plastered to her scalp, and she was going to be sunburned, she could tell.

"This is the end?" she asked.

"This is the end," Katherine said.

Candice and Rose stood at the edge of the circle. When she surveyed who was with them—farthest from the fire about to be lit—she realized almost everyone looked white. She took her daughter's hand and pulled her up so that they were both closer to Katherine.

The mothers—Candice had learned their names, Jean and Patricia—were the ones to light the fire. They used torches tied with cloth at the end, soaked with gasoline siphoned out of someone's truck tank. The women then used their torches to light others' and people disappeared into houses, returning empty handed.

As Candice watched, listening to the cracking wood, looking at all the people around her with somber faces, she felt a terrible regret. They had been here for years, for generations, returning each season to a home that was not a home, and they had been here the whole time. She had never even bothered to think about them.

She realized, as flames started to rise up from within the houses, visible through open doorways, that what was happening had not been a spur-of-the-moment decision. She hadn't even thought about it until just then, but it was likely that some part of what was happening now started not just the day before, with Rita, but maybe with Georgia, and possibly, before her. This was a culmination, she was witnessing, of a timeline of which she'd been ignorant.

Once the houses started to catch, once fire started to engulf walls and roofs, people began to get into cars.

"This is it?" Candice asked Katherine. "They just leave?"

"They already said goodbye," Katherine told her. "Come on, let's go before all this gets noticed."

Katherine sat in the front seat and Rose slid into the back. Candice's car was just one out of many in the caravan driving off Mrs. White's farm. Alerted by the sounds of many engines, the woman had come out onto her porch, standing in her twill pants with her arms crossed, a dog at her side, and watched them drive past. Candice wondered how long it would take before she discovered what they'd done.

26

The Story that Spans Our Lives

—Emily—

I have never made lemonade before, at least, not that I can remember. I am still remembering all sorts of things, and they come slowly, and quickly, depending.

The women in the backyard have not asked for something to drink, but sometimes people don't ask for what they want. Sometimes they don't know what they want.

On the patio, they sit in a square and I set down the pitcher, pouring out cups of what I hope will taste right. "Is Will not coming?" I ask Ms. Donald.

"He's with Alton and his father right now, and I think it's important that they all have some time together at his father's new place. He'll come over soon. I'm sure of it."

"Okay." I sit next to my mother, who puts a hand on my knee.

"Have you been able to find them yet," she asks Ms. Donald.

She is asking about the people who burned down the farm, "absconders from justice," as the newspaper called them. I am beginning to understand that the newspaper is not always a reliable source of information.

Ms. Donald chuckles, and in that sound is the understanding that she may work for the police, but she won't be helping them with this.

"If we *need* to make contact," Candice says, "to warn them, Katherine will be able to find them." Candice is picking a leaf off her skirt, looking up at the sky, wondering where it came from since we have no trees in the backyard. The birds are there, above us, keeping watch as witnesses. Someday soon, I hope, Candice will be able to understand them too.

I feel terrible for Candice. First it was June, and now, her friend Katherine. Katherine's daughter is still missing, and Marlene is second fiddle to the news of the ruined farm. It's been all anyone will talk about for a week, but my mother says it's not the end of the world. That maybe Mrs. White will now have to pay people better to come work for her. I don't care much about what happens to Mrs. White, but I do care about what happens to Marlene, and I worry that she will be forgotten. That the police will find other things to do. I worry too that since Larissa's story is being told all around Texas now, from Dallas to El Paso, a story about missing girls and bonfires in retaliation, whoever did this to Rita, and Georgia, and Marjorie, probably to Marlene as well, whoever took them will go somewhere else. Do the same things there. That history will repeat itself.

I reach forward, picking the book up off the diamond-grated table. It's titled *A History of Larissa, Texas*. It is the book Marjorie Kent had. I open it, but many of the pages are stuck together with mud. When I try to pull them apart, they rip.

"Emily, honey," my mother says, "you're going to ruin it."

Candice grimaces and says, "I think it's already ruined."

She's right, of course. The book is a burned down town, a village with all the people disappeared, like the other book Thomas Gladwell wrote, the one I am going to fix now that I have the missing pages.

Mrs. Habbermire faces the back fence. She doesn't talk much, and I don't know if this is because she is still sometimes confused, or because she does not want to. She sits in one of the wooden patio chairs with her right arm hanging down by her side. On the grass beside her, Lillian sits, her fingers intertwined with Mrs. Habbermire's. Maybe this is how Mrs. Habbermire heals. Maybe, like me, she is just relearning to use her tongue.

Mrs. Habbermire cannot see Them, cannot hear the sweet words of Our language, but she seems to know Lillian talks with someone else—is able to talk with anyone who can listen—now that she remembers. Now that she allows herself to. I'm not sure if Lillian is one of Us, but maybe it doesn't matter. Maybe women cast out of this world and into the one on the other side of the door are linked by something other than blood.

We do not know the full story of the farm. We have what's been said in the papers—"but that's only one side," Candice says.

"Then tell us what happened," my mother prods.

Candice shakes her head. "I don't want to say. Not right now. It's too fresh. Too hard. Too private. I don't want to do that labor, and it's not fair for you to ask, Gracie."

My mother nods, seeming to understand that she's over-stepped. "You're right," she says. "I'm sorry."

And in that moment, with all of us together, it is that simple: the acknowledgement that someone was wrong, and we can still move forward together.

Candice has not come back to work for us. When she received her family and started to care for Della, she also stopped playing with niceties and seemed to become more confident. I like this new Candice. She may not tell the stories we want to hear, but she won't be bullied into telling them before they're ready either.

Mrs. Habbermire's cat comes out from under a bush. It is stalking the bird house, taking halting steps toward us. It does not like Cedar House too much and spends as much time outside as possible.

And now we are all here, the women of Larissa, all of Us, at Cedar House.

•

"There are many kinds of love," Mrs. Habbermire had written over Thomas Gladwell's words.

I understand that there are many ways to love, just like there are many ways to cross, or disappear. This is what I tell Candice when we sit on the porch, waiting for her husband to come pick her up. Mrs. Habbermire has gone to bed with Lillian, and my mother and Ms. Donald are drinking wine in the garden.

They are with Candice and me, and They are weeping too, for Candice's loss. For June, who is gone, but not gone. I have not seen her, but maybe I will, someday.

I hug Candice and then lay my head on her shoulder. I want to tell her that They are all around us, and They are pressing their bodies into us, over us.

"I've been wanting to do something," I tell her. "Can we do it together? You and me?"

She doesn't know what I am asking—how could she? But still, she says, "of course."

Upstairs in my room, I move through Them. The dresser door shrieks as I open it, and from inside I take the wooden box my mother gave me the day after we found Rita. Inside is a history I have not looked at yet.

They follow me down the hallway. Down the stairs. They come out into the night and sit on the ground, on the steps, stand against the wall, in the doorway.

I place the box between Candice and me. "It's stuck," I tell her, "or locked. There's no key."

Candice raises an eyebrow and says, "You don't need a key to open that. How much do you care about the actual box?"

"It's pretty, but not important."

"Well then." Candice steps down into the yard, looking around and then digging from the earth and grass one of the recessed bricks that line the front walk. She comes back with it and holds it out." Smash it," she says, and I do.

It takes eleven strikes of the paver against lock. After the first three, Candice and I start laughing. After the last, when the lock pops open, They sigh and gather closer.

"There has been so much loss, hasn't there," I ask.

Candice nods. And They place their hands on her shoulders. Candice tips her head to the side, almost as if she's learning to lean into Them.

"Sometimes, when I close my eyes, I see Rita," I admit. "I see Georgia, too, sometimes, but not as clearly. There has been so much loss," I say again, "that sometimes I drown in it, too. It won't fix anything," I say, putting my hands on the lid. "Or maybe it will. I don't know."

"What's in the box, Emily?"

"My adoption papers. I hope I'll be able to find my birth mother. It's probably too late," I say, even though I don't completely believe it. I still hope. I do. But I know hope and belief are not the same thing.

In the box, there are a few envelopes. I open them, one by one, a history unraveling, or weaving itself back together.

They tell me to *listen*. They say, *stories have holes, gaps, winding paths through grasslands that lead to groves of trees where more stories are told. Stories that are bridges, long ago abandoned, or broken. Sometimes intentionally, sometimes by accident, by time, or by ignorance. Some stories will never be complete, but that does not mean we stop telling them.*

Candice scoots closer to me and looks at what I'm holding. There, at the bottom of the page in the third envelope, is my mother's name.

Lucinda Clark. The name means nothing. And it means everything.

"Are you going to look for her," Candice asks.

"I wouldn't know where to start."

"I might be able to help you," she says. "Lucinda Clark." Candice leans back and the light coming through the parlor window illuminates her face. "It sure sounds pretty, doesn't it?"

•

At night, I open my window. The Little People are in the cedar tree, and they tell me stories. Sometimes they are true. Sometimes they are not.

Oh, the stories I could tell now. And the stories I won't. All the stories I've heard, that others have told me, that I've plucked out of the night like knotted threads. I've been thinking about *this* story for a long time. The story in these pages. How it is unfinished. How once, Candice told me that I couldn't know everything. How once, I had disagreed with her.

Now I know she is full of wisdom, and that I am only a child, typing here, a story full of stories, on an old typewriter with the I's all misaligned and out of sync with the rest of the letters. I am learning how to tell *my* story, and how sometimes things should be held back, because knowing a story, and telling a story, are two different things.

I am waiting for Them to come home, to find Us. I am waiting *with* Them, too, in the library where I work. One day, maybe soon, maybe a long time from now, We will all be together.

We say of the stories the birds bring, *there are parts. But there are no pieces. Only wholes. Many of them. In the same breast, the same feet, the same landscape of hooves.*

We say, *When people tell you that you are whole, you will know you're not.*

We hear stories. We hear stories of girls running through long grasses. Girls bending their bodies into the memory of wombs. Girls rounding their lips around unfamiliar sounds. Girls hiding. Girls being told they are whole, the wrong whole, full of holes.

I wait for them to bring me *the* story. The one about Marlene. When I have it, I am going to write it. I am going to write the story of Marlene, and of Rita, and Georgia, and Patience.

Remember, We say, and by this, We mean, *do not forget.*

Gwendolyn Paradice is a queer, disabled, Cherokee-Caucasian writer of fiction and nonfiction. A 2024 National Endowment for the Arts Fellow, they're also the author of the Hudson Prize winning short story collection More Enduring for Having Been Broken (Black Lawrence Press, 2021) as well as a chapbook co-authored with poet Kara Dorris, Carnival Bound (or, Please Unwrap Me) (The Cupboard Pamphlet, 2020). Their creative work has been nominated for Pushcarts, Best American Essays, and Best of the Net, and their short stories and essays can be found in Booth, Zone 3, Crab Orchard Review, Tin House Online, The Journal of America Folklore, and others. They retain a PhD from The University of Missouri, an MFA from Bennington College, and MA and BA degrees from the University of North Texas, north of Dallas, where they were born and raised.

Acknowledgements

I'd like to say thank you ...

to Kyle. I'm lucky I found a weird, imaginative, kindred soul in you.

to my grad school friends, especially those who beta read this book, Carley and Kara.

to my students; they are wonderful, curious, smart, risk-taking rebels. I would have a hard writing life without them.

to Anand Prahlad and Sheri-Marie Harrison, whose classes helped give rise to this project.

to Diane Goettel, who published my first book and who buoyed me during the last of my PhD years when I started The Divining Season.

to all the writers who have inspired me and comforted me, writers who make me jealous and who encourage me—with their stories and structures and language—to push, explore, and continue to discover.

to the Native American and Indigenous creatives, craftspeople, and scholars who have helped me understand myself, my communities, and my heritage better.

And finally, an everthanks to my family, who have made this life as a writer and educator possible. Wado.

OUR MISSION Founded in 1982, Aunt Lute Books is an intersectional, feminist press dedicated to publishing literature by those who have been traditionally underrepresented in or excluded by the literary canon. Core to Aunt Lute's mission is the belief that the written word is critical to understanding and relating to each other as human beings. Through the centering of voices, perspectives, and stories that have not been traditionally welcomed by mainstream publishing, we strengthen ties across cultures and experiences, promoting a broader range of expression, and, we hope, working toward a more inclusive and just future.

LAND ACKNOWLEDGMENT We, Aunt Lute Books, acknowledge that we do our work of uplifting marginalized voices and striving toward justice via the written word on the unceded ancestral homeland of the Ramaytush Ohlone who are the original inhabitants of the San Francisco Peninsula. As the indigenous stewards of this land and in accordance with their traditions, the Ramaytush Ohlone have never ceded, lost, nor forgotten their responsibilities as the caretakers of this place, as well as for all peoples who reside in their traditional territory. As Guests, we recognize that we benefit from living and working on their traditional homeland. We wish to pay our respects by acknowledging the Ancestors, Elders and Relatives of the Ramaytush Community and by affirming their sovereign rights as First Peoples.

You may buy books from our website.

www.auntlute.com

aunt lute books

P.O. Box 410687
San Francisco, CA 94141
books@auntlute.com

This book would not have been possible without the kind
contributions of the Aunt Lute Founding Friends:

Anonymous Donor
Anonymous Donor
Rusty Barceló
Marian Bremer
Marta Drury
Diane Goldstein
Diana Harris
Phoebe Robins Hunter
Diane Mosbacher, M.D., Ph.D.
Sara Paretsky
William Preston, Jr.
Elise Rymer Turner

www.ingramcontent.com/pod-product-compliance
Lightning Source LLC
Jackson TN
JSHW070718230226
98184JS00002B/2
9781951874124